The Voyages of the Alexandria

The Voyages of the Alexandria
Book One: The Heirs of Terrison

C.J. Rhinehart

Library of Congress Control Number: 2018906493

ISBN:	Hardcover	978-1-9845-3142-1
	Softcover	978-1-9845-3141-4
	eBook	978-1-9845-3140-7

Print information available on the last page.

Rev. date: 09/04/2020

To order additional copies of this book, contact:
Xlibris
844-714-8691
www.Xlibris.com
Orders@Xlibris.com
722752

To my inspirations for Merik—

Thank you to my family for the unconditional love and support. Thank you for believing in my dream. Thank you for the extra push. Without you, I might still be on page one.

Contents

Chapter 1

In Which Everything Begins

The early morning light cast flickering shadows over the royal airship *Alexandria*. Prince Jovin stood on the airship dock beside the *Alexandria's* captain, Gregory Donald.

"This should be an adventure worth remembering," Captain Donald commented to the Prince.

"I should think so," Jovin agreed.

The first officer, Mister Lewis Carter, bounded down the gangplank stairs from the *Alexandria*. He had been overseeing the crew as they made their final calibrations to the gigantic balloon floating above the airship. Carter slowed his pace and straightened as he reached his superiors, addressing Jovin and Donald with a nod to each. "Your Highness, Captain, we are ready when you are."

The sound of gravel crunching beneath tires filled the air as a sleek, black motorcar pulled into the empty dockyard. Jovin turned to see his father's butler emerge from the vehicle and hasten around the side to open the door for the King of Canston. King Raleigh took in the airship dock, the skies, and the *Alexandria*, proud and triumphant in her slip. Then his eyes landed on Jovin, and he waved to his son.

From the motorcar's open door, there appeared a blond head, soon followed by the rest of the eleven-year-old boy. He scampered out of the vehicle, dirtying his leather overcoat in the process of picking himself up, and raced after the King, grinning from ear to ear.

Jovin's eyes widened in confusion. "He brought Merik?"

Merik was already running to meet Jovin, the tails of his knit scarf flying out behind him. "Jovin!" the boy cried, tackling him in a hug that threw the pair off balance and sent them tumbling into the gravel.

Jovin hurriedly regained his feet before Merik had time to sit up, dusting himself off and hardly glancing down at the boy. Merik pushed his mess of blond hair out of his face and staggered to his feet, still smiling widely.

A bronze blur of flapping mechanical wings flitted up to Jovin and began investigating his face. He blinked and slapped the contraption away before it had a chance to jab him in the eye.

"Sighter," Merik called, and the contraption bolted to buzz around his head instead.

Jovin eyed the flying blur. "I see you have fixed it."

Merik was on his feet, staring at Jovin with the utmost admiration. "I named him Sighter, he's a hummingbird now," he rambled with bright excitement. "I got the miraculous idea to redesign him as I was watching hummingbirds in the Welmonton garden, and I thought, 'why not make him a hummingbird?' they're fast, they're stealthy, and no one would ever suspect them of anything mischievous."

Jovin ignored Merik's enthusiasm and waved for him to follow as he began walking to meet their father. "What was he before?" he asked, more out of duty than actual interest. The last Jovin remembered of Merik's pet invention, it had been loud, wingless, and prickly; usually scurrying about the palace halls, and often making impressive leaps from the floor, up tablecloths, and the random unsuspecting servers' trousers. But all of this had been before Merik's trip to Welmonton over the summer.

"A sort of lizard," Merik answered, plucking Sighter out of the air, where he was once again intent on scanning Jovin's face. "I added wings and changed his shape a bit so he can fly now. He's still under construction, but I think with the new mobility he's—"

"Tell me when I get back," Jovin interrupted.

Merik furrowed his eyebrows in confusion, "What do you mean?"

They had reached the King, who had been waiting patiently for them.

"Hello, Father," Jovin said curtly.

The King placed a hand on Merik's shoulder. "Change of plans," he told Jovin with a kind smile. "You now have a fellow diplomat."

Jovin was silent for a moment. "So you're making me bring the cat?"

"I wasn't allowed to bring him," Merik said dejectedly.

"We got a dog then?" Jovin asked.

"Yes, I *obviously* got one yesterday as a welcome home gift, and you didn't know about this because I'm *so secretive*," Merik said sarcastically. "No we didn't get a dog. *I* am coming with you."

Jovin's nose twitched.

The King patted his younger son's shoulder, "Merik, run along and greet Captain Donald."

"Father, do I *have* to call him *Captain* Donald?" Merik asked.

"Yes, on this voyage you shall call him 'captain'," King Raleigh reminded him, "For the time being, I have given his word authority over yours, and until you return with your brother to our court, he is your superior."

"I understand, Father." Merik replied meekly, shuffling his feet in the gravel. "I'm… I'm going to go say hello to Captain Donald, then," and he ran off to where the captain was speaking to Mister Carter and the second mate a hundred yards away.

Jovin kept his eyes on the King, "Father, please explain."

"My son, I need you to understand that I am not punishing you. Merik has been away from you for three months. Is that not too long to be separated? Surely you have missed him."

Jovin gave his father a speculative look. "And you're sending Merik with me because…?"

The King checked that the boy was out of earshot before continuing. "There is a possibility that our family's personal safety will be threatened. Our sister countries of Ee'lin and Berronatt are experiencing unrest and signs of rebellion, possibly revolution."

"I don't see how their problems will affect us," Jovin said.

"Rebellion is not a tender subject, Jovin," the King said.

"If it is rebellion, then it will stay within Ee'lin and Berronatt. Unless you think it will spread into Canston?" Jovin scrutinized.

"Canston's people are happy, we are in a time of great abundance and peace. We are strong and united. We, as leaders, will always do the right, and just, thing," the King answered. "It is my responsibility to take care of our country and our people, and it is yours also."

"But this is not our business."

"Revolution is everyone's business," the King said. "As a ruler, you must be prepared for everything, good and bad; as a father, I am making sure my children are safe."

There was a static pause while Jovin looked over the dockyard, his eyes landed on Merik, who was showing Captain Donald his mechanical hummingbird with the enthusiasm of an excited puppy.

King Raleigh surveyed his children. "We are a family, we must take care of each other. Canston's citizens are our family. Farmer, merchant, inventor, noblemen, or king; parents love their children the same. I respect any parent who strives to provide a better life for their children. I want mine to grow up brave, strong, happy and healthy; as does the farmer and merchant."

"I understand, Father," Jovin said. "What else is happening?"

"Holy places in both Ee'lin and Berronatt have been sabotaged and dilapidated, there are reports of attacks on travelers, and towns being raided. We have not seen mass panic to this degree since the War of Placate, when you were a child. Communication between our three countries has grown infrequent in the last few days. Berronatt is remaining atop of the problem, but Ee'lin is having difficulties."

"What of the nobility?" Jovin inquired.

"Nothing ill-boding yet," there was something in his father's eyes that made Jovin wary of continuing conversation on the matter.

Jovin's mind flashed back to his brother. "If I am abroad, then Merik is safer at the palace, we protect our bloodline better separated."

His father sighed, "My heart agrees with you, but if the two of you were to stay here alongside me and the country were to be overthrown, we would lose what hope there would be for our survival. A weakened nation is a dangerous one."

"But we are not weak," Jovin insisted. "Our people are strong; our country is united."

"We are strong today, but tomorrow poison may cloud our minds, and our downfall would then begin. I do not know what the future holds, but I *do* know, that if the raids and attacks cross our boarder and escalates, my family *will* be threatened. If Merik stays, and the worst happens, I will regret it every day." The King's attention focused on the *Alexandria,* and the sunlight that gleamed off her windows like a beacon in the patchwork skies.

It was ridiculous, Jovin thought, completely foolhardy to cast Merik upon him in this manner, as though the boy could handle himself. He would probably sneeze at the wrong time and start a war for disrespecting a country's local customs.

"I must say, for your first peaceful campaign, you are not cut any slack. I need you to be my eyes and ears," the King placed an arm around his son's shoulders and began walking towards the airship.

"Why did you not tell me this information sooner?" Jovin asked.

"Because I knew you would disapprove of my decision. You were busy with your goodbyes yesterday, Jovin, and you would have tried to talk me out of sending Merik with you."

"But you told Captain Donald."

"Of course I did," his father said with amusement, "he is Merik's guardian while on this tour."

"But you did not tell your heir?" Jovin said irritably. "I should not be the last person to receive such vital information."

The King watched Merik ramble to Captain Donald as they climbed the gangplank stairs. The smallest of smiles touched his father's austere expression. "You do not need distraction. This is your first mission. I did not want to worry you yet."

Jovin rubbed his forehead. "Father, do not agonize over our safety. I will let you know if something goes awry."

The King focused his attention away from his younger son. "It looks to be about time," he observed. "I think that if everything goes as planned, this will be everything you need. You and Merik will get to spend time away from standard life for a while. It should benefit you both."

Jovin cast his eyes away from his father's gaze. "Maybe it will."

"I know what I have told you will haunt your mind while you are gone, and for that, I can only apologize," the King said, touching his son's cheek with affection, "I advise that you stay vigilant, and have courage. Learn about the world around you, do your best to understand motivations. Try not to focus on that which will cause you pain or fear; times will not always be so uncertain."

Jovin met his father's eye, and in that moment, something went unsaid between the two. He nodded, and with the last exchange of smiles, he turned to climb the stairs to the gangplank. The wind picked up at the top, and Jovin turned to see if his father had left the dockyard. Somehow, it surprised him to find that the King was watching him, a smile still on his face.

Chapter 2

An Unstable Path to a Rocky Conversation

If there ever was an airship worthy of praise, it was the *Alexandria*. Her lines were elegant, sleek and graceful; but she was powerful, made to be a fortress, and to protect her precious cargo. She was a beauty, eye-catching and bold, and drew constant attention, as she was a magnificent, royal, airship.

"Come on! We're taking off!" Merik shouted to Jovin as he ran to the stern and up three flights of stairs to the wheelhouse.

The four landings above deck were devoted to the captain's quarters, the royal quarters, the wheelhouse, and eight passenger rooms that currently stood empty. The belly of the airship housed the kitchens, the greenhouse, and two separate dining halls for royal and crewmembers' use. The crew's rooms and the training room occupied the second level. Lower levels contained storage space, cannons, the engines, and an aircraft hangar in the very bottommost part of the airship. On both sides of the bow, five diagonally curved, diamond-shaped windows stretched from the first to fifth levels, allowing the sky's light into the heart of the airship.

The engines hummed as the airship prepared for liftoff. Steadily, slowly, the *Alexandria* began to rise, leaving her port in Canston. Her hull left the docking braces as she ascended, and a light flashed in the wheelhouse to indicate that they were clear.

"And we're off," Donald whispered to himself. His smile infected Merik, who now stood beside him.

"Whoa!" The young prince rushed out the wheelhouse door and collided with the rail. "We're gaining altitude—and fast! Jovin, look at this!" he shouted back through the open door.

Jovin joined Merik at the rail and looked out at the ground they were pulling away from. "Well, this is a pleasant beginning to an adventure," he muttered to himself.

"I'm really excited," Merik beamed. "It's so smooth! I almost don't feel anything!" He scampered down the stairs to the balcony above Donald's cabin. They were high enough now that the land of Canston was becoming lost below them in the shimmering clouds.

Merik ran down the remaining stairway and sprinted to the bow of the airship, dashing around the passenger cabins and passing crewmen in a hurry. He climbed a few stairs until he was standing at the farthest forward reach of the airship.

It seemed that the whole world was before him, a quilted map of clouds and farmlands. The sky was so blue, the clouds so remarkably white. Merik breathed in elation. The wind ruffled his hair and he closed his eyes, feeling the sun on his face and enjoying the anticipation of adventure as it coursed through his veins. Air had never felt so clean.

Now that he was away from the smell and heat of the palace, away from the ties that held him to the mundane life of a prince, he felt free.

"*Yes!*" he shouted in triumph. Merik failed to notice a nearby crewmember's jump of surprise as he continued to gaze out onto the world below him.

The *Alexandria* glided on into the clouds, gathering moisture on the rails that quickly dried when the sun hit the polished wood. Merik's ears popped now and again, but he did not mind. He imagined he was a great voyager, off to save the world from some terrible evil in his mighty airship *Alexandria.*

Well, Merik reminded himself, *that is not so far from the truth.* His father had only said that he was sending Merik away for his safety. Though he did not know the details, Merik liked the romanticized idea of a dangerous adventure.

Merik stayed on deck all that morning. When he was hungry, he went in search of Captain Donald to ask where he could find a snack. He found Donald in his cabin, which took up quite a bit of space on the top deck, above which Merik's and Jovin's cabins sat, with the wheelhouse over them.

Merik slipped in through one of the polished double doors, and his eyes were dazzled by the morning light from the great window that spanned the entire stern wall.

"Hello, Merik. Have you decided to quit life among the clouds, or are you simply on holiday for the moment?" Captain Donald asked from his place at a wooden desk that was large enough for eight people to sit around comfortably.

"Well, even adventurers get hungry," Merik replied, approaching the window wall and gazing out at the poufs of silvery clouds contrasted against the blue sky. "It's striking,"

A comfortable-looking sofa and a carpet sat across from him. On the wall, covering what Merik assumed to be Donald's sleeping quarters, were two beautifully carved bookshelves filled with books. His eyes flitted over thick leather-bound volumes and smaller paperbacks. There were books in varying colors from golden browns to the brightest blues and every color in between. Merik noticed a scarlet bookmark peeking out of the row of pages and wondered if Captain Donald had read every book on the shelf.

He took in the rest of the room. On the starboard wall, beside the desk, there hung a map of the world, colored vibrantly with remarkable details. A few chairs lined the wall beside it, and above them were locked metal cabinets.

Merik noticed that the flooring had notches to prevent the legs of the desk from sliding in the case of undesirable weather. A few papers were spread across the desk where Donald was marking points on a map.

"What are you working on?" he asked. In his time away from the palace, Captain Donald's mustache had expanded into a goatee, and his dark hair was streaked with a few more strands of grey. But his stature was the same: stately, strong, polite, and proper. His brown eyes twinkled, reflecting the kindness Merik was familiar with.

Donald turned the map around for Merik to see. "I am looking over our flight pattern,"

"I didn't know we were going to Terrison." Merik scrunched his nose.

"We are. They are Canston's allies," Donald said. "However, your father wanted to see if Jovin and Princess Charlotte could be compatible now that they are older."

"That's not likely to happen," Merik snickered, leaning his elbows on the desk. "Do you remember how happy he was with Saphir? She was so fun. She was one of the only people that didn't treat me like I was incompetent." Merik sighed mournfully.

"We are becoming old gossips, Merik; let us leave the subject alone," Donald said with a smile.

Merik nodded respectfully and rested his chin on the desk, "Captain, where can I get some food?"

"The kitchens are on the first level. The side door leads below decks. Walk to the prow; the end door is the kitchen. Chef Mason will be there, he is good natured, but keep out from underfoot."

"I won't pester him. Thank you!" Merik called back over his shoulder as he raced to the front of the cabin and found the side door. His first thought was that it looked like the door to a coat closet, but upon further investigation he discovered that it led to the staircase Captain Donald had mentioned. Merik followed the rest of Donald's instructions, with his inner compass leading him in the direction of the prow, and soon he was at the kitchen door between the two dining rooms.

Chef Mason was kind and genial. He insisted that Merik try his lunchtime masterpiece, and welcomed the prince to the kitchens anytime he had the yearning for a plate full of cookies.

+++++

"Alright," Merik said, casually strolling into Jovin's cabin later that afternoon. "So, I was wondering…"

Jovin set down his book, "What are you doing, Merik?"

"It's been three months since we've seen each other. I've missed you." Merik complained. "Come on! You're my brother, my best friend, the person I can look up to and be proud to be related to, the one I love annoying and laughing with, the person I come to with my girl problems…"

"You're eleven," Jovin pointed out.

"But *still!*" Merik persisted, folding his arms, as though by doing so he had had the final say in the matter. "Anyway, I'm twelve in a couple months," he said, shrugging over to a chair and shuffled his feet.

"Stop," Jovin said, not looking up from his book

"I'm not doing anything," Merik said dejectedly, "hey, did you know that we're going to Terrison? Because I didn't. Captain Donald said that Father—"

Jovin looked up from his book, "You don't have to fill every silence with chatter."

Merik huffed, rose, and walked to the window. As he watched, a cloud obstructed his immediate view of the ground beneath them. "I can't see the palace anymore. Where do you think we are?"

"What is it that you want, Merik?"

Merik felt very small. "I want to spend time with you."

Jovin finally set his book down and joined his brother at the window. "Alright, we've been in the air about four hours, yes? That means that four hours that way is the palace." Jovin pointed northwest. "So, no, you would not be able to see it."

"How far until we get to our next stop?"

"About two and a half days," Jovin said curtly.

Merik wrinkled his nose.

"What's that face for?"

"That's a long time… Where are we going again?"

"Caloricain. Go ask Captain Donald about it," Jovin made to walk back to his chair, but Merik grabbed his arm. "Yes? What is it?"

"I can still stay here, right?"

Jovin pulled his arm free from Merik's grip, "No,"

Merik threw himself at Jovin and hung onto his brother's arm. "Please, Jovin… please!"

"Let go."

"No, you should spend time with me."

"I have things to do, and you're getting in the way."

"Love me, Jovin!" Merik flung his arms around Jovin's torso and pretended to sob into his waistcoat. Merik stuck out his bottom lip and blinked his eyes in a pitiful way.

Jovin let out a dry laugh, "Nice try, but I see that look every three seconds at parties, and you're not doing it justice."

"Meanie!" Merik whined.

"Crazy little wild child," Jovin muttered.

Merik looked up, a mischievous look in his eyes. "Hey, are we bonding?"

"No." Jovin succeeded in pushing Merik away, and the scowl he shot his brother would have been adequate if he had caught a wild fox rampaging through his room at three in the morning. "Get out. Leave me alone."

"But we're bonding!" Merik made to hug him again, but Jovin stopped him and held the boy at arm's length.

"You're harassing me," Jovin sidestepped Merik, who stumbled and plopped down on the floor where he proceeded to pout like a grumpy two-year-old.

"But we're brothers!" Merik insisted.

"And it's been a long day—"

"It's still before lunch—"

"And I am not in the mood," Jovin pulled Merik up and began pushing him toward the door.

"You could at least give me a real hug before you abandon me."

"But you wouldn't leave me alone then, would you?"

Merik's expression twisted into that of concentration. "That is a reasonable question, but the answer is probably no."

Within seconds, Jovin had pushed Merik out of the cabin and slammed the door. Merik heard the lock click.

"At least you've acknowledged my existence!" he shouted at the closed door. "We have the entire voyage to become friends—"

"Then it can wait a little longer, can't it?" Jovin shouted from behind the door.

Merik blew his hair out of his eyes. "Fine then. Bye!" he made a loud commotion as he shot down the stairs, but he stopped on the flight below. Merik leaned against the rail, waiting to see if Jovin would respond.

Jovin's door opened, and he peered out to check whether Merik had left.

"See, some part of your cold heart cares about me," Merik shouted over the winds on deck.

The door closed.

Merik's smile slipped off his face. Even before his summer trip to Welmonton, he had often felt lonely with Jovin. Part of Merik had hoped that this cold and rude side of Jovin would have evaporated in his absence. But this hope was fading.

He scuffed his boot against the stair railing and clomped down the remaining stairs to Captain Donald's cabin.

"You look less than chipper, Merik," Donald commented as Merik came through the door. Donald was looking over a stack of papers while a mellifluous piano piece played from a gramophone nestled in the bookcase.

"I'm fine, but Jovin is..." Merik looked around for the right word. "I dunno, just being unreasonable."

"Hush now; I think you are overreacting." Donald said, smiling.

Merik sighed exasperatedly, "Maybe..."

Donald patted the desk beside him. "Pull up a chair," he produced a pack of playing cards from a drawer.

Merik's disposition brightened, "We should make up a game,"

"What shall we call it?"

Chapter 3

The Phantom of the Regiment

Elias Ganimead sighed and leaned back in his chair. "Their excuses are empty. Iris, they have until twelve tomorrow to answer. Tell them I have grown impatient."

"Yes sir," Iris Shannon nodded. This was her third month working for Ganimead, and so far, she found him to be punctual, precise, and selective. "What if they do not respond?" her voice sounded oddly quiet compared to his.

Ganimead raised his eyebrows in a look that hardly showed his irritation. He went back to his paperwork.

Iris knew this was her cue to exit the office. She set a paper on the desk. "Also, Sir Brenton needs to speak with you," she said.

"If that is all, you may go,"

Iris turned and scurried from Ganimead's office, closing the door softly behind her.

Ganimead took a breath. He leaned back in his chair and closed his eyes.

There was a sharp knock at the office door.

Ganimead sat up, "Come in."

A young man in a wrinkled grey overcoat entered the office. His scraggly hair fluffed around his face dramatically, and his bloodshot eyes told a story beyond sleep deprivation. His coat shifted as he walked, and the four faded tattoos on the right side of his neck were exposed. He adjusted his collar before the darker two on the left could show. "Our group under the name *Arabella* contacted us."

"Wonderful. Thank you, Hadrin," Ganimead said.

Hadrin favored his left arm. He walked forward to set a sheet of paper on Ganimead's desk. "They're estimating twenty-four hours until we have complete access to the security system. The report was sent two hours ago, but the lag time and decoding takes unreasonable amounts of time. *Arabella* has requested to stay among the court for another three weeks."

Ganimead shook his head. "Denied. They know their orders. They need to be out of the country in four days."

"That timeline is unrealistic," Hadrin said coolly.

Ganimead contemplated Hadrin, amused that the former field agent would question his orders. He was beginning to understand the reasoning behind Hadrin's release from his regiment. "They have a week."

Hadrin blinked, surprised at Ganimead's reaction. "I will relay that, but they will not get the message until tomorrow."

Ganimead nodded, "I understand. Send another message to *Arabella* not to act until they leave the court. If the princess is still in the palace, then we will hold operations for a few days."

"I thought the princess was supposed to be there… what made you change your mind?" Hadrin queried.

"Updated intelligence." Ganimead said no more. He jotted down a note on a pad of paper and ignored Hadrin's pestering gaze.

Hadrin felt that he had been dismissed, but his curiosity got the better of him. It had been three years since he had been excused from field work, and his current position as messenger between his regiment and Ganimead was not something he would have willingly signed up for. His tendency to question his peers was something Ganimead frowned upon. "If you don't mind my asking, what information?"

Ganimead set his jaw. "Awfully nosy today." he commented harshly. "I need the princess around longer than we had originally anticipated."

"Why?"

"Legal issues," Ganimead said. "It will get messy if she dies; then we will have to forge signatures, and the country could fall into disrepair. Now go away. You've become a pest."

"Do not treat me as though I want to be here. I have no allegiance to you." Hadrin spoke in a voice tinged with loathing.

"No, but you work under people who *do*," Ganimead stated, "and you report to *me*, not your leaders. Go on. You have things to do."

Hadrin gave it up and walked from Ganimead's office. He passed an open doorway where Ganimead's assistant, Iris Shannon, was telegraphing. From her posture, Hadrin could tell she was strained. He knew how little Ganimead told his supporters, and he was thankful he was allowed more information than the followers of the Landin Favar.

"Haunting the halls again?" one of Ganimead's officers commented to Hadrin as they passed each other.

"These halls don't need to be haunted," Hadrin muttered under his breath, "they're already filled with ghosts."

Chapter 4

Bunny-Basket Jitters

The *Alexandria*'s arrival in Caloricain was seamless. Merik tried hard to maintain his composure, and if one had not known that Merik felt as though he had swallowed a basket of bunnies, they might never have realized the extent of his nerves. Jovin, familiar with the oppressive nature of responsibility, felt nothing out of the ordinary, and hardly noticed Merik's bunny-basket jitters.

The hull of the *Alexandria* bumped gently into four enormous docking braces. The padded braces secured her hull and attached to grooves near the top deck railing. Once properly secured into the braces, the airship would remain in her slip no matter what the weather threw at her.

Duke Mackebury's representative was waiting to greet them, bearing a warm welcome and introducing himself as Armon Cohan. He spoke in an accent unusual to Merik; his was a rolling, punctual dialect. Merik later learned that Cohan was from the small musical country of Venqui across the Gemelle Channel.

It seemed the entire city of Caloricain knew of their arrival. Merik found himself seated between Jovin and Cohan in their open-topped motorcar that carried them from the airship docks to Duke Mackebury's estate. He craned his neck to see banners of the Canston Flag hung from balconies, from storefronts, and all through the streets. People shouted greetings and waved in excitement. Merik suspected that the city had refused to let the arrival of their Crown Prince and his younger brother go uncelebrated.

Merik flinched and clutched Jovin's arm when a group of young ladies started chasing after their motorcar, shouting hysterics at the top of their voices. One girl sobbed unashamedly while her friend slapped her and screamed that she should retain her composure. Merik was surprised when Jovin smiled and waved at them, he then proceeded as though the girl's shenanigans were a normal afternoon occurrence.

The noise of the street increased as they entered the heart of the city. Soon Merik's ears were ringing and the delight of the city became background noise.

Duke Mackebury's manor was set at the edge of Caloricain. The paved driveway was edged in high hedges and vaulting pillars, reminding Merik of the time that he and his tutor, Professor Hopkins, visited the Landen Favar's meditation gardens in Welbern for a history lesson.

Duke Mackebury was kind, possibly arrogant, with a strong infatuation for animatronics. He was a thin man with receding auburn hair and a mustache that looked as though it was trying its best not to fall off of his face. He spoke in a loud manner and waved his hands when he spoke, which increased in vigor when the subject of his animatronics collection was breached. He boasted of his collection of prototypes more than once in a span of thirty minutes, and decided to treat the royal party to a display of his favorites that evening.

Duke Mackebury showed each piece off as if it were his own well-to-do child. The man seemed to cherish each contraption as much as, if not more than, his two daughters. Whether by choice or lack of interest, the two girls had opted out of their father's parade that evening.

The figurines were lined against the walls in their glass cases—some without faces, others with eyes all too piercing. One in particular lacked a face, exposing the polished cogs and gears; it loomed ominously at them from its case. Merik subconsciously shuffled closer to Captain Donald.

"And this one comes all the way from the little town of Bermen, in the southwest of Kaiden. It was a pretty price but, all the same, worth its weight in the extreme." Duke Mackebury had a server open a case and motioned for the man to help the figurine out of its box.

"She is my absolute favorite," Duke Mackebury shooed away the server to activate the automaton himself, pressing a button while turning a crank on the back of the head.

"Would you rather show us another time?" Jovin asked while Duke Mackebury continued to fiddle with the figurine. Merik was sure that Jovin found the whole ordeal to be beneath him. Jovin's time was better spent negotiating the continuation of their contract and assuring the duke's loyalty to the crown, rather than playing with toys.

"If I show you another time, it will be too late and you will have already seen what it is that I want to show you," Duke Mackebury stepped back, grinning. He gestured to the server, who moved to a table at the end of the room. "Not yet, Doani. Wait for my say-so," he moved back to the figurine and pressed a button on the top of her head.

A light came on in her throat. Her posture straightened, and her head rose. Her face changed; the turning gears seemed to create a mask, which one could imagine were eyes, a nose, and a mouth. Her basic shape was humanoid, and she looked rather proud—if a machine could look proud. She stood five feet tall, her arms bent at the elbow.

"Miss Theoloma of the Lower Falls," Duke Mackebury announced. His narrow smile under his greying mustache gave him the look of a proud gopher.

Merik made to move forward and investigate, but Jovin caught his eye.

Merik stayed where he was.

This exchange went unnoticed by the duke, who was saying something to his server again in a hushed whisper.

Merik rocked on his toes, "It's really fascinating. Where is it from?" Merik inquired.

Duke Mackebury smiled, "A clockwork robotics shop called The Ticking Hour, in Kaiden," he pressed a button on the side of her head and stepped back. With a satisfactory nod, he motioned to the server to move a needle onto a record player seated on a table.

Music drifted over them. A soft, haunting melody of violins and piano provided a tentative opening to a lonesome song.

Within the moment, the figure was no longer still. At the first sound of music, she had taken a step forward. Her arms lifted slightly, and her head nodded once.

Merik almost jumped when the figurine moved again. She took another step forward and stopped, leaned back, and gracefully moved her arms.

It took Merik a moment to realize that the machine was programmed to move along with the music. "She's a ballet dancer." Merik took a step forward, but Donald placed a hand on his shoulder.

"Watch just now," Donald advised the young prince.

The dancing figurine spun and made a graceful leap, landing with ease. She stepped in a pattern. Her motions were elegant; her tread was agile. Merik had to remind himself that she was mechanical.

"She is rather wonderful," Donald told the duke.

"Is she not?" he grinned proudly, taking the stunned look on Jovin's face and the eagerness on Merik's in stride. "I have been searching for a few to send as a gift to your father, I do think he would enjoy them. Watch this," he intercepted the dancing machine and bowed to her.

Merik expected him to be hit by the dancer as she continued in her wide pattern, but she halted and curtsied back to him, staying bent in her curtsy.

"Her technology is new to the public," the duke announced, "she has motion sensors to stop her from colliding with anyone. She stalls when she gets close to a living being, and she can sense when she is too close to an inanimate object."

"Are they motion sensors or heat sensors?" Merik asked.

"Is there a difference?" the duke backed away from the dancer. She straightened from her bow and stepped into a pirouette.

Merik silently thought that Duke Mackebury should know there was a definite difference between motion sensors and heat sensors, but he knew that if he voiced his opinion, he would be speaking out of turn.

When the song ended, the dancer curtsied to them and walked back to her original patch of floor.

Merik wanted to inspect the dancer more closely, but Jovin held him back by an arm. "Do not, you are a guest."

Merik stayed where he was.

Chapter 5

The Animated Statue

Later that evening, when the halls of Duke Mackebury's estate were quieted and when sensible people were winding down for the night, Merik found himself wandering the corridors. He had no interest in the tedious conversation between Jovin and the duke's family, and his two grown daughters held no interest or kindness for him. The duke had given his halfhearted permission for Merik to visit the animatronics collection again, but when Merik asked to see them that evening, the duke shooed him and continued his conversation with his flirtatious wife.

So Merik, through a stroke of luck, a scraped-together memory, and a good amount of determination, found himself in the animatronics room again. The machines were locked safely away in their glass cases, their motionless faces were accompanied by the soft light of the chandelier, which cast a ghostly glow over the room and its occupants.

Each automaton possessed a different personality. Some held a stiff mannerism, some seemed only to be people in costumes. There were faces designed into masks of gears, some displayed painted ceramic faces. Every eye, painted or hollow, seemed to follow him around the room. Merik was intrigued by one mechanism that had razors for hands. The one beside it had three legs, the next held a less humanoid shape and resembled a snarling spine-covered animal on its hind legs. Merik found himself doubting their entertainment value. These were trinkets not to be bought on a whim; the bared teeth of the animal convinced him of that.

Merik contemplated running from the taciturn room, away from the vacant-eyed patrons. But he reminded himself that he might never see this quantity of automatons again in his life. He should appreciate this collection before he regretted it.

He tentatively opened the glass door of Miss Theoloma of the Lower Falls. Her controls were switched off, and she bore no face—just an open array of gears and cogs. Up close, Merik noticed two panels of copper that would slide into place to create a mask where her eyes would be if she had been human.

"Alright, what do I have to do...?" he tugged the machine forward a few feet and out of her glass case. She was almost as tall as he was. Merik investigated the back of her head, then he flipped a switch and turned a crank at the nape of her neck.

Nothing of importance happened, other than Merik hitting his finger against a protruding button. "Ow!" he shook out his hand.

Merik gave the machine a long, stern look.

He took Sighter from his pocket and let him investigate the would-be ballerina. "Anything?" he asked the metallic hummingbird. Sighter flew around Miss Theoloma's head once, then came to land on Merik's shoulder. "I'll take that as a no," Merik sighed.

Sighter took to the air again and busied himself searching the room. He darted around each holding box and scanned the contents. Finding no immediate threat, he darted to the gramophone on the table and perched on the horn.

Merik's attention turned back to the animatronic lady; he noticed a button at the side of her head, gave a little shrug, and pressed it.

Her back straightened, and her arms rose. A light in her throat came to life, and her copper mask slid over her cheeks, creating the illusion that she might be a real person.

"Brilliant!" Merik exclaimed. She curtsied to him. Not sure what to do, Merik bowed back.

She stood straight-backed, head held high, waiting.

"Oh, right, you need music." Merik scrambled over to the gramophone on the table and played with the dials.

As before, she started her graceful dance the moment the music washed over the room. She made a pirouette, and then a leap, with every grace of a trained human.

Merik sat down on the tiled floor, watching her programmed routine. Sighter came to perch on Merik's knee and tucked his wings into his body. His head flicked from side to side in time with the music as he watched the dancer with interest.

"Go say hi," Merik prompted with a nudge, "Investigate."

Sighter's head twitched again to show he understood his command and whizzed off to investigate. Sighter flew straight up to the dancer and tried to scan her. However, she was moving so quickly it became exceedingly difficult for him to hover for longer than a moment without a near miss of her hand or a graceful foot.

Merik laughed at Sighter's attempts. "Sighter, abort mission," Merik commanded. Sighter circled Merik once before landing in his hand.

The song faded, and the record skipped, landing on a strangely flat note. Miss Theoloma gave a final curtsy and retreated to her starting point in front of her box.

Merik clapped, but as the mechanical dancer was only a machine, she did not respond.

Sighter zoomed to the dancer, circled her again, and landed on her head. Merik imagined that the little bionic bird was proud of himself.

With a little effort, Merik managed to get the dancer back into her glass box. When he closed the door, he noticed that her face had reset into a display of gears again. As before, she was no more than a statue.

Merik's attention shifted from coffin to coffin. The automatons' vacant eyes seemed to follow him, frozen until the time when the breathing required entertainment once more.

Imaginations run wild in the young, and wilder still when in the grown, although no one cares to admit it. Merik's imagination—not a child's, and not a grown-up's—was wilder still. He could see the terrible lifeless bodies pushing open their glass cases. He could almost hear the scuttering as their multitude of feet struggled over the tiled floor.

The clock in the hall chimed one, reinvigorating his nerves.

The leather soles of his boots sounded all too loudly on the tile floors. His imagination ran with him. For a moment he thought something had followed him from the animatronics room. But he saw no one every time he turned back.

Miraculously, Merik found his way back to the parlor. It was empty now, save for Captain Donald. The warm glow of the fire felt inviting and comforting to the young prince after the electronic lights of the animatronics room.

Donald was in an armchair, staring into the lively fire. There was a ring of liquid on the polished coffee table that indicated the room had been vacated recently. A lone teacup sat in its saucer at the far end of the table.

Merik shuffled to an armchair beside Donald. He kicked off his shoes and tucked his feet up. "I feel lonely," he softly voiced.

Donald looked over at Merik, who thought the captain's eyes seemed sad. "I imagined you might. This is not a city you would enjoy alone. Did you get lost?"

Merik leaned his head against the armrest. "Sort of. It's no fun exploring by yourself." Merik stared at the fire. He decided it was not the greatest idea to tell Captain Donald that he had been frightened by his own mind. "I'm wondering if it really was a good idea for me to come."

"Merik, you did not have a choice this time," Donald reminded him, "but if you had, I cannot imagine you would chose to stay behind; you would have wanted to be here if you had stayed."

"Maybe so," Merik's eyelids began to feel heavy, "how were the negotiations?"

"Jovin did wonderfully. Duke Mackebury complimented your father's leadership, sang your praises, and offered Jovin the pick of his daughters. But everything seems to be in order. As luck would have it, there was little to be arranged. It mainly consisted of trying to keep Duke Mackebury focused on a topic long enough to finalize the re-election contract."

Merik nodded absently. "And what does this mean f-or us?" he yawned. All thoughts of monsters and lifeless eyes were disappearing from his mind like water draining from a wading pool.

"Mostly that we can rely on the Mackeburys and Caloricain for aid if the need should arise. When his nine year term of leadership ends, we will have to assign and settle new contracts with a new candidate; but that is nothing we need worry about at the moment."

Merik was falling asleep, "Where are we going… next?" he mumbled, leaning heavily on his arm in an attempt to stay awake.

Donald rose and helped the prince to stand. "We are heading north to the country of Delliah."

Merik nodded groggily, "Alright… g'night," he stumbled for a step, then regained his balance and walked out the door.

A lump of bronze fell from Merik's pocket and rolled under the coffee table. Donald slipped Sighter into one of Merik's forgotten boots and followed the prince out the parlor door.

Chapter 6

When Life Becomes Boring

The next eight days were incredibly boring. If Merik had had to describe them, he would have said, "I did nothing; therefore, I was useless."

Duke Mackebury and his household treated Merik like the prince he was, doting on the boy and inviting him down to the animatronics room whenever they had a chance. The dancing clockwork was all well, Merik thought, but after sneaking about late in the evening to play with it, an invitation to sit and watch while others showed him what he'd already seen without their help was something he was simply not interested in.

Merik spent much of his time wandering the estate grounds while watching the songbirds and finding new ways for Sighter to be improved. A batch of Retriever puppies had been born in the late summer, and their good spirits and need to play and run about the lawns often consumed Merik's afternoons. His evenings were spent with a cup of hot chocolate in the parlor, listening to Jovin amuse the duke's two daughters with jokes that Merik did not find funny. Captain Donald often joined Merik on these occasions, and on the second night he produced a deck of playing cards.

At last, the day of departure arrived. The morning invited the chilled night air to stay longer now, and the mist clung to the underside of the airships in the dock. Merik thought he had never been happier to leave a place he had been so looking forward to visiting.

There were a few tears, mainly from the duke's eldest daughter, who kissed Jovin's cheek and blushed scarlet while trying to stay dignified. Jovin had a few words with the duke, then he was up the gangplank. Merik scampered after his brother, waving to the party left on the docks and silently thanking the universe that they were leaving.

Jovin waved to the Duke's family for a moment, a smile set in place, then he turned from the rail and sat cross-legged in the middle of the deck, basking in the morning sunlight.

Merik hesitated, then ambled over to sit beside him, "How was your time?"

Jovin's eyes were closed. His back was straight. Merik wondered if he was meditating.

Merik lay back against the polished deck. "I'm so happy we're leaving."

The corners of Jovin's mouth turned up slightly, "Are you, now?"

"You are too," Merik stated. He brought his hands up behind his head. "Don't try to deny it; you were tired of those girls by day three."

"They were fine," Jovin replied. "But it's difficult to charm sisters while they refuse to leave the other's side. The tears today felt a bit unnecessary."

Merik sat up and leaned on his knees. "Captain Donald and I made up a new version of five-card draw—twos are wild, and if you get a four—"

Merik was cut off by two low whistles from the dock, signaling that they were clear from the docking braces.

Jovin got up, "Tell me about it some other time. Depending on the social climate of our next destination, I might join in on a game." Jovin walked toward the stern, his deep-blue coat billowing around him and his hair tossing in the wind.

Merik raised his eyebrows, "Well, that officially makes *one* decent conversation," he looked after his brother. "If we ever get to *two* decent conversations, you might be eligible for an award," he muttered under his breath.

+++++

"You forgot to carry the four," Professor Hopkins said gently.

"No, then it would be eight hundred and seven," Merik stared at the paper, a lost look on his face.

"Not if you subtracted the—"

"That doesn't make any sense!"

"Merik, calm down," Professor Hopkins said. Hopkins had been commissioned as Merik's tutor three years prior, though while on the *Alexandria* he doubled as the botanist and onboard doctor.

Merik slumped dramatically against the table.

"Now, I do not think you are portraying the proper attitude toward the subject," Professor Hopkins mildly scolded, "rewrite the equation, and try it again," he slid a clean sheet of paper to Merik.

"Can I have a break please?" Merik asked. "Maybe I'll be able to get it correct if I come back to it later."

Hopkins had hardly uttered an "if you must," before Merik had scooted away from the table and skipped out of the dining hall.

He gathered up his papers. Hopkins decided that if he had given Merik a break, he, Hopkins, deserved a break as well. *You shouldn't overwork yourself,* he thought. *There is plenty of time for Merik to learn, and more than enough time to work. Let him play now; let him be a child.*

Merik stood in the forward of the *Alexandria*, contemplating life and wondering what Chef Mason would make for lunch.

He mused over the view of the farmlands, green and gold in the filtered midday light. There was a blanket of clouds above the airship, letting through sunbeams like a raggedy patchwork quilt. The few clouds below them reminded Merik of lost sheep. "Of course everyone thinks they look like sheep," he tried for a more interesting metaphor. "How about... the top of a snow-covered icy lake that's been hacked apart by giants who want to destroy all the magical fish..." Merik liked this story better than the sheep-shaped clouds.

Merik looked toward the stern and noticed Jovin some twenty yards down. "Hi," Merik said cautiously, coming to stand beside his brother.

Jovin shot him a temperamental look, and returned to gazing out at the span of endless farmlands.

Merik considered his brother, and decided to keep staring at him until he provided a response.

"I don't like to be gawked at. Stop being pathetic, and find someone else to prod for entertainment."

Merik blanched, "That's rude,"

"There are some things you should learn to get over," Jovin said flatly.

Merik huffed and shuffled into Donald's cabin. Captain Donald was not at his desk but sitting comfortably on the sofa, a book propped open across his knee. "Hello, Merik,"

Merik plopped down beside him, grunting and staring at the ceiling. "Jovin's being a rude, arrogant, ill-tempered groundling… and math is hard."

"Rough afternoon then?"

"The worst," Merik muttered, "and I was so excited for this. So far this whole trip's been kinda lousy."

"It is only just beginning," Donald reminded him, "and do not dwell on Jovin's scouldings; he lives in his own mind at the moment."

"There's still no excuse to act like that."

"Have you thought that Jovin might not be ready for a social demand outside of his requirement? It is my impression that he needs to figure a few things out for himself before he is ready to be social among others."

"Social among *others?*" Merik stared at Donald. "You mean someone who's *not* a girl and *not* important to our father."

"Could it be possible that an expectation of him is too high?" Donald asked.

"I don't like being treated rudely for breathing. It's degrading."

"Only if you allow it to be so," Donald patted Merik on the shoulder, continuing his reading.

Merik watched a patch of sunlight dance across the carpet for a moment, then he sighed and rose.

"Where are you off to now?" Donald asked.

"I'm going back to math," Merik muttered. And, feeling sorry for himself, he slumped out of the cabin.

Chapter 7

Saphir

"Captain," First Officer Carter called though the intercom.

"Just a moment, Mister Carter," Captain Donald said. He motioned for Merik to be silent. "Yes?"

"Silas spotted what looks like a small aircraft traveling north, a few kilometers away. We are set on a near collision course."

"Have you tried to contact them?" Donald inquired. The *Alexandria* had not received a Gliding Warning since their departure from Caloricain the day prior. The nearest settlement with a major airship dock was on the other side of the Ee'lin-Canston border—too far a distance for a small aircraft to traverse alone, let alone past ten in the evening.

"Yes sir," Mister Carter said, *"only static."*

"Make to meet them. We will provide assistance if needed," Donald said.

"Yes, Captain," Mister Carter replied.

Merik yawned widely, "Should I be excited?" he asked.

"It depends whether this aircraft is a threat." Donald rose. "Your significance will remain unspoken," he gestured for Merik to follow him up to the wheelhouse.

"Twenty kilometers until we are in sight," the second mate, Silas McCoy announced as they entered the wheelhouse.

"Prepare the white lights. We do not want to scare this craft," Donald commanded. He turned to Merik. "Please wake Jovin, then wait in my cabin until I fetch you."

"What are the white lights for?" Merik asked on his way out.

"The signal is neutral; it alerts them that we mean no harm," Donald said. When the door had closed behind Merik, Captain Donald turned to Carter. "Is it an enemy?"

"It's hard to tell, sir." Carter tapped the screen inlaid in the center consol. "It's coming from Ee'lin. It hasn't responded to us, and we haven't picked up anything from nearby cities." Carter watched Donald for a reaction. "What are your orders, sir?" he asked.

Donald contemplated the screen where the Ee'lin countryside was mapped out to the coast. "Prepare the men for a fight; arm the cannons. I would rather be pleasantly surprised than endanger us."

+++++

Capitan Donald was looking over a map when Merik joined him in the cabin. "Jovin's on his way," Merik announced, pulling a chair to the front of Donald's desk.

"I find the appearance of this random craft in the middle of the night particularly odd," Donald explained while Merik craned his neck to see the map. "Especially since we are about a days' sailing to the next major city, which would be in Ee'lin."

"Have you tried contacting Queen Venian-Lerlin?" Merik asked.

"I doubt this concerns her court," Donald said.

Jovin entered the cabin a few minutes later, his day jacket flung over one shoulder. "Captain, what's the problem?"

Donald explained about the aircraft and relayed his thoughts about keeping a low profile until they were sure the aircraft was friendly to Canston.

"Well, I agree." Jovin said, seating himself in the chair beside Merik. "And from what father said about the unrest in Ee'lin, it might suit us best if they were grounded by sunrise."

Merik gasped loudly and almost tumbled out of his chair, but said nothing.

Mister Carter's voice over the intercom sounded through the cabin. "*Captain, we're a few minutes off.*"

Donald turned his attention back to the two princes. "Stay here until I fetch you. *Do not leave*," his last words were directed to Merik, who nodded. Jovin raised his eyebrows as Donald exited the cabin.

The boy began tapping his leg in anticipation. "What do you think is happening?"

Jovin leaned back lazily, "They seem flustered."

"You know, we're near the Ee'lin boarder…" Merik prodded.

"Don't start this, Merik," Jovin stood from his chair and walked to the expanse of glass that stretched from one end of the cabin to the other. The railing beyond was nearly invisible against the faded sky.

"Oh come on!" Merik exclaimed. "Don't do that, don't ignore me."

Jovin kept his back to his brother.

The *Alexandria* lurched to the left, throwing Merik out of his chair and knocking Jovin off his feet. Shouts from crewmembers and hurried footfalls came from on deck. The abrasive scrape of metal on wood hit the air, and Merik imagined the aircraft being hauled aboard.

He pulled himself back into his chair, his knuckles turning white as he gripped the armrests.

Jovin stumbled to his feet, his eyes watching the door. "What's going on?" he wondered aloud.

There was a violent crash outside, followed by crewmembers' shouting in panic, and a girl's frightened scream.

Jovin raced to the door.

"What are you doing? Captain Donald said to stay in the cabin!" Merik called after him.

Unsurprisingly, Jovin did not listen.

Crewmen hustled about the deck, illuminated by the white peace lights shining over them, shouting to each other over the wind as it ripped through their ears. Jovin jogged down the stairs, dodging a pair of wildly conversing men at the landing. Stray guns had been tossed carelessly aside and now lay against the rail. The tension on deck struck Jovin's curiosity. A few of the crewmen were crowded in the prow, away from the damaged aircraft that had once been a handsome Ee'landish Windridge. A brilliant blue-and-gold crest embossed the crumpled nose. Its wing had been smashed against the deck, the engines smoked under the bonnet, and bullet holes disfigured the door.

A familiar voice reached Jovin's ears. "I'm fine… please," she was frightened, although she was trying her best to keep up a brave face. "No, really, I'm fine, just… ow!" the girl let out a grunt of pain. She must have stumbled, because the crowd moved aside and someone reached out to catch her.

Jovin cautiously pushed through the crowd.

Captain Donald was kneeling beside her, his words pacifying her. The girl was nodding, pointing at the direction they were flying. Her voice shook as she tried to reply. Jovin noticed the crumpled nightgown, the thrown-on brown overcoat, and the hastily tied leather boots around her feet. Her auburn hair whipped around her in the wind.

"Saphir," Jovin momentarily felt the heaviness lift inside him.

She looked up at the sound of her name. "Jovin," she whispered. Although there were tears in her eyes and she looked exhausted, her face lit up at the sight of him. Saphir reached out a hand for him. He dropped down beside her. Time ceased, and memories flooded in. He was reminded of carefree happiness when life was lighthearted and beautiful and trust was free. But he blinked, and the moment was lost.

"Saphir, what happened?" he gently took her unsteady hand in his.

Her eyes threatened tears. She withdrew her hand to wipe them away before they could betray her.

Jovin was very aware of the watching crew. "We should get her inside," Jovin told Captain Donald, who was crouched beside them.

Donald stood and addressed the watching crewmen. "Everyone is to stay quiet about this young lady," he was stern, almost harsh, making his point clear to each man. "I want no rumors, no false impressions. You will not touch her. You will not disrespect her. You will address her as 'Your Highness' or you will not speak to her at all. Any man who disobeys these orders seeks close acquaintance with the sky spirits."

A few men stared open-mouthed at Donald, some nodded in understanding. Most had never heard their beloved captain speak so gravely. The threat was something uncommon, but no man doubted that at the first sign of betrayal, their captain would act upon his words.

Donald waited until their full attention reverted back to him. "Dismissed."

The men saluted their captain and disbanded, most going below deck, though a few remained to see about the damaged aircraft.

Donald knelt beside the frightened girl, all strict mannerisms gone from his tone. "You are safe here among my crew, they will not harm you."

Jovin straightened up and he held out a hand to her, but she shook her head. "I think I sprained my ankle," she said.

"It can't be too bad," Jovin said.

Saphir regarded him, "I don't think I can stand."

"I'll help you," Jovin told her, "you're going to freeze if you stay out here,"

When she chose not to react to his remark, glancing around at the emptying deck instead. Jovin exchanged a look with Donald, took a breath, and bent to help Saphir up.

She struggled for a moment, then almost collapsed. "I can't walk, I tried. I told you I'm—what are you doing? I'm fine. Put me down. I'm not a child." After a few steps, Saphir seemed to have come to terms with being carried. She tried to look dignified as she clutched his shirt collar, one arm wrapped around his neck to stabilize herself.

Donald opened the cabin door and closed it after them before the frigid wind could force entry into the room.

Merik was sitting in his chair, arms crossed in defiance. "I told him not to, Captain, but he—oh, it's Saphir."

Jovin moved around Merik to the sofa in front of the window wall.

"What happened? Was it only her?" Merik asked.

"As far as we know," Donald replied. He spoke into the intercom and called for Professor Hopkins and Chef Mason to bring something up for the injured princess.

Jovin set Saphir down on the sofa and crouched beside her, "Are you alright?"

Saphir was watching him. She seemed to be on the verge of saying something, and he wondered if his hunch was correct. If she was going to bring it up, then he would talk about it; but if she was going to ignore it, he would not be the one to initiate *that* conversation. Saphir either dismissed the idea, or was thinking something else entirely, because when at last she decided to speak, she only whispered: "I'm frightened."

"You can tell me," Jovin reached for her hand, but Saphir withdrew it. "*Or*," Jovin redirected, now defensive, "you can tell Captain Donald."

"Don't give me that." Saphir sat up and tested her ankle. "I *really* don't need it." Her eyes filled with tears again, but she refused to let them fall. She made a face as she decided that her ankle was not suitable to put weight on.

Jovin's brow furrowed as he watched her, "Sit back down, you'll hurt yourself."

Merik approached cautiously. "Are you all right, Saphir?" his trepidation was evident in his voice.

Saphir smiled for the first time that night. "Hello, Merik," she held out a hand to him, and he gave her hand a loose squeeze. "What are the Canston princes doing on the outskirts of Ee'lin?" Saphir asked, trying to keep her face pleasant.

"Jovin's on a diplomatic tour, and father wanted me to come along so I don't get in trouble," Merik answered.

"Diplomatic tour? Why are you so near the southern border if you were not coming to us—Ee'lin, I mean?" Saphir looked back at Jovin and was surprised to find he had not taken his eyes off her.

"We thought of stopping in Blinley before heading to Delliah," Jovin said, "Saphir, what happened?"

She did not meet his gaze.

Jovin turned her face back to look at him, "Darling, I need you to stop being brave for a moment and tell us what happened."

Saphir took a breath and ran a hand through her hair. When she drew her hand away, it was tinged with crimson.

"That's blood," Merik confirmed in a small voice.

"Go get a towel and a bowl of water," Jovin said, "thank you."

Donald joined them at the sofa as Merik scurried off.

Saphir wrung her hands. She stared up at the ceiling. "We were attacked last night. I don't know who it was… It was late, and I had just gone to bed… Wait, actually, I was still awake…" she spoke slowly, piecing together the fragments of memory that were not a blur. "A siren went off… I remember I threw on my coat… I ran to the door… and my mother was there. She said I had to go, but I didn't know where I was going, she just said, *go.*" Saphir's eyebrows knit in concentration. "She gave me her ring…" her hand went to an inside pocket on her coat and produced a golden ring embedded with the royal crest of Ee'lin. "There were airships over the city and the palace… I think we were being bombed…"

Saphir's story slowed as she tried to recall the night before. "When my mother and I arrived in the aircraft hangar, there were people there that I did not know, and all the staff that I could see were lying dead around us. There was a man with a gas mask… He was wearing a grey coat."

"Rebellion usually declares itself sooner, but grey coats signal the possibility of Landic Assassins," Jovin offered to Donald. "Or what if Berronatt turned hostile against Ee'lin and attacked? Do you know who they were?" he asked Saphir.

"All I remember is that a man tried to grab me but my mother got him off me… I think that's when I hit my head, because it becomes a little blurry after. He went after my mother…" Saphir's hand went to her neck. She tried to pass off the motion as a nervous fidget with the golden necklace she wore there. "But I heard her scream for me to go… I shouldn't have looked back… Afterward, he was going to come after me, but he didn't— I think he let me go… I can't remember…" Saphir put her hands over her temples.

"I retract my statement; the Landic Assassins don't usually let people go," Jovin said to Donald.

Merik returned with a bowl and towel and handed them to Donald. "I'm going to go down to the kitchens," he avoided looking at Saphir and scampered off before anyone could call him back.

Saphir sniffed and steadied her breathing. She motioned for Donald to hand her the bowl and towel, and began to dab at her hairline.

"Is there anything else you can remember?" Donald asked in a hushed voice.

"The airships over the palace, they were military, and there were a few smaller ones over the city. There was fire, and bells were sounding. Then I flew north. I thought maybe Canston could help me, and you did," her voice faltered. "Thank you."

"You are welcome, Your Highness," Donald said. "But we need to exercise caution. If they let you go, they will want to find you again."

"They probably think I'm dead," Saphir tried for a laugh, but it came out strangled. "The winds were strong, and I am not known for being a decent pilot."

"Every reason to keep your whereabouts hidden." Donald rose. "Princess, you shall have my cabin. Please make yourself comfortable. If you need anything, do not hesitate to ask."

"Thank you, Captain, but I think I would feel more at ease in a guest cabin," Saphir responded.

"It is no trouble, I assure you," Donald said.

"Captain, I appreciate your generosity, and your kindness. But while I am aboard, I would prefer a lesser cabin," she said firmly.

"I will have a cabin prepared for you," Donald said.

"Thank you,"

The captain bowed to her. "Please remain here until I return," he strode through the side door.

Saphir stared out into space for a long while. A single tear slipped down her cheek; Jovin hesitated, then wiped it away.

"How's your head?" he asked tentatively.

Saphir snapped out of her melancholy trance. She felt her scalp. "Not all that bloody anymore. Gooey though,"

"That's a bit graphic, Princess."

Saphir took up the towel and bowl again and finished cleaning her hairline. The water became dark and murky as she dipped the towel again. "Well, that's fun," she muttered to herself.

"Let me help you."

"No, I've got it." Saphir averted her eyes.

Jovin was silent a moment, then he spoke: "Why did you think Canston could help you?"

"Canston is a strong country," Saphir said, "my Windridge could not have made it across the Gemelle Channel, and I couldn't turn to Berronatt, seeing as it has its own problems. Ee'lin is on better terms with Canston anyway."

"It makes sense: run to the stronger company—the people you know," Jovin speculated, "the friendlier the face…"

Saphir drew away, "Why must you be so unbearable at this time?"

Before Jovin could reply, the side door opened and Chef Mason entered carrying a tray of soup and a roll of bread. Professor Hopkins followed behind with his doctor's bag. The two bowed to the royals.

Hopkins set about Saphir's ankle before the uneasiness between her and Jovin could be verified. He properly cleaned the wound to her head, dressed it, and placed a bandage over it. Chef Mason informed them that he would be sending Merik up shortly with a plate of desserts. The two left promptly with Saphir's request for tea on Chef Mason's mind.

Jovin stood near the window. He had gotten out of the way for Chef Mason and Professor Hopkins, and, unsure what to do, had stayed there. Now that the cabin was quiet again, he glanced towards Saphir to find her staring intently at him.

She rested her cheek against the top of the sofa. "Merik looks so much older now," She said softly.

"I think he's almost twelve."

"You have the same eyes," Saphir said, "and how is your father?"

"He was fine when we spoke a few days ago." Jovin ran a hand through his hair. He sighed and walked back to her. "Will you be queen, then?"

"Probably… I don't know if I can still rule my country after I ran… or if there will be a choice." Saphir wrapped her arms around herself. "It sounds selfish, but I'm worried about what will happen to me. I… I feel numb. In my head, I feel like I should be afraid, or angry, or *something*, but there's no emotion. Not yet anyway." Saphir's forehead creased, and she took a deep breath. "Talking to you isn't helping, because I'm so confused about what I thought I felt then and what I felt leading up to now. It's too much to handle," her voice faltered, "but I need to be strong; I need to be brave," she said with a firm resilience. "*I need to be brave.*"

Jovin could see the tears forming behind her eyes as she refrained from crying. He moved around the sofa and crouched beside her. "I think you are exhausted and need to sleep," he carefully closed his hand around hers. "I do not mean to confuse you."

Saphir met his eye, "While I am aboard, do not lead me on. Please, I cannot handle it."

There was a knock. Chef Mason was back, apologizing for the lateness of Saphir's tea and ushering along a nervous Merik.

Merik looked slightly ill as he approached Saphir on the sofa. "I brought you these," he murmured, holding out the plate of cookies to her. She took one out of respect.

Merik threw a sheepish glance back to the door, where Chef Mason had exited a moment ago. "I probably ate half the batch of cookies." He waited for a reprimand from Jovin, but Jovin was casting Saphir furtive glances and did not notice Merik's confession.

The concealed staircase door opened again, and Captain Donald reentered. He bypassed the three royals and walked directly to his desk. He rifled through the drawers until he found a leather-bound book and flipped through the pages. He made to walk back to the wheelhouse but stopped before the royalty to address Saphir. "Your room is ready: cabin seven, first door at the bottom of the on deck stairs. Is there anything else we can do for you?"

Saphir shook her head. "Thank you, but no, I have every reason to be content."

Donald replied accordingly and departed to the wheelhouse.

Saphir set her cookie on the arm of the sofa. She straightened up and put her injured foot on the ground. Jovin moved to help her, but she shooed him away, "I'm fine,"

"I understand that you want to take care of yourself, but let me help you," Jovin insisted.

"Persistent, aren't you?"

Jovin ignored her comment and held out his arms to her. She begrudgingly agreed, and he carefully picked her up.

"Open the door, Merik," Jovin said.

Saphir kept her eyes averted as she tried to maintain her dignity.

Merik scrambled to open the cabin door and knocked his toe against the doorframe.

Chilled night air hit their faces. Saphir turned into Jovin's jacket as he walked her down the staircase. Merik hung back at the top of the stairs, then he turned and slipped back into the captain's cabin.

Lamps were lit inside cabin seven, creating a soft, comforting environment. A bed sat in the corner, the coverlet turned down. A folded stack of clothes rested at the foot of the bed.

Jovin set Saphir down in the entryway, "You should be comfortable."

Saphir took in the room, her arms wrapped around herself, "Yes, thank you."

Jovin regarded her, "I'm sorry that this has happened."

Saphir did not speak, and turned her face away from him.

Jovin kissed her hand, focusing her attention back on him, "Good night, Saphir."

She gave him a tired smile, "Good night, Jovin."

Jovin turned to leave. He slipped out the door and began to close it. "Good night," he called back to her.

Saphir humored him, "Good night,"

Saphir's smile faded from her face once the door was closed. She wobbled over to the bed and fell against the soft comforter. Her eyes traveled across the chestnut-colored ceiling and the soft light fixtures. She sat up, wiping her nose and feeling pathetic.

A dressing table and a plush armchair in the corner of the room caught her attention. Saphir caught a glimpse of her own reflection in a mirror; she saw a tangled mass of auburn hair decorated with the bandage Professor Hopkins had placed over her forehead. Her eyes had a vacant light in them. She made herself look away.

Her mind wandered from the room, briefly landing on the boy who had turned into a man since she had come to know him. She had missed him more than she dared to let on. Her thoughts turned homeward; this time yesterday, her mother would have been down the hall and her cat would have been snuggled up at her feet. She wished she could rewind time. Memories flooded her mind and filled her eyes.

Chapter 8

The Report

The flickering shadows cast by the fire were fading. The early morning skies were dotted with fading stars, as the sun had not yet risen. Ganimead was standing at his office window, watching the first strips of color ignite the skies, when there was a sharp rap on the door.

The clock on the wall read 6:13, if it was Miss Shannon, she was early. Regardless, Hadrin was late.

Ganimead strode to the door to reveal the exhausted assassin.

"My apologies, sir; there were complications," Hadrin said, stepping into the room without an invitation.

Ganimead forgave the young man's lack of manners and closed the door behind him. "What happened?"

Hadrin gave his report. "Queen Melba Venian-Lerlin is dead."

"And the princess?"

"You wanted her alive," Hadrin pointed out defensively.

"Yes, alive, but not unharmed. Where is the princess now?" Ganimead asked.

"Flew off in a Windridge," Hadrin replied. "*Arabella* and the battalion are searching the Ee'lin countryside for her."

"They have not found her yet?" Ganimead asked. "She can't have gone far... the aircraft should have broken down by now."

"They send their apologies,"

"Then why did they lose her so easily?" Ganimead turned away from Hadrin and back to the window, where the skies were dancing in orange and gold.

Hadrin sighed, "What else do you want? More than once we have performed above what was promised, yet you pester us. *Arabella* and the Landic have done very well for you. We are not a complacent people. If I were in your position, I would not ask too much of a people who can, and *will*, defy you at the slightest sign of distrust."

"You are in no position to make threats, Hadrin."

"Maybe not. But in the future, we would be willing to accept the slightest appreciation from you. I don't mean patting us on the back, but if we go out of our way to kill someone you want dead, but forget to capture the daughter, then be thankful that the girl will be a weaker ruler than her mother."

"Your employment is not unappreciated," Ganimead said. He turned back to Hadrin, who was glaring at Ganimead without the slightest inclination of humility. "I want updates on the situation. If new information arises and you do not inform me about it, then we will have a problem." He walked to the door and opened it. "When you find her, inform me first, even before your own leaders."

Hadrin's eyes narrowed. "I understand, *sir*," he said, putting disrespectful emphasis on the last word. And with that, he walked through the door without wasting another moment.

Chapter 9

The Scarlet Countryside

Saphir did not leave her cabin all morning. Mister Carter was sent to check on her at one o'clock, but even then she milled about and went back to sleep until Chef Mason brought her lunch at two.

Merik visited later in the afternoon. Saphir took to the armchair for Merik's visit, since lying down made her feel as though she were dying. Her greeting and mannerisms were open, but Saphir's eyes told the story of a restless night barred by disturbing dreams. The young prince cut it short, deciding it was best to let her be alone.

Captain Donald stopped by to see her an hour after Merik, accompanied by the tailor and launderer, Randy Simmons, who presented Saphir with boyish clothes that were closer to her size than the ill-fitting shirt and trousers they had borrowed from Merik. Mister Simmons left soon after taking her measurements, promising to have something more presentable for the princess later that evening.

Captain Donald pulled up a stool from the dressing table. "How are you feeling?"

Saphir shrugged, "I fear I'm slipping into depression," she tried to pass this off lightly, but her eyes gave her away. "When people leave, I have time to think, and… it's suffocating… I'm thinking too much."

"Merik makes a point of commandeering my cabin in the evenings; you are more than welcome to join us," Donald said.

"I don't want to intrude," Saphir said.

"The cabin is a living area," Donald replied, "if the *Alexandria* were a house, think of it as the parlor."

"I doubt I would be an entertaining guest at the moment," Saphir said.

Donald rose and knelt beside her, taking her hand in his. "Princess, I am truly sorry for what you have gone through. Your mother was a brave woman. Her loss is painful. I am sorry we cannot help you more."

Saphir felt like a child. She clutched to Donald's hand. "Did you know her?"

"I did," Donald said, "I met her last year. Remarkable woman—very intelligent. She must have been a fantastic mother. More than once I have met Ee'landish people who have said she was a remarkable queen. I have no doubt that she was."

"She was incredible. Very understanding, and very open to aid those who needed it. She was a wonderful mother… Last year, she knew about me and Jovin before I did." Saphir smiled fondly, and the tears in her eyes were not unwelcome. "The people loved her; they said she was a lioness… Before Father died, they called her his lionheart. I remember when I was little, he said that *she* was what made *him* brave. After he was murdered and she took up complete rule, she called *me* her lionheart… I guess I made *her* brave."

Donald was listening intently. Saphir felt a fondness for the captain that reminded her of her own father. "I don't know why I am telling you this… It doesn't really matter."

"I think it does," Donald told her, "the knowledge that you made her brave is a wonderful thought."

"I guess it is," Saphir wiped her tearstained cheeks.

"What would she say now?"

"Do what is right. Make sure I am taken care of, and remember the people around me." Saphir straightened, her expression resolved to resemble the lionheart they had spoken of—fierce, with the resilience of what is right. "You are one of the people around me; so is everyone on this airship. But I must remember my people. I cannot forget them. I do not know our attacker's motives, but so much is threatened, and I need to be the protector now."

Donald allowed Saphir her moment of resolution to process her thoughts.

She turned to Donald, "What would you say is our next action?"

He hesitated for a fraction of a moment before answering. "The plan is to drop off your Windridge closer to the palace."

Saphir caught on to his train of thought. "Do I need to be thought of as dead? Would it be better if they thought I was alive?"

"They will search for you. If they think that you are alive, they will find us," Donald said, "however, I suggest that you remain with us until we have a better assessment of your country's situation."

"I understand,"

Donald rose. "Would you like to join us for dinner? We will be in the *parlor-living space*," he put a jovial emphasis on the last two words.

Saphir smiled, "Are you mocking me, Captain?"

"I am humoring you," Donald chuckled.

Saphir squinted her eyes and shook her head.

"Well, is there anyone you would like me to fetch?"

Saphir snapped out of her smile. She stared at Donald in silent regard.

"Maybe not?" he offered, "I will leave the option open."

+++++

"Captain!" Merik shouted as he burst through the cabin door.

Donald looked up from his book. "Yes, Merik?"

Merik paused and tilted his head, momentarily forgetting the urgency. "You're reading?"

"I can enjoy myself on occasion; a captain is not always tied to his job." Donald set the book down and leaned across the table. "What is the matter?"

"Oh, right…" Merik fumbled. His eyes glanced up to the left to remember his train of thought. "Oh yeah," he took a deep breath, "Jovin said that we have to dance," seeing the confusion on Donald's face he added, "at the parties," then, seeing as Donald did not understand the enormity of the problem, he added in a small voice, "no one told me about this."

Donald chuckled, "Merik, you love dancing."

"Yeah, but not in public," he scuffed his boot against the edge of the carpet, "not with girls I don't know,"

"You danced with Annalee at the last party, I am confident you can dance with another girl at the next one," Donald said.

"Yeah, but I already knew Annalee, we learned to dance for the first time together. She leads when I mess up." Merik nervously ran a hand through his blond hair. "Anyway, I haven't danced since summer. What if I fail miserably?"

"You will do wonderfully, I am sure." Donald leaned back in his chair. "The dances we use at most parties are group dances; they are easy to learn and simple to fake in case you actually do mess up." He noticed Merik's nervous expression. "Besides, no one is forcing you to dance." Merik's face lit up. "But I would recommend becoming practiced at it. You are the second prince, and one day you will be required to dance at parties. When your brother is king, you will become the diplomat, and it will be mandatory."

Merik sighed. He often forgot about what his life would be like when Jovin was king, these conversations habitually ended with something Merik wanted to forget. "Alright," he walked to the window wall, resigned to the inevitability that he would have to dance at some point in their mission. Merik stared out for a moment. The sky was darkening, and the stars were becoming visible through a layer of cloud. "It's getting cloudy again,"

"A good thing, actually," Donald replied. He stood and took a place beside Merik. "I do not want to be discovered when we drop the Windridge in Ee'lin."

"Who do you think attacked the Ee'lin palace?" Merik asked. "You don't think it was their people, do you?"

Donald paused to think a moment, "We cannot yet tell, but I do not want anyone to know that Princess Saphir is alive; they raided the palace at night for a reason. As long as she is aboard, she is safe. And it will remain that way until we have a lead."

Merik perked up, "Will she have a fake name when we land?"

Donald regarded the boy, "It would be a reasonable precaution,"

"Yes!"

Donald raised his eyebrows.

Merik cleared his throat, moving into a false sophisticated composure. "Um, I mean, that will be fun." Merik glanced around trying to cover his enthusiasm, but failed. "Can I pick it?" he asked, a bit too eagerly.

"What did you have in mind, Merik?"

"Um, what about… Persephone?"

Donald chuckled.

The intercom beeped, and the light flashed until Donald answered it. "Captain's cabin."

"Captain," Mister Carter's voice said over the intercom, *"I strongly suggest that you come up to the wheelhouse."*

"What happened?" Donald's tone lost its merriment.

"We are approaching Ee'lin. We're getting some strange readings."

"I am on my way," Donald answered, "stay here."

Merik protested. "You told me to do that last time and—"

"Merik," Donald's reprimanding look reminded Merik that the captain frowned upon backtalk.

He quickly vacated the cabin.

Merik huffed and got to his feet. Ignoring the insistent voice in his head, he walked out the door.

On deck, the lights were dim. A few crewmembers hustled across the deck, shouting over the wind words that Merik could not understand. A few lights on deck went out.

One crewmember who was a few years older than Jovin stopped beside him. "Your Highness, you may want to remain indoors tonight." The man manually turned off two lights on the wall of the captain's cabin door.

"What's going on?" Merik asked him.

"We are going stealth," the crewman said.

"Oh… Excuse me," Merik scurried up two flights to the wheelhouse and stopped outside the door. He slowly opened the door and slipped in, unnoticed by Donald, but not by Mister Carter. Carter jerked his head slightly, motioning for Merik to move into the corner behind Donald.

"It would devastate her," Donald continued, leaning over an electric map in the center console where points in Ee'lin were lit up red and white.

"She already knows they attacked the palace," Mister Carter pointed out. "There would be no difference in the way she sees it."

"She is young and impressionable," Donald interjected, "her mother is gone, and she has probably lost her country through this. She does not need anything else troubling her."

"*Troubling her?* Gregory," Silas McCoy stared at him, "she's already haunted. She needs to know what happened."

"And she is troubled with Jovin—"

"Of course she's troubled with Jovin, he *would* be difficult to be around, he *messed up*—" Mister Carter broke off, then looked down in shame. "I am sorry, that was out of line."

"You are forgiven. Although the outburst was unnecessary." Donald rubbed his forehead, "I suppose she must know."

Merik shifted from the darkened corner. His voice betrayed his panic. "What happened?"

Donald's eyes lit up with something that was not anger. Merik thought it might be fear. "Merik, you were to stay—"

Merik cut him off. "Captain," he approached Donald for comfort. "What happened in Ee'lin?"

Donald put his hands on Merik's shoulders, "Merik, this is a very delicate situation. It is worse than we originally thought."

"The palace was attacked, what else can happen?" Merik stepped out of Donald's hands and looked over the map displayed in light in the center console. He felt lightheaded. His throat felt very dry. He contorted his face to keep from crying. "How did this happen?" Merik gagged, suddenly feeling very sick. He clutched the edge of the table. "That's a lot of red lights," he ran his hands through his hair, "what does it mean, Captain?" Merik searched Donald's face, hoping there would be another answer than the one he was sure would come.

Donald put his hands back on the boy's shoulders, "Merik,"

Merik's throat tightened, "All the people?"

"We do not know yet," Donald said.

"How…who would do this? It's not… Why would—" Merik was cut off as Donald pulled him into a hug.

Mister Carter looked to Mister McCoy, who had turned away and was presumably wiping his eyes. Between them, the center console's map was aglow where the country had been compromised. Red pixels illuminated the dimly lit wheelhouse, etching a blotch of destruction in the map. Where the capital city had been, there was only an angry blotch of red lights. The entire city glowed red, the farmlands and countryside shone in scarlet. Where the sea met the shore, there was a thin line devoid of light; it skirted the edge of the country like a ring, detaching Ee'lin from the rest of the world.

Donald held Merik tight in his embrace. He looked up, and his eyes met Carter's. Mister Carter shook his head with a pointed look at Merik, and mouthed the words: *"too young."*

Merik pulled away from Donald. "Y-you can't tell her, s-she can't know,"

"Merik,"

"Why do people hurt each other?" he whimpered.

Donald looked down at the boy; his cheeks were red and blotchy. Donald brushed the hair back from Merik's face and kissed the boy's forehead, he gave a shuddering sob and collapsed back into Donald's jacket.

"Breathe, child."

Merik nodded and tried to take in a breath, only to shake and sniffle, gasping in air. Donald produced a linen handkerchief and offered it to the boy. To Mister Carter he said, "Carter, please call to the kitchens and ask them to bring up a cup of strong tea," he looked back to Merik, "I want you to stay in the wheelhouse until I tell you otherwise. Mister Carter and Mister McCoy will be here with you."

Merik sniffed and wiped his eyes. "Alright," he whimpered.

Donald touched Merik's cheek affectionately. He nodded to Mister Carter and McCoy, and vacated the wheelhouse.

Donald hastened down the stairs to the second landing and knocked sharply on Jovin's door. Jovin opened it a moment later. Jovin eyed Donald wearily, "Captain?"

"Jovin, we are over Ee'lin," Donald's tone alarmed the prince, "I need you on your best behavior."

Realization hit Jovin. "Yes, of course," he retreated into the cabin and reemerged pulling on his overcoat. He closed the door and followed Donald down the stairs to the captain's cabin. "What's happened? Have you told Saphir yet?" Jovin asked as Donald opened the door.

"No," Donald ushered him in.

Jovin looked around the cabin. "Where's Merik?" he asked.

"In the wheelhouse." Donald hastened to his desk where he withdrew a map. "There was more to last night's events than the raid on the palace," he traced a few lines on the map, circling the northeast quadrant of Ee'lin's coastline, concentrating on the capital. "Higher devastation in these areas,"

Jovin's gaze dropped. "How many people have died?" he asked softly.

"Our scanners indicate radioactive damage."

"So the injured and ill are fated to die from radiation poisoning?" Jovin moved to the chair in front of Donald's desk. He covered his head in his hands. "Father was wrong; this is not a rebellion of the people. This was an outside attack."

Donald set the map aside. "Saphir mentioned airships, it is a possibility."

Jovin leaned back in his chair. "What will happen to her? She's a danger to us now, as well as to herself."

Donald deliberated for a moment. He glanced to the clock on the wall. It was just before nine. They were to drop the Windridge on the palace's outskirts before dawn.

Jovin stood, "I'll bring her here."

"Be cautious, Jovin."

Jovin hastened from the cabin and treaded lightly down the steps to the main deck. He slowed as he approached Saphir's cabin. The light of her lamp shone through the curtained side window.

Jovin knocked.

Saphir did not answer.

Jovin knocked again, louder this time.

There was the sound of rummaging from within. Then there followed soft cursing as something fell with a low *thump*. After a grunt and an exasperated huff, Saphir opened the door. "Well, it's about time you showed up," she reprimanded.

"What are you doing in there?" Jovin inquired, peeking through the doorway.

Saphir straightened up, blocking his view. She began speaking very quickly, as though she were a child caught and fearing retribution. "Well, I was resting my ankle... and by resting, I mean sleeping, because I am absolutely exhausted. Then you woke me up, and I fell out of my bed and landed on my ankle... Then I stubbed a toe on my other foot, and it is very difficult to stand when you feel you've been compromised... oh, never mind." She saw his amused expression and flipped her slightly messy hair in an attempt to look dignified. "Anyway, is there a reason you knocked?"

Jovin hesitated. He looked down at his boots as the words caught in his throat.

"What?" she asked, suddenly urgent. "You always have something to say; what's the matter?"

His eyes glanced at her. He could not tell her. He would not spoil her spirits. He decided upon the easy answer: "Captain Donald has requested you."

"Are we nearing the palace?" the slight tremble to her voice mingled with the pain Jovin felt.

"Yes,"

She brushed past him, limping horribly but keeping her head held high.

"Saphir, let me help—"

"I'm fine, really," she noticed that he was still beside the door. She turned back to him, "How bad is it?"

Jovin closed her cabin door and said nothing.

Saphir took his silence poorly. She turned and limped away. Jovin followed her up the stairs; he steadied her when she reached the top. She hesitated outside the door, "Jovin?"

He turned his face away from her.

Saphir opened the door and hobbled in to the cabin. "Captain," she painstakingly seated herself in a chair. "What condition is my country in?"

Donald noted the false confidence, and the worried eyes behind the set jaw. She was seated stiffly in her chair. Jovin hung back in the doorway.

"Please, Captain; I cannot stand being the only one who does not know the situation," she implored.

Jovin stood behind her, shaking his head. Donald gave him an apologetic look. Jovin's eyes widened.

The exchange did not go unnoticed by Saphir. When she spoke, her voice was frantic. "Please, tell me."

Donald proceeded cautiously, "It seems the attacker bombed the palace and much of the surrounding coastline."

"Oh." Saphir felt something snap inside her like a twig underfoot. The hope that the damage might have only been to the palace was lost, to be replaced by an intense remorse. She felt dizzy.

"Oh," she repeated. She was vaguely aware that she was falling. Then Jovin was steadying her, asking if she was alright. But she was not alright; how could she be alright when her home, the only place of security she had ever known was gone? Not only had her palace been destroyed, but so had the cities, the families—all the people she had known and loved.

She was alone now. She was all that was left of her past.

As if through a tunnel, she heard Jovin whisper her name. Muffled and farther off, she heard Donald call something into the intercom. Saphir felt herself being picked up and laid on something soft, a pair of green eyes hovering over her, occupying her confused vision. She was taking in shallow, hasty gasps of air. A hesitant hand was brushing her hair away from her face. She tried to say that she was alright, but all that would come out was a stutter of unrecognizable words. The room was silent, save for someone calling her name, calling her back to reality.

"Saphir,"

Chapter 10

The Mark upon a Peaceful Country

"We are going to drop the Windridge within the next hour. She remains here, Jovin. She needs support." Donald closed the curtains on the window wall, and his footsteps receded until the door closed.

The sofa let out a low creak as Saphir sat up. "I didn't faint, did I?"

"Sort of... in a sense..." Jovin faltered.

"I detest feeling powerless," Saphir wiped her nose on her sleeve, "this is weakness, and it's pitiful."

"You are not weak," Jovin told her.

"What would you call this, then?"

"Human." There was a tenderness behind his voice and expression that she was not accustomed to seeing, nor was she prepared for. In her history of knowing Jovin, she had never seen him act so sorry. In their past, she had seen him wildly happy, laughing and smiling with a reckless light to his eyes. She had also seen him lie, dripping in guilt, confused and panic stricken. But now, the remorse that poured out of him, this was new to her.

A voice in the back of her mind reminded her not to confuse her current emotions with those of the past. She needed to remain present, and submissively slinking into the past would only cripple her. Let Jovin be pitiful; let him hold on to her hand and rest his head against her arm while she ignored him.

For a long while, the cabin remained silent. Saphir was beginning to feel hollow inside again. She stared at the ceiling, wondering if she was worth all the trouble she was causing. "Maybe I should have stayed and died with my people," she found herself wondering aloud.

"Don't."

Saphir was startled by the sorrow in his voice. "What's that?"

"Please don't say that,"

From on deck there came the sound of men running to the prow, along with the low vibration of the guilder being dropped from the side. There came the soft hiss of rope cutting over wood and another thwack as something dropped. Another shout echoed through the cabin, this time in surprise. Someone called for the captain; another shouted for the first man to stop yelling. There were footfalls over the deck and astonished cries from the crewmen. Someone was swearing very loudly.

Saphir stared at the door, waiting for someone to come and call them. Her hand slipped away from Jovin's as she unconsciously rose to her feet.

"Saphir," he warned.

"Something's happening," her eyes remained fixed on the door.

"It doesn't matter, the crew will handle it," Jovin rose also, taking her hands in an attempt to regain her attention. "Saphir, darling, stay here."

She took an abrasive step forward, straining on her ankle.

"Saphir, stop." Jovin grabbed her arm.

She weighed her options, but her curiosity got the better of her. She pulled her arm away from Jovin.

Jovin made a beeline for the door.

"Excuse me," she tried to get around him. Jovin sidestepped, blocking her again.

Saphir glared at him, "Let me through."

"What do you think you are doing?" he implored, unmoving.

"I am going out. Let me through," she tried to get around him again, "*please* let me through?"

"No."

Saphir grunted in frustration and made to push past him, but he caught her by the waist. Saphir struggled to free herself, flailing in her attempt to escape. "Let—me—go!"

"Saphir, you're not thinking clearly— you have to stay here," Jovin said.

"I'm fine—let me go!" Saphir brought her elbows back into his stomach and ducked away from him. She stumbled a step, and his hand caught her wrist before she got to the door. "Jovin!"

"No, listen to me. You need to stay here,"

Saphir gave Jovin a filthy look. She leaned back and kicked him in the stomach. Jovin relinquished his grip on her. She staggered to her feet. Her ankle buckled under her, but she kept moving. She threw open the door and sprinted out onto the shadowy deck.

She stumbled down the stairwell in her haste; her mind was set on getting to the rail before her ankle gave out.

Her eyes burned as she stared out into the night. She found herself gagging for air. She felt as though a string inside her had finally snapped. Her knees gave way, her fingers clutching for the rail. She felt herself hit the deck. Everything was wrong. It was all wrong. It was not true. It was her imagination, any moment she would wake up and find herself back home. The air flowing through her felt as though it was drying out her lungs. Her head throbbed. Her heart ached.

She only realized there was someone sitting beside her when an arm wrapped protectively around her shoulder. She gave in to her pride and cried on the shoulder that was offered. Saphir did not know how long she sat there; time seemed to blur into nothingness. Her pain felt hollow inside her, as if it were a creature that was slowly peeling away all that was happy from her world. Hopelessness was a terrible thing.

"Saphir?" Jovin's voice sounded remorseful.

Saphir wiped her eyes with the heel of her hand, sniffling. "Sorry," she mumbled. "It just feels… I… shouldn't be he-ere," she tried to stabilize her breathing, but she could only gasp for air. "I'm falling ap-art. I-I should be s-stronger than this."

Jovin put a hand on either side of her face, looking directly into her watery eyes. "You are strong," he told her. "You are so strong—stronger than you realize."

"You keep saying that, but i-it's not true anymore."

"Listen," Jovin said firmly, "you are here for a reason. You are alive, and you are with us for a reason."

Saphir shook her head.

"You cannot save them now," Jovin implored, "but you are alive to rebuild it."

The vibrant display of light illuminated the darkened skies—a mark upon the peaceful country. Far below, a great distance away, through the air that divided the space of the sky from the belly of the ground, the palace of Ee'lin was in flames.

The *Alexandria* could not see the deeper destruction wrought by the attackers. The city surrounding the palace shone scarlet, with embers of homes and shops glittering as though the stars had turned false upon them. Craters littered the farmlands. Survivors filed out of the rubble. Children cried for their mothers. Mothers cried for their children. Fathers carried their wounded.

The flames from the city spread through the countryside, demolishing crops and farmlands in its wake. The animals stampeded where the fires blazed around them, those who escaped were lost to the remaining survivors. Ee'lin was recognizable only by the lonesome roads and dilapidated houses among the vestiges—the base of what had once been a magnificent and beautiful city.

All of this Saphir could not see, but she was an imaginative girl.

Saphir pulled away from Jovin. She staggered to her feet and wavered at the rail. "What are you doing?" he asked, standing with her.

"Remembering," Saphir said. She was determined to see the remnants of the life she had once loved, now burning in scarlet and creeping their way to the seaside. "This doesn't seem real. I need to remember it as real."

"You don't need to watch it," Jovin said.

"I need to see for myself what I ran from. I would have been among them if not for my mother." Saphir leaned over the rail, a tear slid down her cheek, falling down into the dark expanse between airship and ground. "I need to remember this feeling, because one day I might need to justify it." Another tear dropped from her eye and plummeted down to the ground.

"Justify it?" Jovin whispered. "Saphir?"

She was shaking her head. "What happened?" her voice was losing its melancholy sadness, replaced by a fierce anger that was not hers. "We've been at peace for so long. Who would attack us?" She hit the rail in frustration. "It's pathetic!" she yelled into the night. "It's sick and evil, and I hate it!"

Her voice broke, and her tears returned—hot, blinding tears that made her choke back sobs. When she spoke again, it was in a low, quiet whisper. "Now everyone I love is dead."

She began walking the rail, limping every other step. Her fingers traced the wood, her eyes on the horizon. She spoke softly to herself, as if in a trance.

"All my life I thought I was safe. Come to find out, safety is only a matter of perception."

She took a trembling breath and hung her head. She felt Jovin beside her, but she made no movement to show that she perceived him. "I'll be brave, but my heart will still hurt."

Jovin did not want to leave her, in fear that her grief would cause her to do something drastic. She did not deserve to suffer through this alone.

He enveloped her in a hug, "I'm sorry, I'm so sorry,"

Saphir did not respond to him. She stood like a statue, completely void of reaction.

"Saphir, look at me."

She looked up at Jovin, and her eyes related her hopelessness. "Being strong is difficult,"

Jovin kissed the top of her head and held her close to him.

Saphir was beginning to feel nothing. She was beginning to feel empty again.

Chapter 11

Light

Saphir locked herself in her cabin on the following day and appeared only when Jovin was sent to make sure she was still alive. He stayed with her all evening, reading aloud from a book of Kaiden poems in an armchair until she took a break from staring at the ceiling and began to sob uncontrollably. Nothing Jovin did made any difference to her.

She spoke little on the second day. She limped across the main deck of the *Alexandria* in repetitive circles until she grew tired or Captain Donald made her eat something. Jovin often peered out of his cabin to see if she was still on deck, and was not admitted entry when he went to check on her at nightfall.

The third day, she did not speak at all. She sat on deck in the tepid sunshine, sipping the occasional cup of tea and nibbling at the scones and cookies Merik brought to her. She ignored the puzzled stares of the crewmen, choosing to keep her eye on the skies to the south, where she assumed Ee'lin to be. At night she lay with her back against the deck, gazing up at the starry night sky above the *Alexandria's* gigantic balloon, until she fell asleep.

Jovin was trotting down the stairway on the morning of the fourth day when he noticed Saphir at the starboard railing. Her eyes were closed as she basked in the sunlight. She had braided her long, fiery hair out of her face, and the flyaways whipped around her in the high winds. Jovin was surprised to find that she had come out of her depression enough to dress herself properly. He considered talking to her, but decided to leave her be.

"Saphir's up," Jovin announced, strolling into Donald's cabin, "and she looks better than yesterday."

Captain Donald smiled, "I noticed." He was playing a card game with Merik, who had a smug look on his face as though he knew he was winning.

"Any guesses as to what changed?" Merik asked. He raised an eyebrow at Donald as the captain exchanged a few cards.

"Not really," Jovin said, leaning against the desk.

"I think she has come to terms with her emotions and her situation," Donald said.

Donald put down his cards. Merik grinned, "I win," the boy gloated, and began to reshuffle.

"Probably," said Jovin, ignoring Merik's snickers.

"Speak with her, show that you are there to support her, and invite her to join us," Donald suggested.

"I'll try," Jovin sighed, "what if she doesn't want to talk?"

"You might find that she does, although I would advise caution on the subject of Ee'lin," Donald said. "Patience is a good practice to be in. She will speak when she is ready to. There is no rushing these things."

"You wanna play, Jovin?" Merik asked, holding up the deck of cards.

Jovin took in the array of buttons they had been using as gambling chips and noticed the larger pile lying in front of Merik. "I'll pass," he pushed away from the desk and moved across the cabin. "Captain, do us a favor and teach the kid how to lose gracefully," Jovin said, and slipped through the door before Merik's remark could meet his ears. From the landing he noticed Saphir standing against the starboard rail and jogged down the stairs to the main deck.

He approached with caution so as not to startle her, "Saphir?"

Her eyes were not disheartened, as they had been during the previous days, though they were not as bright as he had once known them to be; they seemed to have come to terms with reality, although they retained fragments of her grief. "Hello, Jovin,"

Jovin tentatively joined her at the rail. "How are you?"

Saphir hesitated a moment. "I am… I am all right," she said finally. "It is a strange cycle, and I just have to sit in it until I can pull myself out. But I feel lighter today."

Jovin felt relieved. This was the most conversation anyone had gotten out of her in the last few days.

"Thank you," she said slowly, "for everything. I appreciate it. You have been very kind to me."

Jovin struggled to reply. "Yes, well, um..."

"Thank you," Saphir said again, straightening up. "Well, I think I'll go find something to eat; I'm absolutely starving. Where are the kitchens?"

+++++

The air became colder as they flew north. Soon it was unadvisable to be on deck without several layers and protective goggles to keep snow from stabbing the eyes. More than once, Merik forgot to put on his goggles, and after being on deck for less than thirty seconds, his eyes were stinging and bloodshot.

Professor Hopkins made frequent visits to check Saphir's ankle. Each time, he seemed content that it was healing rather nicely, though he said she shouldn't go running about yet. While recovering from her trauma, Hopkins's primary concern was how easily Saphir slipped in and out of her melancholy state.

Whatever Saphir's condition—depression or otherwise—these were the first days she felt secure on the *Alexandria*. She played cards with Merik for hours on end, and laughed at the boy's enthusiastic triumphs. She made timid jokes, "*terrible jokes*", according to Merik, but jokes nonetheless. One evening she helped Chef Mason make dinner and dessert—something which earned her "likable points" with Merik.

But when she was alone—either wandering the top decks of the airship or in her cabin, humming old Ee'landish lullabies her mother once sang to her—she would begin to remember what she was running from, what had changed, and how everything she had held close to her was no more. And, remembering hurt worst of all.

Much to the dismay and further confusion of Saphir, the day following her lifted spirits, Jovin grew distant from her. There would be moments when it seemed he wanted to say something to her, but after each of these moments, he would look away or remain silent. Saphir was finding it increasingly difficult to carry a conversation past a few sentences. It felt that his kindness toward her had reached the end of a line. As the days progressed, it seemed that he wanted nothing to do with her. After a lunch of Merik chatting about funny cloud shapes and Jovin not speaking directly to her, Saphir wondered what had happened to Jovin that had caused this sudden closed-off nature.

At dinner on the sixth day, Captain Donald brought up a problem subject. "We are scheduled to land in Delliah tomorrow afternoon, but I do not think it would be wise for Saphir to be recognized." Delliah was a small country situated north and east of Canston that bordered the coast of the Gemelle Channel.

"Do you think I would be in danger there?" Saphir asked. She tried to catch Jovin's eye, but Jovin seemed to have found something of great importance on his dinner plate.

Merik sneezed and wiped his nose on his sleeve.

"If someone let you go, then someone is looking for you," Donald said. He handed Merik a napkin, and the boy sniffled. "I think it would be best for you to stay on board until we know that you will be safe among the people we are with."

Saphir nodded reluctantly, "How long will you be in Delliah?"

"We had planned for two weeks, but with our slight delay and a few other matters factoring in, I would think seven days is plenty," Donald said.

Merik offered Donald his used napkin. The Captain waved it away politely.

Saphir shot Donald a furtive look. "Please do not change your plans for the sake of me; you would be staying longer if you had not come to my aid. I am more than capable of following along quietly until we figure out what is to become of me."

Merik sneezed violently, "Whew, excuse me!" he said brightly.

"You're excused," Jovin muttered to his fork.

"I thought the proper thing to say was 'bless you' when someone sneezed?" Saphir said, completely lost.

"Oh, well then," Merik cleared his throat, "bless me."

"And you have been blessed," Donald smiled. He then turned his attention back to Saphir. "I cannot leave you alone on the *Alexandria*, it would not be fair to you."

Saphir refocused on Donald, "Captain, you have been more than fair to me, and until I have an idea of what I am to do, I am more than happy to go along with what you have planned."

"Just don't do something stupid," Merik said, and he yawned magnificently.

"Like what?" Saphir asked.

"I'm sure you could find something," Jovin muttered.

+++++

When the *Alexandria* docked the next day, Saphir stayed on board. The sleeting sky took a break in harassing the airship long enough to allow it to dock safely, then it turned cruel again. In the afternoon, when Jovin and Merik made ready to meet with the representatives from the castle, both heavily bundled up to keep from freezing, Saphir found that she wanted to go with them—not only for something to do, but also because she enjoyed their company, or at least Merik's company.

"What are you going to do while we're gone?" Merik asked while he grappled with his gloves and his scarf trailed on the captain's cabin floor behind him.

"Oh, I don't know yet," Saphir replied. She took pity on the boy and helped him with his gloves. "What do *you* think I should do?" she began winding his knit scarf around his neck.

Merik made a face while he thought. "If you haven't been down to the greenhouse yet, that's always interesting. Umm, oh! You could go through Chef Mason's cookbook for more recipes- I am *really* getting tired of chocolate chip cookies all the time, and he *always*... Um, Captain Donald has books, if you like that sort of thing..."

Donald interrupted. "Help yourself to any of my books. I have asked Mister Carter to accompany you into town tomorrow to shop for anything you might need. If you require help, or if there is an emergency, Mister Carter has also offered to be on hand. I will be back in a few days after we arrange the formalities. I am sorry to leave you like this, Your Highness, but I do not think it could have been helped."

"It is quite alright; it gives me time to... make myself more at home," Saphir said.

Jovin entered the cabin, bringing with him a gust of bitter air. "They're waiting for us, hurry it up."

"Thank you, Jovin." Donald turned back for a last word with Saphir. "And feel free to purchase anything you like in town, and do not worry about expenses. Make yourself comfortable. Good day, Princess." He bowed to her. Saphir curtsied back.

"Bye, Saphir," Merik said, giving her a hug. "Don't do anything stupid. And remember: if you go out in public, use a fake name. I suggest 'Persephone.'"

"Why 'Persephone'?" Saphir asked.

"I dunno, it sounds interesting." Merik shrugged and followed Donald out of the cabin.

This left Jovin with Saphir.

Saphir stared at a spot on the floor. Jovin cast his eyes around the room.

"So, um, have fun," Saphir said.

"And you as well," Jovin replied.

There was an adamant pause. Saphir hugged her arms around herself.

"Well then," Jovin said at length. "Goodbye."

"Goodbye, Jovin."

Each regarded the other for a very tense moment. Then Jovin said, "Well then," and quitted the cabin.

Chapter 12

The Lies We Tell Ourselves to Feel Whole

Merik's nose smudges adorned the motorcar window, mingled with random fingerprints. He had tried to sit still, but his curiosity was getting the better of him. He moved to look out the window again and smacked his forehead as the motorcar carriage dipped.

"Sit still, Merik," Jovin told him.

Merik rubbed his forehead, "But it's so interesting here," he pressed his face to the window again. "It never snows this much in Canston—at least not in the autumn."

The royal motorcar passed the town hall—a low building with two round, sturdy towers. A thick layer of snow dripped from the slanted roof.

"The buildings are different here too. More like... well, I guess since it gets colder..." Merik murmured to himself.

From the divider in the middle of the motorcar, the representative knocked, and slid the divider door open. "We are approaching the palace," he said, "the King has requested to receive you in the grand parlor. He sends his apologies, but he is not up to a party or banquet this evening. However, he has called for a large banquet tomorrow evening in honor of your arrival." The representative, who had been introduced to them as Sir Arnold Heiton, inclined his head.

Captain Donald's face appeared to the left of Sir Heiton. He exchanged a small look with Jovin. His raised eyebrow might have asked Jovin his opinion of the situation. And the manner in which Jovin's mouth twitched before he looked out the window might have relayed his contempt.

Sir Heiton did not notice the exchange. He did, however, notice Merik's face pressed up against the window again.

"Jovin, look at this one!" Merik exclaimed, pulling at Jovin's arm.

"That is the record hall, constructed thirty years ago by King Pierson I," Sir Heiton said, speaking as tour guide now.

"What kind of records do they keep there?" Merik asked, coming away from the window long enough to ask the question.

"*Merik*," Jovin hissed.

Merik became silent.

The rest of the motorcar ride passed in quiet, and soon they were pulling into the palace of King Pierson II. It was a standard castle and looked to be about five stories high, with a few towers rising above the city. It was a stronghold to withstand all weather; rain, snow, floods and blizzards. For that reason, it was not as graceful as the palace of Canston.

Merik thought it reminded him of a very large meatloaf with smaller meatloaves lined up evenly on top of it; then Merik realized he was hungry and decided to stop thinking about food.

The motorcar stopped outside a large gate and was let in shortly after, stopping again at a pair of great doors under a stone-and-tile canopy. The two other motorcars containing Merik's tutor, Professor Hopkins, their luggage, and a few crewmembers to act as guards, stopped behind them.

Merik noticed Jovin glaring at the castle and heard him huff out a breath a moment after.

Sir Heiton led them inside and into the grand parlor, where King Pierson II was waiting for them beside a well built and blazing stone fireplace.

"And here you are. Welcome." King Pierson had a hard look to his eyes that did not seem to generate any sort of welcome. He was not tall and was rather on the aged side of life. There was a shallow tint to his skin from lack of sunlight, and he shone pale under the firelight. Standing beside Jovin, Merik thought he looked sickly. "I apologize that there is no party tonight; we were not sure when to expect you after we got word you were running a few days late. We decided to wait until we knew you would be here before making arrangements."

"It is quite alright," Jovin replied, smiling kindly. He and King Pierson shook hands. This surprised Merik, as it was not something incredibly normal among royalty, but it helped break the block set up by their late arrival and the lack of a welcoming party. "I apologize that we are later than expected; we ran into a spot of strange weather and were thrown a bit off course."

You liar, Jovin, Merik thought. He did his best to hide a smirk, and failed miserably, though he thought King Pierson did not see.

King Pierson nodded. Jovin was younger than he had expected, and would immediately catch the eye of his daughter, he was confident in that assumption. There was a regal quality about the prince that shone through even when silent, and he respected it.

King Pierson's eyes landed on Merik, who was standing a few steps behind Jovin with Captain Donald. He did not care much for children, even when they were his. He had become close to his daughter and two sons only when they were old enough to stop asking foolish questions, and started behaving like the royalty they were. This boy was not over the age of curiosity; he could tell by the way the young prince's eyes flickered around the room, darting from the crackling fireplace, to the orange tinted windows, to the golden wallpaper, with equal amounts of wonder.

Jovin stepped aside, "I would like to introduce my younger brother, Prince Merik, and our guardian, Captain Gregory Donald, of the airship, *Alexandria*."

Donald bowed, and after a confused moment, Merik did also.

"I welcome you," King Pierson said, and, deciding to ignore Merik's youth, turned back to Jovin. "Would you care to discuss the continuum of the peace treaty tonight, or wait until a further date?"

"I would appreciate it if we were to hold off for the moment," Jovin replied.

"Of course, I am sure you are weary from traveling." King Pierson inclined his head.

Merik, who was awake, hungry, and excited about being in a different country, privately thought that King Pierson was mistaken, but he knew not to point that out to the King.

"I will have dinner brought to your rooms. Let us discuss it after you are rested," King Pierson continued, "Captain, if your airship requires any maintenance or resupply, my people will take care of it. You may leave any request with my dockworkers and we will have them taken care of before your departure."

Donald bowed, "Thank you for your kind hospitality, Your Majesty. It is greatly appreciated."

The King inclined his head. "It is an honor," to Jovin he said; "if you would excuse me, I will retire. Please make yourself at home; Mrs. Brown will show you to your rooms."

At a wave of the King's hand, a middle-aged woman came forward from beside the doors. Mrs. Brown curtsied. "Good evening," she smiled. "This way to your rooms, Your Highnesses."

Jovin nodded to King Pierson, "Thank you again for your hospitality. Good evening," he turned and followed Mrs. Brown out the door. Donald bowed to King Pierson, and Merik made a quick bow before scampering after Jovin and out the door.

+++++

Saphir timidly knocked on the door of the wheelhouse.

When there was no answer she knocked again, a little louder this time.

"Just come in, nothing indecent going on here." Mister Carter's voice shouted through the closed door.

She slipped in. "I wanted to let you know that I'm ready to go," she announced.

"Just a moment, Princess," Mister Carter said. He was frantically pressing buttons on a control panel and staring intensely at a screen. A headset covered his ears, and his blue uniform coat lay over the back of his chair.

Saphir peered around at the array of buttons and switches. The center of the room was occupied by a large electronic map where the *Alexandria* was marked by a small, blinking light. She contemplated relocating the map to show Ee'lin's topography instead of the Canston-Delliah boarder, but stopped herself by flattening her new skirt and folding her hands.

"You appear nervous," Mister Carter said plainly, without glancing at her. He continued to tap a few buttons, then consulted a stack of paper, and referred to the screen again.

Saphir forced out a laugh, "It seems that I am obvious,"

"If I thought nervous was your usual disposition I wouldn't have mentioned it, but from what Merik says, you're pretty level headed." Mister Carter said, turning away to finish tapping on the keyboard.

"I used to be," said Saphir, "It's easier to remain calm under stress when you're naïve."

Mister Carter let out a grunt of amusement. "Well, there's a statement," he picked up a pen and jotted a note on the stack of paper. "It's difficult to know how to react in every situation. Those who think themselves wise are often just experienced in the ways of hardship, those who are not, have only been spared the cruelty of the world."

"Am I graced with the presence of a poet *and* a philosopher?" Saphir asked.

"Silas and I exchange books from time to time, he's got me reading a little book of poetry that was published amid the War of Placate. It's in my coat pocket if you want to take a look at it."

Saphir dug around in the pocket and produced a small green book. "Oh, I recognize this! Isn't the author from Kaiden?" she said, thumbing through the pages. "Have you read the poem that talks about bloody flowers? There are a few that are really inspiring and rally the reader to fight oppression. Jovin read them to me a few days ago—" Saphir stopped short, her smile fell from her face, and she quickly set the book down.

Carter gave her a sidelong glance. "*Pray we survive what we have created,*" he quoted from the book.

"Yes, that poem." Saphir said, shifting onto her stronger ankle, and looking anywhere but at Carter.

It was a few minutes before Mister Carter straightened up and shrugged on his long, blue uniform jacket. He placed the book of poems on his station, and made a note informing Mister McCoy not to move it.

"Alright, if anyone asks, you are my stepdaughter. You are a passenger on the *Alexandria*; your mother is back in Canston. This was your chance to see a bit more of the world. You have never spoken with Jovin. You work in the kitchens with Chef Mason and help when needed. What would you like your false name to be?"

"Um… Merik suggested 'Persephone,'" Saphir offered.

"Absolutely not. We're calling you Miranda. Last name? We need to decide upon it beforehand." Mister Carter checked his brown hair in the window's reflective glass, ratted it a moment, and shook it out.

"I don't know," Saphir said.

"Let's go with Lester," Mister Carter said, finally deciding his hair was decent enough.

"Miranda Lester," Saphir tried out the name. "But why a stepdaughter?"

"If anyone suspects something, it would be much harder to track a stepdaughter than a real daughter. And this way if they try to find us again, or me, and you are not with me, or I without you, it will be easier to make up excuses as to why we were separated. Your mother could have gotten mad or something, took you with her… endless possibilities. Anything unclear?"

"No, I understand." Saphir straightened her coat.

"Brilliant." Mister Carter held out an arm to Saphir, "Ready then?"

It was just beginning to snow again when the two finished their mandatory shopping. They had started out the venture alongside four crewmen who had assisted them in carrying packages, but they had quickly been sent back to the *Alexandria* with arms laden with boxes and bags full of daywear and dresses. On Mister Carter's insistence, Saphir also purchased a large down bed coverlet, a heavy carpet, a couple of fluffy pillows, and a few lightbulbs to provide softer light in her guest cabin. Carter kept up a reminder that if she was to stay with them, no matter for how long, she should at least feel comfortable; and for this, Saphir was grateful.

Saphir and Mister Carter emerged from a shoemaker's shop near the upper circle of the city and decided to warm up in a tea shop.

"Well, let's see," Mister Carter said as they picked out a table with a clear view of the street. "You've got the basics: a couple of dresses, new boots and party shoes, that fantastic purple coat; you have a few things to make your cabin a bit more homelike and less generic. Is there anything else you might want, anything at all?"

Saphir smiled, "I think I have enough. Thank you for taking the time to do this for me. It is very kind of you."

Carter waved it away, grinning kindly. "It is my honor, Princess."

Their tea arrived quickly and they were looking out at the streets when it began to snow. Carter looked up at the sky through the window. "But it's only four, don't start that now."

Saphir regarded him. "Has the weather disappointed you?'

"It should have started later than this," Carter said, still staring up at the clouds, "I was expecting snow around seven, not this early. When you've lived in the clouds as long as I have, you start to catch on to the patterns of the sky… But apparently it's still not enough time."

"Which is?"

Carter counted silently. "About eleven years? Maybe twelve?"

Saphir starred into her tea cup and silently pondered his answer. Her mind was calm, then it glitched, reversed, and fogged with unwanted thoughts. Horrid, nauseating thoughts. She closed her eyes in an attempt to expel them.

In a moment of panic she felt herself knock her entire undrunk cup of tea off the table.

The crash pulled her mind back into place, she took a breath and opened her eyes, suddenly aware that Mister Carter had been watching her with concern.

"I'm so sorry," she said to the waitress as the woman scrambled to pick up the pieces. The waitress assured her that there was no problem, and offered to get her a fresh cup. Mister Carter offered to pay for the damages as Saphir tried to calm her breathing.

When she was stable and able to piece together reality again she realized they had delivered her a piping hot cup.

"I understand that it is not my place," Carter said, "but if something is troubling you, it can help to talk about it. You don't have to talk to me, I might suggest the Captain, or Professor Hopkins. You should not have to bare your sorrow alone."

"I'm having a difficult time," Saphir admitted softly.

"Sometimes tea can help calm anxieties." Carter said kindly. "When I feel uneasy I like to stand out on the airship's deck and count the clouds. If it is a cloudless day, I try to count the birds that are gliding beneath us. Silas writes. Grinnings exercises. Pippin sings. Colter breathes. Philbert dances around the main deck in the moonlight until Ibsen throws his old, smelly socks at him; for a while he was buying a new pair every time we made port. Parness started painting the crews' quarters a year back, and that's the reason we have strange and beautiful designs all over the walls. When you're falling asleep and stare up at the ceiling, all you see are geometric shapes. Elsmere used to recite poetry at the top of his lungs, or break out into song; not happy, soothing songs— loud, boisterous songs about conquering fears and tromping mountains." Carter paused as Saphir cracked a smile. "Everyone has a way of finding their own personal happiness. Sometimes it helps to have someone to hold your hand through it, sometimes you need to hold your own hand and drag yourself out. But if you don't know how to find yours," he held up his mug, "sometimes a good, strong cup of tea can calm the heart's aching."

+++++

The alliance was reaffirmed between Canston and Delliah the following day. After a pleasant afternoon of chatter, King Pierson II commented that he was grateful that Canston had sent the princes rather than a folly of courtiers.

Four times in the week that followed, Merik and Captain Donald visited Saphir on the *Alexandria*. They spoke of the court, the security of the castle, and the business of town. Saphir did not care for talk of the Delliah castle, but was pleased to hear of the new card game Merik was inventing, and about how he was working on training Sighter to dodge and hide behind icicles.

She and Carter visited the tea shop daily, chatting about his life before he came to work for Captain Donald, and about his mother, who tried to get him to follow his father's path of being a tailor, and of the hoard of books that Mister Silas McCoy seemed to have smuggled aboard.

"I swear on Ira and all that is good, no one can own that many books. He tried to get me to smuggle five or six different renditions of the exact same book among my things, and I do not kid when I say that, if my mother had heard my curses, she would have banned me from ever again entering her house. You laugh, but Saphir, it was the exact same book!"

"Oh hush, cut him some slack, Lewis, I'm sure there is an explanation."

"I'm sure there is, I've just yet to hear it." Carter grinned.

On a chilled morning one week since their arrival in Delliah, Merik came bounding into the captain's cabin, his hair bore dustings of snow, and his cheeks were flushed and rosy. He would have been comical, bursting in with his scarf tails flying behind him, his heavy coat buttoned haphazardly, and his gloves on the wrong hands. But he was not. There was a look of sheer panic across his normally jovial face. "Jovin's with a girl!" he shouted, stopping short before he skidded over the carpet and ended up on Saphir's lap where she was curled up with a book on the sofa.

Saphir felt her throat tighten. "Well… good for him."

"They're outside," Merik said breathlessly, as though he had run all the way from the palace to tell her this unnecessary news.

"I really don't care," Saphir said tartly, and turned her attention back to her book.

"She wanted to see the *Alexandria!*" Merik nearly screamed in frustration.

"Fine." Saphir replied simply, and added under her breath, "I won't get in her way then."

"Saphir, have you gone mad?" Merik yelled. "*She can't see you!*"

"Wha… oh goodness gracious!" Saphir said, cottoning on. She leapt to her feet, the book flying out of her hands and landing with a dull *thud* on the carpet. "What do I do?"

"Hide!" Merik seized her arm and began dragging her outside. "They were a few minutes behind me at the gate, got caught up—doing whatever—and

I got here first to warn you." He flung open the door. "Go hide in your cabin! Go!"

"This is ridiculous," Saphir muttered, clomping down the stairs to the main deck. She peeked over the rail to be greeted by a barren dock. "Merik, how did you get here?" she called back to him.

Merik came flying down the steps, tucking his gloves into his pocket. "Jovin invited me to accompany them into town."

Saphir peered over the railing again. Merik threw his head over the rail also, she caught him by the scruff before he tipped over.

"Who is this girl anyway?" Saphir asked.

"I think she's Delliah's princess. Jovin always goes for the ones that are influential." Merik looked glum a moment, then threw his hands in the air. "There they are! Run! Hide!"

Saphir crouched down so her eyes were level with the railing. She could see Jovin walking from a corner of the dock, arm in arm with a giggling girl who was tossing her dark, silky hair over her shoulder.

"This is ridiculous," Saphir said, now crawling back toward her cabin door a few yards down the line.

Saphir made it to her cabin door and slipped in, ignoring Merik's remarks about staying hidden. She agreed to stay and then grumbled something unprincesslike that she hoped Merik had not heard.

There was a moment in which Saphir seriously considered ignoring everything and walking out on deck. *A bright white, stupid, blinding moment!* She wondered what their reactions would be. She wondered what she would do. "Probably something unadvisable," she murmured aloud. "No, stay here." Her eyes wandered around the room. Saphir had spent so much time here in the last week that it was part home, part prison cell.

"I'll just go to the kitchen," she told herself, walking to the hallway door. "I'll stay out of sight. I'm just going… to find something to do. Yes, that's right." She stepped out of her cabin and into the drafty hall, she pulled her new purple coat closer around her. "Why in the world are you talking to yourself? You're being completely childish. It's not like anyone can hear you."

She tread lightly, her boots hardly made a sound as she crept down the stairway, weaving through doors and halls until she found herself pushing open the kitchen door. She half expecting to see Jovin and his dark-haired friend waiting for her there, but there was only Merik, who screamed at the sight of her. His hand flew out of the cookie jar. "I didn't do anything!" The cupboard slammed behind him with a loud *bang*.

Saphir raised her eyebrows. "Of course not,"

Merik had recovered from his shock. "I thought you were Chef Mason coming back to reprimand me." Merik glanced at the cookie jar cupboard and stuffed his hands deep in his pockets. "What are you doing down here?" he asked. His expression changed in sudden realization. "If they see you—"

"They wouldn't come in the kitchen," Saphir said, walking to the cookie cupboard and taking out the ceramic jar. "What princess wants to see the kitchen when she can be distracting Jovin?" she took out a cookie and bit into it viciously. Her face changed in an instant. "These are really good."

"'*Distracting*'?" Merik snorted. He took a cookie and finished it in two bites. "I kno-ow... I ate half the batch yeshterday." He said thickly through a mouthful of crumbs.

Saphir took out three more cookies and slid two across the counter to Merik. She then returned the nearly empty cookie jar to the cupboard. "Yes, I used '*distracting*' because there are children present."

"I didn't realize you considered yourself a child." Merik snickered through a mouthful of chocolate chip cookie. "I think we need more cookies..." he said after a moment.

"Did you preheat the oven?" Saphir pulled the baking sheets out of the drawer.

"Ah, I didn't!" Merik exclaimed, and scrambled across to the oven.

Saphir went back to the bowl and stirred the thick goop of cookie dough. "I guess we'll just have to wait for it then," she said, hopping up onto the counter.

Merik hopped up across from her. He stared at the toes of his boots. "There is literally nothing to do," he said at length.

Saphir yawned, "Sure there is."

"We're stuck here waiting for the oven to preheat," Merik pointed out.

They heard a flirtatious giggle nearby, followed by Jovin's amused voice. The female voice said something again and Jovin replied as their passing footsteps echoed softly on the wooden planks.

There was a brief moment during which Merik and Saphir stared at each other; then, with a little squeak, Saphir slipped off the counter and onto the floor, hiding behind the large butcher block that occupied the middle of the kitchen. The door opened, and Saphir held her breath, watching Merik for the sign to flee.

"It's just Jovin," Merik announced.

Saphir shot back up. Her hair was pulled back, and there was flour over her apron, but she stared at Jovin unabashed. "Yes, what is it?" she said curtly.

"Keep your voice down," Jovin muttered. He shot her a warning look that turned to amusement as he took in her post-baking getup. "Do I dare ask?"

Saphir ignored his previous comment. "Where's you newest catch?"

"Her name is Felicity, and she likes the windows in the dining hall," Jovin corrected unemotionally.

"So easily amused?"

"She finds them charming," Jovin said coolly. "And you're no different."

Saphir went scarlet at the thought, wondering if Jovin knew how much time she had spent staring out the dining hall windows. Even now, as they were stationary in port, the windows offered a pretty sight of the harbor and an appealing view of the town.

Saphir changed tactics. "Planning on leaving anytime soon? I would like to be able to walk around my dungeon freely again."

Jovin made no reply and walked past her to the dish cupboard. He took out two glasses and filled them with water. "Not sure yet," he told her simply.

Saphir looked him straight in the eye. Her nose twitched.

Jovin looked as though he was about to make a longwinded reply, but he checked himself and swept the water glasses off the counter. "You've got flour on your face," he mused as he passed her.

Saphir glared at Jovin until the kitchen door swung shut behind him. She brushed her nose with the back of her hand, and a little dusting of flour sprinkled onto her apron and fell to the floor.

Saphir lurked in the shadows outside of the captain's cabin, her eyes fixed on a spot where two people were occupying the docks. The wind picked up and Saphir tightened her coat around her. Her forehead creased as she gnawed at the inside of her cheek.

Merik materialized in the partial lighting beside her. "I've come to say goodbye. Jovin said I shouldn't waste time… Saphir?" Merik followed the line of her gaze to where Jovin and the dark-haired girl were trifling beside the motorcar in their wait of Merik. "Idiot brother," Merik muttered in disdain. "Look, Saphir; don't get attached to him. Don't take it personally, he's always like this."

"I remember. I just… I guess I forgot."

Merik shuffled his feet. He patted her shoulder awkwardly.

Saphir suddenly burst into speech. "Did Jovin ever actually love me? Did he ever say anything that might have caused him to… to… did I mean anything?"

Merik's surprise at this question was all too evident. "Wha? Oh, um… I don't know if he ever actually loved *anyone*." Then Merik became silent.

The two watched Jovin kiss the girl's hand and move to exchange words with the driver beside them. The man opened the motorcar door for the girl, and she slipped in. Jovin started making his way back toward the *Alexandria*.

"He used to smile at me like that," Saphir said.

Merik scoffed. "You're not the only one."

Saphir froze as Jovin came aboard. The smile had slipped from his face and he looked tired, squinting in the fading light. He spotted Merik beside Saphir, who was hidden in the shadows.

"We're leaving," Jovin said, ignoring Merik. He went to take Saphir's hand, but she pulled away and swept past him. He trotted after her and stopped her by the arm. "Saphir?"

Saphir turned sharply to him. "Let go of me," she said calmly.

Jovin released her. "Saphir, darling, what is it?" he asked.

"Please. *Don't.*" That was all she seemed able to say.

"Don't what?" he asked, staring at her with his eyes full of concern.

The voice of reason became silenced. In a fraction of a moment, Saphir's patience snapped and the avalanche of emotions fell through. "*Don't.* Just stop. Stop with everything. I don't want it, and I don't want to see you. Stop with the dramatics and the two-faced sweetness and the lies. I need space. Please, leave me alone." She turned on her heel and started walking to her cabin again.

Jovin was rendered speechless for the space of three agonizingly long seconds, and then realization hit and he began to chase after her. "What are you talking about? Space from what?" he caught up with her, and Saphir stopped.

She made to speak, but her words got caught in her throat. She clenched her fists over her eyes and took a shuddering breath, unable to convey what she needed him to know. All she seemed capable of doing was to stare at him in condemned silence.

Her silence was enough.

Jovin's concern dropped. In barely the space of a heartbeat, his whole demeanor changed. He backed away from her. "Alright, I get it," he said flatly. "I'll leave you alone then. Have fun being miserable. Send a letter if you get a chance. Just don't resort to missing me too much in my absence, you'll only hurt yourself further," he paused, "see you in a few days."

Saphir felt as though she had been knocked over the side from aloft, and was now plummeting to the ground. Jovin left the deck, calling to Merik to hurry up. And without a single glance to her, Jovin was tromping down the gangplank, his silhouette dark in the feeble glow of the lamps.

Merik ran to Saphir and embraced her. "I'm sorry," he pulled away quickly to follow after Jovin.

Chapter 13

A Congregation of Circumstances

A few days following Jovin and Saphir's squabble, it was time to be off again. The morning the *Alexandria*'s passengers prepared to depart, King Pierson II called for a last word with Jovin. "There is unease across the Channel," the King said. "Yesterday the Crown Prince of Venqui was murdered. The whole country is in panic. As they border Terrison, I feel I must warn you that Venqui has been hostile to their neighbors in the past. If I were traveling across the Channel, I would exercise the utmost caution. We do not know what the people of Venqui feel toward royalty at the moment, and that could be dangerous for you. I advise you to stay where you are protected."

"Do we know who killed him?" Jovin said.

"Nothing is confirmed, it seems the culprit did not leave a calling card. If it had been the Crove, they certainly would have made it known." King Pierson II said.

Jovin nodded. "I will take this into consideration. Thank you, it is appreciated."

King Pierson's mouth formed a tight-lipped smile. "You are a valuable ally. Take care, young man, from what I can tell, you will be a decent ruler. I look forward to our next meeting—albeit without my daughter, if you do not mind," his forehead contracted, "I have no wish for Delliah to be swallowed up by Canston. To avoid putting us into a precarious situation, I think it is best to cut romantic ties today, before any wounds become fatal."

+++++

The *Alexandria* left port later that morning. Jovin filled Captain Donald in on what King Pierson had told him on the motorcar ride from the castle, Merik listening intently beside them. Captain Donald found the information disturbing and far more fascinating than Jovin did, but let the matter drop once they reached the docks.

To celebrate their homecoming onto the *Alexandria*, Merik insisted on having Saphir on deck when they took off. She laughed and clung to the railing as the airship started its gentle slope upward. It was heartwarming seeing her smile like that, and Merik thought she looked best with her eyes shining from excitement and her hair flying around her, all the while laughing and exclaiming at the wonders of the world. Merik was reminded of his first flight on the *Alexandria.*

When the airship was stabilized and flying south on their course a half hour later, the two found themselves in the captain's cabin.

Captain Donald was poring over a map on his desk with Jovin, who looked up and promptly dropped his gaze again, pretending to be deeply emerged in the map. Saphir ignored Jovin and said a good morning to Captain Donald, who nodded in acknowledgment and smiled back.

Merik sat on the rug in front of her, taking Sighter out of his home in his pocket along with a handful of tools that he laid on the carpet. There was a moment when Merik stared intently at Saphir. "I see you are wearing girl clothes again."

Saphir flattened the skirts of her soft green dress. "I've been wearing girl clothes for about a week, but good observation nonetheless."

Merik nodded his understanding and went back to tinkering with Sighter.

Saphir's eyes wandered the room to the map on the table. She stepped up beside Jovin, cautious not to bump into him. He did not acknowledge her presence and stared at the map with intrigue.

"Where are we now, Captain?" Saphir asked.

Donald pointed out where they were in regard to Delliah and their path south. "Around *here*, we are going to stop in Blinley before we cross the Channel to Terrison."

Saphir glared at the silhouette of Terrison as though the scribbled shape had done her a great personal wrong. "Have we decided what to do with me?" she asked the captain.

"I suggest that you stay with us until we have somewhere to send you," Donald addressed her, leaning around Jovin, who was scratching his neck and avoiding her gaze. "Of course, only if you are comfortable with that."

"Would it be unwise to try to contact Ee'lin?" she asked in apprehension.

"We certainly could try, but I deem it best that no one knows how alive you are," Donald said.

A twitch of a smile touched Jovin's features.

Donald went on, "I will see what news I can find of Ee'lin when we get to Blinley."

Jovin eyed the captain, "What does my father think of this?"

Saphir felt the color drain from her face at the mention of his father.

"I have requested to speak with him this evening," Donald answered.

Merik let out a huff of frustration as Sighter's wing fell apart in his hand. "Ow!" he exclaimed.

"Are you all right?" Saphir asked.

"Sharp." Merik sucked on his hurt finger. He stared down at the lifeless hunk of metal in his hand and sighed. "This pointless thing," he muttered at Sighter. "Fix yourself!"

Saphir thought it best to sidetrack Merik from his frustration with the trinket. "So as of today, how long is your trip so far?" she asked, kneeling on the carpet beside the young prince.

Merik shrugged and called over to Captain Donald. "What do you think? A month?"

"Thirty-three days," Donald replied.

"That's a long time," Saphir said. "Is everything going well?"

"I think so. I almost got into trouble in Caloricain because I suggested that I should acquire one of the Duke's puppies, and his oldest daughter was not happy about that."

"She wasn't happy about too many things, though." Jovin muttered to himself.

Saphir restrained from making a rude comment to Jovin, and turned her attention back to Merik. "That's too bad."

"I wouldn't even be allowed to have a puppy anyway," Merik went on, "it would be too much work while we're abroad, and you can't exactly let it outside. And then all the castles and halls are confusing, and one has a tendency to be late for dinner in such cases."

"*Tendency* might be an understatement," Jovin muttered, though Merik did not hear.

"Well, since you don't have a puppy; what is a day like in the life of Merik?" Saphir asked.

Merik's eyebrows scrunched as he thought. "I have school with Professor Hopkins, I sometimes hang around here… food… I build things too. There's a training room on level two, it has an obstacle course and a place to invent things. It's interesting enough. I'm trying to learn the dying art of sword fighting, but I kinda stink at it."

"I'm sure you are better than you think," Saphir assured him.

"No, he's pretty bad," Jovin called over.

Saphir chuckled, "Well, you're probably better than me,"

"But no one sword fights anymore, so I think it's a bit pointless," Merik said confidently, "I think it's a waste of time, to be completely honest."

"Maybe that's why you are not as good as you think you should be—because you think you will never use it," Saphir suggested.

"You have a point," Merik agreed. He called over to his brother, "Hey, Jovin, have you ever used fencing in a real situation?"

Jovin peered at them over the notes he was now writing, "Not as of yet,"

"Hmm..." Merik thought for a moment, "Captain, have you?"

Donald regarded Merik, "I have," he replied simply before going back to looking at the map.

Merik straightened up. "What? When?"

"Maybe you will find out if you continue to learn this 'dying art' you speak of," Donald said, "I find it best to be prepared for whatever life may throw at you; that way, when something unexpected happens, you are better prepared than you would be otherwise."

"Also I bet it helps you to live," Merik said.

"Also that," Donald agreed.

Saphir grinned at Merik, "Now I feel like the odd sheep out. You'll have to teach me how to fight sometime."

"Yeah…" then he shook his head, "I'm not so great," he held up the mutilated form of Sighter. "This is what I am good at."

"Which is?"

Merik hopped up on the sofa to sit beside Saphir, his excitement so obvious he had become giddy. "It's my secret affliction," he whispered, a wide grin plastered over his face. "I made this."

"What is it?" Saphir leaned forward to get a better look.

Merik moved the wing to make Sighter's shape more recognizable. "He's a hummingbird,"

"He's very pretty," Saphir said.

"When he's working, he can actually fly."

Saphir straightened, "You're messing around now."

"No, really, he can fly," Merik affirmed. "But right now he's a complete catastrophe."

Saphir looked over to Donald, "It can fly?"

"Of course he can," Donald's eyes gleamed with pride for the boy. "Merik, tell her what you are adding."

"Yes, and when did you make him?" Saphir asked, her eyes alight with her excitement.

"Yes, so," Merik said. "I started about two years ago. For a while, he was a little bug-lizard thing. I added wings this last summer. He's going to be pretty amazing when I'm done, but I sat on him a while ago, and his wing snapped. Plus he falls out of my pockets all the time, so he's not flying at the moment." Merik flipped Sighter over to show her the underbelly. "His purpose originally was to be a useful little tool for everyday life. You know, opening locked doors and eavesdropping—things like that. But then I realized that if I made a few changes, I could possibly create an artificial life force."

"*What?*" Saphir's jaw had gone slack. "And you're what, twelve?"

"In about a month, yes. But I'm still figuring out how to make him completely independent from me. I'm close, but he'll get nervous and fly back to me, or malfunction and fly the wrong way. He has sensors in his eyes that can recognize people. I've figured out a way to record conversations too. It's all really exciting, but he keeps breaking, so it's been difficult to advance him any further than where he is at. But I'll get there in the end. The troubling part is trying to keep him small, because if I keep modifying and adding newly discovered technology, he'll just keep growing, and I am trying to avoid that. The issue has been converting the new features to make them 'Sighter sized' and that has been *extremely* difficult." A miniscule bolt fell out in his hand. Merik looked Sighter over to see where the bolt belonged, but came up short.

"So what you're saying is that you are ahead of our most brilliant engineers and inventors by decades," Saphir said.

"Actually, the technology already exists, but it's not readily available to the public," Merik said. "And then there's a ruddy license you need to order supplies. So unless I operate under an adult's name, I'm not allowed to order anything or buy from shops. It has been a *grueling* struggle," he fitted the bolt back into the socket, "because not many people want to sell to an almost twelve-year-old."

"But you're royalty; don't you have some authority over them?" Saphir asked.

"Not unless I make myself known as a prince. But I'm the second son, a kid, and less likely to be recognized, so I'm allowed to go a lot of places." Merik tried to fit the wing back into its place, but it went slack and hung limp from Sighter's side. "But father doesn't want me hanging around in inventors' shops *all* the time."

"What do you use to power him?"

"He currently operates on solar energy, but I want to convert him to fusion. We've started powering some of our motorcars and parts of the palace with fusion energy; it's leading us away from our electric and steam-powered age. But Professor Hopkins said that the world is not ready to convert power sources yet." Merik noticed Saphir's puzzled face, "Fusion energy has a better battery life, it's made by colliding something or other. I have to keep looking into it, but I bet it's better for Sighter than other energy source."

"But where did you learn all this?" Saphir's jaw hung loose in her amazement.

"When you ask a lot of questions, you get a lot of answers. At least that's what Captain Donald says. I've taken to hanging about with the inventors at the palace and copying them. I've learned loads." Merik shrugged.

"Well, I'm impressed." Saphir smiled. "I cannot wait to see where you go with your inventions."

"Thank you, *Your Highness*," Merik mocked a little bow from his seat, "I will let you know if I ever win a national science prize or a prestigious award." He placed his hand over his heart and waved his nose in the air, almost as if he could hear the applause of the prize-givers. "It is such an honor to be here, accepting this award for most accomplished child ever to walk the face of the earth." He said, adopting a superior, pompous tone. "I would like to thank only one person, and that would be Saphir, because I owe it all to her. Through my long and difficult years of inventing, trying to find the one thing that would work, she had been my greatest supporter. Thank you," he wiped a fake tear off his cheek. "I am so honored," he covered his face with his hand and fell into false hysterical sobs.

Saphir found herself laughing. "Lovely speech. You should write it down."

Merik shot back up, dropping the hysterical act, "Did you see the engine room yet?"

"I cannot say that I have. I've stayed on the top two floors," Saphir answered.

"*Why?*" Merik shot up, stuffing Sighter into his pocket. "Come on, I'll give you the tour."

"What, right now?" Saphir asked.

"Yeah, unless you want to wander around forever not knowing where you're going," Merik said. "Anyway, it beats hanging around here."

Saphir shot a glance over to where Jovin and Captain Donald were still discussing the map. Jovin was scribbling away again, a stern expression upon his face. He said something to Donald that made the captain shake his head and point to another spot on the map.

Saphir soon realized that the *Alexandria* was a lot larger than her initial impression. Hidden behind a door in the captain's cabin was a staircase that led down the entire hull of the airship. The stairwells were disguised differently on each deck; in many cases, their doors appeared to be part of the wall. If it had not been for the doorknobs, Saphir thought that the doors might have gone completely unnoticed.

She already knew the first level: kitchen, the guest and crew's two dining halls, and the greenhouse. She and Merik only peeked in on the second level, as the prow belonged to the crew and the stern was occupied by the training and fitness room. Merik's invention space was there also, but he suggested seeing it another time.

Level three was storage.

Saphir got lost in the engine room on the fourth floor when Merik stepped away to greet Mister Grinnings, an engineer whose job it was to maintain the cannons on every floor. The engines' gentle hum from levels four and five were soft enough that they could not be heard on other levels.

Saphir accidently set off a cannon on the fifth floor. It was with many apologies and uncomfortable smiles that she left Mister Grinnings to see to it, all the while Merik roared with laughter.

There were a multitude of windows on every level, shining bright, dazzling sunlight into the hull of the airship. When the *Alexandria* was designed, Captain Donald had insisted that there be light on every floor. Years before, he had served on an airship that had too few windows and found himself avoiding the claustrophobic lower decks. As a result, he had placed windows wherever it was possible, and whenever it would not compromise the hull's integrity. In the common ocean-sailing ship design, a wall of thick glass in the stern covered the greenhouse on the first level, the training room on the second, and the top of the third floor where the cannons began.

Saphir found great interest in the gigantic windows in the prow. They stretched from the top floor all the way down to the lower deck in five diagonal rows of colossal diamonds. Standing against one of the window walls of glass, she was transported into the folklore of the sky spirits who escort great travelers to Heaven.

On the sixth level in the prow, there were ten unoccupied passenger rooms. Saphir found this floor rather ominous. Apart from two obvious stairwells, the rest of the level was bare except for the U-shaped line of plasma cannons on either wall.

"It's hard for an airship to be traced in the higher atmosphere, because the radio towers and communication signals don't reach too high," Merik said brightly. "Captain Donald says that it's harder to track an airship in a fuzzy field of energy; it creates static on their instruments. He said that the *Alexandria* flies in the medium range. However, we would be easier to track if we dropped altitude, and harder to track we kept going straight up. That's for emergencies," he pointed to a line of white safety bins beside the stairway door. *Oxygen. Life preservers. Flammable. Caution.* "They are on every level just in case of a water landing or fire, or any reason we have to blow up something to get out of the hull."

The seventh and final layer of the airship was the aircraft hangar. This was where the escape vessels and recreational flyers were located. The bottom of the airship opened inward to allow smaller aircrafts access to the skies. It was all ladders and catwalks here, connecting to the stationary escape flyers. The room seemed far too large to be the last layer of the airship, and as far as Saphir could tell, this was the only place where there were windows of stained glass. The strips of color ran along the top of the hanger's perimeter, casting an otherworldly glow over the polished fliers and planes.

+++++

It was nearing evening on their second day of travel after leaving Delliah, and Blinley was a few hours off. For Merik, the days were growing boring.

Saphir had spent the day reading on deck in the fleeting sunlight, and when the weather grew cold, she relocated to her cabin. Jovin took to the training room that afternoon, as he had the evening before, and had not been seen since. Merik saw less and less of his brother each day. Jovin did not seem to care; he made no effort to acknowledge Merik's existence apart from at mealtimes, and even then Jovin retained his distance.

In his boredom, Merik had taken to watching Captain Donald pore over paperwork in his cabin.

"How is Sighter coming along?" Donald looked up from his work, startling Merik in his chair.

Merik blew his hair out of his eyes, slumping in his armchair. "Really problematic. Sometimes he spazzes and turns off, not to mention that he's getting beaten up because I keep dropping him. He's just too fragile."

Donald nodded in understanding, "If you would rather have another project, I am in need of an invention."

Merik perked up, "Like what?" All thoughts of his dilapidated hummingbird flew from his head.

"An undetectable tracking device," Donald leaned over his desk slightly, "also a way *to* track the device."

The way in which Donald spoke made him feel that this matter was of the utmost importance. "Why?" he asked the captain. "Any of your crewmen could make one, and I know *you* could; so why do you want me to do it?"

"Busywork mainly. You find yourself in need of a side project, and there may be a time when we are in need of it," Donald replied.

Merik thought for a moment. "Alright, I'll do it. When do you want it by?"

"Let me see your progress in one week. What with the change in our routine, I do not know how much time you will have to work," Donald said.

"It'll be done sooner than that," Merik said boldly, "give me a couple of days. It might be done by tomorrow—that is, if nothing interesting happens." Merik crossed his arms in pride and leaned back in his chair.

"That confident?" Donald asked.

"I know things," Merik said. "What's it for?" he asked as an afterthought.

"Oh, nothing major. Emergencies and such."

"What type of emergencies?" Merik speculated.

"The situation has not yet arisen, so I cannot answer that yet."

"It's for Saphir, isn't it?" Merik asked.

Donald gave a worn smile, "I suppose we shall see."

+++++

Blinley was a large city on the far eastern coast of Canston. Originally a fishing village, it was later taken over by large corporations who bought the land and built the shack-style homes into mansions. The streets were clean, although the air was not. And the people, much like their ancestors, were those with a love of the sea. For that reason, there were only two public airship docks in the city.

Captain Donald went out at five and did not return until after eleven. By that time, Merik had nodded off on the sofa and Saphir's eyes were heavy with the strain of staying awake. She was considering going to bed herself, but before she had made up her mind, the cabin door flew open and Captain Donald strode in, bringing with him a gust of chilled ocean air.

He took off his coat and hung it on the rack by the door. "I have news for you, Princess," he said, walking into the room and turning the overhead light up brighter. "Merik, wake up."

Merik flinched. "*Don't kill the birds!*" he cried, jerking out of sleep. He blinked at them through a daze.

Donald beckoned Saphir over to the map on the wall. Saphir pulled her coat around her and ruffled her hair to get it out of her face. "What is it, Captain?"

Donald pressed the intercom button, "Mister Carter, wake Jovin and get up here."

"But we're docked, wouldn't Mister Carter be asleep?" Saphir asked.

"He addressed the entire second level," Merik said with a yawn, "someone will wake him up." His hair was matted to his forehead and sticking up in the back. "But it would be faster to wake up Jovin right now," he laid his head down on the sofa and promptly fell asleep again.

"What's going on?" Saphir's face had drained of color. "Captain?"

Donald moved around his desk and jotted down a note on a pad of paper. "Do not allow yourself to overthink; take a deep breath,"

Jovin came bounding into the cabin a few minutes later, "What's wrong? You're back late."

"Did you see Mister Carter on your way in?" Donald asked.

"I'm here," Carter yawned, entering from the side door. He closed the door on his coat ends, sighed and tried to pry them from the closed doorframe. He pulled his arms out of his coat and yanked on the fabric, but the coat stayed stuck in between the door and the frame.

"Mister Carter, open the door," Donald said.

Carter nodded sleepily and retrieved his coat from the now open door. He staggered over to them, his eyes half closed. He rubbed his nose with the back of his hand. "I've barely slept this week. Everyone is out, and the rooms are quiet. What is going on?" he demanded through a fog.

Every eye was on Captain Donald. "No one I spoke with from Blinley has traveled south to Ee'lin in almost a month. Now, remember that we are not close to the Canston and Ee'lin borders, but we are close enough that news would travel. More than a few people have spoken about sky bandits and terrorists who sabotage anyone trying to cross the borders, but people with family in Ee'lin are hard pressed to get a response, telegraph and telephone alike." Donald pointed to the borderlines on the map. "They say that the eastern coast of Berronatt is completely blocked off."

Saphir rose from her chair, moving to examine the map with the rest. "I did not think we had bandits that far north."

Jovin scoffed, "Don't assume you know everything."

Saphir clenched her fists in her pockets but did not reply to Jovin. "What do they say about me?" she asked Donald.

"No one in Blinley knows that you are with us, and quite frankly, I do not think they realize you are missing yet," Donald said.

"Peachy. Simply grand," she walked away from the crowd. "All this destruction and no one seems to notice?" She stared out at the towns streetlamps through the window wall.

"Not in Blinley," Donald said. "However, if we were closer, there might be another story."

Mister Carter shook his head. "If Blinley doesn't know, they're not gonna know about it if we fly a couple hours south," he looked at Saphir with apprehension, then wiped a hand across his face. "This whole thing is screwed up."

"What do you think Captain, should we leave in the morning?" Jovin said, glancing to Saphir, who still had her back to them.

"As soon as we can pay for the slip," Donald said.

"Father dearest needs a call first," Mister Carter muttered under his breath. "Captain, you wanted to contact our King while we were moored," he reminded them.

"Yes, thank you, Mister Carter." Donald said.

"We're still in Canston, we could send Saphir back to our palace," Jovin offered.

They turned to Saphir.

"I rather not go," she said cautiously.

"Why not?" Jovin asked.

She bristled, "I *am not* going to go stay in your palace."

"So you won't stay in my *palace*, but you're *fine* staying on my *airship?*" Jovin asked accusingly. "Why is that, exactly?"

Saphir straightened, *"I do not want to be sent away."*

A long, ringing silence followed her words.

She heard Jovin whisper to Donald, "Fine, she can stay," but when her gaze landed on Jovin, he looked as though he had not said a word.

+++++

"I want you to drop her off as soon as possible," King Raleigh said through the radio's speaker.

"I understand, Father," Jovin replied.

Captain Donald raised an eyebrow at the prince. Jovin pretended to ignore the captain's silent judgment.

The *Alexandria* needed to remain in Blinley until they were finished contacting the King using the radio towers the docks provided. The airship's messaging system was limited to surrounding aircrafts, nearby cities, and immediate radio towers. Captain Donald had explained to Merik, the *Alexandria*'s communication limitations were based on weather patterns and topography. Many airships operated short range, and the *Alexandria* was not exempt. In order to reach across the entire country of Canston and communicate with the palace, they needed to be docked.

The King's voice spoke again, his tone softened, *"Jovin, I do not want your emotions to cloud your judgment,"* his father said, *"I do not want Canston's fate entangled with Ee'lin's. We spoke of this. Merik is with you for the sole purpose of keeping my children safe from Ee'lin's dangers. Inviting the target of the attacks to stay, with open arms, is unwise; surely you see that. As your king, I command you to continue your mission without the Princess aboard."*

"Where would you leave her?" Jovin's tone dropped in volume. "She has nowhere to go."

"I suggest sending her to Caloricain. She can stay there. She will be safe with Duke Mackebury. She will not be found," the King said.

"Father, you know Saphir, she would be miserable there," Jovin said.

"*She will not remain aboard the* Alexandria. *Do you understand me?*" the King threatened. "*She is a danger and will be searched for. If she is found with you, Canston will have no choice but to take the brunt of it. You will be made a target to those who wish her harm. I am not willing to put my people, or my sons, in danger. Jovin, you must do your best to understand.*"

"Father—"

"*You are my people. I will not allow you to seek a problematic situation.*"

"I understand." Jovin said flatly.

"It is a decision that must be made as King. I will await your message relaying her shipment to Caloricain. Good day, Jovin, Gregory."

"Good day, Your Majesty," Donald replied.

The line disconnected.

"We need to make arrangements for her departure," Donald voiced.

Jovin was silent.

"Shall I call for Princess Saphir?" Donald asked.

Jovin's brow furrowed, "Are you to send her away now?" he stared out the wheelhouse window.

Donald refrained from speaking.

"Caloricain is too proud to keep her presence a secret," Jovin said, "all manner of people walk the halls; she would be found out within the month."

Donald considered the prince. "Jovin, may I remind you of your father's ruling?"

"I remember his words, but I also remember that I am Crown Prince. He has trusted me and my judgment with this mission, as such, I have ruling over what to do in difficult situations. She stays until we arrange the safest house for her to reside in. Until we have taken in the measure of her threat, she remains our guest." He made himself meet Donald's expectant gaze. "This is my decision, not yours."

Donald watched resolution form in the young man's eyes. "If we act upon this, what will I tell your father?"

Jovin flashed a smile. "I will relay what needs to be said to the King. Do not worry yourself about it."

Chapter 14

Ashes of the Past

Iris Shannon opened the office door cautiously. A pungent smell reached her nose. "Sir?" her voice seemed quiet under the howling of the wind and the crackling of the fire.

Ganimead's voice came from across the room. "Come in, Iris," his silhouette was etched against the fire. He tossed a paper into the flames. The room burned brighter for a moment while the paper was consumed, then the light faded again.

"Um, sir, we have more information from Ee'lin." Miss Shannon found that her voice was quavering. She set a file on the corner of the desk. Her attention fell on an ornate picture frame that sat sideways on the desk. "What is…?" the firelight glared off the glass, blocking the photo from her view.

"Speak up."

She took a step back as Ganimead swept another stack of papers off his desk and proceeded to burn them. She thought she caught the glimpse of a blueprint for a building before it was tossed into the fire with the rest.

"Yes sir," she consulted her clipboard, but her eyes flitted to the picture frame again, if she moved a couple feet forward she would be able to see it.

"Did you find the date for the masquerade?" Ganimead's tone had changed to deadly cold. He turned his back on the fire, his eyes narrowed.

"Do not snoop, Miss Shannon; you will get yourself into trouble," he walked around his desk and opened the window behind it. A wave of freezing air hit the room. Ganimead did not seem to notice the chill; his eyes stared out into the fading sky.

Miss Shannon was stumbling over her notes, her mind racing to gather her thoughts away from the photograph on the desk. "They are planning to hold the masquerade ball on the fifteenth, sir," she said.

Ganimead had not moved. Miss Shannon thought that his mind was somewhere else entirely. But no sooner than she thought this, his whole demeanor changed. "Alright," he turned to address her. "We have our day." Authority was back in his stance, no longer lost in thought. "Find me Garrett Kellan, have him here in two days. Garrett Kellan."

"Yes sir," Miss Shannon's eyes swept back to the picture frame on the desk. She took a deep breath to summon her bravery, "Um, sir, what is the picture?"

"New life, new ties. Old life, dead ties." Ganimead answered without the slightest hint of emotion. "Move along before you ask another impertinent question."

Miss Shannon nodded sharply. "Yes Sir," she quickly left the office. She thought her heels clicked far too loudly in the silence that followed behind her.

Ganimead's eyes landed on the photograph. He hated the reminder; he hated that Iris was curious, and he hated that she could not be disposed of yet. "*Stupid girl*," he tossed the picture frame into a drawer without a glance at it.

Ganimead opened the file Miss Shannon had left and thumbed through it. "I need to know where she is, not what they found. If there's no body and no bones, she's not dead."

He needed Ee'lin to come quietly. The country was in panic. They needed a ruler, a strong ruler, but it appeared that the princess was the only known heir. Ganimead knew that Kellan could change that if he was given the opportunity. Ee'lin would be a great ally, and a fantastic resource. He guessed that there were people he could use as leverage to manipulate the princess into handing over her county, but he would rather have her public consent. Proof was preferred over assumption. He could take control illegally and finish her off later, but he wanted her alive for now. He liked the idea of her signing her abdication in person; signing away her rights to rule… to someone who would do better than she.

Hadrin knocked and was summoned in an hour later. He looked better kept then he had of late; his hair was combed back, and his eyes appeared rested, though he was holding his mechanical arm a bit gingerly today, braced to his chest, the forefinger occasionally twitching.

"Problem with the arm?" Ganimead rose from his desk to meet the younger man.

"Got shocked earlier from a light switch in the infirmary. Strange thing. Seized up an' all. I'm going to get it looked at later." Hadrin stood like a soldier, straight-backed, head held high. The black Landic eviction tattoos contrasted sharply against the pale skin of his neck. He looked the part of a mercenary, although the tight hold of his false left arm and Ganimead's knowledge of his expulsion ruined the image.

"I need you to relay a message to all your Terrison contacts," Ganimead said.

"Yes sir, what's the message?" Hadrin said.

"Two things." Ganimead held up his hand. "Find the royal airship, *Alexandria*; there are two Canston princes aboard. There will be talk when they land, so it won't be difficult to find them. Your people probably already know about it."

Hadrin nodded, "And the other thing?"

"Make sure they do not leave Terrison."

Chapter 15

Old Strings Become Tangled

"We're almost in Terrison!" Merik had run around the *Alexandria* in search of Jovin for the last ten minutes to give him the good news. He had finally found Jovin reading in Donald's cabin when he retraced his steps. "We're almost there! It's going to be amazing!" he babbled.

Jovin gave a dry laugh at Merik's rambling. "Calm down, we're not there yet."

"But we will be by tonight!" Merik's excitement could not be stifled. "Oh my goodness, I cannot wait! The masquerade... Jovin, I'm so excited; it's one of the most beautiful countries in the world. I've seen pictures."

The midmorning light shone brightly though the window wall, bouncing off a mirror by the coat rack and reflecting onto the center rung. Captain Donald was in the wheelhouse, and Saphir was still in her cabin. Merik had been up early in anticipation. He had not been sleeping through the night since the dismal news of Ee'lin, but the thought of a masquerade, in one of the most beautiful countries in the world, was an idea so promising that it drove all worries right out of his head.

Saphir entered the cabin, yawning, but looking reasonably well rested. "Good morning," she said sleepily. She had on one of her new ensembles from Delliah, a light blue skirt and corset duo, accented and with trimmed with white lace.

Merik ran over to her, "Saphir, we're going to be in Terrison by tonight!"

He reminded Saphir of an excited puppy. "You're awfully chipper about it, Merik," she walked over to the map on the starboard wall. "So where do you think we are right now?"

"Blinley is here." Merik pointed to a town on Canston's eastern coast, near Ee'lin's border. "And we're probably… here?" he pointed to a spot on the edge of the Terrison coast, horizontal to Blinley.

"The palace is farther south than that," Jovin appeared beside Saphir and Merik.

"Oh, there it is." Merik's tone was absolutely giddy.

"I didn't realize we were flying south," Saphir thought aloud. "I guess it makes sense, but I didn't really process it."

Merik stared at the map. "And after that where are we headed?"

"Simport," Jovin replied.

Merik found it on the map and traced his finger from the palace in Terrison to the Simport palace in Tavenly. "That's really far out of the way," he said.

Saphir grinned, "You're zigzagging a bit, aren't you?"

"What happens to Saphir then, after we're done with your mission?" Merik asked.

Jovin leaned on Donald's desk, regarding them. "She can stay with us until she has a home to go back to. We'll figure it out," he spoke nonchalantly, as if the matter was of no importance, but Saphir was pleased all the same. "Unless, of course, if you would rather live on the streets, but that's your call." Jovin added.

"No, I'm good, thank you,"

Merik, who was not paying attention in the slightest, was staring intently at the map, commenting that two countries together looked like a ferret wearing a chef's hat. He stepped back to get a better look at the map and tripped over his feet, falling into Saphir and Jovin and knocking the three of them to the floor.

"Ow!" Saphir exclaimed. In vain attempts to save herself from falling backward, she had spun in midair and ended up falling face-first onto the wooden planking, both boys landing over her.

Jovin propped himself up so he was not crushing Saphir. Jovin gritted his teeth. "*Merik, I swear…*"

Merik's boot had caught in the hem of Saphir's skirt. He was having trouble untangling it. "I didn't mean to do anything!" he got his shoe out and stood rather hastily. "Ta-da!" he shrugged pathetically.

Jovin found his footing. "Sometimes I think you do things just to cause trouble," he grumbled, dusting himself off.

Saphir held her arms out to them. "Help a lady up, won't you?"

Jovin did, and she thanked him. There was an uncomfortable pause.

Merik noticed a subtle look that passed between the two, he grinned widely. He started backing away toward the door. "I'm… I'm just going to go and tell the world of this great discovery."

"Great discovery?" Jovin repeated.

Merik kept backing up, tying to look casual in the act. "Yeah, um… that we'll be in Terrison soon. That's big news. I have that tracking thing for Captain Donald I need to work on anyway, so… bye." He bolted for the door and was gone a moment later.

Saphir turned to Jovin. "Did that seem normal?" she gestured to the door where Merik had just left.

"Honestly, I do not know," Jovin replied. He retreated to pick up his book from the desk and turned back to her. "Are you going to be all right once we get to Terrison?"

"What? Oh, I'll be fine." Saphir laughed dryly, and as though she was convincing herself, she continued: "We've had a few issues in the past, but I'm sure they don't mean anything anymore. We were sort of friends at one point, but I'm sure we'll be fine."

Jovin eyed her with apprehension. "Are you talking about Charlotte?"

Saphir backpedaled, "Yes, sorry. I just mean that we are not children, and I am sure she will agree to let our disagreements remain in the past."

"I'm sure she will agree since you seem so insistent," Jovin said.

Saphir bristled, "There is nothing you can do, if that was what you were implying."

Jovin's eyebrows contracted. "I am not sure that I was."

There was a pause. Saphir stared down at her shoes, Jovin glanced around the room.

A thought struck Saphir, "Just don't do anything that will make the whole situation even more awkward."

Jovin gave her an amused look, "Anything I need to know about?"

Saphir shot him a furtive glance. "At the beginning of last year, Charlotte and I were acquainted… then I found out she fancied you." Saphir passed it off lightly. "This was at the time when whatever happened between *us* had just finished, and she laughed at my actions..."

"You smashed a vase on my butler's foot. I would have laughed too."

"Is he alright?" Saphir asked nervously.

"Fulton tried to quit, but Father insisted that he remain on staff," Jovin said.

"I am sorry about that," Saphir said sheepishly. "Anyway, long story short: Charlotte and I are not close. So that's that…" she sounded a bit more chipper now. "It's just foolish girl things, do not worry yourself."

"Are you saying that this is somehow my fault?"

"I never said that," Saphir said tartly.

"But you've implied it."

"Jovin," Saphir placed a hand on his arm, "it is *always* somehow your fault." It came across as more of a joke than the actual truth, which was what she had intended. She realized that her hand was lingering on Jovin's arm and quickly withdrew it.

This had not gone unnoticed by Jovin, for he gave her a knowing look, "Saphir, are you still *helplessly, desperately* in love with me?"

Saphir flinched violently and stumbled back a step, folding her arms over herself defiantly.

Jovin chuckled and stuck his hands in his coat pockets. "You are, aren't you?"

Saphir flushed redder than her hair, flustered for a moment, then she burst into speech. "I am not! How could you even say that? You think too highly of yourself."

"Alright," Jovin smirked.

"I *am not* in love with you," she said unabashedly.

"Sure… well. You'll figure it out," Jovin said casually. He winked at her and began moving toward the door.

"That was a really fantastic answer. Incredibly enlightening, Jovin. Where *do* you come up with them?" Saphir sassed.

"You'll figure it out," Jovin said, turning with a grin. "What else do you want me to say?"

Saphir hugged her arms tighter around herself. "I don't know, maybe how *you* feel?"

Jovin shrugged, "Honestly, I don't think it really matters."

Saphir scanned Jovin's face, "Well then, feel free to flirt with Charlotte when we get to Terrison. I'll try not throw up in front of you. I'll save it for whatever pair of shoes you're planning on wearing that night. Good day," and she hastened by him and out of the cabin.

Chapter 16

Fairy Lights

Terrison was known to be one of the most beautiful countries in the world. It was a land of profit, wealthy in minerals and green farmlands. Snowcapped mountains stood high in the air, under which were nestled emerald landscapes dotted with boulders and quaint towns populated by cheerful people. Music and creation occupied the gigantic cities, although they did not compare to the beauty of the wilds. The palace in which the royalty lived, stood on a hill overlooking the culture-filled city of Flinith on the western coast.

Unlike their other stops, where the *Alexandria* had been required to dock in the city, the royal port in Terrison was attached to the hill on which the palace stood. Sixty years beforehand, a half-moon shape had been carved into the western side of the hill; there they built the castle's private airship dock. A tall white-and-red-striped lighthouse looked over the airship yard and connected to the dock house. A high, electric fence joined at each end of the building, lacing its way around the mouth of the port, serving to keep unwanted persons out of the palace grounds. From the harbor, the only safe way into the grounds was through the dock house. Anyone looking to climb over the electric fence would have been mad. Even in power shortages, the fence was always buzzing, and the backup generators were always charged and guarded.

The *Alexandria* bumped gently into the docking braces, the clamps were secured, and a light in the wheelhouse buzzed to confirm that the *Alexandria* was successfully docked. At the controls, Mister Carter commented to McCoy, "I like this port, I like it a lot," he was grinning widely, looking out at the green lawns and hedges of the palace beyond.

"Pretty smooth landing for a private port," McCoy replied. He tapped a few buttons, and the men in the dock house verified that they were secure.

Jovin was standing in the forward of the airship, reaffirming his purpose with every deep breath as he prepared his mind for what was expected of him. He knew he would miss the relaxed schedule on the *Alexandria* and knew that in a few weeks their trip would be over and he would be back to his royal life in Canston. There was a part of him that wished he could stay aboard forever and give everything up, traveling from city to city, to other countries, and beyond. To remain in the sky, and live among the clouds.

But that would never be. He was reminded of that fact every time he saw Merik, every time he opened a book his father gave him to study, and every moment he was with another person who knew and remembered, what his title and status truly meant. All of that, was a reminder of the inherited obligation to the elaborate way of life that was set before him.

It was easier to pretend his title meant that he was better than everyone else, he was beginning to believe it… up until the reality check that was Saphir. She was a handful, hard to get along with, and hard to be alone with. At least that was what Jovin told himself.

+++++

Saphir was waiting by the railing in front of Donald's cabin when she noticed Jovin; she could tell by the way he was standing—hands behind his back, feet apart, and head held high—that he was uneasy. He was not looking around at the new scenery, not admiring the lawns or the pond beyond the dock house; he was looking off the starboard rail, directly at the palace, as if it were a deadly enemy.

Merik appeared beside her and leaned against the balcony railing. "He's preparing to be perfect again," he mocked a whisper.

"How do you mean?" Saphir asked.

Merik gave an apologetic shrug, "He's got this whole regal and commanding persona he puts on before meeting high officials; it charms the ladies and impresses the men, and it usually keeps us on good terms with everyone." Merik cleared his throat, "Of course, he probably doesn't realize he's doing it because it's a newer development. He didn't do it when—" the curious look on Saphir's face made him cut short, "never mind."

There was an awkward few minutes where Merik looked down at his boots and Saphir investigated the view opposite the palace, where the puffed silvery clouds impressed the illusion of a white sea.

Captain Donald came from his cabin. "Are you both ready?" he asked. "As a reminder, please do not make the royalty angry." Donald gave a sidelong look. "*Merik*, my words are directed at you."

The boy scoffed, "Are you kidding? *I'm perfect*," he held his hands under his chin and blinked in a dramatic way that ended up looking sarcastic and rather foolish.

"Let's not get too arrogant now," Saphir reminded him.

"*Arrogant,*" Merik said childishly, "arrogant my foot!"

"I almost feel that you're sassing me," Saphir said airily.

"*Me? Sassing you?*" Merik exclaimed. He turned away from her and folded his arms. "I have nothing left to say to you," he stuck his nose in the air, making a point to continue with the overdramatized attitude. He gave a dignified little "*Humph!*" and walked down the staircase to the main deck.

Saphir looked to Donald. "That is normal, right? It's not just me he does that to, right?"

"He also boasts of his exceptional luck at apprehending card cheats," Donald chuckled.

"That little gossip!" Saphir exclaimed. "That was *one* time and he had won *fifteen* games in a row! It doesn't make sense to win that many times. I think *he* was the culprit," she looked after Merik, who let out a shriek and broke into a run, pausing to wait in the bow. He then hid behind a few of the crew who were checking the docking braces, in an attempt to avoid retribution. He kept making obvious glances towards Saphir, seeing if she would chase after him.

Saphir glowered playfully at Merik and then turned to Donald. "What should I expect today?" she asked.

"You should expect the concern of your allies. Act with every bit of kindness and grace you possess. If complications arise, I will see that you are not mistreated." Donald inclined his head. "Also, Mister Carter has offered to take you into town for a masquerade dress."

"He is so sweet. And yes, I have nothing nearly flamboyant enough for a masquerade in Terrison, so I guess it cannot be helped," Saphir said. "I can't imagine that Merik is thrilled about what he will have to wear. I bet Jovin doesn't mind." She half expected Jovin to materialize just to patronize her, but he did not, and her glancing around was in vain. "Captain, maybe this isn't a good idea; it might be easier to pretend I'm not here."

"I do not think there can be any backing out at this stage. It is possible that the people of Terrison have a better answer about the situation in Ee'lin than we heard in Blinley. You are allies, are you not?"

"We are," Saphir said. "I'm just getting cold feet."

Mister Carter came down the stairs from the wheelhouse. "All locked in and safe to go ashore!"

"I didn't realize that you say 'ashore' when you're on an airship," Saphir commented.

Mister Carter shrugged. "I've been saying it all my life, and no one has stopped me as of yet. It's still the shore, so why not?" he turned his attention to Donald. "Are we waiting for anyone else? Or is it just us?"

"I have asked Professor Hopkins to accompany us today to keep an eye on Merik. I have given most of the crew shore leave, although I have asked them to continue to use the *Alexandria* for their sleeping arrangements."

"That'll light up their socks," Carter muttered.

Professor Hopkins came up the center deck stairwell and waved the group onto the first-level stairs. He was better dressed than Saphir had seen him, in a black and white pinstriped suit and baby blue vest; his glasses were on the outside of his coat pocket, giving him a relaxed, yet sophisticated look. Saphir thought he looked semi-similar to a penguin.

Merik came out of hiding and approached Hopkins. "I just wanted to let you know that if I wander off, I will not hold you accountable," Merik declared.

"What?" Hopkins sputtered.

"If I wander off and *die, never to be seen again by man or machine,* you should know that I do not hold you responsible, but rather *this thing*"—he pulled out Sighter from behind his back—"for *not* navigating me to safety."

"But you did not put *in* a navigation system," Hopkins pointed out.

"*Exactly!*" Merik concluded. "How could I get to safety without a navigation system?"

Hopkins eyed Merik with suspicion, "If this is a new way to mess with me, it will not work. How long have you been thinking *that* one up?"

"A couple minutes," Merik shrugged, "I thought it would be funnier... Anyway, if you can make a joke, you should make one... although that one sounded *way* funnier in my head."

Hopkins patted Merik's hair, "Please do not wander off and die."

"No promises,"

Captain Donald, Mister Carter, and Saphir joined them on the main deck. "Yes, Merik, I would rather you stay with the group this time," Donald said.

"I think there's a story here I'm missing," Saphir commented, looking from Merik to Donald and back again.

"Merik wandered off in Caloricain. Big fiasco. Had to lock him up afterward." Jovin walked over to meet them. He seemed to be in a decent mood and gave Saphir a sideward smirk.

"Well, the machines were cool, and I thought I should be able to look at them," Merik muttered very quickly. "And anyway, Duke Mackebury was fine with it. I didn't break anything."

Jovin raised his eyebrows. "I wasn't talking about that."

Donald interjected before Saphir had a chance to question them. "I believe they are waiting for us."

Jovin gave Merik a look that showed his contempt, and he then led them down the gangplank to Terrison.

Merik thought, and maybe he thought correctly in thinking this, that the people of Terrison were clinging to the old ways and were not fully embracing the technology of the quickly advancing future. Although they had electricity and other luxuries that befitted the royalty in the palace, he felt, as an aspiring inventor, that the air of progression was lacking. Merik wondered if the palace would have looked exactly the same if he had been there three hundred years ago. He later noticed the lightbulbs, the occasional automatic door, and the intercom system that seemed to be in every room, and he had to admit to himself that maybe they were up with the times, but maybe they had a better way of hiding it than those in other places he had visited. At least they had not gone to the extreme of flaunting just how advanced they were, as Caloricain had so poorly done.

There was definitely a part of Merik that liked the old architecture, the high ceilings, the soaring towers, and the sparkling glass windows that took up the whole wall. It felt as though there was a mystery behind them—something that called out to Merik, offering him the world starting at page one.

Walking through the palace entryway was like stepping into a pastel painting. The palace was decorated in gold and ivory. The black-and-white marble floors shone, beaded drapes framed windows, and large mirrors reflected sunlight, refracting it throughout the halls.

The herald led them to a grand hall. Waiting for them on the raised platform next to the unoccupied thrones, was a beautiful girl who Merik thought looked like an angel from Heaven.

Princess Charlotte had curled blonde hair that fell to her waist, dazzling eyes, and painted red lips. She held herself with such grace, poise, confidence, and pride, that although she wore no crown, there was no doubt that she was a princess.

Unsurprisingly, it was Jovin who approached her first. He flashed a smile and bowed to her while the rest of his party waited a few steps back and bowed accordingly.

"Princess Charlotte," Jovin said, moving forward and kissing her outstretched hand.

"Prince Jovin," Charlotte spoke with an air of gentleness and genuine happiness. "I trust you have fared well since out last meeting."

Jovin smiled. "Indeed, although it seems that you have grown more beautiful since the last I saw you; I did not know it was possible."

Charlotte laughed, a musical laugh, like that of a fairy or nymph. "You always were a charmer."

"And you were always quick on the uptake," Jovin inclined his head.

"Well, you have to be," Charlotte mused. "In the court, it is important to know what is going on and how to avoid speculation. I would say being aware of oneself is practically mandatory."

Jovin only smiled. He turned back to his party, "May I introduce my companions: Captain Donald of the *Alexandria*; the first mate, Mister Carter; my brother, Merik, and Merik's tutor: Professor Hopkins." Each bowed as he was called upon. Merik bowed a split second later than expected. "Also with us is Princess Saphir of Ee'lin, and we would be ever so grateful if her presence here was not announced to the public." Jovin then whispered to Charlotte: "I'll explain in further detail later."

Charlotte curtsied to the group. In pure curiosity, her eyes flitted for a moment over Saphir. "You and your party are welcome. We are pleased to be your host for the duration of your stay." She smiled her most dazzling smile that often won favor. "My brother is unavailable at the moment, but he and my father will be present later this evening for dinner. I believe your rooms are available if you would like to a moment to settle before dinner," she motioned to an attendant who was waiting by the door. "Monique, would you please show our guests to their rooms?"

"Yes ma'am," Monique curtsied and beckoned for them to follow.

"Thank you, Your Highness." Donald bowed and led his group out of the hall after Monique. Merik was looking around in excitement, Saphir stared ahead of her, and Mister Carter and Professor Hopkins followed.

Jovin kissed Charlotte's hand again. "I shall see you for dinner,"

"Yes," Charlotte smiled, "you are welcome to come find me beforehand if you would like."

"I might," Jovin winked. He bowed and joined his group, who were waiting at the end of the hall for him. He blatantly avoided making eye contact with Saphir.

+++++

Saphir paced her room, huffing, her face bent into a grimace. "You really shouldn't care, you're being childish. You know better than this. You're smarter than this. You know how these situations are, you need to prioritize and not fall into that ridiculous wallowing feeling. *Get over this,*" she told herself for the umpteenth time, plopping down onto her mattress and falling back into the comforter.

There was a knock on her bedroom door, and without waiting for an answer, Mister Carter entered. "Are you all right?" he asked.

"Of course I am," Saphir answered, but it came out more sarcastic than intended.

Mister Carter sat down next to her, the expression on his face somehow made Saphir feel worse. "How about we go looking for a party dress tonight instead of going tomorrow?"

"Why?"

"Get your mind off things. We'll go get a look at the town before everyone goes for a tour; that way if you need to, you can decline by stating you've already seen it. Gives you an escape option if needed."

"I guess that could be fun," Saphir said. "But am I allowed to miss dinner?"

"Quite frankly," Carter said in a quieter tone, "you're not supposed to be here, so I don't think it matters what you do, as long as you don't get found out and you don't die, as Merik so plainly put it."

"Well, if you put it like that." Saphir hopped up.

"Right," Mister Carter stood, "I'll leave you to get ready. I'll also tell the Captain that we will be missing dinner and not to wait up."

"Mister Carter, thank you," Saphir said, "I cannot begin to tell you how much I appreciate all you've done for me."

"Of course," he said, straightening up, "and anyway, you're more fun to hang around with. Beats polite dinner conversation," he flashed a kind smile before slipping out the door.

+++++

Dinner was an elegant affair that evening. The long table was prepped with the finest cutlery, the best dishes, and silk napkins. The food was excellent; there were multiple courses and an array of desserts that ranged from miniature cakes to decadent pies with whipped cream.

The king and queen of Terrison were not present this evening, Merik had not heard a reason for their absence, but it made him feel slightly uneasy. Conversation was light and boring; Merik got lost trying to figure out what topic the party was on. He kept wishing that Saphir was there so they could make fun of the baby forks and spoons—rather than the likeliness of a drought over the coming years.

Merik's only consolation was the splendid food. But his ears did perk up when the conversation turned to the Vanderbon taking over towns in the north.

"But I do not see how it could favor them," a man with spectacles said. "They are peaceful, and while not completely docile, I doubt they would invade."

"But all the same, if they continue to march through the mountains and cross the borders, we may find our cities in trouble," an older gentlemen said.

"Are they that much of a threat?" Conrad, Charlotte's twin brother, asked.

"Not always, but there have been incidents," a baron remarked. Merik thought his name was Weveal, although he thought he may have misheard.

"Such with any race," the spectacled man said. "Remember: ten years ago, the Landin Favar threatened to invade both of our countries and wipe us out."

"But that was a different time," the Baron-that-Merik-called-Weveal said, "I believe the offenders were found out and imprisoned. Popular news suggests that the Landin Favar has been peaceful ever since."

"But they weren't imprisoned for that long," Merik piped up. Everyone turned to look at him, and though the stare was not angry nor judgmental, Merik felt nervous. "They were captured for a while, but then the young radicals rose up from within then found and executed them. It was only after the old religious leaders were gone that there was peace."

Professor Hopkins beamed with pride.

Princess Charlotte leaned forward. "I am not as familiar with this recent history. Who remained left to them?"

Under Charlotte's curious wide-eyed gaze, Merik felt speechless. "I am not entirely sure, but I think a few of their generals rose to power. It's not my religion or culture, so I don't know the details."

"I find it intriguing. If you remember anything else, I would love to talk it over with you." Charlotte smiled at Merik.

Merik sat up a little straighter, a new confidence in him. Jovin caught his eye a few seats down; he gave Merik the smallest of nods. Merik beamed.

The conversation was back on the Vanderbon. "All the same, it does not matter how similar they are to the Landin Favar; the Vanderbon are becoming a problem," a boisterous official said.

"In what way, Sir Rille? I do not see how they are anything more or less than is to be expected of them," Prince Conrad said.

"They are unruly and uncontrollable," Sir Rille replied.

"But I fail to see how they are a problem if they are uncontrolled," said Prince Conrad, "is that not the way they have always lived? They do not belong to Terrison or any other country; they are their own people, and furthermore, while they are harmless, they should not have to be *controlled* under our rule. Unless they offer a severe threat or nuisance, I cannot see a reason to dislike them."

Jovin nodded, "I have to agree with you, Conrad. What reason is there to dispel them?"

The Baron-Merik-called-Weveal leaned forward, "But what if they were starving towns out of food? They could become a threat, they could become unreasonable."

Conrad tilted his head, "I am under the impression that they pay for themselves and provide entertainment to the towns they inhabit. I see no problem with them."

"What if they were a threat to us?" the Baron-Merik-called-Weveal continued, "what if they were not as virtuous as they appear to be?"

"There is no proof that they have ill intentions," Conrad insisted, "they do not seem to be a threat."

"Not that I mean to blatantly target them, but there *is* always a first time for something," Charlotte pointed out.

Conrad gave his sister a low look. "Please, let us *try* to be optimistic in light of the evidence we hold."

Charlotte said nothing in reply but held herself proudly, subtlety showing her contempt with her brother.

Merik scrunched his face, "I'm confused; what have the Vanderbon done to make us doubt them?"

"Nothing yet," Sir Rille answered Merik, although it was clear that his words were directed to the party as a whole.

"But there is always a possibility," another official interjected, "now, the Crove on the other hand..."

"Let us turn away from such vulgar subjects onto something more cheerful," Conrad said with a curt smile.

+++++

It was late in the evening. Dinner had ended, and the majority of the party had gathered in the parlor. Merik had decided to turn in. Jovin and Charlotte segregated themselves away from the noise and clatter of the royal gathering and slipped out into the palace grounds.

They walked arm in arm along the veranda rail, taking in the lamp-lit lawns to where the grass sloped into the pond near a rose garden. "We should walk that way," he mused.

Charlotte nodded, but it was obvious her mind was elsewhere. She did not look at Jovin and kept her eyes trained on the castle grounds. Jovin took up her hand gently. They stopped at the far end of the veranda, overlooking the lawns. Even at that distance, Jovin could hear the raucous laughter coming from the parlor.

Charlotte turned to Jovin. The soft spell they had been under was broken and her tone was deadly serious. "I need to know something,"

"And what is that?" Jovin asked as he lolled against the rail.

"I am confused," Charlotte folded her hands. "Princess Saphir, what do I need to know, and what do I need to stay quiet about?"

Jovin pushed off the rail, "You don't have to worry about anything,"

Charlotte raised her eyebrows, "Somehow I feel that is not the case. Jovin, please explain what is going on."

"It is a rather confusing story, I have fewer of the details than I should," he said, "I believe Captain Donald has explained it to your father."

"I must have been absent," Charlotte's expression remained still. "Explain to me what you understand. Now, at this moment I will listen, I will not interrupt. And you, Jovin, will explain to me what I need to know."

Jovin took a breath and looked out over the grounds again, his mind turning over on itself. He blew out a breath. "Alright," he focused his attention back on her confused face. "A couple weeks ago, Saphir's palace was attacked. We were in the vicinity, and we were able to rescue her. We are not certain who attacked, but she *is* the only known heir to the Ee'lin throne. She is under out protection until we can find her a safe haven." Jovin said.

Charlotte regarded him silently.

"That's as much as I know," he added to let her know he was done speaking.

"This must be strange for you," Charlotte said after a moment. Her tone was softer than expected.

"What?"

"I was under the impression you were fond of each other at one point. I assume, now that you have gone your separate ways, it can be uncomfortable," Charlotte said airily.

Jovin was not sure how to reply. "It's been interesting," he said trepidatiously.

Charlotte took up his arm and started walking them down the stairway to the lawns. "Come along. You wanted to see the pond, did you not?"

Jovin stared at her, awestruck. "You're taking this surprisingly well."

"How else would I have taken it?" Charlotte asked. They came to a stop at the foot of the stairs. Charlotte looked at Jovin, an amused expression over her face. "I am not unreasonable; I understand, or at least, I want to." As an afterthought, she added, "What is your take on Saphir now?"

Jovin gave a little shrug. "We're fine… It can be awkward," he added, as though by saying this he would save himself from the ditch he had dug.

He felt comforted by Charlotte's smile. "But such is life," she said. "There is a gazebo around the palace, and a garden, if you would like to see them. They are magical at night."

Jovin's eyes lit up at the change of subject. He took Charlotte's hand. "Let's go then." He picked up into a jog, Charlotte trailing behind him.

Jovin was amusing, Charlotte thought. She had known men of all sorts: the rouge gentlemen, who were secretly softies; the sweet, quiet sorts who showered women with every compliment just to earn a smile; the ones willing to make fools of themselves for a laugh; and the men she considered to be untouchable—the "too good for anyone" sort she classified Jovin under. A moment ago he had been flustered like a child caught with his hand in the cookie jar, now he was running off to look at the garden lights with a shining smile on his face. It was a break in character that surprised her more than anything had that evening.

In a short time, they were in the rose gardens. The tiled gazebo was lit up by strings of lightbulbs. Ornamental solar lights littered the garden, reminding them of mystical lands from their childhood stories. The palace cast a golden glow over the scene, and the moon winked at them from her perch in the heavens.

"This is lovely," Jovin grinned, and turned to Charlotte, who was giggling at his reactions. "What?"

"You are positively giddy," she chimed, "like a young child."

"I don't get that very often," he mused, gazing around at the garden, spinning in a circle.

"I would assume not," Charlotte started down along the path, walking slowly enough to give him time to catch up with her.

And he did, a smile still plastered across his face.

Charlotte pointed to the gazebo. "When I was younger, I would play that I was a fairy, I would dance around the gazebo pretending to cast spells..." her voice trailed off. "Of course there came a time when I no longer played, I remember wondering why. I thought that maybe I had amused the garden fairies... that, or I had annoyed them."

"Do you still dance here?"

"Not in years," Charlotte replied.

"*Would* you dance here?" Jovin asked.

"Not unless I was asked," Charlotte grinned.

Jovin took up her hand, "Will you dance with me?"

"I would be delighted."

Jovin led her by the hand up the gazebo stairs, their shoes clomping lightly on the wooden planks. He paused in the middle of the floor and drew her close. "And *one-two-three, one-two-three...*" he counted, waltzing her in a wide circle. "And *spin,*" Charlotte spun, her contagious smile slipping onto Jovin's face.

"Just like childhood," Charlotte said, coming out of her spin to become level with Jovin again.

"The fairies are surely amused," Jovin said, "we're off tempo. *One-two-three, one-two-three,*" he chanted again. "She spins again, and… *one-two-three,*" he slowed their waltzing, and they revolved slowly on the spot.

They stared fondly at each other under the gentle lighting, swaying in time with the sound of the breeze through the garden, the thought of fairies and magical childhoods fresh on their minds.

Jovin brushed her cheek gently.

"I know what you are doing," Charlotte took Jovin's hand away from her face. "You are not going to kiss me. I apologize if you were under another impression, Jovin."

Jovin's jaw had gone slack. To Charlotte's increasing surprise and confusion, he started to chuckle. "I wasn't expecting that,"

"I would assume not," she said gently.

Jovin blinked in astonishment. A moment later, he resumed the vivacious attitude again. "Shall we finish our dance?"

Charlotte smiled gently, "That would be appreciated."

Chapter 17

Swirling Skirts and Vacant Memories

The morning of the Masquerade arrived, and the palace of Terrison was undergoing a rush of organized chaos. Servers and decorators bustled their way through the palace, running from one end to the other. The palace had transformed overnight, and it was difficult to imagine the outcome while the halls remained under construction.

Not knowing her place in the wake of it, Saphir found herself pacing the corridors. She felt lost the majority of the morning, her mind wandering with her feet. Her conversation with King Aldrich drifted into her head now and again. *"We are delighted that you have joined us. Your presence shall remain unannounced. We are old allies, your country and mine; Terrison holds no harm for you."* Saphir was grateful for all of this, although she found it difficult to ease her puzzled mind.

Her skirts swished as she walked. The sound reminded her of other times, her mother's smile, her dearest friend Madeline, her aunt Clarissa and her uncle Roben, as well as the cemetery where her father was buried; now doubtless a heap of rubble, a blackened husk of her old life. *So many tragedies, so many memories, all in the sweep of a skirt.*

Her feet led her to the entrance hall. The checkerboard marble floors were occupied with visiting nobles, all of whom were chattering in anticipation for the Masquerade that evening. Saphir spotted Charlotte mingling among them. She had not spoken to Charlotte yet and had no desire to put herself in a potentially uncomfortable situation. She stepped behind a group of young girls to avoid Charlotte's line of sight.

Near the entrance doors, Saphir noticed Jovin in deep conversation amongst a group of older noblemen who seemed enthralled with him. One man laughed, and another gave Jovin an approving slap to the shoulder. She found it settling to see Jovin communicating with people who appreciated him for something other than his looks and rank.

She hovered beside a sunlit window wishing she could consider herself a guest, and not a tagalong. At that moment, she wanted nothing more than a friend—someone who would *not* silently judge her. For reasons she could not understand or explain, a friend seemed impossible to obtain. Maybe it was because she had little interest in the Terrison nobility, all of whom were clamoring on about the ball. Or maybe it was her; maybe she was closed off and had not realized it. "'Maybe *created a thousand reasons, and* maybe *could create an infinite trove of answers,*'" she quoted softly from a Kaiden poem.

Jovin excused himself from the gentlemen, leaving them laughing and tipping their top hats. His eyes scanned the crowd and landed on Saphir, giving her the smallest of smiles and nodding her over.

In response, she shook her head and remained beside the window.

A confused frown crept over Jovin's face. He made his way over to her, excusing himself and nodding politely as he passed through the crowd. "Hey, Saphir," he playfully greeted, "are you all right?"

"Yes,"

"You sure?" he scrutinized. "You look like you need a hug."

"I will not permit you to give me a hug," Saphir stated.

"Well, actually, I was going to find Merik and ask *him* to give you a hug," Jovin smarted.

Despite herself, Saphir's mouth broke into a reluctant smile. "You look like you are enjoying yourself."

"Well, yeah, when you're not being goggled over every two-point-three seconds, there is actually fun to be had," Jovin said, looking over the crowd beside her.

"I'm glad." For the first time in a long while, Saphir felt at ease with Jovin. She thought that maybe Jovin could tell, because he bristled a moment later, cleared his throat, and stood with his hands behind his back.

They watched the crowd for a bit. Saphir not daring to start up a conversation for fear of backfire.

Jovin cleared his throat again, "Have you met Miss Carlise yet? She's a novelist from Amelia."

"I have not, you will have to point her out." Saphir's face paled as she surveyed the throng of people.

Jovin noticed the sudden change in her. "What?"

"Charlotte sees you," Saphir stepped away from Jovin.

"So?"

Saphir shuffled around to the other side of Jovin so if Charlotte looked their way again, she would see only her back and not immediately recognize her.

Jovin's face was now alight with amusement, "Saphir, are you really—"

Saphir waved her hand to silence him. "No, I just… I do not wish to speak with her. It's awkward for me. I'm not even supposed to be here. But here I am… *here*… with *you*."

"Is that all?" Jovin asked, "I'm almost surprised… Well, actually no, not really."

Charlotte was chatting animatedly with a crowd of courtiers, her eyes paced over the room and landed on Jovin; they nodded in acknowledgment, and Charlotte continued her conversation.

"I think I'm going to leave; have a good day," Saphir said, her panic slowly elevating.

He caught her hand as she turned away, "No," Jovin said, "hang around for a bit."

"I shouldn't, really, I should go,"

Jovin smiled softly, "You don't have to,"

Saphir turned her face on the room, "But isn't she watching you?"

"Everyone is," Jovin said, "but they're starting to notice you as well."

Saphir took a breath, "If you won't let me go, at least pretend to be talking to me."

"Not fond of silence anymore?" Jovin asked.

Saphir bristled, "Not fond of being thought of as silent."

Jovin's eyes landed on a few nobles who had taken interest in Saphir. A few gentlemen were conversing beside a group of young ladies who appeared to be defaming the princess. Jovin recognized them as a bunch whom he had excused himself from earlier that morning.

His brow furrowed, he moved closer to Saphir and brushed a lock of hair off her shoulder. "Pretend to flirt with me for a moment."

Saphir blanched. "*What?* No."

Confliction paralyzed her. She decided to leave. She did not have to stay here, or with him, any longer than she wanted to. But she thought she heard him whisper, although it might have been her imagination: *"Forgive me for a moment and trust me?"* and she felt her resolve waver.

"This is ridiculous," she let out a nervous laugh. "Fine, you win. Happy?" she batted her eyes, smiling as though she wanted nothing more than to smile and smile for the rest of her life.

Jovin was utterly bewildered. "I've seen you flirt, and that is not flirting. Try again, maybe?"

Saphir gave an exasperated huff and made her smile less obnoxious, settling for gazing sweetly, albeit irritated, at Jovin. "Better?" she asked. "Now, what *shall* we talk about? How astonishingly uncomfortable this is? How about how awkward I find my entire existence at this moment?"

"Well, what did we talk about way back when?"

Saphir found it difficult to look at Jovin. "I forget," she said, casting her gaze around. She could feel more of the surrounding nobility's attention on them now and was rather unsure what to do. "First off, I cannot remember. And secondly, how does this benefit *anyone?* We're in plain view here. I'm just going to get myself into trouble like I did before, and I really—"

"Saphir, you're rambling." Jovin's eyes fixed on a spot beyond her, his forehead creased. His eyes tracked a movement behind her.

"Do we have an audience?" Saphir asked.

"Considering how many people have asked about you today, I think they're starting to piece it together. Stop acting as though you notice them,"

There was a commotion, and the people around them were becoming louder. She heard someone mention their names, and someone else mentioned Ee'lin. A woman gasped and announced that she remembered seeing Saphir at a gathering a few months past. The rush of excitement grew as the crowd began realizing who Saphir was.

"This gossip will give you away..." Jovin's tone was close to worry as he took in the crowd. "I'm making a decision," and he grabbed her by the waist, pulled her close to him, and kissed her.

Saphir's initial impression was shock, which was quickly replaced by a guilty satisfaction that drove all else from her mind. Her mind regained itself and was flooded with memories of her and Jovin: their silly sneaking about under their parent's noses, the late nights dancing under the festival canopies, long walks through the palace gardens. Every memory she had been too in love with to forget, and too heartbroken to want to remember.

From far away, Saphir heard a pair of young girls croon, "Ooh, that's so adorable!" Her friend shrieked out a giggle. The crowd shifted their intrigued tone as they began to lose interest, save for the folly of ladies cursing her name.

Jovin was making a show of kissing her and had made no sign that he had noticed the shift. In Saphir's mind, it was as though a light switch had been flicked off. She broke from Jovin, and stared at him, dumbstruck at his satisfied expression.

She took up his hand and dragged him from the crowd and through the side hall she had entered by. She made sure they were out of earshot before turning on him.

"What the hell was that?" Saphir hissed.

"I was saving your neck," Jovin said with a smirk, "I also put myself in a very precarious position by doing that, but there you go."

"Always thinking of yourself first." Saphir felt her cheeks burning. "I cannot believe you would do that."

Jovin had noticed a movement over her shoulder and led her farther down the hallway. "By the way, darling, you owe me one."

"What are you talking about? *You* kissed *me.*" Saphir glanced back the way they had come. She noticed a group of young girls hovering around the doorway, failing to be inconspicuous. Behind them, a few nobles were observing the pair with curious expressions.

"I saw them," Jovin muttered.

"We're making a scene," Saphir warned.

"Exactly. Lean against my shoulder. Walk slower," Jovin advised.

Saphir obliged, still angry and outwardly trying to appear calm. "*You kissed me,*" she repeated more calmly.

"I saved you." Jovin replied, leading them through a doorway and into a side hall. He glanced back to make sure no one had followed them. "No, listen—" he said when Saphir tried to protest. "Now, no one will question why you are here. You can do whatever you'd like now, they won't try to intimidate you. I made them envy you. I made them *all* envy you. If they know our history, they'll think you're with me. If they *don't* know our history, *they'll think you're with me,"* he grinned. "This gives an *actual reason* for the Ee'lin Princess to randomly be here in Terrison with me. They'll forget about the attacks, they won't try to solve it, it actually draws attention away from you and places it on me. Or, if they don't know much, you could be anyone: a courtier, a server, a random quiet girl I took a fancy to. I've given you a mask to hide behind. Do I hear a thank you?"

Saphir was skeptical. "That *is not* what you did."

"Sweetheart, think about it."

Saphir averted her eyes, looking anywhere but at Jovin's satisfied expression.

"*Anyway,*" Jovin went on smugly, "you kissed me back." And with a wink and a proud smirk, he walked away as though he knew a magnanimous secret.

"What the hell are you doing?" She muttered at his receding form.

+++++

Charlotte's eyes narrowed as Jovin approached her, albeit cautiously under her scrutinizing gaze. When he reached her, she turned and walked away down the corridor, leaving him to chase after her. "Wait, Charlotte."

"You have some explaining to do," Charlotte said curtly. "*Again.*"

"Charlotte, please wait. I can explain."

She paused, folded her hands, and observed him with a taught smile. "Do not waste my time, Jovin. I have no patience for boys who play with heartstrings, mine or otherwise."

"Look, I really…"

"I had made up my mind to trust you," Charlotte's forehead creased. "You are one confusing fellow."

"I'm sorry," Jovin begged.

"There have been too many excuses," she turned away, blinking back her irritation. "How about this," Charlotte said, taking a breath. "For the time being, I will forget. I will not inquire any further regarding you or Saphir."

"You don't have to do that."

"No," Charlotte said tartly. "I really think I do," she gave him one last patronizing look. "Good day, Jovin. I shall see you at the Masquerade tonight." And she walked away, leaving Jovin alone beside the glaring window.

Chapter 18

Masquerade

The Masquerade ball that evening was one for the history books. In a vain, and successful, attempt to cling onto the splendor of the past, Terrison had gone to every extreme in preparation for the grand event. Gold and purple strands of silk hung from the ceilings. The great glass dome above the dance floor gleamed like a portal into the heavens. The chandeliers sparkled, polished to perfection. Every lightbulb shone brightly; every floor tile had been cleaned with care. The music of the orchestra floated through the air, inviting the attendants to dance under the stars.

The lavish costumes reminded one of sorcerers and enchantresses, majestic and regal in brightly colored ensembles and splendidly decorated masks. Curled hair was piled high and pinned with diamonds, and top hats bobbed among the crowd of feathers and tiaras.

Merik thought he had never seen a place so beautiful in the whole of his young life.

+++++

Jovin met Charlotte at the foot of the staircase in the entrance hall. She looked dazzling in her pale pink and ivory embroidered ball gown, a matching mask clutched loosely in her hand. Her hair was pinned half up, allowing the rest to fall in immaculate curls down her back. Charlotte's angelic face held a smile that grew at the sight of Jovin.

Jovin offered her his hand, "Absolutely beautiful."

"You are always the charmer," Charlotte's mellifluous laugh flitted though the air.

Jovin smiled. He was dressed handsomely in a goldenrod waistcoat and a knee-length ebony jacket. Like Charlotte, he wore no mask.

Charlotte noticed this. "Where is your mask, Jovin?"

"I don't know what you're talking about," he mused, pretending to take interest in the high vaulted ceilings.

"Jovin, humor me for a moment,"

Jovin produced his golden mask from his inside pocket. "I have it, but I won't wear it."

"And why not?"

"Care to dance, Charlotte?" Jovin asked, changing the course of the conversation.

Charlotte took his hand, inclining her head. "I would love to."

+++++

"What *does* she see in him?" Saphir muttered as Jovin and Charlotte took up their places on the dance floor.

"I really don't get what *you* see in him," Merik commented back.

"I do not know what you are talking about." Saphir turned away from the dancers, contemplating the chandelier across the room.

"Sure," Merik teased slyly.

The two observed Jovin smile his charmingly sweet smile at Charlotte, she blushed and batted her eyes so amiably, that Saphir's nose scrunched, and her brow furrowed.

"And that annoyed expression is not because the *famed, devilishly handsome, heart-stealing Prince Jovin Flayarti Raleigh of Canston who stole your own heart many moons ago* is dancing with another girl?" Merik prodded.

Saphir turned a shifty glare at him. "Of course not."

"Uh huh, sure," Merik said, obviously not buying it. He looked casually around the ballroom, "Oh look, the *Baron Weveal of Boringness* is headed our way." Hoping to avoid conversation, he stepped behind Saphir and out of the Baron's line of sight.

Saphir had replayed the last few seconds in her mind, and her face now split into a scowl. "*Jovin did not steal my heart!*" she protested, "I never—"

Merik gave her a sardonic grin, raising a finger in a superior manner. "Silence is a virtue."

"*Are you sassing me?*"

Merik did not respond. He flattened his lapel and pulled his mask down from his forehead, giving her a sidelong smirk. "Of course not, Princess," and he slipped through the crowd.

Saphir watched in stunned silence as Merik picked his way through the sea of masks and gowns. She straightened the shoulder cuff on her ornate sapphire ball gown and contemplated the room.

"Fantastic party, would you not agree?" Captain Donald had materialized beside her.

Saphir jumped slightly, then, realizing that it was only the captain, fell into a false impression of happiness. "Oh yes, fantastic."

There was a pause during which Donald stood tall and swayed to the music. Saphir's attention went back to the dancers, she tore her eyes away from them when Jovin dipped Charlotte. The song ended, and a new one began.

Donald inclined his head to Saphir, "May I have this dance, Your Highness?"

Saphir was touched at his offer and accepted.

Throughout the dance, Donald watched Saphir intently. He noticed her smile as she spun, her laugh when her dress skirts flared, then her straight back and gritted teeth when they passed Jovin and Charlotte. Jovin's eyes would automatically move to Saphir, and every time, he would make some small blunder in his dancing—something that both Donald and Jovin hoped would remain unnoticed by the two princesses.

When the song ended, someone tapped Donald's shoulder. Both he and Saphir turned to see a tall, lean, sandy-haired young man dressed handsomely in a navy and golden suit. "May I cut in?"

Donald's eyes moved to Saphir, who behind her painted mask seemed mildly interested in the person. "Yes, of course," Donald bowed to Saphir and left her with the young man.

The stranger bowed, "Princess," he greeted.

"Sir, *whose-name-I-do-not-know*," Saphir curtsied.

"Conrad," he replied. His decorative golden mask hid most of his face, but his blue eyes relayed his happiness at introducing himself.

"Saphir," she answered.

"A pleasure," Conrad replied, and he kissed the back of her hand.

The musicians struck up a lively tune, and the dance began. Conrad and Saphir kept in time as the dancers began a new step.

"Where is your title, sir?" she asked. He had not introduced himself as '*Sir Conrad of anywhere in particular*', and as he already knew who she was, and seeing as her identity had not been announced publicly, she was curious.

"I do not appreciate titles in introductions; they distract from decent conversations," replied Conrad. "But if you must know, I am the crown prince of Terrison."

"*Oh.*" Saphir was a bit taken aback. That made him Charlotte's twin brother. She stiffened, lowering her gaze to her feet.

"I am not planning on beheading you, if that is what you are concerned about," Conrad reassured her. They had been following the dance throughout their conversation, and now they turned away from each other. Saphir spun and changed partners for a very brief moment, then she was back with Conrad.

"I am glad you would not," she replied as she took his hand again. "But that was not exactly what I was worried about."

"You are most intriguing, Princess." Conrad grinned, "I mean that as a compliment."

Saphir returned his smile, "Then I shall take it as a compliment."

The dancing continued.

Saphir danced with Conrad for seven dances.

+++++

Donald regarded the two with approval. Saphir seemed to be enjoying herself, and Conrad could not keep a grin off his face as they danced. Having met Conrad at dinner the previous night, and having later struck up a meaningful and a humor-filled conversation, he deemed Conrad to be a kind, good-natured young man—a much needed companion for Saphir.

Merik spotted Donald among the masses of covered faces and colorful costumes. He picked his way over to stand beside him. Merik removed his mask from his face and let it rest on his forehead. He looked up at the captain and gave a dramatic shrug, blowing out a little spurt of air in exasperation. "I am very confused right now," he told Donald.

"How so?"

Merik gestured to the dancers. "Saphir was mad a minute ago, and now she's unexpectedly *happy*. And *now* Jovin seems to be utterly and completely ignoring her existence."

Donald contemplated the young prince. "It seems that Jovin is jealous of the princess's new suitor."

"*What?*" Merik shrieked so loudly that a passing waiter upended his tray. Donald caught it and helped steady the man, who looked mildly traumatized. "Sorry," Merik muttered to the waiter, who bowed and said that there was no problem but scurried off the moment the boy had turned away. Merik glared at Donald. "*What do you mean 'new suitor'?*"

"You look rather invested in this," Donald observed.

Merik threw up his hands, "I *am* not, I'm just confused by women."

"You are not the first."

Merik adjusted his mask, took it off, put it back on, and tried to fix it again.

In the next moment, the Baron-Merik-called-Weveal appeared out of the colorful crowd. "Captain Gregory Donald!" he exclaimed with gusto. "How wonderful to see you here! I thought you would not be attending our little escapade tonight. I am so glad you could join us." The man carried his lavish indigo mask on a rod in his right hand. His greying brown hair was combed neatly back and off of his pruned beard.

Merik pulled his mask low over his face.

"As well you, Wallace. I follow the advice my late wife left behind, which was to 'never pass up a reason to celebrate.' I strive to follow her wisdom."

"Ah, wives and their uncanny knack for knowing their husbands," the Baron chortled.

Merik wondered if the kind expression on Donald's face was forced, but a moment later the captain turned the Baron's attention away from himself by reintroducing Merik. "Wallace, I believe you have been acquainted with Prince Merik of Canston, although you may have not been introduced properly. Merik, this is Baron Wallace Von Lorian, a common friend of your father, as well as myself."

He bowed to Merik, who remembered his etiquette and bowed back. "Always an honor, young master," Baron Von Lorian said.

"It is great to meet you sir," Merik replied. *Where in the world did you get the name Weveal from?* Merik asked himself. *Now you're just making things up. Don't call him Weveal in real life, or you're dead.*

There was a quick moment where Merik contemplated continuing a conversation, but Captain Donald picked it up.

"How is your family—your daughter, Malory, and your brother, Benjamin? I have not seen them since Merik's christening." Donald said.

"Oh, they are wonderful!" the Baron said. "Malory just became engaged to a nice fellow from Kaiden. They are so happy it makes me proud. She is past the days of taking her beauty for granted. I do not see Benjamin as much as I used to; he has become slightly bitter since his wife passed."

"And your wife, Samantha?" Donald asked.

"She has decided to stay away this time as her sister is expecting a child any day now," the Baron answered.

"How wonderful,"

Baron Von Lorian spoke of uninteresting things. Uninteresting to Merik in any regard. The Baron seemed typical among barons: jovial, in a constant good mood, quick to turn a sticky situation into a pleasant one, and a close friend of the royal family. Donald tried to keep Merik in the conversation but quickly realized that Merik was bored, and made a gap in the conversation to allow the boy to excuse himself, which Merik did.

Merik slipped through the crowd and out of the ballroom. There was a balcony on the west side of the ballroom that overlooked the city of Flinith. He walked along the marble railing to the far end, keeping away from the guests and wishing there were more people his age present. The few children he had met had been rather snooty. Merik had distinctly heard one girl whisper to her friend that she made a point of not speaking with strangers—Merik found this comment odd, seeing as they were at a ball, where it was common for attendees to socialize with one another, acquainted or not.

Merik leaned against the balcony rail. The temperature had dropped since the sun had set, and there was a light breeze. But Merik was not cold. If anything, he felt as though the stuffiness of the ballroom was still lodged in his lungs, no matter how he gulped down the chilled autumn air. His splendid knee-length scarlet jacket was a pretty sight, but after wearing it for two hours, it had grown itchy and irritating. His mask was always too hot, and the chatter of the partygoers rang like the unending cry of an infant in his ears.

He pulled out the crumpled form of Sighter from a hidden inside pocket. He tugged on a wing, mimicking a flapping motion. He pressed a miniscule button on the back of the hummingbird's head, and Sighter's chilled copper panels warmed slightly. Sighter tried to flap his wings, but only one worked, while the other lay trembling in Merik's hand. He sighed and turned off

Sighter, setting him in a side pocket where he rested against a pack of playing cards.

His attention moved over the city of Flinith, which was alight with glowing homes and shops. This view reminded him of the view from their palace balcony back in Canston.

There was a bright light in the distance. Just as carnival lights are always brighter than the rest of the lights in the town, this light was bigger and brighter than those in the rest of Flinith. Merik wondered if the light had always been there; he thought maybe it had and he had not noticed it until then. He stared at it for a moment, contemplating it. The light looked odd, but Merik could not place the imperfection in his mind.

Merik's curiosity prompted him to watch the light, but after a few minutes of unchanged activity, he turned away and decided it was nothing to be worried about. He pulled the pack of playing cards from a pocket and started to shuffle them on the wide railing. He picked a card at random and put it face up into the deck. He shuffled and looked for the card again. Merik decided that this game was even more boring than the party and stuck the cards back into his pocket.

Merik yawned. Subconsciously, he checked the light at the end of town again. "Wait, what…"

Merik's surprise increased when the light expanded upward, flashing a vibrant golden glow across the sky. For a moment, the light dimmed to a flicker.

Merik took a step back from the rail. "What was that?" he wondered aloud.

Another bright flash illuminated the sky, larger this time. The flames clawed upward, hungry to burn and ready to devour.

Merik was frozen on the spot. He could not find it in himself to move his legs; they seemed to have melted into the ground.

The light continued to grope for the stars. It grew larger, spreading across sideways until it was a livid burn on the town's horizon. Merik knew for certain that this light was not a carnival.

"It's a fire," he whispered to himself. "Someone's home burned, and the fire is spreading." Feeling that he should do something, but unsure what, Merik unstuck his legs and retreated into the party.

No one seemed to have noticed that anything was out of the ordinary. Merik darted though the shifting crowd and sidestepped a waiter carrying a tray of champagne. He searched the crowd for Captain Donald but found no immediate trace of him. After a moment of scanning, he spotted Saphir's mane of curled hair.

She was dancing with Prince Conrad and seemed to be enjoying herself. Merik stopped for a moment, watching the dancing couple; he decided that it would be too hard to try to force his way onto the dance floor, and he had no desire to be shunted aside by haughty guests.

Merik was starting to feel anxious, but he kept up his search, pushing through the crowd. He ran over the entirety of the hall twice and failed to spot the captain—or Jovin, for that matter. He gave up his search attempt and ran back out onto the balcony.

Merik now knew for certain that it was a fire. It had spread in a wall of flame, tearing through the distant streets. The skirt of the city was rimmed in brightest orange. Merik could see the flames beginning to lick at the clock tower. He could imagine the panicked shouts and cries of children as they screamed for their parents. Innocent people were down there. Families. A high-pitched siren evolved into the night, screaming out in distress.

Merik felt nauseated and rushed back into the palace, pushing past an extravagantly dressed lady and ducking as she reached to hit him over the head with her fan. Merik's mask had dropped a long time ago, and as Merik's focus flitted from masked face to masked face, his nausea turned to terror.

"Captain Donald!" Merik shouted out. He was desperate. He kept looking around in faint hope that he would see Donald, hoping beyond hope that somewhere his cry had not gone unheard. "*Captain Donald!*" He shouted again, louder this time.

The musicians stumbled over their music. The conductor eyed Merik with arrogant suspicion but continued to conduct, urging the musicians on. Hordes of eyes stared at Merik, whispering covertly behind glittered and gloved hands, but Merik did not care. He was more frightened than he had ever been in his entire life. No one seemed to realize what was happening, they were all too caught up in their gossip and merrymaking to give him more than a disgusted glance.

Merik was about to shout again when Baron Von Lorian appeared beside him, a horrorstruck look on his face. He seemed flustered by Merik's impertinence. "Prince Merik, what are you—"

Merik saw a familiar head of dark hair and pushed past the Baron. "Captain!" Merik stumbled over his own feet and collided with Donald. "There was… and it exploded… fire… I couldn't find you—" Merik broke off his speech, realizing that he was jabbering. "There was an explosion at the far edge of town. It wasn't just a fire… it was huge, and the fire is spreading… There's a siren… *I fear people are dead now…*" he added in a strained whisper, shaking with emotion.

Donald was quick on the uptake. "How long ago was this?" he asked firmly. His tone made it clear that he needed facts without added complaints.

"It just happened," Merik answered.

"Alright," Donald straightened up. He dashed through the crowded ballroom to the balcony, Merik and Baron Von Lorian close on his heels. Donald took one look and blew out a pent-up breath.

From the near edge of town, a large crowd of people were marching up the paved road to the palace gates. Their numbers were revealed by their illuminated electric lights and gleaming weapons, a long, shifting horde that snaked the winding road to the palace.

Donald addressed the Baron, who looked astonished and altogether bewildered. "I need you to find King Aldrich and tell him to evacuate the palace. Either that, or to prepare for a fight. Tell him that we have minutes. There is no time to waste. Hurry."

With a nod, Baron Von Lorian ran to deliver the message.

Merik looked to Donald with worried eyes. "What are we going to do now?"

Donald took hold of Merik's arm to keep him at his side as they rushed back into the ballroom. "Look for Jovin and Saphir; we need to find them as swiftly as possible."

The lights in the ballroom flickered to a dim glow. Then they went out. Some guests fell; others screamed. The musicians stopped playing. All was still.

The darkness was broken via handheld pipe lighters and candles servers supplied to the ill-tempered guests. Someone was talking very loudly, explaining the situation to the nobles and reassuring them that they would be fine as long as they remained calm.

But that was a lie. Everything was moving quickly and in slow motion all at once. Merik heard someone shout for a family member. There was a shatter of glass. A gust of chilled air flew over the crowd. People scurried to find each other in the dim light. There was the low hum of voices who were scared to speak too loudly.

The grip on his arm was still strong, and Merik was glad of it. Donald pulled him near a window and spoke firmly, "You, your brother, and Princess Saphir are my priority. We are going to find them and get to the *Alexandria*.

You will stay with me and not leave my side." Donald looked Merik in the eyes, "You are being very brave, Merik; I need you to continue to be brave."

"Yes sir," Merik said. He did not feel brave—not anything close to it. He was frightened and worried for his brother and Saphir. He wanted to rewind the whole adventure—to be home in Canston—but Merik knew it was beyond his power. He nodded and followed Donald around the crowd to the door at the other end of the ballroom.

The room beyond was cast in shadows, and the faint glow from Donald's lighter did nothing to penetrate the vast darkness. Three figures scurried toward them, one holding an electric torch. Merik could see that one was Baron Von Lorian, the other two he assumed were palace staff. The Baron recognized Donald and halted. "I alerted the King, and he has taken a few precautions. He wishes to speak with you."

"I imagine he would. Where is he?" Donald replied.

"Down the hall, the first door on the left," the Baron said. He and the servers continued into the crowded ballroom.

Donald and Merik found the King, who was accompanied by Princess Charlotte and Jovin. The room was small—hardly an office for a clerk, let alone the King. In the center of the room stood a desk with three candelabras casting a ghoulish light over the occupants.

Some of King Aldrich's worry relaxed upon his seeing Donald, and he beckoned them closer. "I was worried I would not be able to speak to you beforehand."

Merik ran and hugged Jovin, who, for his part, looked slightly relived to see Merik and placed an arm around the boy's shoulders.

"Your Majesty, I plan on leaving as soon as possible. I advise you to accompany us," Donald stated.

"That is very generous of you," the King replied.

Princess Charlotte took a step forward. "Father, must we flee?" she stared at him, an anxious edge behind her eyes. Merik was not sure whether she wanted him to leave, or whether she thought the idea to be absurd.

"I am not leaving Terrison, Charlotte," the King said to her. He turned to Donald, "However, I ask that my children accompany you."

"I will not leave you here!" Charlotte protested, "If we leave, we must leave together."

"I think not," the King said to Charlotte, who seemed to be holding back tears. He spoke to Donald, "I need my children to survive. If the mob takes the palace tonight, then I need to know that my heirs are safe."

Donald nodded curtly, "Yes. Where would your son be now?"

"I saw him about ten minutes ago," Jovin said. He moved away from Merik, closer to the table and the King. "He and Saphir were in the ballroom."

There was a distant scream from the ballroom. King Aldrich turned to Donald as a wave of alert washed over him. "Find Conrad and leave. Get out of here. I will let you know when it is safe for them to return."

"Yes, Your Majesty," Donald bowed quickly and motioned for Merik and Jovin to follow him out.

Charlotte rushed to her Father, "Father, no, I do not want to leave you!" her voice broke, but her tears had not yet dropped.

The King hugged her and kissed her head. "My daughter, my beautiful light, I love you. But now," he released her, "you must go."

Charlotte broke into tears. "*Father, no—*"

"Get out of here!" he commanded. Charlotte took a startled step back. *"Get out of here!"* her father's pain shone through in his voice.

Charlotte recoiled. Jovin took her by the waist and led her from the room. Charlotte strained to keep eye contact with her father until the very last second. Once in the hall, he let go of her. Charlotte wiped away tears and gratefully accepted the hand Jovin offered her.

In a blurred moment, they were back in the ballroom. Donald stopped the group with a raised hand, "Jovin, take Charlotte and Merik. Tell Mister Carter to ready the engines if he has not already. With any luck, I will meet you there with Saphir and Prince Conrad before anything tragic happens. Get to the *Alexandria* as fast as you can," he looked directly into Jovin's eyes. "*No one stops you.*"

Jovin nodded curtly. "I understand," he turned and, with Charlotte still clutching his hand, walked briskly across the room and through a doorway. He paused and retraced his steps, "Come on, Merik, hurry it up."

Merik had not moved from Donald's side. "Oh, um, right," he gave Donald a fast hug and scurried across the floor to Jovin. "Be careful, Captain!" he shouted over his shoulder as he caught up with Jovin and Charlotte.

They walked hurriedly down the hall, guided by the moonlight and feint glow of the city's fire that penetrated through the occasional window.

Jovin stopped at a corner and looked to Charlotte. "Left," she said. And they followed her down the left hall.

The halls were frigid now, a continual draft of night air sent shivers down Merik's back. The sounds of panicked partygoers receded with every step, and the only sounds were the clicks of Charlotte's high heels and the swish of her dress.

"This way," Charlotte said again, and they turned a corner.

Charlotte was frightened more than she cared to admit. She had stopped crying, but her eyes felt teary all the same. There was no one around: no servers, no guards, no random people. It was so very odd. She was used to the palace in all its glory. There had hardly ever been a soundless moment; now there was too much silence, and what had once been her lively home, was now reduced to a hollow shell.

"Wait," Jovin caught Charlotte's arm, stopping her in her tracks. She had been lost in thought and had not realized that they had passed a window that over looked the front gates.

"What is it?" Merik backtracked to them.

Under the bright streetlamps outside the iron gates that protected the palace, there stood a mass of people dressed in grey coats and carrying weapons. A second group behind the militia appeared to be shouting to the soldiers—whether encouragement or insults, it was impossible to tell.

"So it's only the palace without power," Merik observed.

"Where are the guards?" Charlotte whispered, her eyes trained on the gate.

"Damn, we need to move," Jovin reached for Charlotte's hand and dragged her and Merik behind him. "They may have seen us. Come on. We are in danger unless we get out of here soon," he released their hands, and they continued down the hall.

Charlotte focused on keeping pace with the two princes. They rushed down a staircase and through the still entry hall. Jovin flung open the door to the veranda, and they passed into the bitter night.

They raced down the lawn to the airship docks. Charlotte's high heels got caught in the grass, and she discarded them without a second thought, running out of her heels and leaving them stuck in the turf. The cold dew stained the hems of her glittering dress, and her feet began to feel numb.

For the first time that evening, they heard the roaring crowd, which had grown restless at the gates. For a panicked moment, it felt as though they had been spotted. A gunshot fired, and the crowd became eerily quiet.

Merik reached the dock house first and sprinted down the concrete sidewalk to the polished brass front door. "It's locked!" he shouted. "Great, we got here without dying, but we can't get in."

"Hush, Merik," Jovin said, trotting around the side of the dock house to inspect the sides.

Jovin returned half a minute later and beckoned to them. "I think I found a way through the fence; hurry though." There was another shout from the crowd as a battering ram struck the palace gates.

Merik scampered around the building, Charlotte close behind him. Jovin motioned to the corner of the building where the wall met the fence. "Look, there and there," he pointed to the high roof of the dock house, where a large rock protruded out of the stone-inlayed wall. "I think we can climb over it."

"Are you crazy? We can't do that! It's thirty feet tall!" Merik said exasperatedly.

"The electricity isn't on. We have to get over," Jovin said.

"I do not think I can, Jovin," Charlotte said meekly. Her teeth were chattering, she was shoeless, and in her party dress, which was made for showing off rather than keeping out cold, she was turning blue.

Jovin removed his jacket and wrapped it around her shoulders. "Alright, we can find another way."

"Oh, thank you," Charlotte replied, pulling the jacket tighter around her and pushing her arms though the sleeves.

Merik stuck out his tongue and made a face at the exchange. Then, losing interest, he looked along the wall of the dock house for a way in. He spotted a small door and decided to check it, hoping it was miraculously unlocked. It was not. "Why do you have to be locked?" he grunted to the door.

"No luck then?" Jovin asked.

"Everything seems to be against us right now." Merik kicked the door and then checked the handle again to see if it had somehow unlocked itself in the time since he kicked it. "Open!" he rattled the handle again. "Just open!" he turned to Charlotte. "Is there a key? Maybe it's hidden over here somewhere? Charlotte?"

She shook her head, "I do not know. I do not come down here very often."

"So we're dead then?" Merik sighed.

"No, it means that we need to find another way," Jovin said.

"I think we should go around the building to check the other side," Charlotte said.

"Good idea," Jovin agreed.

"No, it's not," Merik muttered, but his comment went unnoticed. He trotted after them to the other side of the docking house. There was another side door, accessible by a keypad lock. Merik tried to pull it open, but the door held fast. There was also a keyhole, but no key.

Jovin looked to Charlotte, "Any chance you might know the combination?"

Charlotte searched her mind, "I have no reason to know it," she said apologetically.

Merik swore under his breath.

Jovin smacked his arm.

"Ow!" Merik rubbed his arm.

"Princes do not curse in front of ladies," Jovin reprimanded.

"*Princes are kind of stressed out at the moment!*" Merik exclaimed rudely.

Charlotte investigated the keypad, tapping in a few combinations.

"I doubt disfiguring it would help," Merik muttered.

Jovin gawked at him, "Are you going to blow it up?"

"I have nothing to blow it up *with*," Merik replied sarcastically.

Charlotte sighed and walked to the high fence, which had so often been alive with electricity. She tentatively reached out a hand and touched the cold metal. It was just a fence, nothing more, but it blocked them from their freedom.

"Any ideas?" Merik muttered.

"Not at the moment,"

Merik's voice dropped in volume, "Jovin, are we gonna make it?"

"I hope so," his brother replied emotionlessly.

"Do you think Saphir and Captain Donald are okay?"

"I really hope they are," Jovin said, quieter this time.

"I wish we could pick the lock," Merik muttered. "Is there any way we could kick down the door?"

Jovin gave him a look, "I won't stop you trying."

A wind blew from across the cliffs. Merik shivered and put his hands in his pockets. "Ow!" he pulled out what had startled him and examined it. "Sighter!" he exclaimed.

"What?" He had caught Charlotte's attention. "Merik, are you all right?"

"Sighter—he's my hummingbird. But he broke, and I haven't fixed him yet, so I put him in my pocket because I was running late and forgot and parties are boring and... never mind." He began tinkering with the pieces, unscrewed the bird's head, and then detached a wing.

"Can he help us?" Charlotte asked.

"*Yes*," Merik replied. He twisted and continued to disfigure the mechanical hummingbird. "I've picked four locks in my time, and two times I used

Sighter to help me." He moved pieces around for another thirty seconds and then stepped closer to the door. Sighter's smooth design that had changed remarkably; it now resembled more of a pin cushion than a hummingbird. Merik inserted a piece into the keyhole, and in another twenty seconds he had the door open.

"You are a genius!" Charlotte exclaimed.

Merik beamed with pride. He held the door open for Charlotte, "After you, Princess."

Jovin held out an arm to stop her, "Nice job, Merik, but I am going to go in first, just in case."

"I was trying to be a gentleman," Merik said sardonically.

"And I can appreciate that," Jovin stepped through the doorway. After a few seconds of silence, he reappeared. "Nothing yet. Come on."

They followed him in.

Patches of moonlight littered the tiled floor, casting the rest of the dock house into shadow. Merik stayed close to Charlotte and Jovin as they walked across the entry hall to the opposite side. They found a pair of glass doors and quickly exited through them.

Once out, Merik let out a pent-up breath. "I almost expected something."

"I think we all did," Jovin looked over to Charlotte, who was staring at the giant shape of the *Alexandria* three hundred feet to their left. Soft lanterns and low windows gave the entire airship a homelike glow.

"She's beautiful," Charlotte breathed.

"She is," Jovin agreed, taking up her hand again. "And now we board."

Merik raced ahead of Charlotte and Jovin, and paused at the top of the gangway stairs. Ahead of him was the bridge connecting the hull and docking braces. "Come on!" he shouted down to them.

"Oh no," Charlotte murmured, staring between the airship deck and the flimsy gangway. Her eyes flicked to the endless void beneath them.

"Charlotte, you have to," Jovin said, climbing up after his brother and taking her hand as she reached the platform where the railed bridge began. "You go first, Merik,"

Merik took a breath, "Just make sure she gets aboard before the mob gets us." He started across the plank, getting across quickly and tore down the main deck stairwell.

Charlotte was frozen in place. "Jovin, I-I cannot…"

Jovin took her hands, "Charlotte, look at me. You will not fall. It is perfectly safe. You will be fine."

"I just..."

"Heights?"

"A little bit, but if the bridge gives out, the drop—"

"It will not give out."

"But—"

"Hurry or the mob will kill us."

Charlotte nodded, "I understand." She took a step.

Jovin held her hand and started walking across the gangplank. Charlotte's bare feet shuffled on the boards, feeling for flaws that would make them fall. She decided that she was brave enough to look away from Jovin to glance behind her. Her eyes shifted to the dark cavity of space beneath the gangplank. Charlotte let out a squeak of fright and clutched onto Jovin's arm. He turned her face away to keep her from looking over the edge. "We are almost there; just keep going," he assured her. "You can do this."

Charlotte was shaking, apologizing profusely. Jovin held out his hands to her and slowly guided her over the remaining planks.

She had just stepped onto the airship when the lights came back on in the palace. They gasped in surprise, staring out at the blinding display of light perched on the hill.

Merik came running from the stairwell and skidded to a stop beside them. "I just woke Mister Carter, he's getting the engines ready. As soon as Saphir and Captain Donald get here, we're ready." Merik looked out at the palace. "Do you think they can still get out?"

"I really hope so," Jovin replied.

Charlotte stared open-mouthed at the palace; its lights were glittering and illuminating the skies. It would have been beautiful had it not been for the mob at the gates.

Another gunshot fired. Someone screamed.

Chapter 19

A Familiar Scenario

Saphir was frantic. She had lost sight of Jovin a long time ago while he had been dancing with *Perfect Princess Charlotte,* and had not seen Merik since long before that.

She gripped Conrad's hand tightly to avoid being separated in the throng of people. In truth, she was more frightened by the thought of being alone than of losing Conrad in particular. The irregular light from electric torches and candles was making it difficult to identify whose face belonged to whom. She kept scanning the crowd in hope of spotting Captain Donald or Merik; and although she did not care for the way the evening had progressed, even Jovin would have been a welcome sight then.

Then the power returned.

Every person in the ballroom fell silent. A few people blew out their candles. The crowd held their breath in anticipation.

Saphir looked to Conrad, who appeared composed. "I need to find Captain Donald," she said evenly. In the ringing silence, she knew that almost everyone had heard her.

"Yes, you do." Conrad said, and led her through the crowd.

At the edge of the ballroom, an important-looking man caught up to them. "Your Highness, I have orders from your father," he said, flustered.

"You are to accompany the Canston party on the airship *Alexandria* right away. They are moored in the royal airport. Your father will have you return when it is safe."

"I understand; thank you," Conrad replied.

"Baron Wallace Von Lorian," the man stated with a nod to Saphir, who nodded back in greeting.

Conrad looked to the Baron. "Charlotte—where is she?"

"With any luck, she has already boarded," Baron Von Lorian drew a deep breath. "I strongly suggest that you waste no time."

Conrad began leading them in the direction of the docking yard.

Saphir let go of Conrad's hand, "Wait, where is Captain Donald?" she asked the Baron.

"I do not know; I think—"

"Saphir, Prince Conrad, it is time to leave." Captain Donald had just rounded the corner and was trotting to meet them.

"And here he is," Baron Von Lorian finished, relieved at Donald's miraculous timing.

"Come along now, we have very little time." Donald ushered the two royals along, looking back over his shoulder he called to Baron Von Lorian. "Wallace, are you coming?"

"Oh, um, yes, of course," the Baron wasted no time in following them down the corridor.

"But what about everyone else in the ballroom?" Saphir asked Donald. She was now gripping Conrad's hand again, and for his part, Conrad was not objecting.

Captain Donald's expression relayed his concern. "I do not know," he told her. "At this moment, we have to focus on getting the five of you to safety. One priority at a time."

The power pulsated, then went out for the second time. Saphir yelped.

"Are you all right?" Conrad's voice asked through the darkness.

"Fine," she replied. "Just… it startled me."

"This night cannot end well," Baron Von Lorian whispered.

"We are still free, so we move." Donald waved them on through the moonlit hall.

They reached the veranda doors and were out of the palace faster than Jovin, Charlotte, and Merik had been, partly because Donald kept them moving, and partly because Conrad knew the halls better than Charlotte did.

There was a loud yell from the gates, followed by another sound: metal hissing on metal. The sound seemed to reverberate through the air, echoing in her chest and causing her to recoil in distress. The world was still for a moment, then there was chaos.

+++++

"They broke through!" Merik exclaimed. He suddenly felt very alone and very afraid.

"They broke through," Charlotte softly echoed. She put her head in her hands, "I cannot believe this."

Jovin put an arm around her shoulders and stared out at the tangle of people running toward the palace. They had watched the palace lights fail, heard a volley of gunshots from the gates, and listened anxiously to the silence that followed. "I know," was all he seemed capable of saying.

"Donald and Saphir are still out there!" Merik suddenly exclaimed, running to the gangplank. "We have to go find them—"

Jovin caught him by the arm. "No, we stay here. Captain Donald said he would get them to the *Alexandria*, and we will stay here until he does."

Merik turned anxious eyes on his brother. "What if he doesn't? What if he needs our help but we aren't there? He could di—"

"My brother is out there," Charlotte said softly. "My family..."

Merik stopped his protest, pacing to the port side of the *Alexandria*. Beyond the rail, there was nothing but the open sky and the full moon, reflected over a blanket of clouds that lay beneath them.

+++++

Just keep running. Saphir and her companions had left the palace behind and crossed the lawn. She almost retwisted her nearly healed ankle in her decorative party heels, and had resorted to carrying them. A few hundred yards more and they would be at the dock house.

Run. Don't stop; just keep moving, she told herself, stumbling as they crossed onto the pavement of the dock house.

Donald produced a key ring and opened the front door quickly. "Inside," he told them. They filed in. He locked the door to slow down anyone who might follow them. "Get on board; I have to unlock the braces!" Donald shouted to them. He ran across the floor to the control room, where he engaged the release of the docking braces, hoping they could make it across the gangplank before the *Alexandria* drifted away from the cliff line.

Conrad reached the stairway first. "Saphir!" he held out his hand to her and allowed her up the stairs before him. She stopped at the top of the stairs, staring at the gangplank as it rocked in the wind. The braces were unlocked now, and there was nothing to keep the gangway steady. Conrad came up behind her. "Are you alright to go across by yourself?"

"Yes," she replied breathlessly. She took a nervous step and reached out her hand to the railing. She looked up at the *Alexandria* and spotted three figures at the railing: Merik, Charlotte, and Jovin. They had seen her, and now they raced to the gangplank's exit point. Merik waved to her. Saphir took one step, then another. She focused on the figures on the other end, which were steadily coming into focus. The look on Jovin's face made her breath catch in her throat. Her feet moved forward.

Saphir stepped off the gangplank stairs and ran to Jovin, burying her face in his shoulder. It felt all too familiar—the panic, the fleeing. "We lost you."

"I know. But we're all here now. You're safe," Jovin said, "this isn't the last time; this isn't Ee'lin. You're not alone."

Saphir nodded and let go of Jovin. Their eyes met again, and he dropped his gaze from her. Saphir bent to scoop up her shoes.

Conrad and the Baron stepped onto the deck. Conrad crossed to his sister and hugged her. "Charlotte, are you all right?"

"I am fine, but Father—"

"We will talk later," Conrad said, cutting her off.

The deck lurched, throwing everyone off balance. The gangplank unlatched and disconnected with the airship as the braces were retracted. The *Alexandria* hit against the side of the cliff with an awful *clop-clump-thunk* as the metal of the braces hit the wood of the hull.

Saphir dropped her shoes again, Merik stumbled and fell over, landing on the sharp and disfigured form of Sighter. "Ouch," he mumbled.

Jovin righted himself and looked over the rail at the dock house. "Captain Donald must have detached the braces; we will float free if we don't take off soon."

"Where is he?" Merik asked, leaning over the side to stare at the doors of the docking house.

Baron Von Lorian pointed a silent finger.

Donald was sprinting full-out from the dock house to the gangway. He was up the stairs in seconds, running across the violently rocking gangplank and was on board in a fraction of the time the others had taken. He completely ignored the royals and flew up the stairs to the wheelhouse, bursting through the doors, startling Mister Carter. "*Go. Go now*!" he commanded.

Mister Carter wasted no time in replying. He engaged the engine and slowly guided the airship away from the cliffs and out of the braces. "We're gonna pull the—"

"Leave the gangplanks, any attachments— let them fall!" Donald commanded.

"Yes, sir."

Donald took a deep breath, his eyes trained on the darkened palace, where lights were moving from room to room and over the lawns.

The *Alexandria* slowly glided away from the port. Without restraint, they floated freely, drifting like a prodigious kite.

Mister Carter looked down at a screen and pressed a few buttons. He voiced his worry, "Captain, engine three is not engaging."

"*I knew it.*" Donald tore his attention away from the window. He moved to the controls and took over from Mister Carter. "They would not have let us go so easily; they will try to track us," he glanced out the side window toward the Terrison palace. The mob had flooded the palace now and must have realized that the *Alexandria* was casting off. Some of the rioters were running down the lawn, foolishly thinking they could stop the airship before it left port.

"Captain?"

"Alert the crew; get the children inside. We are going *up*. Engage High Elevation Protocol."

+++++

The oxygen mask was tight against Merik's skin. His ears had popped, clogged, and popped again, then clogged and refused to pop further. He was in extreme discomfort. Saphir fidgeted with her hands, her eyes flitting around the room uneasily, not taking in any of it. Charlotte remained composed and had her hands folded in her lap while she stared at her bare, dirt-caked feet, Jovin's dress coat still around her shoulders. Baron Von Lorian sat quietly, eyes closed, breathing evenly and playing with the wedding band on his left hand. Both Jovin and Conrad seemed to have mutually decided not to make eye contact, or even to acknowledge one another. They stared in opposite directions.

All the passengers sat in a row on the floor of Donald's cabin, oxygen masks around their noses and mouths. Their backs were to the starboard wall, the breathing tubes connected to an oxygen tank hidden inside a cabinet.

For the past few minutes, everyone had been silent, and except for the faint hum of the engines and the rustle of cloth when someone moved, the world around them remained still. Merik wondered what the world looked like beyond the shining sheet of metal that had replaced the window wall.

Merik, sitting beside his brother, turned to him now, "Jovin, how high up do you think we are?"

"Not a clue."

"Do you think we are able to breathe without the masks now?"

"I don't know, keep it on."

"Do you think people are following us?"

This time Jovin hesitated, "It is highly probable."

"Oh." Merik pulled his legs up to his chest and rested his chin on his knees, taking a deep breath through his oxygen mask.

How did they know people were following them? And if there were, was it not obvious that they had flown upwards, rather than away?

He did not want to think on that. Instead, he focused on keeping his breathing even, and searched for another thought to distract himself. He leaned around his brother, and contemplated their Terrison companions. He returned to his back to the wall a moment later, as it was rude to stare at people who had just been run out of their country by their own subjects.

Relief came in the form of a flashing green light above the door. Captain Donald's voice sounded over the speakers: "*We are descending now, you are free to take off the oxygen masks.*" Sheets of metal slid away, revealing the window wall and the darkened sky.

Princess Charlotte removed her mask with a mumbled: "Thank goodness."

Conrad rubbed his face where the mask had cut into his cheeks. "I'm confused. Wouldn't we have been better suited to fly away?"

"It's harder to track an airship in the higher atmosphere; the radio towers and communication signals don't reach high enough," Jovin answered. His eyes were half closed, he looked as if he was about to fall asleep. "If someone was trying to follow us, it would be harder to track us in a fuzzy field of energy. It creates static on their instruments. In theory, we should be safe."

Charlotte set her mask down and rose. She swished her ruined skirts, then retreated across the room to stare out the window wall at the small speck of yellow light that was the city of Flinith.

In silence, Conrad followed her. So did the Baron.

This left Merik with Jovin, who was leaning against the wall with his eyes closed, and Saphir, who had her knees pulled up and was staring vaguely across the room, her forehead creased in contemplation.

Merik rose to his feet, deliberated on what to do, then decided to go up to the wheelhouse, where Captain Donald was.

Saphir watched Merik leave, then her attention turned to the three by the window. *Well,* she thought, *at least they have each other, and at least their palace is still standing.*

She put her head in her hands. This catastrophe reminded her of her own escape: the lateness of the hour, the quick getaway, the abandonment of a parent—two parents in this case—and the guilt that would hang over the heads of those fleeing, as though they had committed the crime themselves.

Saphir knew what that felt like. She almost rose to console the three by the window, to reassure them that there was still hope for Terrison. But she did not.

Saphir shook her head in an attempt to clear her thoughts and decided to go to her cabin until there was a reason to be around people again. She rose, setting her air mask on the shelf in the wall.

"You alright?" Jovin asked quietly.

"Huh?" Saphir looked down at Jovin, who was watching her with apprehension.

"You look distressed."

Saphir almost shot back that Jovin looked far worse than she felt, but she ultimately decided against it. "It's like living it all over again."

Jovin stood, "Why don't you stick around for a little while? I am sure Captain Donald will be here shortly. I think it is probably best if you know where we are headed next."

She nodded and seated herself gingerly on the edge of the sofa. Jovin hesitated, then he moved to Donald's desk, leaned against it, and kept his back to the room.

Charlotte sighed, and, after exchanging an exhausted glance with Saphir, joined her at the other end of the sofa. She found her hair in a matted tangle and pulled out pearled pins until she could comb her fingers through it.

"I am so sorry," Saphir said softly.

"I never imagined that it would be... overrun." Charlotte blinked, remembering something. "Conrad," she called over her shoulder, "did the palace appear empty to you?"

"Not in the ballroom, but now that you mention it, yes, the rest of it was," Conrad replied, walking around the sofa her and taking up his sister's hand. "You think the lack of security was not incidental?"

Charlotte shook her head, "We must have been set up. Someone must have planned it from the inside and dismissed the staff for the evening. It would explain the power outage as well."

"Who would have the audacity to do that?" Baron Von Lorian asked. He came around the sofa and stood before it, his arms crossed in disapproval.

"I do not know." Charlotte breathed out a sigh. "But they must be callous enough to threaten all of Flinith."

Except that you and your brother got away and your parents might be alive, Saphir thought to herself. She kept her mouth closed.

Conrad was thinking along the same lines as Saphir, "Do you think they are still alive?"

Charlotte turned to him, pure panic on her face. "Of course they are. *They have to be.*"

"But what if they're not?"

"*What if they are?*"

"Charlotte," Conrad looked her dead in the eye. She set her jaw and stared back at him, "Our home was overtaken. Unless there is a miracle in the works, people have died tonight, and there is no saying who."

"You want to give up hope that our family is alive?" Charlotte stood, suddenly fierce. Pearled hairpins spilled from her lap across the heavy carpet.

"No, I am telling you not to get overly attached to low possibilities," Conrad said softly.

Charlotte turned and walked away to stand beside the window wall again, staring out at the speck of light that was the city of Flinith. Her shoulders drooped, and her hand came to her cheek.

The side door opened, and Captain Donald entered, flanked closely by Merik. Captain Donald bowed to Charlotte and Conrad, and he then approached the Baron. "The Prince and Princess, along with yourself, are more than welcome to stay aboard; however, I should warn you that we already have one sought-after royal aboard, and it might endanger them further if we are being pursued."

Baron Von Lorian eyed Merik with suspicion.

"Merik isn't the threat," Saphir said.

The Baron looked at her for a moment, back to Donald, and then back to Saphir. "What did *you* do? Should I be concerned?"

"Has no one told you?" Jovin said from the desk.

Donald explained Saphir's story to the Baron. Conrad looked sadly at Saphir, "My father must have forgotten to explain the life-threatening part."

"Unless there is another reason…" Charlotte said in a carrying whisper.

Saphir tuned on her, "Excuse me?"

Charlotte stooped low enough to throw Saphir a contemptuous look, then to glance at Jovin. "*You never know…*"

Saphir leapt to her feet, tripping over the hem of her torn dress. She straightened up, staring intently at Charlotte. "*No.* Do not make assumptions. My worth, and reason for being where I am, has nothing to do with you. I am not worth less than anyone else, here, or anywhere. And you *will not* look down at me with the contempt I have so often seen in your eyes."

Charlotte did not answer at first. No one spoke. No one dared move too hastily. It was as though they were waiting for a bomb to ignite and blow them out of the sky.

At long last, Charlotte took a shuddering breath. "I believe I owe you an apology," she said calmly. "You are correct. I am sorry if I wronged you; it was not originally the intent."

Saphir's eyebrow flicked upward, but she said nothing. She resumed her seat, tucking her feet up to her and rearranging her dress.

"What…?" Merik whispered, dumbstruck.

Donald gave Merik a withering look that clearly stated *"Behave yourself,"* and he turned his attention back to the Baron. "We are scheduled to arrive in Simport next, but we have to make a supply stop beforehand, as we did not have the time to resupply in Terrison." He continued as though the exchange between the princesses had not taken place.

"Yes, well…" Baron Von Lorian looked to Conrad, who nodded, and then to Charlotte, who pursed her lips in a tight smile. "Yes, I think we will accompany you until there is a time we can return safely. Thank you for your hospitality."

"It is an honor," Donald said. "I have arranged your rooms; they should be ready shortly. In the meantime, I have ordered tea from the kitchens."

Merik looked around at the melancholy group, and an idea popped into his head. He grinned mischievously, "Anyone want to play a card game?"

"Merik, now is not the best time for cards," Jovin said, shooting him down. Merik's shoulders dropped, and he hung his head.

Conrad regarded the disappointed boy. "I'll play,"

"You will?" Merik's face lit up.

"Yes, why not? I could use a pick-me-up," Conrad looked expectantly at Baron Von Lorian. "Wallace?"

"Uh, yes, that sounds lovely," he replied to Conrad rather than to Merik.

Jovin sighed and ran a hand over his face, "Fine."

Conrad looked to his sister, "Charlotte?"

Charlotte flustered, "Oh, well, I… Oh, alright."

They gathered chairs around Donald's desk. "Saphir, come sit by me," Merik said. Saphir did not deny the boy his request and moved a chair around the desk. "Captain?"

"I shall play another time, Merik; I have a few things to attend to." Donald answered graciously.

Merik fished out a pack of cards from a coat pocket and shuffled them wildly.

Conrad gave Merik an inquisitive look, "Do you always keep a pack of playing cards in your pocket?"

"Parties get boring," was Merik's answer.

+++++

"How is it possible to win eleven games in a row?" Merik tossed his cards down on the table.

"Well, it's not my fault you keep losing," Conrad shrugged.

"Hmm," Merik speculated.

"Shall we play again?" the Baron picked up Merik's cards and shuffled them into the rest of the deck.

Merik was eyeing Conrad with suspicion, "I don't think you'll win again, though, just saying."

"Oh really?"

"Yes, really," Merik said. "And I'll make you a bet too! Hey, Captain," he leaned back in his chair to call to Donald, who was studying the intricate map that adorned the starboard wall and occasionally jotting notes down on a piece of paper. "Do we have anything we can bet?"

"What did you have in mind?" Donald replied.

"I dunno, playing chips, buttons… chocolate chips. How about cookies or something?" Merik offered.

"You would just eat them all before we started," Saphir observed.

"Probably," Merik agreed. "Alright, how about whoever *wins* this game has to go get cookies."

The Baron finished shuffling and started passing out cards.

"That seems a bit backwards, don't you think?" Saphir said.

"No, because if the loser had to get them, we'd all be in the kitchen, and it would be pointless. And this way Conrad won't want to win. But if he does, he has to go fetch the cookies." Merik said, as if it were obvious. "It's a *win-win!*" he chuckled, then sighed, "Ahh, I'm funny."

"Alright, whoever *wins* gets the cookies," Charlotte agreed. "But what if we do not know where the kitchens are?"

Merik wrinkled his nose, "Oh, come on, how am I supposed to have any fun when you guys are asking silly questions?"

The Baron finished dealing the cards, and everyone began examining their hand.

Jovin noticed that Donald was still consulting the map. "You know what? I think I'm going to sit this one out," he said, handing in his cards.

Saphir smirked, "Are your cards really that bad?"

"Not in the slightest; they are actually really good, but I don't want to be the one to play a game of fetch." Jovin rose from the table and joined Donald who was studying the map. Behind him he heard Merik say, "I bet he actually had really bad cards." Charlotte replied, "I do not think he even looked at them." And Merik sighed and said, "Well then…" And Conrad chuckled.

Jovin approached Donald, "Captain, what are your thoughts?"

Donald looked at Jovin, then back at the map. "I fear for your safety. This uproar, on top of Ee'lin's condition, makes for two precarious situations within a month of each other."

"Coincidence?" Jovin asked.

"Not what I would call likely," Donald said. "Either someone has pulled at a spider's web and is trying to cause you and your brother harm, or we have been in the wrong places at the wrong times."

"Who would want to do that?" Jovin crossed his arms and regarded Donald with puzzlement. He lowered his voice, "The situations could be linked to each other. Maybe it was *Terrison* who attacked Ee'lin, and then the people rebelled because they thought it was wrong."

"But why would King Aldrich not arrest Saphir or try to stop her leaving? He sent his children with us, after all," Donald said. "No, they are allies. The friction between Ee'lin and Terrison in the last one hundred years did not stop them siding together in the War of Placate. And all complications considered, I am pleased to see that Saphir and our Terrison companions are communicating so nicely."

Jovin snorted a laugh and ruffled his hair. "Yeah, well, Conrad seems to have taken fondly to her, so I doubt there will be as much discomfort between their countries after this."

"Is there something on your mind, Jovin?"

"No," Jovin replied very quickly. He then realized he had spoken too hastily, and backtracked. "I mean thank you, but no."

From behind them, Jovin heard Merik shout, "You can't do that!"

Conrad replied, "Why not?"

Merik explained in his most dignified voice: "Because, according to the 'winning cookie legislation,' purposeful losing clearly contradicts the agreement of which was made most recently, meaning that by losing *on purpose*, you are convicted of cheating, *which* is punishable by banishment!" There was a short silence, followed by giggles from those at the table.

Jovin smiled to himself. "New theory: the attackers are enemies of Ee'lin or, alternatively, Canston, and they are following us and targeting our allies."

"*Cheatery!*" Merik stood abruptly, jarring the table and scattering the cards. "I saw that!"

"Merik, what are you talking about?" Conrad asked, plainly confused.

Merik ignored Conrad and peered suspiciously across the table at Saphir. "I think there is something in your pocket that shouldn't be there."

"Why, I do not know what you are talking about." Saphir's innocent voice was all too phony. "I don't have pockets."

"Don't play games with me, missy—cards on the table."

Saphir gave Merik an annoyed glare and tossed her cards on the table. "See? Nothing suspicious," she stated.

"King, jack, ten, nine. Where's the *queen*, Saphir?" Merik turned on her. "Your hand is missing a card."

Saphir huffed, and from her lap she tossed another card on the table—a queen of spades—the card she needed to win, under normal circumstances. "Happy, Merik?"

Merik sat back in his chair, a smug look on his face. "I am satisfied, yes."

Saphir rose, "I guess I am off to fetch cookies then," she announced. As she passed Jovin and Donald on her way out, she commented to Jovin, "Your brother doesn't miss a thing."

"I almost wish he would," Jovin replied.

"It might have saved me a trip to the kitchen." She smiled in amusement and continued on her way.

"So in all fairness, Saphir won. I finally lost. See? I wasn't cheating." Conrad said to the proud prince.

Merik grinned broadly, "Oh, sure, not this time you weren't."

Chapter 20

Under the Circumstances...

Everyone arrived for breakfast at different times on the day following their hasty departure from Terrison. Captain Donald and Baron Von Lorian were the first in the dining room, followed shortly by Conrad, who had gotten lost, even though Merik had explained to him in great, albeit confusing, detail where to find the kitchen and royal dining room.

Conrad was dressed in a jumble of Jovin's clothing; his blond hair and tan complexion were offset by the borrowed maroon waistcoat. The effect was not unfashionable, but Merik thought that the haughty arrogance of the previous owner still clung to the clothes and did not altogether suit Conrad.

Conrad fought to keep his voice chipper to make up for his sleep-deprived eyes. "Do we have a plan?" Conrad asked Baron Von Lorian and Captain Donald as they tucked in to eggs, rice, and ham over toast. "I thank you for your hospitality and kindness to us, Captain, but I do not want to become a hindrance to your party. I suggest that you drop us off; that way we do not endanger you in your task. I am confident that we can lie low until this blows over."

"Your Highness, my respect is to you, but I do not think that is the best option," Captain Donald replied. "If you were discovered, I fear you would be handed over to the attackers you are running from. You are more than welcome to remain aboard until the threat is neutralized or we return to Canston; then you can stay in our palace until we can assess our options thoroughly."

"I do not want to be found running," Conrad persisted. "The situation was probably just a riot. We can contact an ally, get back, and pacify the problem before too much time has elapsed."

"But Your Majesty," the Baron cut in. "We do not know whom we can trust at this time. It may be an ally who arranged the riot, if we were to return we could be walking into a trap."

Conrad was silent while he considered his options. "I see your point," he agreed after a moment of thought. But another matter was weighing on his mind. "The situation with Princess Saphir…"

Baron Von Lorian gagged on his toast.

"She is our guest, as are you." Donald explained.

"Yes, of course," Conrad backtracked. "I did not realize that their condition across the Channel was so extreme."

"Has there been any communication with Ee'lin?" Baron Von Lorian asked, swallowing his toast with difficulty.

"The *Alexandria* is hardly the first place survivors would contact." Donald passed the Baron a napkin.

With the sounds of a half-sedated horse, Merik came clomping into the dining room, yawning and sporting the bedhead of a freshly cleaned kitten. "Morning," he yawned sleepily. He took a seat beside Donald and put his head in his hands. "I had a dream about strange purple animals… they wanted to see the ballet, but it was already sold out. So we snuck in and got caught… after that we were turned into turkey vultures, and Sighter started attacking us… then we were wagering something… I lost a bet… and the *Alexandria* was flooded." Merik looked up at their bewildered faces, realizing that he had interrupted a conversation. "Sorry, I'll go back to sleep."

As if to save Merik from being reprimanded, Saphir came into the dining room looking better rested than Merik by a long shot. "Good morning," she said as she bypassed them on her way into the kitchen.

"Everyone seems a bit scattered. Is it always this way?" Conrad asked in hushed tones.

"We all have a lot on our minds," Baron Von Lorian muttered back.

Saphir returned from the kitchen carrying two plates and set one in front of Merik, who perked up enough to see food, take a bite, and fall into semiconscious eating.

"What have you decided, Captain?" Saphir asked, taking a bite of eggs.

Donald drummed his fingertips on the table. "That is a very good question," he replied absentmindedly. "Jovin is intended to meet with Tavenly next, in the city of Simport. Truthfully our arrival is not scheduled for two weeks, but after the events of last night, I might suggest that we abandon the tour altogether and flee back to Canston. If we turn around today and head south, we might be able to cross the Channel before the sky grows treacherous."

"We can't do that." Jovin came into the dining room and stood beside Saphir. She scooted over for him on the bench, munching her toast and deliberately not acknowledging him. "It's our last stop, I owe it to the Tavenly government to show up. And, if there *is* trouble coming, I need them on our side."

"We cannot bring the five of you into another country without someone noticing. It would become a game of chance, and while buttons and trinkets are fine, lives should not be used as playing chips." Donald said.

"But you *would* drop everyone off and leave them? Isn't that is a risk, also?" Jovin replied. "But if *I* do not go to Simport, we not only break a promise, but also set ourselves up for unsteady relations with Tavenly."

"What do you suggest?" Donald asked Jovin, his forehead bent into a line.

"At the moment, I am not sure." Jovin reached across the table and took a slice of Merik's untouched toast.

Merik, who was half asleep and hence slow on the uptake, shot up. "I'm too promising to die yet; let's not do anything stupid."

"So humble, so considerate of others. It would be a shame to kill him." Saphir teased quietly, grinning down at her toast.

"I'm not sure I quite understand what the dilemma is," Conrad said, "you're going into Tavenly. Well, then, take us with you. Tavenly and Terrison are allies; Charlotte and I will be safe there. Actually, you can probably leave us there."

Charlotte came through the door. Her hair was down, and she wore a soft blue dress belonging to Saphir. "Good morning, everyone," she said, taking the seat beside her brother.

"Why, Charlotte, you look lovely," Jovin flattered.

Merik rolled his eyes, and Saphir made a point of looking anywhere but at Jovin.

"Thank you," Charlotte said. She folded her hands in her lap and tried to keep her tired eyes from conveying her hidden anxiety. "Captain, when are we returning?"

There was silence around the table.

"We're going to Tavenly, Charlotte," Conrad said slowly.

"Conrad, we left our *parents* in that *mess*," she replied softly.

Jovin excused himself to fetch breakfast from the kitchen.

"They could still be alive." Conrad tried for optimism, despite his words on the matter the night before.

Charlotte took a breath and decided not to engage in an argument at the breakfast table. "Maybe they are." She did not look at her brother but directed her next question at Donald, "Where will we go after Tavenly?"

"With luck, back to Canston," Donald said. "Then we can arrange to see you safely home, or we can arrange safe lodgings. Of course, you are welcome to stay as long as you like; there would be no rush to send you away."

"That is greatly appreciated," Charlotte said.

Jovin returned with two plates and set one in front of Charlotte with a wink. She gave him the slightest of smiles in reply and picked up a fork, although she did not eat.

Baron Von Lorian addressed Donald, "Tavenly may know that Charlotte and Conrad are with you by the time we arrive."

"Do you think the news will travel that quickly?" Saphir asked.

"It very well might," Baron Von Lorian replied. "But they will see us as guests, we are no threat to them."

"Unless they think we are bringing the rebellion with us," Charlotte said, still looking at her plate.

"For safety reasons, might I suggest again we postpone the occasion and head directly to Canston?" Donald asked.

"*No*," Jovin interrupted. His fork clattered on the table, "I will not abandon it. *I have decided*. I have an impression to make. Reasoning good or bad, *I have to go*."

"Let us think this over before we draw a conclusion," Donald said.

"Captain, we started this mission to retain peace. If I do not arrive in Tavenly, we risk losing their trust. I will not have it."

"Jovin, I appreciate your honesty, and I agree with you, but in light of our current situation, we might be better suited to skip Tavenly for the sake of the trust you already have," Donald said.

"Well, let us think about it," Jovin said blandly. He pushed away from the table, gathered up his plate, and exited through the kitchens, leaving a nonplussed silence behind him.

"Dramatic maniac," Merik muttered, though only Saphir had heard him.

+++++

It was shortly after breakfast when Jovin spotted Conrad on the way back to his cabin. "Hey, Conrad, can I have a moment?" Jovin called, jogging to catch up to him.

"Oh, sure." Conrad stopped outside his cabin door. Baron Von Lorian and Conrad's cabins resided on the port side, while Charlotte had been given guest quarters on the starboard side beside Saphir's.

Jovin cleared his throat, "I feel I should warn you, it would not be wise for you to remain close to Saphir."

"I'm really not that close to her," Conrad eyed Jovin. "By why not?"

Jovin's smile did not reach his eyes, "She has been confused enough with everything that has happened, and she doesn't need to be confused further."

"Oh. Well then, I see." Conrad did not seem to be fazed. But his eyes narrowed. "You continue to mess with her, and yet, you also mess with my sister… at the *same time. Very regal.*" Conrad gave Jovin a penetrating look. "So… here is my question: which are you going to abandon first?"

"Wait, what?"

"You cannot continue to mess with both of them; they will see it. And *you* may not realize it yet, but girls are smart—*a lot* smarter than you're currently giving them credit for. Sooner or later they'll gang up on you, and you'll be in a very sticky situation, my friend." Conrad stuck his hands in his pockets. "So you can either tell me what's really going on, *or* you can be thrown overboard by a couple of angry princesses."

"It's not like… There's a complicated history, and the fate of her country is weighing on her."

"Alright, got it," Conrad said, turning to open his cabin door.

Jovin stepped forward, "I *am* making sense, right?"

"Yes," Conrad said. "Don't get involved with Saphir, because she's already been through enough emotional trauma, *especially from you*, added to the fact that her country is probably in shambles, her mother has passed and she is alone, *and* you continue to neglect and manipulate her. She needs nothing to pain her further. *I get it.*"

"Aren't you going to say something else?" Jovin mused.

"Oh, yes," Conrad looked Jovin dead in the eye. His sarcastic tone had gone deadpan. "I will only say this once: *do not* get involved with my sister. *Got it?"*

This sudden mood swing surprised Jovin enough that he retreated a half step.

Conrad remained glowering, "Charlotte can be a delicate person; she is easily won and easily lost. Depending on how long we stay aboard, I want to know that she will be as happy as she can be, under the circumstances, for as long as possible. And if—sorry, *when*—you break off whatever little game you're playing, I don't want to see her hurt." Conrad gave Jovin a stern look, "So, for all of our sakes, leave her alone."

Jovin scrutinized Conrad, "Are you threatening me?"

"Yes, I am, good of you to notice," Conrad said firmly. "She needs to stay happy. I will do all in my power to keep her so."

"I understand,"

Conrad seemed pleased, "Good. Then I think *someday* we may see eye to eye."

Jovin stepped away, "Have a pleasant day, Conrad."

"And you also," Conrad stepped into his cabin. He gave a single wave and closed the door.

+++++

"Done." Merik announced. He set a coin-sized metal object on Donald's desk, followed by a thin, metallic, black-screened box the size of a slice of toast. "It took longer than expected, but it's finally done," Merik swelled with pride. "And for the record, Professor Hopkins *did not* help."

"I was not under the assumption he would," Donald said, picking up the small, blinking, tracking device. On the back, in thickly marked black letters, Merik had written the word "BUG", Donald hid his amusement and took up the thin-screened box.

Merik watched in anticipation while Donald surveyed his inventions, bouncing back and forth on his toes impatiently. "So..." Merik asked in a hesitant whisper. "Do you like it?"

Donald beckoned Merik around the side of the desk. "What are the buttons for?" his tone had not changed to mirror Merik.

The boy was getting nervous. "Oh, I added another option to track more than just the one bug I made; that's what this does," Merik pointed to the farthest left button and took the control panel from Donald to better his presentation. "This one will connect to the *Alexandria* once we program it, or to another power system; that's what this outlet is for," he pointed to the cable port on the side. "It should give us a map of the area through the computer and help navigate the best route to find the bug," he pointed to the second button on the right. "This one doesn't do anything yet. And this is the power button," he pointed to the last button from the left. Merik flipped the box over to show the back side. "The transmitter is behind this plate, along with the guts. I haven't tested it yet outside of the training room."

Donald's complacent expression split into a fatherly smile. "Shall we give it a test run, then?" he rose and, with a grinning Merik in tow, ran up to the wheelhouse to download the tracker into the *Alexandria's* system.

+++++

"Captain?"

Randy Simmons, the crewman in charge of laundering, entered the wheelhouse. In his hands he held a new, freshly ironed brown coat. At their stations Mister Carter and McCoy passed an inquisitive look, in which Carter's eyebrow rose up into his hairline.

Simmons brought the coat to the captain. "Just finished," he offered it to Donald.

"Thank you, Mister Simmons." Donald took up the coat, gathering the fabric in his hands and shaking it out so the ends fanned in the air.

Mister Carter watched with amusement, "It's a coat, Captain; what're you expecting?"

Donald politely ignored Carter's remark and investigated the sleeves. "Merik's coat, actually," Donald corrected. He furrowed his forehead, "Where did you put it?" he asked the tailor.

Simmons showed Donald a pocket on the inside flap of the jacket. "Right here, the fabric doubles over on the other side, so unless you were looking for it, it would be difficult to stumble upon."

"What in the world are you gonna do with Merik's coat?" Mister Carter interrupted. "Wear it next holiday?"

"Well, no, actually," Donald said slyly. "I do believe that *you* are going to wear it."

Mister Carter flinched. McCoy set into snorting laughter.

"*Me?*" Carter shrieked.

"Put it on, Lewis, it'll match your eyes," McCoy faked a dreamy expression.

"Can it, McCoy," Carter shot back.

Donald tossed Carter the coat, "Go walk around."

"I'm not going to—"

"You do not have to wear it; just hold it," Donald told him.

Carter grudgingly drew the child's coat around his shoulders and tied the sleeves around his neck like a cape. "Ta-da," he gave Donald a pointed look as McCoy continued to roar with laughter. "This is officially the worst thing I've ever done under your captainship."

Donald waved him away. He produced a flat grey box from his pocket. "Walk around on deck, and then go below to the hangar."

Mister Carter sighed, but clomped down the stairs to the main deck none the less. From the wheelhouse, Donald, McCoy, and Simmons had an excellent view of Carter as he skipped around the main deck in a mocking impersonation of Merik. Carter pretended to play hopscotch, then laid down in the sun and rolled around as though he were a child rolling down a grassy hill.

"Isn't he breaking a load of rules by mocking royalty like this?" McCoy asked Donald.

Carter was pretending to yawn now; his parade seemed to have ended. He patted his stomach to indicate hunger and pranced over to the middeck stairwell that led into the heart of the airship. With a flourishing wave, Carter disappeared below deck.

McCoy and Simmons stood in stunned silence. Neither spoke, awaiting their captain's reaction.

"Well then," Donald said, examining the screen on the box. "I can see him; it looks as though he has taken to running the full length of the third level in his attempt to replicate Merik."

Simmons cleared his throat, "Um, yes, well, if that is all, Captain…"

"You are dismissed,"

Simmons left in a hurry. McCoy ducked his head and returned to flying the airship.

Mister Carter reappeared ten minutes later, his hair askew and his face flushed. He bowed low to the captain and removed the coat from his shoulders. "As you requested," Carter said, unabashed.

Donald raised a single eyebrow, "I believe I said to *walk*, not gallivant like an excited pony."

Mister Carter took it in his stride, passing Donald the coat. "Well, if it is Merik's coat, why not introduce it to what it will be living every time he wears it. I was breaking it in." Carter reclaimed his seat at his station. "And anyway," he went on smugly, "running around isn't horrible when you pretend to be someone else."

"Who said to pretend to be Merik?" McCoy asked. He was still waiting for Donald's reprimand of Carter.

"It was in the job description," Carter said.

"Mister Lewis Carter," Donald chuckled.

Carter's neck snapped his attention to Donald. "Captain," he replied as a professional officer.

"In the future, I would advise you not to impersonate royal personnel without their consent, and never again in such boorish fashion." Donald paused to allow Carter to take in his words. "However, seeing as Merik is not aware of your actions, and you have been mildly amusing, I will overlook this one-time slipup."

Chapter 21

The Problem with Airships

Mister Carter's voice came over the intercom. *"Captain?"*

Donald moved through the captain's cabin to reach his desk. He pressed the return button. "Yes, Mister Carter?"

"I strongly suggest your presence in the wheelhouse." Mister Carter's voice sounded strained.

"Be there in a moment," Donald replied. He looked back at Merik, who was sitting on the rug in front of the sofa, tinkering with scraps of metal in the faint hope that he could fix his invention.

Merik had noticed the conversation and was curious. "Hurry up, Captain; the sooner you go, the sooner I can find out what that was about,"

"And the sooner I find out what you are up to," Donald said in good humor. He pulled on his overcoat and hastened out the door.

Mister Carter was standing over the control table. Lights flashed from the large screen that covered the tabletop. Mister McCoy was at his seat, inspecting the flight patterns of the airship. Donald pushed open the door and joined Carter over the control table.

"Engine two is failing." Mister Carter pointed to the two red lights blinking on the screen. "It's functioning at twenty percent."

"And the other engines?" Donald asked as he took over the control table from Carter.

"They're all right. What… no! Engine three was stable!" Mister Carter rushed to the starboard wall and investigated the screen where a new array of lights were flashing. Carter swore under his breath. "Engine three is now faltering. We won't have enough time to repair the engines if we shut them down while we're in the air. If we free float that long we will be blown off course. Simport is still too far to make it without stopping for repairs. What would you like us to do, sir?"

Donald studied the flashing screen. "How far can we make it until it is mandatory to stop?"

Carter took off his cap and ran a hand through his neatly combed brown hair, messing it up considerably.

"A few days, but I doubt we will make it more than two." McCoy piped up.

"Is anything else malfunctioning? How about the stabilizers?" Donald said.

"Nothing else yet. We can limp along on the other engines, but I can't see us moving faster than ten knots anytime soon," Carter relayed.

Donald nodded to Carter, preparing to leave the wheelhouse. "Manually shut engines two and three down. Keep North and East on our current course. I will give you landing orders within the hour."

+++++

"So what was the problem?" Merik asked, leaning over Donald's desk.

Donald had a map spread out in front of him and did not look up to reply. "What makes you think there is a problem?" the captain replied.

"Just a few things," Merik's forehead furrowed as he watched Donald measure distances on the map. "That's pretty far," he commented. "You know, from our current position."

Donald dragged his finger from one point to another on the map. "Two days, maybe closer to three," he murmured to himself.

"What's the problem, Captain?" Merik asked.

Donald jotted down a note and slid the notebook away from Merik, who was trying to get a glimpse of it. "Sometimes it is best to remain oblivious."

"And sometimes, there is a *very curious kid* asking his *very wise mentor* what is going on." Merik stated matter-of-factly.

Donald raised his eyebrows, "Do not look into this."

Merik sighed in exasperation. "If I don't hear it from you *now*, I'll find out later. If it's important, you're gonna tell us at some point."

"If it was of your concern, I probably would." Donald went back to the map.

"*And* when you do, I will already have figured it out." Merik moved away from the desk, heading for the door. "If you won't tell me, I'll find out from someone else," he called over his shoulder before opening the door and racing out. "Every other person on this airship would be more than glad to tell me whatever I want to hear."

Donald sighed and pressed the intercom to the wheelhouse. "Mister Carter?"

"*Yes sir?*"

"Please refrain from mentioning the engine problem to Merik; he has the idea that there is a big secret that I refuse to tell him and that he must find it out for himself."

Mister Carter chuckled. "*Yes sir, if he asks, I'll make something up.*"

"Good man," Donald said. "That is all. Thank you."

+++++

"A water shortage?" Merik exclaimed. "A *water* shortage?"

"Yes, our exit from the palace yesterday occurred before we had resupplied a few important items, drinking water being one of them," Mister Carter replied.

Merik scuffed his shoe on the floor, "Goodness gracious, I was looking forward to something exciting."

"Bored?" Carter asked. He was busy tapping a control panel at the starboard wall, to their left McCoy was steering the airship. Two crewmen Merik did not recognize were working at a line of screens on the port-side station.

"Haven't seen anyone all day," Merik stated. "Jovin locked himself in the training room and said that *he wanted to be left alone*. Saphir's off somewhere… I don't know where she is. I don't want to annoy our new passengers yet; they're stressed. I refuse to do math. Actually… I'm avoiding Professor Hopkins."

"Why don't you go down to the kitchen, maybe Mason could use some help," Carter offered.

"I'm *tired* of cookies… I'm tired of sweets… I'm tired of mindless eating from sheer boredom," Merik grumbled. "But maybe… yeah, I'll do that." Merik's mind was whirling. *Chef Mason will know if the airship is low on water, and if he says that we have plenty of water, then…*

Merik smiled to himself as he trotted down the stairs to the kitchens.

"I knew it," Merik stated. He closed the cabin door behind him and walked purposely across the room to Captain Donald, who was looking over a pile of paperwork. "I knew it," he repeated.

"Knew what?" Donald asked.

"There *is* no water shortage."

"And why would there be?"

"Because Mister Carter said there was, and he said that's why you're looking for a place for us to land," Merik rambled. "But Chef Mason said that we have *plenty* of water. So by that logic, and the *sheer intellect* that is myself, I have come to the conclusion that you are not telling me the whole truth because there is no reason for us to stop."

Donald set down his papers. "Merik,"

"I want to know what—"

"Merik, there might come a time when I need you to blindly trust me. Sometimes not knowing keeps everyone happier. You are only allowed part of the picture, and sometimes it is a good thing."

"But—"

"I needed you to trust me right now," Donald said.

Merik felt small under the stern gaze of the captain. "I understand… I'm sorry."

"You are forgiven. But please, in the future, if I ask it of you, I need you to follow orders the first time," Donald said.

Merik nodded sheepishly.

Donald felt that he had made his point. He patted the space of desk beside him, "Come pull up a chair; you will figure it out eventually. I might as well tell you now."

Merik, surprised but delighted, pulled a chair around the desk next to Donald.

"Take a look," Donald handed a stack of papers to Merik.

Merik read the top paper in puzzled silence. Curiosity got the better of him, and he scanned the second paper, then flipped through the rest of them. "They all say the same thing," Merik said, reading the eighth paper.

"The problem—the one I was trying to keep from you—happens to be in your area of expertise." Donald held out his hand for the papers, and Merik obliged. "Inspections—a week ago, two weeks, three. The *Alexandria* is a remarkable airship, her engines are thoroughly inspected a few times each week," he gave Merik a pointed look, "very recently, there have been a few issues."

"Like what?"

"Problems that cannot be solved aloft," Donald replied. "We have to stop to make repairs before the problem worsens; considering our present companions, I am doubtful that the engine difficulties are coincidental."

"Do you think someone tampered with the engines?"

"There is that possibility," Donald set the papers down. "The *Alexandria* was accessible while the majority of the crew was roaming about Terrison."

Merik considered this. "It would make sense; everyone leaves for a while to stretch their legs and get supplies, the crew was gone, and we were in the palace—it would be a perfect opportunity to sneak aboard and wreak havoc." Merik gasped in realization, "Captain, what if they *knew* of the masquerade, and that there would be an attack on the palace? And what if they *knew* we would have to get away, and they purposely planned for our engines to be ruined so we wouldn't be able to go too far and would have to stop for repairs? It was all a plan!"

"I thought something very similar," Donald agreed. "The troubling notion is that they could find us wherever we stop. If we were purposely sabotaged, then they would have calculated how long the engines would last after damages. They would be able to predict the general vicinity of where we must stop for repairs."

"But we have representatives from three allied countries aboard the *Alexandria*." Merik's face went very pale, his eyes wide. "They'll be waiting for us. They could have shot us down by now, but maybe they want to kill us in person." Merik tried to breathe calmly, but it was becoming difficult.

Donald rested a hand on his shoulder. "If they wanted everyone dead, then Terrison's fate would have mirrored Ee'lin's," Donald kept his voice even to calm the boy. "But they did not."

"Who are *they*?"

"There are suspicions, but nothing is certain yet," Donald said.

Merik shook his head, "This is just bizarre. I don't like it. Too many escapes, too many whacky people. *It's unsettling and frightening.*"

"It is," Donald said. He decided it was time to divert the boy's attention. "How is Sighter coming along?"

"*Why* would you ask *that* when *my life is in danger?!"* Merik exasperated.

"Merik, at this point in time, no one has tried to kill *you* in particular. You have just been around people who are targeted."

"But my friends are in danger... my brother might be next," he muttered. "Why are people so... so thoughtless and awful and..." Merik slumped in his chair, and let out a grunt that sounded more like a growl. "Ugh."

"Would you like me to answer that? Because if so, we will be here for a very long while..."

+++++

Donald motioned Baron Von Lorian to the chair across from him in front of his desk.

Baron Von Lorian leaned back in his chair but found it either uncomfortable or too relaxed of a posture and sprang up again to perch on the edge of his seat.

"Engines two and three have been shut down. We plan to stop for repairs," Donald said.

The Baron nodded vaguely. "That is very... where do you plan to stop?"

"Somewhere in northern Terrison," said Donald. "I have my reservations about landing. It is not as though we make port without drawing attention. We *look* like a royal airship, and word of our arrival may travel faster than we can land and make the repairs."

"Not if we land somewhere where royal airships are common," Baron Von Lorian suggested.

Donald consulted a map on his desk between them. "We could make it to Tinseenwell in approximately two days."

"If we do not drop out of the sky first," the Baron reminded him sardonically.

Donald was reminded of Merik at this comment. He smiled in spite of the situation, "I do not find that likely. If every engine were to break down, we would stay aloft until we were towed to a port."

Baron Von Lorian contemplated this for a moment. "How does the engine situation effect your timeline?"

"Repairs in Tinseenwell will only take a few days if we are in luck. We sail two days, and repair the engines in another two. From there, we sail southwest to Simport, arriving six to seven days from now," Donald said.

"Well, if there are complications, it gives us something to do in the meantime," the Baron's eyes saddened as they fell on the shape of Terrison on the map. "No need to be *too* early for a rendezvous with destiny."

+++++

Merik asked Jovin, "But what good can be gained from a treaty with Tavenly, when it isn't anywhere near Canston?"

"If war were to break out, it is good to know your allies, and your enemies." Jovin explained as he leaned back in his chair.

"Very poetic," Merik muttered.

Donald had called Merik, Jovin, and Saphir to his cabin to discuss their options. So far, Saphir had remained silent. She sat with her feet tucked in under her on the sofa, staring out at the clouds through the window wall.

Merik was seated against the wall by the bookshelf, tinkering with the disfigured form of Sighter. After using Sighter to pick the lock in the Terrison palace, he had fallen into further disrepair, added to the fact, Merik had set him on the dresser and later thrown a book on top of him.

Merik twisted a wire. Sighter's wing fell off and landed with a sad little *thunk* on the wooden floor. "That's it," he muttered, picking up the wing and shoving it into his pocket along with the rest of the dilapidated creature. "Captain, I need a sterosimp for Sighter. When can we land?"

"You can look for it when we land in Tinseenwell," Donald said.

A knock came from the door, and Charlotte entered, followed by Conrad and Baron Von Lorian. She walked up to the map on the wall beside Donald's desk, and inspected it a moment. "We are still in Terrison?"

"That is correct," Donald replied. "If you need anything, we will resupply there. From there, we have a few decisions to finalize."

"With respect, Captain, there is only one," Jovin straightened in his chair. "Whatever the threat is, they are not the target. It's not for Terrison, and it's not directed at Ee'lin," he kept his eyes trained on Donald. "It is us. It is Canston. *Me.*"

"But we weren't close to Ee'lin during the bombing, so they weren't after *just* us, even if we were part of their plan," Merik pointed out.

"They may have been luring us in," Jovin said. "And it worked, didn't it?"

Saphir looked up from the teacup she held clutched in her hands. "Do you think they'll be waiting in Simport?"

Jovin turned to Donald, "We need to drop everyone else off. They cannot come. Where's the nearest place they will be safe?"

Donald picked up on Jovin's train of thought. He looked over the map, "Lady Locksley lives four days from Tinseenwell."

"Perfect," Jovin ignored how sheepish Merik suddenly appeared. "Could we have her meet us? Or send them via train."

"Who is this person?" Conrad asked.

"Lady Eleanor Locksley of Ariden, a very close friend of the Canston crown," Jovin answered.

"But Jovin, you cannot drop us off and leave," Saphir said amicably. "What are you going to do, go to Simport by yourself?"

"You are not coming," Jovin stated.

Saphir rose from the sofa and tossed her empty teacup onto the cushions. "And *you* should go?" Saphir implored, walking across the cabin to him. "What if they *are* after you? It would be the perfect opportunity—"

"Which is why you need to go into hiding. I see no reason to abort my mission. You, on the other hand, need to stay away from people who will recognize you," Jovin retaliated.

"*But Jovin—*"

Saphir was cut off by Donald raising his hand. "I will send a message to Lady Eleanor when we land. Until then, we will assume that everyone of royal importance will be vacating the *Alexandria* in Tinseenwell," Donald affirmed. "Merik, that possibly includes you."

Merik made to protest, but remembered what Donald had said about following orders the first time, and kept quiet.

Chapter 22

Mending Patterns

Merik eyed the cabin door. It was the second day since their departure from Flinith, and Merik thought that maybe it was an alright time to ask for a friend. He knocked and then retreated a step.

Conrad opened the door. Merik thought he looked rather unwell; his shirt was creased, and his eyes showed signs of restlessness. His blond hair stuck out in odd places, as though he had been licked by a farm cow. Merik was reminded of his own head of hair in the morning.

"Do you wanna play cards?" Merik asked shyly.

Conrad gave Merik a reluctant smile, "Not now, but thank you, Merik."

Merik felt a bit degraded and turned to leave, but then thought better of it. "*One game?*"

Conrad gave the smallest of chuckles, "Are you really that bored?"

"No, but I think you're nice, and I think my ego needs to be beaten at something every once in a while," Merik stated.

With a bewildered and contemplative smile, Conrad opened the door wider for Merik to enter. "Alright, *one* game."

Merik shuffled, "Six outta ten?"

"But you've lost six times already," Conrad pointed out. He drew a hand across his face in covert exhaustion. "If we play to ten, you've already lost."

“Not if we start over…” Merik made a face and clasped his hands in a pathetic, pleading manner.

“What is that face?” Conrad snorted. He picked up his cards, “You look like an injured seal.”

“Really,” Merik went deadpan. “I don’t know what is more bizarre—that statement, or that you’re questioning my pitiful face.”

Conrad replied only with a halfhearted smile, “Fine, we can start over; but *I’m* shuffling.”

“Why?”

“That way you can’t cheat.”

“I cannot believe you would accuse me of cheating,” Merik said, exasperated. “I am an honorable and trustworthy person.”

“Maybe under normalcy, but based on recent events and your deep desire to win, I’m not taking chances,” Conrad said.

“Fair enough,”

+++++

“Oh, hello, Charlotte.” Saphir stopped in the kitchen doorway. Her thoughts for a cup of tea vanished from her mind.

“Hello, Saphir,” Charlotte looked around the empty kitchen—everywhere but at the other girl before her. “Please, do not let me prevent you from your mission,” Charlotte said stiffly.

“Right,” Saphir stepped into the kitchen, and the door swung shut behind her. She tentatively made her way to the stove and filled the tea kettle. She set it on the stove and stepped back.

There was a forestalling pause between the two girls while they avoided each other. Charlotte picked at a cup of soup she had been toying with. Saphir puffed out an uncomfortable breath.

Charlotte cleared her throat. “Saphir, I would like to apologize for how I have treated you. It has been very rude of me,” she paused, thinking Saphir would interject, but Saphir stared at the tiled floor as though she found the scrubbed spotless grout interesting. Charlotte was unsure what to say and took a breath, “I have to pull myself together eventually, and it would be best if I know where I stand.” Charlotte took another breath, “Once I understand what the situation is, I can better myself and be friends with you… If that is what you desire.”

"Well, I don't know anymore," Saphir muttered under her breath. She turned to Charlotte, and there was a strange tone in her voice that did not belong there. "Tell me, Charlotte, is it possible to be friends with someone who is not as *perfect as you?*"

Charlotte stiffened, "I am not perfect in the sense you assume me to be; I am perfect in the way I need to be."

"What does that even mean?" Saphir shot back.

Charlotte straightened defensively, "It means, that I am who *I* should be, just as you are who *you* should be. We are very different, and that is good. But you are failing to see how similar we are because you cannot focus on anything but our differences."

"Do not blame me. I have tried for peace. But I don't understand your hatred for me, or how it has vanished overnight?"

"I misunderstood a situation, but I would never say that I hated you," Charlotte said. "I believe we have a bit more mending to do."

Saphir realized she had forgotten to turn on the stovetop and turned it on before Charlotte noticed.

"What do you do for entertainment around here?" Charlotte asked at length.

Saphir gave her a confused look of empathy, "There is literally nothing."

"That cannot be,"

"Unless you enjoy long card games and making and eating endless batches of sweets, you're out of luck." Saphir selected her teacup and set it on the counter.

Charlotte played with her soup spoon, "That must be difficult."

"I have Merik," Saphir answered defensively.

Charlotte tapped her spoon on the side of her bowl and set it on a napkin. The kettle began to sing, Saphir removed it and poured herself a cup of tea.

"Saphir, I am sorry for being rude to you; you did not deserve it," Charlotte said. "I do wish to make amends."

Saphir gathered her teacup and walked to the door. "We will mend, it just might take time. Have a good day, Charlotte," Saphir said, and she strode quickly out of the kitchen to sequester herself in the greenhouse for the remainder of the afternoon.

Chapter 23

Tinseenwell

The two days it took to arrive at Tinseenwell passed slowly. The threats on their lives loomed over them like a cloud hanging over their heads.

The dinner before their arrival in Tinseenwell was a quiet one. Marred by the possibility that Lady Eleanor Locksley would agree to take them in, the atmosphere was subdued.

Near the end of dinner, there was a knock on the dining room door and Mister Carter entered. He bowed to the royalty, "I am sorry to interrupt. We are nearing Tinseenwell, arrival time is estimated at two hours."

"Very well, thank you Mister Carter," Donald said. Carter bowed and dismissed himself. "I will contact Lady Eleanor tonight after we arrive," Donald informed the table.

"How will you contact her?" Baron Von Lorian asked.

Jovin was making it a point not to look at anyone, and seemed to be incredibly interested in a piece of lettuce on his plate.

"Telephone, or telegraph if it comes to it," Donald replied.

"And if she does not answer?" Conrad asked.

"If there is no answer by our third day, then I will have everyone stay hidden and remain on board when we arrive in Tavenly. I plan to send a message to Simport to inquire about recent attacks or suspicious behaviors," Donald explained.

"Should I start shopping for a party dress, just in case?" Charlotte said, trying to lighten the mood.

"I would advise it. On the possibility you go with Eleanor, you may need it," Donald said.

+++++

"No one picked up," Donald said.

"What now?" Jovin asked.

The postage office in Tinseenwell was empty, save for the clerk sorting mail in a back room. Each attempt to reach Lady Eleanor Locksley via public telephone was failing. When they called, it rang and rang. Donald continued to hang up and try again, but both he and Jovin were getting discouraged.

The post office was just a few minutes' walk from the airship yard where the *Alexandria* was under repair. The airship's mechanic estimated it would take two days to repair the damaged engines. As a cautionary measure, he planned to partially rebuild engines two and three in hopes that it would be enough to get them to Simport. He planned on making further repairs while in Simport to assure their safe passage across the Channel on the journey home to Canston.

Donald hung up the telephone, "I will send a telegram. If I do not hear from her by the day after next, then they will have to come with us."

"I am sure they'll be fine. Saphir and Merik don't want to be sent away," Jovin stated.

"But the others should not be mixed deeper into this," Donald lowered his voice as the Clerk behind the counter moved nearer to finish sorting letters. "We need to do what is safest for them."

"You almost done, sir?" the Clerk asked Donald.

"Yes, thank you," Donald replied. "I need to send a telegram."

The Clerk looked up, "Yes, of course." The man ducked down behind the counter and reappeared with a piece of paper. "Now, what would you like to say?"

Jovin looked at Donald. "We need formalities," he muttered just loudly enough that Donald could hear him.

"Yes, but it is also urgent," Donald replied. He was very aware of the Clerk's curious eyes watching their discussion. "Write this: 'Lady Eleanor, greetings.'"

"Uh huh, got it," the Clerk muttered as he scribbled.

"'I am carrying passengers which require safe lodging. Please contact us in Tinseenwell, docking space number twenty-seven. If we do not hear from you before the twenty-first of October, we will assume you have not heard from us,'" Donald looked to Jovin, who nodded in agreement. "And please sign it 'Gregory Donald.'"

"Huh... hmm... yes," the Clerk looked up from the paper. "Anything else, sir?"

"That will be all."

The Clerk counted the words and rang up the amount on the cash register. "That will cost eighteen trilla."

Donald paid and waited while the man shuffled into the back room to send the telegram.

Jovin leaned closer to Donald, "Is this safe? I mean, are we endangering ourselves by sending this?" he asked in hushed tones.

"There is always a risk, and if we do not hear from her soon, we will have a problem anyway. Considering whom we are traveling with, it is only a matter of time before something goes awry."

"What about resending the message from the airship?" Jovin asked.

"I am trying to avoid using the dock's radio towers. We do not know who might intercept our message," Donald said. "We will have to wait to contact your father until we are somewhere we can trust the signal towers, probably in Tavenly."

Jovin nodded, then a thought struck him. "Captain, we're slipped in *fourteen*; why did you tell them twenty-seven?" Jovin asked under his breath.

"I have a man standing-by in twenty-seven in case someone intercepts the message," Donald said.

Jovin stared around the postage shop, taking in the aged wooden walls, exposed air vents, and bare lightbulbs that each hung by a string from the ceiling. It was a little run-down, but Captain Donald had explained that by going off the beaten path, they would be less likely to attract attention. That was also the reason they had abandoned their wealthy clothing, choosing instead to change into common colors of browns, blacks, and discolored whites, in hopes that if the *Alexandria*'s passengers were in fact targets, they might overlook Jovin and Donald in their street clothes.

Donald checked to see that the clerk was still punching in the telegram before taking out a golden watch. "Quarter past ten," he said softly. "They close our dock gate at twelve."

"Do you think it is safe here?" Jovin asked. "Does a closed gate really deter people?"

"Not if the people causing trouble are determined enough, or moored in the slip beside you."

The Clerk returned, and Donald stuffed his watch away before the man's eye could catch a glimpse of gold.

"All done. The Ariden post office confirmed that they received it; you'll have an answer soon enough," the Clerk smiled at them. "Here's your receipt."

"Thank you, have a good night," Donald double-checked it, and the receipt joined the watch in his pocket.

"What do you reckon?" Jovin asked as they rounded a street corner.

"If Eleanor replies tomorrow, we will be in luck," Donald and Jovin turned another corner. "But if she has to wait to respond, or they cannot stay with her, we will have a problem."

"Isn't there anyone else they could stay with in the area?"

"Not that I trust with this secret," they nodded to the grizzled man on guard outside the docking gate, walking quickly through the unoccupied guardhouse toward the back gate. The *Alexandria* came into view, lit up by the streetlamps and ambient lighting, she was easily the most impressive airship on the lonely dock.

Jovin glanced back over his shoulder, "Do you think anyone followed us?"

"I doubt it; we have not been docked long enough to rouse suspicion," Donald replied as they climbed the gangplank to the *Alexandria*.

Everyone was waiting in Donald's cabin. Merik had tricked Conrad and Baron Von Lorian into playing cards again, while Saphir and Charlotte sat at opposite ends of the sofa and tried their best to exchange conversation without being uncivilized. They looked up when Jovin entered and did not look at each other for a few minutes after.

"I hope to hear from Lady Eleanor tomorrow," Donald moved to the table and pulled up a chair along with Jovin. Conrad won the game, and Merik dealt Donald and Jovin in.

"And if we do not?" the Baron asked over his cards. He exchanged a card and took a new one from the deck.

"Then everyone is in need of new party clothes," Donald made a face at his cards and placed one in the discard pile. He drew another.

"And we should be here, what, two days?" Conrad asked. He exchanged three cards, then smirked, causing Merik to wrinkle his nose and frown at him.

"Three days at the most," Donald replied.

Merik glared at Conrad, "You better not win,"

"No one yet knows what the future holds," Conrad replied smugly.

"You better not," Merik muttered, exchanging two cards.

"And then to Simport?" Conrad asked Donald.

"Unless you go with Lady Eleanor," Donald said, placing his card on the table. "There you go."

"Three aces and a pair of kings!" Merik exclaimed. "Not fair!"

Everyone set their cards down. It was clear that Captain Donald had won. Conrad had a rubbish hand and had smirked only to bother Merik.

Jovin looked across the room to where Charlotte and Saphir were not speaking on the sofa. "What's up with them?" he asked no one in particular.

"I dunno, been talking off and on for twenty minutes. No shouting yet," Merik said in a hushed tone so the princesses would not hear. He gathered up everyone's cards and shuffled.

"Think they're plotting something?"

"You never know with girls," Conrad said. He handed Merik the cards to cut and let out a yelp when Merik smacked away his hand, apparently not amused by Conrad's winning streak. "I guess you never know with boys, either," Conrad muttered. He handed Baron Von Lorian the cards to cut instead.

Jovin did not seem to have heard. "I swear, if I wake up in a pile spiders tomorrow..."

"I don't think they'll be able to find any spiders," Merik pointed out. Conrad dealt the cards.

Jovin drummed his fingers on the table.

"No need to worry, they are just getting to know each other," Baron Von Lorian tried to reassure Jovin.

"They've barely spoken to each other before now," Merik pointed out unhelpfully.

Charlotte and Saphir had not heard a word of the boys' conversation, and were now speaking in soft, carrying giggles.

"At least they're talking," Merik observed. He patted Jovin's shoulder, "Maybe you *should* be worried."

+++++

Jovin went with Captain Donald to the postage office the next morning. Instead of the aged clerk from the previous night, a young brunette was behind the counter. She smiled radiantly as Jovin and Donald entered the shop. "Good morning," she called to them.

"Morning," Jovin replied cheerily. Her smile grew wider.

The captain approached the counter, "Miss, have there been any telegraphs this morning? We are expecting a message from up north, for the name Gregory Donald."

"I'll go check," the girl said, and disappeared into the back room.

Donald eyed Jovin, who avoided his gaze by glancing around the post office in an attempt to look innocent. "*Jovin*,"

"What?" Jovin said, unabashed. "I flirt with everyone, it's not uncommon,"

The captain gave Jovin a look that was worthy of Merik ten times over.

Jovin let out a strangled sort of laugh as the shop girl returned.

She smiled again and set a paper down, "There is nothing for Gregory Donald. Would it be under a different name?" she asked.

"I think not," Donald's forehead furrowed. "If you do not mind my asking, has anything come in from the north in the last ten hours?"

"Nothing. I have a few from the locals: one from southern Terrison, one from Blinley, a couple from Ee'lin…" Donald and Jovin exchanged a look. Thankfully it went unnoticed by the girl, who was trying to recall her memory. "But nothing north of Terrison," she said. "*Where* in the north, if you don't mind my asking?"

"Ariden," Donald replied. "My wife is staying with her sister in a noble household; we were expecting word from her by now."

"*Oh*," there was something in the way her face fell that was not conversational.

"'*Oh*'?" Jovin repeated.

"It's just that, um, Ariden is having trouble on the outskirts. I heard that they are not letting anyone over the borders…" she looked troubled.

"Anything else?" Jovin prompted. "Sorry to worry you, but it's my mum, and I want to make sure she's all right."

The shop girl looked between Donald and Jovin, clearly pondering whether or not their relation was biological, but surpassed her thoughts on their varying appearances as she found his concern for his fictional mother endearing. "I shouldn't share this, but there have been some funny telegraphs coming in lately," the girl glanced over her shoulder, obviously worried that someone else would come in and reprimand her for speaking openly. "A few from Ariden, saying strange things like *'do not come back'* and *'it's dangerous here'*—lots of startling messages."

"And how do you know all of this?" Donald asked her.

"I help translate telegraphs when they come in. I see lots of messages. I try not to think too long on any, but when there are so many from the same place with the same message, you can't help but wonder," she wrung her hands and looked ashamed. "There has been nothing on the radio about it. No one's taking about it; they're all too chatty about the princess from Ee'lin stepping down."

"Wait—*what?*" Jovin's face was stricken. "What do you mean?"

Donald looked between the two but said nothing, knowing that this girl would let more information slip if she was talking directly to Jovin.

"How do you not know?" the girl looked confused.

"We've been traveling," Jovin replied shortly. "What about the princess?"

"It was announced two days ago, Princess Saphir of Ee'lin has renounced her throne."

Chapter 24

Fear Gives Way to Bravery

"Who's ruling her country?" Jovin's throat felt dry. He knew for certain that Saphir had done nothing of the sort; she had been aboard the *Alexandria* the last four days with no way to contact her court—*if* the court was still functioning after the attack.

"Sir… what was his name… Kellan… he's her uncle on her mother's side. Apparently the queen became very ill, and the princess just decided she was not going to rule. He's remaining in the court until they crown him officially," the girl said.

Jovin and Donald exchanged a look. *Saphir was the* only *known heir to Ee'lin.*

A cataclove of images rushed into Jovin's head: Saphir kicking and screaming, being dragged from the *Alexandria* by a man whose face was not clearly visible… Saphir being thrown over the side of the rail… a shot and a bloodied mess in her cabin…

Jovin resisted running from the post shop. *Someone kidnapped her in the time we have been gone. They planned it out. What if…* Jovin blinked. The *Alexandria* was guarded on the docks, and Donald had instructed the crew to remain alert and wary of strangers nearing the airship. No harm would befall anyone aboard. It was unlikely Saphir had been kidnapped in the ten minutes they had been gone.

The girl looked between Jovin and Donald, "Is everything all right?"

"I've been to Ee'lin, once glimpsed the princess. It just seemed that she loved her country; I can't see why she would abandon it," Jovin covered.

"You must travel a lot. What did you say your name was?" the girl asked.

There was a split moment where Jovin's mind went absolutely blank. *His alias—what is it?*

Jovin covered his mind laps by moving his shoulder slightly, causing his bag to fall with a *thud* on the tile floor. He hoped the girl was not familiar with the sound of weapons dropping in canvas. He scrambled to pick up the bag again; thankfully nothing had gone off or fallen out.

"Sorry," Jovin said, straightening up. The girl giggled, covering her smile with her hand. "Yes, I am Gairen, Gairen Donald. Good to meet you. I don't think I caught *your* name?"

"Oh, I'm Leanna Porter." They shook hands, Leanna smiled again.

Donald felt that the conversation was getting a bit too friendly, "Gairen, we should get back to your brother, we will be back later to see if your mother has responded." Donald made for the door, and Jovin followed him.

Leanna's eyes filled with panic, "Wait, Gairen, do you want to… have you seen the town? There are a thousand places for dinner…"

Jovin turned back, grinning at her. "You're adorable and very pretty," Jovin replied, "but you don't want to get mixed up with me. We're scheduled to leave tomorrow anyway."

Leanna blushed pink. "I understand. At least you let a girl down easy," she gave him an affectionate wave.

"See you around, though, we're still waiting for mum to reply," Jovin winked at her and followed the captain out the door.

Donald waited until they were out of sight of the post office before stopping Jovin and pulling him by the arm to the side of the street. "Alright, we need to talk about something," he said sternly.

The young man raised his eyebrows in a way that made it clear that he was proud, if not boastful, about the situation. "I know what you're going to say," he said, "but I couldn't have done anything; she started it."

"You played along," Donald said in a fatherly tone.

"And it was completely innocent. I told her that it wouldn't work, and she backed down, what else should I have done?"

"You need to stop attracting attention. We are trying to keep a low profile," Donald reminded him.

"And traveling on a gigantic airship is *definitely* the way to go about that."

Donald put a hand on the young man's shoulder, "I am serious, Jovin."

Jovin stepped away from Donald, "I understand where you're coming from, but I don't always agree." After a moment of silence, Jovin added, "she had guts though,"

"She liked you," Donald sighed, running a hand over his face.

Jovin shrugged and put his hands in his pockets. "I'm surprised she bought the father-son thing… Nice save, though, with the brother story and the mother in—oh my gosh… *Saphir!*" Jovin took off sprinting down the crowded street to the docks.

"What? *Gairen!*" Donald called after him.

Jovin did not falter. He kept running. Soon he was out of sight among the sluggish morning crowd of Tinseenwell. Donald walked faster, deciding it would look suspicious if a grown man was seen running in the streets, whereas a young man might any day. Donald picked up the bag of weapons that had slipped off Jovin's shoulder and followed after Jovin to the docks.

+++++

Jovin's feet pounded up the gangplank. A few crewmembers on break gawked at him in surprise as he raced across the deck and up the first staircase to Donald's cabin. He burst through the cabin doors, startling Merik and Saphir, who gaped at him.

"Jovin, what… is everything all right?" Saphir rose from her seat beside Merik on the sofa.

"Saphir!" he ran to her and embraced her. "Thank God you are all right," he released her and stepped away hastily. "Sorry, I didn't mean to…."

She was staring at him, eyebrows furrowed, her jaw hanging in surprise. He regained his composure and spoke more calmly: "People were saying strange things in town."

"What kind of strange things?" Saphir asked.

Jovin hesitated, and he was sure that Saphir noticed. He could not look at her without feeling an immediate wave of guilt. He pretended to take interest in the chandelier behind her. "Things… um… Captain Donald should explain it. I don't think I'm the best person to tell you…" he glanced back to the front of the cabin, hoping Captain Donald would walk through the door and explain.

"Jovin," Saphir spoke softly. Her hand touched his cheek, and she gently guided his face level with hers. "What is it?" she implored tenderly.

"I..." Jovin had no choice but to look at her. What else could she lose at this point, when she had already lost so much? What would the throne be to her if she was on the run? He could tell her. He might as well; she wanted to know, and it was nothing she would not be expecting.

But no. This could not come from him. He had already dealt her enough pain.

He realized he had been gripping her hand and released it. Unable to look at her, he moved silently to the window wall where he stayed until Donald opened the door a few minutes later.

"Saphir," Donald said calmly. She was still beside the door where Jovin had left her. Donald motioned her to a chair in front of his desk. "We found something out that is of concern to you."

"I noticed," Saphir said as she took her seat.

Donald cleared his throat, "Someone has claimed your thrown and right to rule your country."

Saphir stood, "*What?* Who?"

"A man named Kellen who is supposedly a brother to your mother. To the people in Tinseenwell, it seems you have stepped down, giving permission for your uncle to take rule of Ee'lin while you tend to your *ill mother*," Donald said.

"Then they are greatly mistaken," Saphir said. Instead of feeling sad and pitiful, as Jovin had thought she would; she stood before them, her voice was strong, and her eyes held a fierce determination. "What should I do? How do I stop this imposter?"

Jovin stared at her in admiration.

Donald considered the question, "Presently, I think we need more evidence than we gained from the shop girl. While we are out today, I must ask you to remain cautious, we must keep our ears open. Do not speak of Ee'lin in public. I am doing what I can to keep you safe."

"I understand, Captain," Saphir said. "Mother didn't have a... no, wait..." she sat back down, shifted in her chair, and then stood up again. "This is just so strange," she said finally. She moved to the door, then turned back. Saphir opened her mouth as if to speak, closed it, opened it again, and left the cabin.

"To be honest, I think she took it rather well," Merik said after a pause. Jovin had forgotten about him. The boy had remained quiet throughout the conversation, choosing instead to tinker with a new contraption Donald had suggested he create. He held up a slightly bent metal disc, covered in wires and buttons. "I think it's done," he told Donald with a grin.

"What have you made now?" Jovin asked.

"At this point in time, I'm not entirely sure," Merik said, "but I think it's a time bomb. We'll see; we have a few things to test in the next couple of days."

"You're teaching him how to build bombs?" Jovin regarded Donald and Merik, and then, after seeing that neither intended to reply any time soon, he said, "surely not." Merik scratched his head sheepishly, and Jovin sighed, "Why, may I ask?"

"It started as a conversation that became a project," Donald had moved to investigate the metal disk.

"Something to occupy my time when I am done studying." Merik handed the disk to Donald. "I made a tracking contraption, and that was pretty interesting. Now Captain Donald and I are improving weapons."

"So you've been making bombs in your spare time," Jovin gave his kid brother a twitch of a smile. "Well then," he said, turning to Donald, who had observed the exchange between the two. "Carry on," Jovin said, and he left the cabin.

Merik exchanged a look with Donald, "That was an improvement."

"I think the responsibility and change of scenery have been good for him," Donald sat down next to the boy and held out his hand for the metal disk and turned it over a few times. "It looks workable; what are your thoughts?"

"I see no reason for it not to work," Merik replied. "Can I buy supplies in town today for Sighter?" Merik asked.

"I do not see why not," Donald replied.

"Great, because Sighter is falling apart, and unless I find something to fix his wings, I'll have to start from scratch."

Chapter 25

The Missing Piece

Merik was bored. He yawned and stuck his hands in the pockets of his new brown coat, staring around mindlessly, and waiting for Captain Donald to finish talking with a leather salesman so they could move on to the next uninteresting stall.

They had left the *Alexandria* just after one o'clock and had been shopping for the better part of four hours. Accompanied by Baron Von Lorian and a few crew members, Saphir and Charlotte had broken off to look for new dresses and clothing. Merik was left with Captain Donald, Jovin, Conrad, and three other crewmen who acted as personal guards. Which was just as well, Merik thought, there were all sorts of crooked-looking people about. More than once, Merik was appreciative that Captain Donald had had them change into common attire, rather than stay in their eye-catching clothing.

Merik liked the heavy brown overcoat Donald had acquired from the tailor, Mister Simmons, though he missed the comfort of his worn leather coat, but Donald said the golden buttons would attract too much attention. Even so, their whole party attracted attention. Their casual attire could still be considered upper class, and most boys Merik's age were enrolled in boarding school. In Tinseenwell, it was common for the locals to have dark hair, as opposed to the lighter hair of the southerners. Saphir's auburn hair was hidden under a scarf to keep from attracting attention, and Charlotte and Conrad's light hair was hidden under a hat, but it was not common for children to wear a hat, or even a cap, and Merik stuck out as a foreigner.

Tinseenwell was home to a gigantic bustling city marketplace known as The Swap. It spread three miles in diameter, and had a reputation for drawing folks from all over the world. This was where the locals bought their daily supplies and where travelers were often cheated out of better deals. Carts and stalls were parked end-to-end in every which way, reminding Merik of long trains with unmoving cars. Hundreds of carts bordered the streets and checkerboard shops. Often there was scarcely enough room to move from the shops into the flow of the crowd without bumping into someone. The hubbub in the streets felt like controlled chaos. As evening neared, the side allies and foot traffic of the street became more populated. Merik tried his best to stay beside Captain Donald, but it was a maze, confusing and untidy.

They had been in The Swap for what felt like an eternity; but their shopping was not yet complete, and Merik still needed to find a piece for Sighter's wing. There were plenty of inventor's carts, and they passed a few displaying rare parts for weapons, animatronics, and coils of strange electrical wire, but his party remained on the move, and Merik was unable to investigate.

His eyes began to droop, and he shook himself to stay attentive. Captain Donald was debating with yet another leather salesman about buckles and buttons and topics that did not engage the boy's interest. Jovin was entertaining Conrad with a pair of stunning spheres he had purchased three stalls ago; apparently they were effective on immediate contact, renowned for knocking the offender out for half an hour in unfortunate cases. The stealth weapons cart they had been acquired at had held nothing for Merik, and nothing to fix Sighter.

Merik's eyes landed on a counter across the foot traffic, displaying a machine he was not familiar with. Merik looked around at his group; everyone was caught up in conversation, and Merik deemed it reasonable to slip over to the inventor's stall for a moment before they had time to call him back over.

The cart owner analyzed Merik as he approached. He was shorter than Merik, with small eyes and multiple piercings in his nose, eyebrows, and around the edges of his ears. His right arm was missing from the elbow down, replaced by a working forearm with nimble mechanical fingers plated in brass and leather. The man's smile seemed kind enough, but Merik had learned better than to trust anyone selling something here in Tinseenwell.

Merik nodded to the man in greeting and looked over the counter. The boy's eyes went wide as he found the missing piece he needed for Sighter's wing. Merik calmed his face. "What is this piece for?" he asked, trying not to sound as though he had been brought up in a noble home.

The man's ringed eyebrow raised as he caught the foreign Canston accent. "They're used in small objects—usually things such as clocks and replacement limbs and such. I've got one in each of my fingers, see?" he stretched his mechanical arm out to show Merik the gears under the leather glove he wore over it. "But it's not a very common piece, I'll tell you."

"I'll give you three trilla for it," Merik said. He saw the man's eyes rake across his clothes. Merik became very aware that, even though he considered his clothing casual, it was still high-end garb for the Tinseenwell population. His jacket alone was probably worth three new pairs of boots.

"Twelve," the merchant said.

"Six."

"Ten."

"Eight, but that's as high as I'll go," Merik said flatly.

"Nine."

"Really, I'm out; eight is all I have."

The man squinted at Merik. "Eight it is then," he picked up the fingernail-sized silver piece. "If you're looking at this, I'd 'spect you know what it's for?" The merchant watched Merik feign surprised amusement. "Not just anyone would pick up a sterosimp out of all of this," he motioned to the array of parts placed perfectly on the white tablecloth. "If I'm not mistaken, I'd say you're an inventor."

Merik, who thought the merchant had figured out that he was a prince, breathed a sigh of relief. "You caught me," Merik smiled. "I live with my uncle, he invents things for the baron. Sometimes he lets me tinker with his tools." It seemed to be a decent story; it explained his clothes being those of a higher family but did not give away his lineage. It also explained why he knew so much about machines. Merik *really* hoped that the merchant would not ask which baron his uncle worked for. "I lost a sterosimp about a week ago, and my uncle can't finish the toadstool he's making without it." *Toadstool? Really?* Merik silently cursed his last few words. The merchant would never buy it.

"*Toadstool?*" the merchant was not buying it.

"That's what we're calling it so far. It's like a, um… toad catcher… We have a toad that lives in the house, and we can't catch it, so…" Merik trailed off. His story was spiraling, and he knew it. "Look," he said, "I just need the piece. Here," he reached into his pocket and pulled out five silver trilla, pulled three more out of his back pocket, and placed them on the counter. "That is literally all I have."

"You don't have to explain things to me, boy," the merchant handed Merik the piece and swiped the money off the counter. "Now get lost, kid; there are some people giving you offbeat looks," he nodded slightly to Merik's left and leaned across the counter. "There's a man down there that's been eyeing you for a while. Go meet your uncle and get out of here. Better be careful, young master. Don't get lost."

"Thank you," Merik tucked the piece into his pocket and looked the way the merchant had indicated. He noticed no one in particular that seemed to be watching him. Everyone was in too much of a hurry. He turned to regroup with the others, "Uh oh."

They had moved on from the leather stall and had vanished from the street.

Merik scanned the crowd of darkly dressed people. "You'd think that Jovin would stand out," Merik muttered, thinking back on Jovin's blue jacket. He scanned the crowd and decided to go back to the leather vender he had last seen them at. "Excuse me, could you tell me which way—"

The man eyed Merik suspiciously, taking in Merik's clothes. He gave a little snort, "The wealthy people?" the vendor waved lazily to Merik's left. "Some of 'em went that way; a couple said something about meeting Alexa or someone."

"Thank you very much," Merik nodded to the man. Maybe *"Meeting Alexa"* was a code phrase, or maybe the man had overheard incorrectly.

Merik hopped between people, moving faster than the crowd and drawing odd glances from the average passerby. He knocked into a man carrying a small wicker basket, the man kept his hold on the basket but threw Merik a dirty look when Merik uttered an apology.

"And who're you to apologize like you're somewhat important? Get a move on, boy," the man snarled. He had a long, thinly waxed mustache and dark eyes. "I said get a move on."

Merik scampered away without another word.

There was no sign of Captain Donald or his brother. Merik was getting nervous.

He passed a man exclaiming loudly while advertising a new radio that showed moving pictures and played music, Merik was reminded of the palace in Canston where they always had top-of-the-line entertainment long before the common people did. This radio was outdated by Merik's standards. He immediately felt guilty for comparing himself.

Heads turned at the quickly moving, sandy haired kid, who, in his fancy day clothes and straight-postured manner, stood with the dignity of a noble, although he was only a boy.

The merchant's words about someone watching him began to flood his brain, and his warning to not get lost panicked his mind's eye.

Merik found a sign for the airship docks. Merik turned right, but as he did, he glanced back at the crowd. The mustached man with the wicker basket Merik had bumped into was talking to a man dressed in grey. He was pointing to where Merik was standing.

Merik told himself to stay calm, but his heart hammered in his chest.

The Man in Grey nodded and handed the other a small leather pouch. The basket man shifted and was lost in the crowd again.

The Man in Grey started walking down the crowded street. Merik saw the man shoulder through a family of locals. The grandmother took up her granddaughter's hand and shrunk away into the street. A father shielded a young child from the Man in Grey. People in the crowd recognized him, or maybe they realized he was going to get through whether they moved or not. The man's eyes searched the crowd. Merik saw the man shoulder through a few more people. Deciding that he had waited long enough, Merik turned and ran.

The Man in Grey saw the young prince's priceless expression—a mixture of fear and surprise. The boy's sheltered life had made him curious; otherwise he would have fled long before. Even in Canston, the young prince should have known what the man's grey attire meant: the black insignia over the heart of his jacket, the three scarlet lines that ran from the right shoulder. People stepped out of his way, not wanting to be caught in between. But the young, sheltered prince was clueless to what the man's uniform meant.

The Man in Grey pushed a young woman aside. She turned to retaliate, but ducked her head when she saw what he was. She mumbled a quiet apology and scurried away.

The young prince pushed past a girl standing beside a group of small children. The girl exclaimed and dropped her doll. The children looked around to see the reason behind the girl's yelp, but by the time they looked around, the young prince had passed.

Merik ran for the better part of ten minutes. Each time he glanced back, Merik saw that the Man in Grey was keeping a steady pace with him. The man did not seem to be running, he was moving at nothing more than a quick walk from the looks of it. Merik was sprinting full out, moving as fast as he could while maneuvering through the crowd.

"*Ow!*"

Merik had collided into a slim girl, sending them both tumbling to the ground.

"Oh, sorry," Merik said, helping the girl to her feet. He kept his eyes fixed on the crowd. For a shining moment, it looked as though he had lost his pursuer.

"Where you think you're goin'?" the girl shot at him, straightening her wide-brimmed, dirt-colored hat. She was a few years older than he was, maybe fourteen; Merik could not tell, she had one of those faces that made it practically impossible to define an age. She was decently pretty, and would have been more approachable had she not been scowling at him in irritation.

"I'm—" Merik caught a glimpse of the Man in Grey over the heads of the moving crowd. "Sorry again, I have to go," and he took off down the street again.

Merik made an attempt to lose her, but the girl followed him. "Hey, kid, what're you doing?" she shouted after him. "You look lost. I can 'elp you. I know my way around. Where're your people?"

Merik stepped in between two vendors' stalls in hopes that he would be overlooked between the new black coats and trick photography. He craned his eyes to catch a glimpse of his pursuer and could just see the Man in Grey over the tops of brown top hats.

The girl tapped him on the shoulder.

Merik flinched and shot a mile into the air.

"Jumpy, aren't you?" she snickered. "Who're you? Where's your family? Where're you from? What're you here about?" she pestered. She had an odd accent to Merik that was not like anything he had yet heard in Terrison—nothing like the proper, delicate way that Charlotte spoke, or the less delicate, but still proper, manner of Saphir. Definitely not anything he would have heard back in Canston. She reminded him of an inquisitive puppy; if a puppy could talk, it might sound like this girl.

"Um…" Merik backed away from her. "I'm um… um…ah…" his mind had gone completely blank and he was unable to string a coherent sentence together.

The girl eyed him suspiciously, "Are you all right?"

"Please leave me alone,"

"I can't! You're too interesting. What's wrong?"

Merik just pointed down the street. The vendors on either side of him were becoming irritated at the two kids chattering between their booths.

The girl peered back the way they had come. The Man in Grey emerged from the crowded street, scanning the masses of faces. Her face split in shock. She seized hold of Merik's wrist and began dragging him back into the crowd. "You're in trouble, kid," she nagged. "You're a dead one."

Merik tried to pry his wrist out of her grip, but her grip was surprisingly strong. "Let go!"

"Notta chance. You need to get out of here, I can help." She kept her focus straight ahead of them, pulling Merik through the unending crowd. "I'm Angela," she called over her shoulder.

Merik was too bewildered to reply. His brain was muddled. He let himself be lugged along behind her like the frightened child he was.

Angela darted onto a narrow side road between two high, three-story buildings, taking Merik with her. She continued down the street, making turns and backtracking on parallel roads until Merik's sense of direction was utterly lost.

"Where are—"

"What'd you do to get into trouble with 'em?" Angela asked, cutting him off.

"Where are you taking me?"

"Away," Angela said. She did not look back at him, she just kept walking. They passed a grubby door with a peephole and a tarnished doorbell. Merik tried to reassure himself that he was all right, but he felt uneasy.

"Stop!" Merik yanked his arm free.

"Hey, *king of the scared kids*," Angela replied, a perturbed expression over her face. "Don't think I don't know what's going on; I probably know bed'er 'an you."

"What?"

"Tall man, dressed in grey, scary-looking face, looks 'ike he eats rats and toenails for a treat, probably has invisible tattoos over his collarbones, in 'n army of spies all ready to continue if 'is mission fails. You won't outrun him, no one ever does. But you can outsmart 'im."

"What?" Merik was flummoxed. "Who... how much do you know about this guy?"

Angela froze, watching him with apprehension. "You don't know... Where're you from?"

Merik folded his arms over himself, "That doesn't matter."

Her long brown hair flipped over her shoulder and her hat's brim flopped as she glanced over her shoulder. "He's part of the Landic Assassins. They usually wear grey like that, carry weird weapons. They have their information branded into their skin. It's black when they're dismissed, but it's invisible otherwise."

"You know a lot about them," Merik stated.

"My family lived next to a dismissed 'ne for twenty years before I 'as born," Angela said. "Bad things happened in 'is house… to his house, and him, once the common people decided he was no good. The town tried to kill 'im. It was a massacre, I lost two uncles that day. I know just what I need to know."

"You know more than me."

"You know nothing. A snail knows more 'an you," she said sharply. "You're a noble, 'nd not from this country; your accent gives it away. You're dressed too colorful to belong to the idiot duke that rules Tinseenwell." She turned suddenly and peered down the darkening alley, "Did you 'ear something?"

"No," Merik jumped and stared back down the empty alley.

"Oh, 'ell then," she continued to stare down the streets as though she were the rabbit being chased by the wolf.

Merik shuddered and took her in for the second time. She was taller than he was by about a head, and lanky, as though she had grown very quickly in a short space of time. Her dress and frayed overcoat showed signs that they had once been very nice, though now they were covered in a layer of grime that extended under her fingernails. Merik found himself taking a step away from her.

"You need to get out of 'ere. He'll be after you again if you're not gone. But you'll get caught faster without a guide. I know my way around," Angela said.

"Can you tell me where to find the airship docks?" Merik asked.

Angela looked perplexed a moment. "Oh," she whispered, "you're from the pretty 'ne that pulled in yesterday," she wrapped her mangled coat closer around her. "I *knew* you looked too nice to be frum 'ere."

Merik hesitated in answering, "Can you tell me how to get there?"

Angela pointed the direction they had been heading, "That way." Angela turned to Merik and eyed him with suspicion. "Though I'm wondering what you did to get in trouble."

"I didn't do anything," Merik objected. "I lost my uncle and my brother in the crowd, and I can't find them now. Then that man began chasing me, and I got scared."

Angela snickered, "You got scared."

"Yes," Merik insisted. "*I am not used to being chased.*"

Angela ran her tongue over her teeth. "Well, if you admit to being scared, I guess you're braver than most, and stupider than the rest."

Merik blinked. "Can you please just show me how to get to the airship docks?"

"And he uses fancy words like 'please', well, I'll be. You're some'in, kid." Angela waved her hand. "Sure, hurry it up, that guy won't stop to smell the pipes or not'ins." She chuckled at her joke, and she ran down the street.

Merik dogged after her. They passed a run-down purple apartment on the side street they were following, a large sign in faded golden letters over the doorway read, "*The Great Tarinii Fortune Teller: Predict, Admit, Rediscover!*" Merik could have sworn he glimpsed a pair of eyes at the window as they passed.

Farther down the street, they passed the back door of a noisy pub. A crowd of men sat outside on the steep steps under a door. The red paint was peeling from age and weathering. The man nearest promptly vomited upon seeing Merik and Angela.

"Ignore 'em," Angela whispered as they drew closer. "They're gone past reasoning,"

Merik hastened away from the spreading pool of sick.

One of the men was crying in hysterical sobs, and two were smoking from strange wooden pipes; the excess smoke hung in heavy troves around the shabby door. Another man stared at them maliciously as they passed. "Who's the runt, pretty face?" he called after Angela. He laughed drunkenly while the sobbing man continued blubbering and the sick man retched again.

Angela said a few nasty words that Merik had not known, but whose meaning he understood.

The drunken man did not take kindly to her words, and rose. He ignored Angela, and his meaty fist grabbed the front of Merik's clothes. "You look scared, kid."

"I *am* scared," Merik replied evenly, staring back into the one glazed eye of the drunk man. The other eye had been replaced by a contracting brass ball of inlayed panels.

The one-eyed-man's eyebrows disappeared into his bush of tarnished hair. "Who's this one?" he laughed. His friends joined in, and their revelry filled the alley. He released Merik, "Little tyke, good for you, ba-raver-ing." He stumbled back to the steps and fell into his sobbing friend.

Angela grabbed Merik and pulled him away from the reach of the men. "Shove off."

The man seemed unperturbed by her. He toasted to Merik and took a swig from a bottle beside them.

"See you 'round, pretty face," he slurred.

Angela grabbed hold of Merik's wrist again and stomped him down the street.

Merik said nothing and let her rage boisterously as she ripped down the side roads. The dilating hunk of metal that was the man's eye had burned an image into his own retina. Merik would not forget it anytime soon.

+++++

Jovin turned his back from Donald, who was haggling with a hat salesman, and meandered two carts over to join Conrad at a stall that was supposedly selling time traveling dust.

"It's odd though, don't you think?" Conrad was saying to Jovin, reiterating their conversation as to why no one had yet recognized them.

"Not really," Jovin said, picking up a small vile titled *Dream Dust*. "You are in the far north and people are not accustomed to what you look like." He set down the vile and waved for them to follow Captain Donald to the next stall.

"Even so, Merik and I stick out," Conrad said, as they passed through a few stalls and delved deeper into The Swap.

"Yeah, you're definitely blond, but they don't know you're… Where did Merik go?" Jovin glanced around. "Did he follow us?"

Conrad spun around in alarm. "He was with the Captain, wasn't he?"

"He was a moment ago," Jovin said.

Conrad followed Jovin back through the stalls to the main flow of people. Neither could spot Merik's blond head through the moving crowd.

"Great," Jovin muttered, irritated. "Absolutely brilliant."

"Where would he have gone?" Conrad asked.

"Stay here. I'll be right back." Jovin shouldered his way through a few people to get to Donald. Jovin stepped up beside Donald and covertly nudged his arm. "Captain, the kid's gone." Jovin said, casually so the hat vendor would not hear.

Captain Donald blinked in surprise. "Ah yes, thank you, Gairen." Donald followed Jovin back through the path of stalls to where Conrad was waiting at the mouth of the street. "When did we lose him?"

"I'm not sure, we just noticed he was gone," Jovin said.

"Alright, you will go meet Alexa. I will see you there," Donald said softly.

"Let me help you find him," Conrad said eagerly.

"No, you go back," Jovin said to Conrad, "I'll go with you, Captain."

Donald sent Conrad with the three crewmen who had accompanied them, they turned down the crowded street and disappeared into the flood of Swap-goers.

Donald and Jovin were left at the stall. "We need to move out of the crowd for a moment," Donald told Jovin, taking out his communicator and searching for a signal.

"What are—" Jovin stopped short. "Is *that* Merik?"

Donald followed Jovin's line of sight up the street.

Jovin's eyes followed the blond head of a child as it moved along with the crowd. "Wait, no, it has pigtails," Jovin sighed.

"I need to reach Mister Carter," Donald said. He fiddled with his communicator. One light blinked feebly. "I cannot do that with this noise."

Jovin followed Donald down the busy street and into the mouth of an alleyway, where the stream of people was considerably less dense. Donald turned a knob on the side of the handheld communicator. "Mister Carter?"

There was static. Then Carter's voice came through the speaker, muffled at first, "*Captain, what's wrong?*"

"Merik is lost. We are going to find him. I sent Conrad back with the rest of the crew," Donald conveyed.

"*Understood, Captain,*" Mister Carter replied.

Donald turned off the communicator. To Jovin he said, "I had an idea this might happen."

Donald produced a thin-screened box and pressed a button at the bottom. A small blinking green dot appeared on the corner of the screen, accompanied by a white dot near the center.

"There he is," Donald said proudly.

"What is…? Is that supposed to be Merik?" Jovin asked, dumbfounded. "What have you done now, Captain?"

"Actually, it was all Merik's doing; I merely suggested it," Donald replied. "He is moving. Come."

Donald waved Jovin after him, retracing their steps back down the side road. The moment they were back among the crowd, the screen began to spaz. The grid on the screen glitched, and Merik's light vanished.

"What's wrong?" Jovin asked.

Donald furrowed his brow, "I think the receiver has too much interference."

Jovin stepped up beside the captain so as not to get swept away by the bustling crowd. There was a vendor across the channel staring at them as though he was trying to remember where he knew them from.

Donald tapped a few buttons on the screen. "Well, that is as good as it is going to get. He went this way, I say we try to get into his general vicinity, then we can get out of the crowd and—"

"We're getting strange looks."

Donald did not look up from the screen. "Merik headed toward the end of the street."

"Captain, he's talking to someone," Jovin muttered casually.

Donald glanced up at the vendor. "He is curious, we appear wealthy." Donald waved Jovin after him and slipped into the crowd.

It was slow going. They lost each other now and again, and by the time they found each other, the possibility that Merik was getting into further trouble had increased. Donald stopped at the bend in the street to locate Merik again. For a short second the screen worked properly, showing Merik zigzagging away from them.

"Where does he think he's going?" Jovin said, voicing his mind. "Wouldn't he be trying to get back to the… to Alexa?"

"I cannot tell," Donald said. He blew out a breath as the screen continued to glitch. "Why is there so much interference?"

"There're about a thousand different inventions in this town that could block the receiver," Jovin suggested.

"Wait, he moved," Donald said suddenly. "He is heading down Fenway, towards…"

"Towards what?"

"We need to find him," Donald said. "Merik is headed into the slums."

+++++

Merik could hear the far-off sound of the bustling vendors and passersby, mingled with the occasional shouts from inside buildings and the dripping of drain pipes.

Angela continued trudging straight ahead, not acknowledging Merik.

They found themselves in a dirtier part of the city. Their path was caked in thick layers of grime, Merik wondered if stone actually lay beneath it. Tall buildings, homes, and forlorn shops all had the same greying walls and peeled paint. Graffiti protesting the ruling class made regular appearances. Merik's eyes picked out a peculiar triangular symbol in most every scrawl. He felt nauseated at the sight.

They passed a little lady peddling fine jewelry who shrank back at the sight of them, hanging her head so as not to make eye contact.

Angela seemed not to have noticed the woman. She yanked Merik by the arm down the dodgy side streets. "Almost there," she assured him.

The narrow street came to a dead end of abandoned shops with blackened and cracked windows. Scorch marks adorned many of their storefronts, and Merik noticed bullet holes in a few of the doors.

Merik stared at Angela. "Where are we?" he asked.

"Shortcut to the docks," Angela said. She walked straight up to a faded grey door and knocked. "We can get through to the other side, and then it's only a couple of minutes to the airship harbor."

Merik reached his hand into a pocket and felt the cool metal of Sighter, somehow, he found that its presence calmed him. "Are you lying to me?"

Angela looked confused. "No, I'm not. We'll get you back," she said confidently. She knocked again, glancing around impatiently.

Merik wondered if Captain Donald had noticed he was missing. Jovin probably did not care. The thought saddened him. Jovin had probably noticed he was missing only after Conrad or Captain Donald pointed it out.

"Do you have any family?" he asked the girl.

Angela turned a skeptical face to Merik. "I don't see why you care, but sure, loads."

"Loads?"

"Large family," Angela said shortly.

"Like, actual family, or lots of friends?"

"Does it matter? But sure, you could call them friends, I guess," she spoke dryly.

By her tone, Merik felt that he was getting into hot water. He backtracked, "Close friends?"

"No." Angela's eyes were darting around the horseshoe of abandoned shops. "And I think I'm an only child, so don't ask about siblings."

"I have a brother," Merik said conversationally.

"You do…" her reply was a mix of statement and question, and it confused Merik further.

Fear was creeping its way up his chest. This was not right. He should not be here. He needed to get away from this strange girl, and soon, before he got lost in this chaotic city permanently.

"You're not taking me to the docks, are you?" Merik asked.

Angela turned an intolerant eye on him. Another expression flitted over her face, he wondered if it could be amusement. "Took ya a minute, didn't it?"

The next thing that happened should not have taken Merik by surprise, but it did. The grey door behind Angela opened, and a large figure darted out.

Merik had barely a second to squeak out a scream before he ran, making to scamper back down the ally, and almost stumbling in his haste. He did not know the way back through the allies and side streets to the market, all he knew was that he must flee.

A nimble hand caught his shoulder and yanked him backwards, sending him tumbling to the ground. He started to fight off Angela, but a new and stronger figure pressed a hand over his mouth and took a tight hold of his arm. Merik was struggling, thrashing in desperation to fend off his attackers; then something cracked him on the skull, and he felt himself slump forward, and into unconsciousness.

Chapter 26

The Tipping Point

"Well done. You have exceeded my expectations," a man's voice said.

"He was scared to begin with," a familiar girl's voice replied.

"Next time your victim will not be so easily swayed, but you did well today."

The clinking of coins reached Merik's ears.

"Thank you, I did fine. Wait, what is this? I wanted gold, not silver!" she protested.

"Shut up," the gruffer voice commanded. "I shouldn't be paying you for your training. Be grateful for what you receive."

Clump!

"I'm grateful! I'm grateful!" she cowered and sniffed. "I'm sorry, sir. I didn't mean to disrespect."

"Silence your mouth, child," the man retorted.

Merik tried to look around, but his vision was impaired by a silk sack covering his head. He made to move, but found that his wrists were cuffed together. He could feel the gears click as he struggled; the more he moved, the tighter the shackles became. The ankle binds were simple and old fashioned, but they would work well enough to keep him from running.

Merik felt his breath quicken and he reminded himself to stay calm, it would not do to start hyperventilating.

"Gather everything. We leave shortly," the man said.

"Yes sir."

"Did you clean up yet?" the man's voice was farther away now.

"I thought maybe just leave it open, they won't catch it that way," the girl called back. Her footfalls drew closer. She prodded his arm and he flinched involuntarily.

"Hey you," the girl said. She removed the sack from his face.

Merik stared up in shock at the brown-eyed gaze of Angela.

She called back over her shoulder, "He's awake, sir."

"Bloody brilliant," the man cursed. Merik did not see his face, only the swish of a grey coat as he moved into a side room.

Merik stared at Angela in horror. He found himself unable to speak, for they had muzzled his mouth.

"Sorry, Merik," Angela said. She had removed her ragged overcoat, and Merik noticed a burn scar at the side of her neck. Angela removed the gag and let him sputter for a moment.

"What's going on?" he whimpered. The light from the overhead lamp barely illuminated the guilt-ridden expression on Angela's face. Another thought struck Merik, "*You kidnapped me.*" His mind whirled. His only hope was that someone had seen him and was now looking for him.

Angela gave him a pitying look, "Too innocent and young to understand." From a bag she produced a brass object that looked like a gas mask.

Merik eyed it wearily.

Angela then took a small bottle from inside the bag and screwed it into a hole on the side of the mask until it clicked into place. With a sorry smile she pressed the mask over Merik's mouth and nose. She flicked a small lever with her thumb, and the sticky gas started to fill the chamber.

Merik's eyes went wide. He held his breath. He thrashed for a moment, desperately trying to get the mask off his face, but the cuffs on his wrists only tightened. With surprising strength, Angela held his head, keeping the mask firmly in place.

"Don't struggle," she hissed between her teeth as she held him down. "Breathe,"

Merik was running out of breath. He was scared of dying, but he knew he would have to breathe eventually. It was either now, or in the very near future when he would become unconscious from lack of oxygen. He took a shallow breath through the mask.

It did not smell horrible. It smelled odd, though. It reminded him of cough syrup from his toddler days—the sticky, sweet smell of something dreaded.

The fumes began to make Merik drowsy, and after a second breath, his eyes closed.

"He's out," Angela called to her teacher.

The side room door squealed on its hinges, and he reappeared. He bent to study Merik. He poked a long finger into Merik's stomach. "You're almost underweight, aren't you?" he commented. To Angela he said, "Get the bag in the kitchen, we need to move out of here." As soon as she was gone, the Man in Grey picked Merik up and tossed him over his shoulder like a flour sack.

"Have you left anything for them to find?"

Angela held up a lifeless ball of scrap metal she had found in Merik's coat pocket. "What better than this?"

+++++

"It's being finicky again," Jovin said begrudgingly and handed the screen back to Donald.

Donald's ears picked up on a conversation between two people at the mouth of an alleyway. "Hold on to it for a second, I will be right back." He moved away from Jovin and discreetly walked close enough to hear the two people better.

"Just a kid, he was, rambling about finding the airship docks," the girl tossed her long brown hair over her shoulder. "Real fancy, too, new coat 'n all." She sounded like a troublemaker, a pickpocket, and a thief.

Her companion grunted. He was a tall man with most of his face was hidden by his upturned collar. "Most unusual. Where did he get off to?"

"He went that way," she pointed down the alley. "He'll get lost down there unless someone helps him soon."

Donald waved Jovin over. "Merik went this way."

"How can you tell?"

Donald shot his eyes over to the man and girl who were still talking about the strange well-dressed child. "Come on."

Farther down the alleyways, Jovin and Donald came across the same group of drunken men that Merik and Angela had run across. They eyed

Jovin and Donald's unrumpled clothes with some interest. One man hocked up a great wad of spit and dislodged it in their direction, but the rest made no move to confront them.

Jovin stepped around a pool of sick with distain and avoided making eye contact with any of the men. Donald nodded once in acknowledgment to the group and followed Jovin down the alleyway.

The screen came back to life now and again, steering them deeper into the heart of Tinseenwell. Occasionally, when they passed an apartment, the screen would freeze and go black, the two tended to give these dwellings a wide berth.

There was a scuffle as they passed a side alley and a pair of grubby looking men emerged from the shadows. One held a tarnished dagger and was pointing it directly at Donald. "Whatcha got of worth?" he sneered.

Jovin's hand inched for an inside pocket, he disguised the motion by standing with his arms folded over himself.

The second man had a hard look on his face, he was broadly set, with a deep scar that stretched across his jaw. He pointed a short sword at Jovin that gleamed in the soft light of the descending sun. "Turn out your pockets," his gruff voice filled the tense air.

Donald exchanged a glance with Jovin, and slowly raised his hands in a nonthreatening manner. "Gentlemen, please, abandon your weapons and walk away. We need not fight," Donald said coolly.

The second man, the larger of the two, chuckled maliciously. "You isn't in a position to be a-giving orders, you're a-thinking we're filth to your polished boot," he lumbered forward, glowering over the prince.

Jovin stood his ground, his eyes flicked from the blade point on his chest to the man threatening him.

"On the contrary," Donald said, the first man still holding the dagger to his eye level. "I think nothing of the sort. However, I assume that you are either low on pocket money or you have a particularly interesting backstory that has brought you into this situation. Regardless, I would advise you to leave us be."

The larger man let out a raspy bark of a laugh. "Skin him," he ordered the tramp.

In a flash of steel and flying coattails, Jovin withdrew a knife from inside his coat pocket. He darted forward and blocked the strike aimed at his neck. He kicked the larger man in the stomach, who then lumbered back a step, and, enraged and snarling, sent another wide swing at Jovin's head. He blocked and caught the man's wrist, twisting the hilt of the knife around the man's hand, causing the short sword to fly out of his grip and scutter to the ground a few feet away.

Jovin held his knife to the larger man's throat. "Stand down."

The thug's sneer returned. "Little young warrior wanna play a man's game?" he growled, although he did not move, for Jovin's knife remained embedded into the unbroken skin of his thick neck.

"Stand down," Jovin repeated. He was all too aware of the tramp still threatening Donald. He wondered why the captain had not disarmed the man yet. *What is he waiting for?*

The larger thug's eyes gleamed maliciously. "You're scared."

"Actually, I am not," Jovin said calmly. "I am determined."

"I bet you've never killed a man before."

"I have not yet needed to," Jovin replied.

Jovin slowly slipped his hand into his side pocket and found the metal spiked spheres he had bought earlier that day.

The larger thug noticed the motion and took his chance to make a wild dash for his short sword a few feet from them.

Jovin's first stunner hit him square in the back, sharp talons digging in through his tarnished clothes and electrocuting him. He fell to the ground with a *thud*, his nervous system frozen in shock, rendering him unable to move. The corners of his mouth twitched, his eyelids fluttered.

Seeing his partner in this weakened state, the tramp made a mad slash at Donald with his knife. Jovin's second stunner hit him on the side of the head. He too, like his fellow, fell to the ground. He jerked violently for a few seconds before submitting to stillness.

Jovin straightened up and tucked his knife into the scabbard sewn on the inside of his jacket. He turned to Donald, "I could have used a hand," he said flatly.

"You handled it decently," Donald replied. He picked up the tramp's knife and examined it in the partial light.

Jovin found the larger man's short sword, stepped on the flat of the blade and yanked the hilt upward. The cheaply crafted weapon broke cleanly in two; Jovin tossed the hilt aside. "We're running out of daylight. In the future, let's take less time." He retrieved his stunners from the two motionless men, folded the talons in on themselves, and tucked them back into his pocket.

"I was curious to see what you would do," Donald said. He pocketed the tramp's knife and pulled out the screen again. "This way," he pointed down the forward alley.

Jovin followed Donald at a trot, leaving the two thugs lying unconscious in the alley.

The end of the street smelled like a rancid rat decaying in coagulated pond water. The air hung in murky layers and clung heavy to the skin. Even the light seemed strained in this depressing place.

"You think he's here?" Jovin asked, bemused.

Donald bent and picked up a shining bronze object from the grime-covered street.

"No one lives here…" Jovin noticed the mechanical hummingbird in Donald's hand. Jovin huffed out a breath in frustration. "Damn it, Merik," he turned away from Donald, running his hands through his hair.

Donald pocketed Sighter and pointed to a run-down storefront. A shuffling of fresh footprints over undisturbed dirt led up to a small veranda. A grime-crusted window covered the better part of the shop face. Scratched lettering had been chipped off the glass in places, but they were able to make out where the lettering had been.

Kaiden Imports
141407 Bineven End
Tinseenwell, Terrison

The grey door stood slightly ajar.

Jovin hesitated. "Who do you think we're dealing with?"

Donald stepped onto the first of the three stairs to the shop front. "I have a few ideas. I hope it is only a petty thief, but I think that assumption would be mistaken."

Jovin glanced back the way they had come. "Is this a trap?"

Donald paused before the jarred door, "I would almost count on it."

Chapter 27

The Lightless Passage

Donald pushed open the door.

The room was dank and chilled, and smelled strongly of mold.

Jovin muttered a curse. "No one's here, how can this be the place?"

Donald crossed the floor to another jarred door at the other end of the room, it swung forward to reveal the top of a dusty metal staircase. "Footprints," he told Jovin, indicating the recent places where the dust had been displaced.

Jovin peeked over the stairs while Donald relayed a message into the handheld communicator. The narrow spiral stairway was scarcely large enough for a person to stand upright, but the light from outside the rundown shop was not strong enough to show more than the first three steps. Jovin fished in his pockets. "You don't have a light by chance, do you?" he asked Donald.

Donald produced a small electric lighter from an inside pocket.

Jovin nodded in appreciation. "Ready?" he fished in his jacket and raised his knife to eye level. "Here we go then." Jovin took a step onto the stairs, Donald close on his heels.

+++++

Conrad joined the two princesses in the dining hall after he and the guard returned from town. They were seated at the end of the wooden table beside the port side windows, which were showing the skies, rather than the depressing display of the harbor. Charlotte held her cup of tea in front of her while Saphir picked at a scone, her own teacup still full and presently cold.

"You're back early," Saphir observed. She shifted in her seat and pulled her woolen coat closer around her.

Conrad looked over the pot of tea and a plate of blueberry scones. "It's just me. Merik got lost, and Jovin and the Captain went after him."

"He got lost?" Charlotte asked.

"Merik is a very smart kid, I am sure it was an accident," Saphir retaliated.

Conrad deemed it wise not to upset either at the moment. He took a teacup from a platter farther down the table. "I think he just looked the wrong way and wandered too far, turned around, and we were gone. But it's all fishy. Who knows, there could be a possibility of kidnapping." Conrad poured himself a cup of tea and took a sip. "Oh great, cold tea, just what I wanted."

"Is that sarcasm, Conrad?" Saphir asked.

"As a matter of fact, it is." Conrad sat on the bench across from Saphir, on the side of his sister.

Charlotte furrowed her brow, "But no one knows who Merik is, why would they kidnap him?"

Conrad shrugged, "Maybe there's an underground slave trade in children, and no one wants to mention it."

"*Conrad!*" Charlotte reproached.

"It was just a thought."

Saphir's face paled, "It could have been an accident…"

"There is no slavery here in Terrison," Charlotte stated sharply.

"We don't know that for sure," Conrad said.

"I think we would have heard something about it by now," Charlotte said, exasperated.

"We are royalty; we get the filtered news," Conrad muttered.

Charlotte looked disgusted. "Conrad, that is not a subject you should talk about—"

Saphir rose suddenly. "I'll get us more tea," she scooped up the teapot and practically ran to the kitchen door at the end of the room.

Saphir heard Charlotte whisper, "Really, you should watch what you say," and Conrad replied, "But then *I* would be giving you *filtered* conversation."

Saphir pushed through the kitchen door, and their debate was lost to her.

Chef Mason was standing with his back to her, stirring up soup for dinner. He turned at the sound of the door, "Why hello, Princess,"

"Hello, Chef Mason," Saphir replied, setting the teapot on the counter and moving the kettle to one of the many burners.

"More tea?" Chef Mason asked, amused.

"It's much needed," Saphir hopped up on an empty counter—a very unprincesslike action indeed.

"What's the situation about now?" Chef Mason asked, setting the soup ladle on the counter.

"Merik got lost in town," Saphir replied evenly.

Chef Mason gave her a startled look. "Our Merik? That is odd indeed."

"That seems to be the common thought," Saphir picked at her nails.

Chef Mason busied himself chopping up vegetables. The end of a carrot flew off the chopping board and rolled under a cabinet. Saphir hopped down from the counter, found it, and deposited it in the sink.

"Is the Captain back yet?" Chef Mason asked as he began spicing the soup.

"Not that I know of, and neither is Jovin."

+++++

The staircase shook under their feet, the dust floated through the air and blinded them as it became displaced. The walls were tight against the staircase, only a few inches from the metal of the stairwell.

The stairs kept coming, spiraling counterclockwise into a deep unknown. Their footsteps echoed on the metal steps.

"Wait," Jovin said after a few minutes. He stopped, and Captain Donald stopped behind him. "It's completely silent. Turn out the light for a moment."

Donald obliged.

As their eyes adjusted to the dark, Jovin began to see a faint light somewhere beneath them. After a few more seconds, Donald turned the light back on.

"I apologize; claustrophobia was kicking in."

"Likewise," Jovin said, and started down the stairs again.

After what Jovin guessed to be three flights, they came to the bottom. There were footprints here also, leading to a door a few yards away.

This door too stood slightly ajar, a muted light spilled out from its frame. Jovin exchanged a nod with Donald, and went through.

Chapter 28

In Which What Is Hidden Remains Unseen

The air was split by a sharp *Beep! Beep! Beep!* from a small speaker over the kitchen door. Chef Mason looked up from the minced carrots.

"What does that mean?" Saphir shouted over the din.

"It means you should all go up to the captain's cabin and stay there until further notice." Chef Mason gave her a look that left no room for discussion. When Saphir continued to stare at him, he added, "I'm not talking about in ten minutes." The alarm's forceful clamor resided.

"Oh, you mean now. Sorry," Saphir slipped through the door and back to the dining room. Conrad and Charlotte looked at her expectantly. Saphir held up a hand. "Captain's cabin," she said, and they followed her without another word.

Once inside, Conrad walked to the desk and called Mister Carter over the intercom. "Hello there!" Conrad said, speaking very loudly.

"*Hello, Your Majesty,*" Mister Carter replied with amusement in his voice.

"Wait, am I talking too loudly?" Conrad asked in the same obnoxiously loud voice.

"*I would be able to hear you just fine if you spoke in a whisper.*"

"Oh, well then, um, sorry about that," Conrad stammered. "Anyway," he said at his normal level of speaking, "what's going on?"

"*That's a good question.*" Mister Carter replied. "Captain Donald sent us his whereabouts; usually it would be a distress call, but he hasn't called for aid yet."

Conrad glanced up at Charlotte and Saphir, both wore the same expression. Saphir turned her face away.

+++++

Merik was lying unconscious on the dirt-covered tile, his hand and ankles bound.

Jovin rushed to his brother. "He's alive," he relayed to Donald.

Captain Donald inspected Merik, who was breathing steadily. Apart from the scratches across his face and a bloody splotch at his hairline, he looked all right. Donald opened Merik's right eye and waved the lighter close to his face. "Pupils are dilated, not constricting. I would say that they drugged him. Whoever took him wanted to keep him alive."

Jovin's eyes darted around the dim room. "It looks like a smugglers' hold," he ran a finger over the floor, it came away covered in a thick layer of dust. "You still don't think it's a trap?" he whispered in a voice barely audible.

"Not sure," Donald replied. "If it was, I think something would have happened by now," he looked around at the footprints circling Merik. "Keep your guard up."

"There's another door," Jovin whispered.

Donald sat Merik up, and the prince's head bobbed. "We need to get Merik back to safety. Then we can discuss what to do."

Jovin noticed that Donald said "safety" and not "back to the *Alexandria*" or "airship", and gathered that Donald was being precautious in the case of concealed microphones or another form of listening device. "I'll carry him." Jovin handed Donald his knife and scoped up his brother. Merik remained the consistency of a limp noodle.

They started back up the staircase, Donald following closely behind. The tight-cornered stairs caused Jovin to miss a step, but Donald steadied the two before they went tumbling back from whence they had come.

+++++

"What happened?" both girls asked as Donald opened the cabin door and Jovin entered carrying the lolling form of Merik, whom he placed on the sofa.

Saphir leaned over Merik and took a pulse. She lightly tapped his shoulder and stood up straight when he did not wake. "What happened?" she asked again, more quietly.

Jovin did not answer her directly but turned to look at Donald, who was speaking with Mister Carter over the intercom while Baron Von Lorian listened nearby. Charlotte and Conrad had both come to investigate Merik for themselves.

"Where did you find him?" Charlotte asked in a small voice.

"In a storeroom at the bottom of a staircase," Jovin said. "The kidnappers left us a trail and everything."

Charlotte touched Merik's scalp where a small amount of dried blood was visible. She ran to the washroom for a damp cloth and returned a moment later to clean Merik's forehead with motherly concern.

Saphir leaned over the back of the sofa, staring blankly into space. "You're sure there's not an underground slave trade in Tinseenwell?" she asked Conrad.

"Not legally," Conrad said.

Charlotte heaved a sigh, "*Filtered news*, Conrad, you said it yourself."

"It's probably connected to everything else," Conrad said, watching the unconscious boy with concern.

Jovin took a seat beside Donald's desk and rested his head in his hands.

Captain Donald approached the prince. "Jovin," Donald said.

"They didn't kill him, and they didn't try to kill me when we went after him," Jovin said softly. "There's no way we can protect all of us."

"Lady Eleanor has not replied to our plea," Donald reminded him. "We cannot travel across the Channel on a weakened engine."

"We can't just keep everyone on board," Jovin said, raising his head and starring imploringly at the captain. "We're scheduled to stay in Simport for fifteen days."

"Do you doubt our ability to stay undiscovered?" Saphir asked.

Jovin rounded on her, "*Yes*, I do. This is too much of a risk."

Charlotte gazed doubtfully at the group. "What if it is not connected? What if it is a coincidence that danger has targeted the governments?"

Conrad turned to her, "You knew that theory was false before you said it."

Charlotte dropped her gaze, "Yes, but where is the optimism?"

Conrad ignored her and addressed Donald. "Simport likely knows that we are with you; the escapade in Terrison does not leave many options for our escape," Conrad pointed out. "It is not safe for us whether we stay aboard the *Alexandria* or find lodging on the ground. But Jovin has a mission to conclude. We are his guests, and if he decides to reveal us, then we will be at the mercy of Simport and their friendship—or betrayal."

Donald assessed the air of unease that lingered among the cabin's occupants. "I will check the post office tonight and again in the morning, but we must leave tomorrow before noon to avoid being found and targeted again. We told the post office that we were in slip twenty-seven, but the airship in twenty-seven left three hours ago; that could cause suspicion if we are not carful. Jovin, I want you to stay on board tonight. You are to accompany me tomorrow on the chance that the young woman is there again, she will be more likely to give up information if she is speaking to a younger face."

"Captain, you're not that old," Jovin mused from his chair.

Donald's mouth shadowed a smile. "But not young and flirtatious, either." Donald walked to the door and pulled on his heavy woolen overcoat. "I will take care of our slip and check with the crew to see how the repairs are coming along. Keep out of sight. And please, call on Hopkins to attend to Merik." Donald did not wait for a reply, he gave the group a curt nod, and exited the cabin.

Baron Von Lorian looked around at the solemn faces and then down at the still unconscious Merik lying on the sofa. "I will go in search of the doctor," he said, rising from the carpet. "Try to look a little happier; he is still alive. And everyone looks better without tears in their eyes." He walked to the front of the cabin and slipped through the side door that led down to the first level. The four remained in a thick silence.

Charlotte took another look at the cut along Merik's hairline, and, deciding there was nothing to be done about it until the doctor arrived, turned and leaned her back against the sofa, tucking her feet up to her. "There is a line somewhere in a poem: '*The air was thick with memory*'. It feels like that now, except it is not memory..." Charlotte went silent and started at the carpet.

"We have nothing to fear by a visit to Tavenly," Conrad corrected.

Charlotte's voice was hardly above a whisper, "Allies can be persuaded."

Saphir shifted from foot to foot. "Do you think they know?"

"Probably," Conrad replied. He looked from his sister back to Saphir.

"Then they probably know I'm here too," Saphir hugged her arms around herself. "I just don't want to be separated. Right now, so many things are uncertain, but it's safe here. Right now, this is all I've got."

Jovin was slumped in his chair, resting his head against his arm. "That's cheerful: you, me, a handful of proper royalty, and the kid lying unconscious on the sofa. What an excellent party." His tired eyes flicked from Saphir to the two around Merik.

No one made a reply.

The silence continued until Baron Von Lorian returned with Professor Hopkins. Hopkins stated that Merik had been drugged into sleep, but would wake within the next few hours. He cleaned the wound on Merik's hairline and wrapped the boy's head in long strips of gauze. Hopkins left shortly after, promising a full recovery and smiling like an optimist.

Charlotte took a shaky breath. "I think I will check on dinner," she said softly as she rose. "Saphir?"

"I'm not leaving Merik," Saphir answered.

"That is sweet of you," Charlotte then addressed her brother. "Conrad, would you please accompany me?" Conrad rose silently and followed his sister from the cabin.

Baron Von Lorian straightened up, and on the pretense of clearing his head, he also left the cabin.

Saphir remained staring out at the fading light of the sky port. "Are you all right?" her words were directed at Jovin.

Jovin arose from his chair and moved to where Merik was still lying on the sofa. He crouched and hesitantly touched the bandages to his brother's head. Jovin watched as the boy's chest rose and fell steadily, his face devoid of pain. "Merik's fine," Jovin answered. There remained a nagging realization in the front of Jovin's mind that he could have lost Merik that afternoon.

"I asked about *you*," Saphir said softly.

"I'm alright," Jovin's voice was somber. He rose to his feet, straightening his lapel and looking utterly overwhelmed. "I'm gonna go see if the Captain has returned."

"Jovin,"

Jovin turned back to her. "Yes?"

Saphir hesitated before answering, "You couldn't have prevented this."

He shook his head, "He's just a kid, I should have been paying attention."

"But you don't have to blame yourself," she said.

For a moment, Jovin seemed as though he wanted to say something, then he took a breath, and did something that surprised her; he placed a hand to his heart, and bowed to her. "We don't deserve you, Saphir." And with a sad smile, he left the cabin.

Chapter 29

Talk in Riddles

Ganimead drummed his fingertips on his desktop. "So what you're telling me is not actually good news; it's just news I expected to hear. You know, when they say something is good, it usually comes as a surprise."

The Assassin's hard face remained emotionless. "Sir, I am giving my report. This should be good news."

"*It should be.* But seeing as I am already aware of it, it is now *old* news." *Talk in riddles; it confuses them, and you get the truth more often.*

The Assassin was getting irritated, and his gritted teeth showed it. "Then I *apologize* for wasting your time."

Ganimead looked lazily around his office. The fire was dying in the grate, and the midnight skies stretched endlessly through the window. "You confirmed what I suspected. Is the boy unharmed?"

"Yes, we left him in the smugglers' cellar—everything you requested," the Assassin said.

"When did they come looking for him? What time was it?"

"About six in the evening. He had been gone two hours when they found him."

"Not bad. They are quick on the uptake. I'm surprised they found him at all in Tinseenwell." Ganimead twirled a pen between his fingers absentmindedly, "And you are sure that they have the Terrison twins with them?"

"Yes," the Assassin reported. "I recognized the princess easily enough, and her brother let slip to my apprentice that they are from southern Terrison. They will not be difficult to identify again."

Ganimead's eyes flicked over the report on his desk. "Anything else?"

"My apprentice requests to stay behind on the next mission; she knows the younger prince will recognize her," the Assassin said.

"Yes, very well," Ganimead muttered vaguely. "She can help Hafner shape up my older recruits."

"I am sure she would like that very much."

Ganimead was only partially listening. His eyes skimmed the assassin's report. "Are they taking everyone to Simport?"

"They have not heard from Eleanor Locksley."

"*Obviously.* So to Simport then, into the arms of their allies?" Ganimead's eyes flicked back to the man before him. "I appreciate your service," he stood from his chair and held out his hand to the assassin.

"It's been good practice for my apprentice," the Assassin replied, taking the hand that was offered. "If that is all, I will be off. Good evening, sir." The Assassin nodded his head once and vacated the room.

There was a knock at the office door. Ganimead sighed and called to enter. "Brenton, hello, what do you need?"

"Good to see you too, Elias." Brenton gave a slightly uncomfortable smile and handed Ganimead his report. "They haven't left yet, but wherever they decide to go, they will leave tomorrow."

Ganimead reminded himself that he needed to be polite to Brenton. "Thank you,"

"No one in Tinseenwell knows much about what happened to the Terrison palace, we are keeping it quiet until we have complete control of Flinith. The king is being especially difficult, the queen has not spoken, and we have the courtiers on lockdown. I have word that one of the nobleman considered our presence *so repulsive* that he became deathly ill. The whole court assumed that there was peace."

"What else?" Ganimead said.

"One of our contacts let slip to the Canston Prince that the Ee'lin princess is no longer the face of power in Ee'lin. According to her, it was very amusing; the prince had a little heart attack and practically ran to the princess. Our contact is going to leave Tinseenwell tomorrow morning." Brenton took an envelope out of his pocket. "Here's her report. She said they are still trying to contact Lady Eleanor Locksley in Ariden."

"Damn it, they're catching on," Ganimead looked over the letter. "Thank you, Brenton, I appreciate it."

"Another thing: the newer Elite want an audience with you. The Falangies are getting a bit restless and they want more information about what will happen to their clan hiding out in Ee'lin."

"Again with all the questions, that is always the problem with Falangies," Ganimead sighed. "Very well. Ask Miss Shannon to arrange a replacement meeting."

"Will do." Brenton hesitated and took a step closer to the desk. "Also, the Landic Assassins are under the impression that we have agreed to take on and lodge the entire Eastern Clan's new recruits."

"You have got to be kidding me!" Ganimead slapped his hand across the desk. "The last thing I need is a bunch of murderous seven-year-olds running about the grounds!" he exclaimed. "Fine, we'll take them, I'm sure there's room somewhere to set up their barracks in the valley."

Brenton shrugged apologetically, "Yeah, sorry about that."

"They're pushing their luck," Ganimead muttered. "Put them next to Decor eight."

"Will do. Anything else before I leave for Venqui?" Brenton asked.

"No. Thank you, Brenton," Ganimead sighed, feeling slightly overwhelmed and wishing he could just do away with the entire Eastern Assassin Clan. "More trouble then they're worth," he muttered.

"Eh, at least they're not asking questions this time," the door closed behind Brenton.

Chapter 30

Slipping into the Hurricane

"'*Dear Gregory, I am entertaining many high levels at the moment and cannot take in more. My most sincere apologies. Ask me again in a week. Love to all, Eleanor.*'"

"So that's it?" Jovin asked. A wind blew through the unpopulated street. He pulled up the collar on his overcoat.

"That is it," Donald replied.

It was the third day in Tinseenwell. The weather had been growing steadily colder since they arrived, now the wind bit through their coats, and pricked at their exposed faces. Jovin and Donald had gone to check the post office at eight that morning to find a reply from Lady Eleanor. Now they stood outside the docks, having waited to open the telegram until they could discuss it without being overheard.

"'Entertaining'? What does she mean by that?" Jovin asked.

Donald stuffed the paper into his pocket. "'Entertaining high levels.' She means that there are people around that could threaten your lives further. She wants us to stay away."

"But what do we do now?" Jovin looked over his shoulder. His nerves had not yet settled since the news from Ee'lin, and had only heightened when Merik had been taken. Even now, with everyone safely on board the

Alexandria, he could not help but feel that they were in danger of being found out.

"We have to take them with us," Donald said.

Jovin had noticed something in the post office that morning: Leanna, the flirtatious post office employee, had not been in. She had worked the morning shift the day before, and he had expected her to be there again. The older man that had taken her shift had not given any indication to where she might have gone.

There were few people about the town that morning, and fewer airships on the docks. Being Tuesday, the merchants from the weekend were gone, and the incoming merchants would not arrive until Wednesday or Thursday. Donald had confirmed with the airship's mechanic that the engines were functional; the crew had tested them all morning, checked everything, logged it, and checked them again. The engines were not in prime condition, but the crew's handiwork would be enough to keep the *Alexandria* aloft. As long as they were able to obtain the engine parts they needed in Simport, they would be able to cross the Channel back to Canston without a problem.

By nine that morning, everyone was situated in Donald's cabin; it had become their usual gathering place and was the most fitting room for their party of seven.

Merik tinkered with Sighter by the window, a sheet of tools and mechanical bits laid out on a towel. After missing the sterosimp for so long, he was finally able to resume repairs on his injured mechanical hummingbird. His head was wrapped in bandages, and his eyes retained an exhausted, slightly bloodshot look. His mood remained calm, though he had not spoken to anyone other than Captain Donald about his kidnapping.

Charlotte was reading from Donald's collection of books at the end of the sofa while Baron Von Lorian sat beside her, conversing with Saphir and Conrad who were sorting through a deck of cards on the rug.

"Lady Eleanor cannot take you in," Jovin announced upon entry.

Unnoticed by Jovin, Merik hid a grin.

"She does not think it's safe for you there—not yet, at least," Jovin plopped down on the sofa next to Charlotte. "Personally, I can't imagine that you are any safer with us; but now, there is nothing to be done." Jovin commented to the ceiling.

"You're being dramatic, Jovin," Saphir mused.

"You didn't *want* to bring us anyway," Merik piped up.

"Considering that you were *kidnapped* yesterday, it would be beyond foolish to send you anywhere," Jovin snapped. "I don't know what the right thing to do is. I'm looking for any alternative at this point."

+++++

Captain Donald looked up from his desk, "Good afternoon, Princess."

"May I borrow a few minutes of your time?" Saphir asked hesitantly.

Donald inclined his head, and Saphir pulled up a chair to the desk. They had been airborne for a few hours and the cabin was empty, as everyone was shut away in their rooms or below decks.

"I am concerned for Ee'lin," Saphir confessed, shifting uncomfortably in her chair. "I feel powerless. I feel confused. For the last few weeks, I've tried to pretend that it doesn't bother me, but I am completely torn up. I have abandoned everyone," she took a breath. "I trust you, Captain, and I need your advice."

Donald set aside a stack of papers and focused his attention on the princess. "Wringing your hands only causes more pain," Donald spoke softly. "Do not choose to suffer about this. Choose to accept it, and to beat it. No one benefits if you tell yourself that you are powerless. You are not powerless, and you never have been."

Saphir's eyes were welling of their own accord. Her throat felt tight. "Am I not powerless in this position? *I am.* I feel that I have failed not only myself but also my mother, and every person who might have looked to me for answers. *And I have none.*"

Donald produced a handkerchief and handed it across the desk to her. "Maybe it is time you decide what you want."

She reflected on his words. She felt her confliction taking hold over her and took another breath to calm it. "I want my country back." Her voice sounded strange to her, a declaration, more than an answer to his question. "I want to help my people. I want to lead them, and to protect them."

"And how are you going to do that?" Donald asked her.

"I will figure out a way," she said. "I have to trust that everything will work out, but I can't wait around for it to right itself; I have to do something. Life won't fix itself for me, no matter how much I want it to."

"I see determination now," Donald told her. "Once we get back to Canston, we will be better placed to aid you in reclaiming Ee'lin, if need arises, and diplomacy does not work."

Saphir tried to smile. "Thank you," she sighed. "The thing is, my mother *did* have a brother. We just never saw him. I thought he left the family to travel before I was born. If he has returned now… well, I think the timing is awfully convenient." Saphir straightened, "Thank you for speaking with me, Captain. I will let you get back to your work," she made to set her damp handkerchief on the edge of the desk but then thought better of it, and stuffed it into her pocket.

"Saphir, might I suggest speaking with Jovin on this?" Donald advised. "My suggestion of Canston's aid will be nothing without the crown backing it."

"I probably should speak with him," she stated after a moment's thought.

"And a stronger friendship between Ee'lin and Terrison would not go amiss."

"Eh…" Saphir shuffled her feet. "We're getting there."

"Saphir, friendship is the only way to ensure that you will be safe here. If you make enemies with the people you are constantly surrounded by, you may only harm yourself in the future."

"Right again," Saphir grimaced. "Well then, I think I have some thinking to do."

+++++

Merik found himself standing on deck, his overcoat was pulled tight around his shoulders and he wore his goggles to protect his eyes from the bitter wind and the sprinkling raindrops. He stared into the clouds in the direction he imagined Simport to be.

Merik was not excited.

After being tricked and kidnapped and chloroformed in Tinseenwell, this next adventure sounded rather boring. Although Merik had been frightened at the time of his kidnapping, he now looked back on it with a sense of wonder. *Why him? Who were Angela and The Man in Grey, and what did they plan to gain from his capture? Why did they leave him for Captain Donald and Jovin to find? It made far more sense to take him away and sell him, or hold him for ransom. Did they not know who he was and how much he was worth? Did they care? Maybe not.* Merik reminded himself that he was lucky to be alive; he knew he should be grateful that he had been found in time. But these questions haunted him.

Merik felt something brush his shoulder and looked around to find that Conrad had joined him. Conrad was also bundled up to keep out the cold, and his coat bore droplets of rainwater.

"What are you thinking about?" Merik asked Conrad.

Conrad pulled his scarf down to answer, "I don't know, really."

"How can you not know? You are the one thinking it," Merik remarked.

"Maybe because there are so many thoughts going through my mind that every time I see one clearly, another pushes it aside," Conrad said lightly.

"Mother and father?" Merik asked.

Conrad's goggled eyes seemed to glaze over, "Yeah."

"I'm sorry that this happened," Merik told him. "I lost my mother a few years ago… I can imagine that the worry is really scary."

Conrad's eyes scrutinized the cloud layer. "The hard part is… I was thinking about it, and a large part of me wonders… maybe if I knew they were dead, maybe I would feel better? If I knew what condition they were in, even if they were gone, I would feel better just knowing. This waiting and wondering is the worst of it all."

Merik shook his head, "No, Conrad. Trust me, you want to keep hoping they are alive. You don't want to hope they're dead. When people are dead… they are gone. But if there is a chance they might be alive, you want that chance."

"I'm sorry, Merik, I sounded rather insensitive," Conrad said.

"It's alright," Merik said. "But don't try to judge it yet." Merik's last words came out strained, and in the high winds on deck, he hoped that Conrad had not heard him. Merik did not want to be thought of as childish or weak.

But Conrad had heard him, and he understood. And he hugged Merik as if he were his own brother.

+++++

Donald entered the wheelhouse, bringing with him a gust of frozen autumn air.

"Shut the damn door," Mister Carter muttered from his seat at the controls. His back was to the door, and he had not realized whom he had addressed.

Mister McCoy glanced up from his book and made a noise like that of an injured cat.

Carter turned in his chair. "Oh, my apologies, Captain."

If Donald was amused, he upheld the composed manner required of him. "Please show some class, Mister Carter." He strode to the center table where the electronic map was aglow in white, relaying the populated cities and terrain beneath them. Donald compared notes between the map and a stack of papers he had brought with him.

McCoy glanced over to Mister Carter, who seemed completely unabashed by his reprimand. Carter was fidgeting and tapping his fingers on the control panel in contemplation, his attention fixed on a patch of clouds through the window.

"Lewis," McCoy muttered. "Tell the Captain."

"Tell the Captain what? Oh," Mister Carter blanched. "No, I think you should."

"I was having a reading break, it's your turn."

Captain Donald speculated the pair. "Have you disrespected another authority figure?"

Mister Carter cleared his throat, "Sir, Tavenly replied."

Donald raised a single eyebrow, "When?"

McCoy set his book aside and pressed a button on his screen. "They sent a voice message a few minutes ago."

"You may play it."

McCoy turned a knob, and a speaker beside the control panel crackled to life.

"*Greetings to the Canston airship* Alexandria,*"* the man speaking sounded pompous, and a little too jovial to be the sender of a governmental message. "*This is the government of Tavenly. I am Wendell Jackaby, representative of King Phlurus and Prime Minister Twill. We are thrilled to be receiving your representatives tomorrow in our capital of Simport. Safest travels to you all,"* the recording ended.

Donald observed the uncertain faces of his crew. "They have replied, what causes you this panic?"

"Well, *I think*," Mister Carter said. "That since we carry important foreign diplomats; the prime minister himself should be contacting us."

"That is not always how these things work," Donald replied. "The message was to confirm that we are expected tomorrow." His forehead contracted. "Well, there is only one thing left to do, then."

"You're going to tell them to—"

"No, Mister Carter," Donald said, cutting him off. "We must reply."

McCoy set about connecting the *Alexandria* to the signal airwaves. A flashing green light appeared beside a microphone and speaker. "When you're ready, Captain."

Carter shifted uncomfortably, "What are you gonna say?"

Captain Donald motioned for silence, "This is Captain Gregory Donald with the Canston airship *Alexandria*. I am attempting to reach the palace of Simport in Tavenly."

"*This is Simport, Tavenly. Whom does this message concern?"* another voice called through the line.

Mister Carter exchanged a shifty glance with McCoy.

Donald held up a hand to his crewmen. "Mister Wendall Jackaby contacted the *Alexandria* recently; we wish to return the favor."

The man on the line paused for a long moment. "*Yes, he can be made available. Do you wish to speak to him now?"*

"Please." Donald stepped away from the microphone while the contact delivered Jackaby. "What is with that face, Mister Carter?"

Carter screwed up his face in a different way; this time he looked like a flattened hedgehog. "This is peculiar," was Carter's reply.

The line rose to life again, "*This is Wendall Jackaby. Am I addressing the Captain of the Canston airship* Alexandria?" he asked promptly.

Donald turned back to the microphone and pressed a button, the green light flashed again. "You are correct," he replied. "I apologize for not receiving you earlier."

"*Quite alright*," Wendall Jackaby replied. "*We are concerned about your time of arrival. We had to make new arrangements for your stay, what with the new royalty you bring us."*

Mister Carter stood suddenly, knocking over an empty mug and causing it to fall from the table and onto the tiled floor with a shattering crash.

Donald shot him a silencing look. He held up a hand to Carter, and returned to the microphone. "Oh?"

"*Yes, the Terrison royalty—prince and princess. We were told they are with you*," Wendall Jackaby said.

"Who is your informant?" Donald asked.

"*The palace in Terrison contacted us yesterday, but the more the merrier. Simport is delighted to host any number of royalty, and this occasion shall be one for the history books*," Jackaby said boisterously.

"If you do not mind my asking, who in Terrison contacted you?" Donald said.

"A duke… what was his name? Frightenfeld? He informed us of the Terrison royalty's sudden and unfortunate departure. But we are here, ready to welcome them with open arms," Jackaby stated proudly. He cleared his throat. *"However, we were not sure whether Princess Saphir of Ee'lin is still among your party."*

"Did the duke also mention the princess?" Donald said, delaying his answer.

Wendall Jackaby spoke up quickly, *"He mentioned that she might be with you, He suspected she was. We are expecting her now as well, and have made accommodations for her just in case,"* when Donald did not immediately reply, Jackaby went on more gravely*: "We mean no harm. I have a job to do, and if you are in doubt of your quarry's safety after the week's startling events, I must assure you that you need not be."*

Carter and McCoy waited in rapt attention for their captain's answer.

"Yes, thank you," Donald finally said. "She is safe with us, along with the Terrison prince and princess, Prince Conrad and Princess Charlotte. Our arrival is estimated to be late afternoon tomorrow. We look forward to meeting with your court and negotiating terms in continuation of the treaty with Canston. Thank you for your time, Mister Jackaby."

"Not at all, Captain," Jackaby replied. *"Safest travels."*

The line went dead.

Chapter 31

Act like a Princess

Saphir turned away from the window wall and tried to let her concern about Merik's sudden headache release from her mind. He had mentioned it was too much for him to be around any amount of noise, so he had retired to his cabin. This bothered Saphir, although she did not know why. "Alright, so whether or not they are fully aware of our situation, we need to act as if we are fine and nothing is wrong,"

Charlotte gave up a strained little laugh, "Act like a *perfect princess*?"

Conrad looked confused, "What are you talking about?"

"There is a saying that part of being a princess is maintaining a level head in the spotlight, it is to conceal your own thoughts and to never let on that anything is troubling you, no matter who has wronged you, what the threat may be, or who is trying to intimidate you." Charlotte explained.

Conrad shifted uncomfortably while he waited for someone to expand upon the topic, or to smile and laugh it off, saying that it was meant as meant as a joke, not something they actually had to deal with. But as the silence stretched on, and neither girl spoke against the statement, he felt the strange tightness in his chest that he associated with disparity, and decided to let the topic drop.

Jovin had been resting his head in his hands and now fixated his attention on Captain Donald. "Captain, this situation is potentially hostile. We cannot endanger ourselves to better our pride. There is no guarantee that we can trust them."

"It is very possible we cannot," Donald agreed. "The representative mentioned a court member named Frightenfeld."

"Frightenfeld? He must have meant Ferrenfele." Conrad's boots clomped softly over the wooden floor as he began pacing the cabin. "He is a member of the high court. If he's able to communicate with Tavenly, what does this mean for the rest of the court?"

Baron Von Lorian eyed the prince with apprehension, "I see where your thought is traveling, but do not jump to conclusions yet. We were asked to stay under Canston's protection until we have been released by the Captain, or your father, and not a moment before."

"But what if they are alive!" Conrad exclaimed, his face lit up in a wide grin. "Charlotte, our parents—all of our friends; Mindyann and Riler and everyone! And grandfather and grandmother. This news makes everything better."

Charlotte was smiling too. "We could leave you after we reach Simport and find another way home, there would be no need to safeguard us any longer," she told Captain Donald.

Baron Von Lorian gave her a withering look, "Princess, we do not leave the *Alexandria* until I hear your father's voice commanding you to come home, not a moment before."

Conrad retreated a pace, "And what authority gives you the right? My apologies, but we outrank you, Baron, this is our decision."

Baron Von Lorian did not shrink. He stood tall, a parental light in his eyes as he surveyed the twins. "I am your elder, I know more of this world than you. I would suggest that you listen to my reasoning and not jump into traps of sand before thinking it through."

Conrad's forehead contracted. He looked to Charlotte, who cast her eyes down. "If that is what you think is right," Conrad said slowly, "then I must give way."

Charlotte folded her hands, "Our apologies, Baron, Captain."

+++++

Jovin found himself rambling into the captain's cabin later that evening. He had stared out his cabin windows at the cloudy night sky for a while, trying to make sense of his thoughts; but he did not know where to begin to dissect this strange web they were caught in. The airship's passengers were winding down for the night, and it was only Captain Donald in the cabin. He looked up from his book when Jovin entered, a large mug of tea steaming beside him. Jovin found it odd that the habitually poised captain was seated cross-legged on the floor beside the window wall. His back was against the supporting frame and for the first time since they had left Caloricain, he looked peaceful, and without worry. His feet were bare, his tie was undone and folded neatly on a leather bound journal on the floor beside him.

"I'm sorry to bother you this late," Jovin said.

Donald sat up straighter, setting down his book. "Come in, Jovin."

"Am I wrong to fear for the future?" Jovin sat with his back against the sofa, facing Donald. "Even if everything goes as planned, what will we do when we depart Tavenly? The engines are weakened, and you said so yourself, it would be too dangerous to travel back across the Channel to Canston. But we are not likely to find a city in all of Tavenly where we will not be recognized."

Donald regarded Jovin with intrigue. "You make a fair point. What would you propose we do?" the captain asked kindly. "Think about this, Jovin. You will one day be king, these decisions will be yours."

Jovin blew out a long breath, "I don't know what the right thing to do is, or even if there is a right thing. I don't see a compromise, and I don't see an option that doesn't offend someone, or harm us."

There was a knock on the front cabin door, and Merik padded in on rainwater-soaked socks. The improved version of Sighter flitted around his head lazily. Sighter's wings moved so quickly that all one could see was a blur of bronze. Sighter darted past Merik, gave the room a once-over, then returned to guarding the young prince.

"Oh, hello," Merik took a seat beside Jovin. Merik pulled off sodden socks and tucked his feet up under him.

"I thought you went to bed," Jovin commented.

The boy's face was pale, and the aura about him was utterly exhausted. "I couldn't sleep, and any type of noise makes my head hurt. Then I started worrying...." he ruffled the already messy hair that poked through his partially bandage-wrapped head. "I was hoping I could get a few words of kindness."

Jovin thought aloud, "How about—"

"Not from you," Merik protested. "You'll say something like 'stop worrying and just go to sleep,' and I need something encouraging that won't make me irritated."

"But what if I said something useful this time?" Jovin objected.

"Then we will simply have to live without whatever wisdom went unsaid by your brilliant brain," Merik sassed, he turned his attention from Jovin to stare intently at Donald. "I am looking at you."

"Well, what if Captain Donald doesn't have anything useful to say?" Jovin went on.

"Then I will go and ask Saphir, and if she doesn't have anything, I might annoy Conrad until he says something."

"Just how low am I on the list?"

"Behind the cat you didn't want to bring," Merik pouted.

Jovin was about to protest, but Donald held up his hand. "I think Merik has made his point."

"That he doesn't think I give good advice?" Jovin scoured.

"That we should have brought the cat," Merik rebutted.

Jovin considered his brother with amusement. "How does the *cat* give better advice than me?"

Merik turned slowly to stare at Jovin. "Have you met Bentley? He just smiles and gives you hugs."

"Only because you feed him."

"Anyway," Merik carried on, "I had a question. What are *we*"—he pointed to himself—"going to do when we get there? Do we have to stay on board the entire time?"

"You are not going to," Donald told Merik. "We all must go ashore."

"Then what?"

"Do not fret on it now. Put the future from your mind, because when it comes, it will be different then how you are imagining." Donald said.

"It always is," Jovin muttered. "Well… good night," he rose and left the cabin.

Merik looked at the door Jovin had vacated. "Maybe he was the one who needed advice." Merik scooted across the floor to Donald and leaned against his shoulder. Sighter landed on Merik's knee. "Captain, is it right that I am not as scared as I think I should be?"

"How do you mean?"

"In my head, I keep thinking that I *should* be scared more than I am, but I'm actually kind of curious," Merik sighed, "but part of me is still a little scared."

Chapter 32

Simport

The *Alexandria*'s hull rested against the docking braces, the latches tightened and locked firmly into place around the airship. Led by Captain Donald, Jovin and Merik marched down the gangplank to meet the man awaiting them on the shore.

Wendall Jackaby was an enthusiastic man with a prominent nose and crinkled eyes. His tone and manner of speech matched how he had sounded through his message. He took no notice of Captain Donald, or Merik for that matter, and spoke directly to Jovin as though they were the only two present. "Wendall Jackaby, representative of Prime Minister Twill, and secretary under King Phlurus," he announced, bowing deeply. Rising and glancing over Jovin's shoulder, he asked, "But where are the rest of you?"

"Good to meet you," Jovin said, drawing the man's attention back to him and noting Jackaby's disregard for his present companions.

Jackaby started a long-winded tirade about lovely weather and how grateful he was that the recent snow had not hindered their arrival, about how much he honored and respected his King, and how it was Jovin's honor, he was sure, that they had been so warmly invited into Tavenly. Jovin nodded and agreed until Jackaby announced in an ill-mannered tone, "I apologize for the inconvenience, but the King cannot see you tonight." Jovin was thrown off his guard by this and did not speak until the remaining royalty had filed down the gangplank to meet Jackaby. Jackaby's elation at everyone's "glowing presence" was second only to Merik's annoyance at being blatantly ignored. "We apologize for the cramped conveyance, but I assume you are used to it by now," Jackaby exclaimed as he escorted their number through the gates of the airship yard to a pair of awaiting motorcars.

Baron Von Lorian and Captain Donald were offered the second motorcar as their means of transport and the royalty crammed into the first. After they had filed in and the driver had closed the motorcar's door behind them, Jackaby stated, "It is so exciting having the five of you here; it is as though the holidays have come early."

"We are happy to be here," Saphir replied, avoiding her companions' eyes as she said this.

"And you have every reason to be, Princess Saphir," Wendall Jackaby went on, flourishing a hand as the driver started the motorcar and they pulled away from the airship docks. "You will have to meet Lord Avery; he is particularly charming, you could even go so far as to call him Simport's newest celebrity. He recently agreed to be patron sponsor and paid a long overdue wage to the… a sort of outreach program for the proper training of young minds and such. The pair of you must meet, I do believe you will like him, he is a perfect companion for a noble lady such as yourself."

"How lovely," Saphir said dully. "I will have to—"

"You will adore him." Jackaby did not appear to comprehend Saphir's distaste at being cut off, and continued his flattery.

Merik pressed his face up against the motorcar window and watched the dock until the *Alexandria* was out of sight, then he slumped against Saphir's shoulder and took to staring at the carpeted floor.

Conrad picked up the lapse in conversation and went into a long, drawn-out question concerning the communication between Tavenly and Terrison, and whether or not he would be able to contact his father that evening.

Saphir withdrew her attention from Conrad's tirade and took to gazing out Merik's side window at the cobblestone road. When she turned back, she realized that Jovin had been watching at her, he raised his eyebrows in a questioning fashion.

She averted her eyes, hoping he would leave her be.

"And you will be staying the full fortnight, so you might have time to see the Ice Crystal Castle finished in its grandeur," Wendall Jackaby droned, "it is a beautiful homage we construct each winter to honor our ancient sovereigns and their struggles with New Zyroo in the more recent times of revolution. There was a time it snowed eleven months out of the year, and the only building materials Simport had was ice. We taught the barbarians from New Zyroo a lesson during the two hundred year war, nearly wiped out their forces. They could not penetrate our fortress; so that is why we rebuild a tribute to our history every winter. They are almost done now, although it has been warmer than we had hoped, and the ice keeps melting, dear me. But it is a fantastic sight at sunset, what with the colors shining through the Ice Crystal Castle's walls. We shall see, maybe you will need to stay longer just to see the Ice Crystal Castle completed."

The motorcar came to a halt, and a server held the door while the royalty and Wendall Jackaby hustled out. A chilled breeze bit at their faces as they followed Jackaby up the stone steps. The scarlet doors opened automatically, and the party moved into an entry chamber where servers took their heavy coats.

Jackaby was explaining the history of the castle's architecture in confusing detail to Jovin a few paces ahead of the group. His droning tones caused Conrad to fall into step beside Saphir and Merik. "Whatcha thinking?" he muttered discreetly.

"It's going to be very boring here," Merik said with a pointed look.

Conrad mumbled an agreement as Jackaby stopped them beside a pair of grand staircases at the end of the hall. A server in emerald attire awaited them at the foot of the left staircase. Jackaby grinned at the royalty. "If you would like to rest before the gathering tonight, we have arranged your rooms. If there is anything I can answer before I send you off with Diann…?"

"One question," Jovin said, "would your king be willing to see us tonight, or is he going to make us wait until tomorrow?"

"Oh, I do not have an answer to that as of yet," Jackaby smiled at Diann, who looked politely confused. "The King is very busy with meetings and political matters at the moment; he just agreed to a partnership with the Landin—"

"*We are* political matters," Jovin cut across him, "I suggest he rethink his priorities."

Jackaby looked as though he was not sure how to respond to this. He cleared his throat before beaming again. "I shall appeal your request to the King,"

"Thank you," Jovin said curtly.

Jackaby motioned for the group to follow Diann up the stairs, "Good to meet you all."

Merik walked slowly up the stairs beside Saphir. Halfway up he stopped and peeked over his shoulder at the entrance hall. Jackaby was marching down the floor in an obvious rush. At the end of the hall, he paused to brush a hand over his head, took a moment to glance back at them, and then disappeared through a side door.

Chapter 33

Never Trust a Rumor

A tall man in a vibrant red coat moved forward from the party gathering, his hand outstretched to the prince. "Lord Avery of Simport and the Wildes to the East," he smiled a toothy grin that did not reach his eyes.

Jovin shook his hand, "Prince Jovin of Canston."

Lord Avery went off on a long-winded lecture about mundane matters of little importance to Jovin: his take on the winds while flying, their swift arrival, and "*how wonderful*" it was that everyone was all together in the safety of the Simport castle. "We were unsure if you would make it, what with the weather and all. There were bets on whether or not you would be tossed out of the sky," the man laughed, "I suggested that it was an ill-stated argument; however, I know some who could care less. Anyhow, we are not displeased that you are here. Gave us all a good laugh. I cannot imagine the trip you have had."

"It has been more than decent, although a little draining," Jovin replied.

"Wonderful. You have been traveling a very long while, I know," Lord Avery said.

Jovin was having a hard time keeping his own face pleasant. "About—"

"I don't think I would find it draining at all. When I travel, I travel long distances, and I hold up splendidly for long periods of time without rest," Lord Avery said, "I am sure I would find your journey pleasant."

"No doubt you would," Jovin said civilly.

"Oh, dear boy, you sound drained. Never fear, travel is beneficial for the soul, and your travels have been so light and easy, and I am sure all of your destinations were more frivolous than the last; a good night of rest on solid ground will charge you right back up. You are honored to stay in our castle, no more tossing airships tonight, you are to stay in the most splendid and luxurious location in all of Tavenly."

"We are—"

"Oh, and *of course,* you must introduce me to your companions," Lord Avery mused, "the princesses who accompany you must be *so* entertaining,"

Jovin felt stricken. "I am sure I do not know what you mean."

Lord Avery laughed as though Jovin had known *exactly* what he meant.

Jovin did not laugh.

Lord Avery went off on another topic: "I have just signed another deal to sponsor the ball in your honor. I must say, it was a pretty price, but you are appreciative, no doubt."

Jovin kept a close watch on Lord Avery's face—mainly his eyes. His eyes would shift upward when he said something was 'wonderful', or uttered a compliment, displaying that he had no real interest in the subject in question, and found his own words on the matter to be nearly demeaning.

"Everyone here practically worships the ground I walk on, it is as though my small feat of donating and sponsoring has saved them from complete and utter ruin. They *do* need me, although, I do not need them. I enjoy their debt and praise immensely. If one is to be proud, it must be for right, and honest reasons, not made up, deceitful reasons. Falsehoods bring shame. There is no room for shame in my life, I am simply too good for it. If I were to be shameful, it would rip apart my whole being. No, I am much too knowledgeable to fall into a network of fabrications and deception. My awareness is unmatched. You must tell me, what faults are you best known for? For these attributes are the reason that one is gossiped about, whether we like it or not. But alas, even the most hateful and revolting chatter is better than being forgotten entirely. You smile, but you know this to be true, don't you, lad? This way or that, I am sure you find a way to stay in the wagging circles. I have heard copious stories. Truth or no, the tales are impressive, although, I am sure they are *significantly* exaggerated. I deem you reasonable, but not without fault."

There came a point in their one-sided conversation where Saphir materialized beside Jovin. "Jovin, we are moving into the parlor," she said, tugging lightly on his arm.

Lord Avery plucked her hand from her side and kissed it. "You must be the girl I have heard so much about. Saphir, am I correct?"

"*Princess* Saphir," Jovin corrected.

"Absolutely riveted," Lord Avery said.

Saphir placed a smile on her face. "And you are?"

"Lord Avery of Simport and the Wilds of the East. I must say, your beauty is that of no comparison. Your fellow did not mention it enough." An evident thought washed over his face. "How is your mother? I heard that she was taken ill, but she must be better if you have the confidence to leave her side."

Jovin cleared his throat. "Well, uh, Princess Saphir, shall we try to find our companions?" Jovin took up her arm. "Excuse us," and he led her away though the crowd of nobles.

"Who was he?" Saphir asked Jovin in a hushed tone.

The crowd slowed as people began to file into the grand parlor. "A certain Lord Avery who thinks he's made of money," Jovin told her.

"He took to me rather well," Saphir commented, "a bit straightforward, though, isn't he?"

"Just the cut of your dress," Jovin muttered irately.

"I noticed," she said. "Did you mention me?"

"Hardly," Jovin said.

Saphir snickered, "Oh, you didn't like him,"

"Not in the slightest," Jovin glanced sideways to ensure that they were not being overheard. "He thinks many strong thoughts and cares nothing for a word anyone says."

"It is a common theme here then," Saphir agreed. She spotted a gaggle of girls quietly whispering to each other across the room, they caught her reproachful stare and revoked their attention quickly before she could decide if she was, in fact, their topic of discussion. She tightened her grip on Jovin's arm.

They passed through the parlor doors and squeezed past an elderly lady who had dyed her greying hair a gentle shade of lilac. The lady bumped into Saphir, but hastily scurried off before she could utter an apology.

"How do you mean?" Jovin asked her.

Saphir pulled Jovin toward a fireplace, slightly away from the mulling crowd. "I was speaking with a duchess, and we probably spoke ten words in our entire conversation," she said. "The rumor of my abdication is really pressing a nerve, I've heard a lot of apologies and people have told me countless times that they think it was for the best. It's just... they either don't speak, or they laugh a lot, which I don't have a problem with, but the laughing over every little thing is tiresome."

"Have the others reflected these thoughts?" Jovin asked.

Saphir craned her neck to see over the crowd. "I don't know, I lost Charlotte a while ago…"

Jovin spotted a haughty figure across the room. "I don't see our party… why don't you stick close to me for a while..."

Saphir smirked. "A little protective?"

Jovin kept his eye on the crowd, "Making sure that you are safe here."

Saphir's amused smile dropped. She stiffened and turned her back to the room, fixing her eyes on the fire in its place.

"What?" Jovin asked.

Saphir blatantly did not look at him. "That girl over there is the Prime Minister's daughter, Olivia Twill. We aren't on good terms."

"Saphir, as the future queen—"

"Shh," Saphir pulled Jovin closer to her to shield her from the Prime Minister's daughter.

"Well, this is familiar," Jovin whispered from beside her, their backs to the room. "You were on bad terms with Charlotte, and now this girl; as a ruler, you cannot have enemies around every corner."

"I know," Saphir shot back, "but Charlotte and I are fine now, and this girl is hard for me to handle."

"What do you mean?"

Saphir casually looked over her shoulder and smiled as if they were in deep conversation. "Jovin, what do you think I mean?"

"Is this about me again?"

"You'd like to think this is about you, wouldn't you?"

Jovin contemplated her, then broke out into a hearty chuckle.

"Oh, stop it," Saphir snipped.

"How many people are you in trouble with?"

"I don't want to talk about this," Saphir said.

"Come on, Saphir," Jovin prompted, "I could give you the upper hand over her. I could give you the upper hand over everyone here…"

"You had better not kiss me again," Saphir shot back.

"Why so defensive?" Jovin countered.

Saphir bit the inside of her cheek to keep from saying something stupid.

Jovin brushed a curl of hair away from her face. "Sorry," he kissed her hand in apology, "I didn't mean to make you defensive."

Saphir found it difficult to look at him, "I know,"

Jovin took up her arm and stood with her.

"What are you doing now?" Saphir asked.

"This could mean anything you want it to mean," Jovin told her. "I can be your first line of defense. We have been traveling on an airship... I'm sure they think we have grown to be somewhat close... or whatever they want to think." Jovin noticed a few people watching them. "And if not, I am here to support you."

"Thank yo... *what?*"

Thankfully for Jovin, Merik found them in the crowd. "Couldn't... find... anyone," he huffed. "I've tried to get away from four different conversations, two of which were about my hair. What's wrong with my hair?" He turned to Saphir for an answer, but her response was only muddled confusion. "They keep saying I'm getting blonder and blonder every time I see them!" in a strained whisper, he added, "I've never met these people *in my life*." Merik gave a whimpering grunt. "I don't like this. It's freaky."

"There's Charlotte," Saphir said, perking up and separating from Jovin to meet her friend. The two girls exchanged words over the churning crowd. Charlotte's stern expression did not leave her face as she gripped Saphir's hand mercilessly, speaking fast and not taking her eyes off her friend.

"Something is wrong," Jovin observed.

The two princesses joined them. Charlotte looked as though she might be sick. "I believe I found out what happened to my parents."

Jovin looked over the crowd. "Let's talk in the hall, I see another door—"

There was the loud tapping of a champagne glass, and a gentleman called for attention. The crowd silenced. "Welcome, everyone!" the four of them turned to the front of the room, where the Prime Minister was holding an empty glass and spoon. "What a magnificent night it is to be gathered for this special occasion," he went on. "Not only do we have a host of very significant people here, but we have a few royal guests here as well—and not only the ones we were expecting!"

The crowd guffawed at this feeble joke.

Merik and Jovin exchanged a checkerpoint glance.

"We are honored, not only with the presence of Prince Jovin and Prince Merik of Canston, but also with that of Princess Saphir of Ee'lin, and Princess Charlotte and Prince Conrad of Terrison," the Prime Minister announced. Many people looked around to find the royalty he spoke of. A few pointed the royals out to their friends. The upside of this was that they could easily spot Conrad in the crowd.

"The night after next, we will have a wonderful ball in their honor, sponsored by our own Lord Avery."

There was another round of applause, a few people cheered.

Merik glanced at his brother to voice an observation, but Jovin held up a hand to silence him.

The Prime Minister continued: "Let us now go about the evening as we please. Thank you for your time," he smiled and gave a little bow. The crowd cheered as though he had just accomplished a complex operatic aria.

A band began to play the moment the prime minister was finished. And it was not long after that the four royalty were bombarded with eager nobles wanting to hear the every event of their voyage thus far.

In this way, it became exceedingly difficult to end a conversation, for the moment one made to move on, they were pulled aside and made to start another.

Merik was overlooked and was able to slip into the crowd to find Conrad. Jovin failed to extricate himself from an exceedingly soft spoken, but clingy, group of girls, while Conrad, in a similar situation, had to excuse himself multiple times before he could follow Merik through the crowd to a less populated space of floor.

"What's going on?" Conrad asked as soon as they were away from the crowd.

"Charlotte's looking for you." Merik pointed to where the princesses were patiently sidestepping the pretentious nobility. Conrad began to reply, but Merik cut him off. "You stay here, I'll be right back." Merik said, and began pushing his way to the other side of the room.

The princesses had laced their arms, and their light responses made them sound ill at ease. "Princess Charlotte, can I borrow you for a moment?" Merik asked, sounding quite innocent and silently praying he had not attracted the attention of the several ladies and noblemen surrounding the girls.

"Yes, of course," Charlotte excused herself, loosely promising to try to find the nobles again. She made to follow Merik, then doubled back and politely stole Saphir away from the conversation.

Jovin had found Conrad in the time since Merik's departure and was waiting with less than the usual party smile and more worry than Merik had ever seen on his face in public.

"What's the matter?" Conrad asked when they were in earshot.

Charlotte's smile melted away. "There is a rumor that Father and Mother have gone away to the country manor."

"I don't see a problem with that,"

"*Conrad.*"

Merik looked between the two, "Wait, is this a code, or do you not have a county manor?"

Conrad waved the comment aside, "No, we have one, and this isn't a code we have agreed on," he added with a puzzled glance to his sister.

Charlotte took a breath. "I know for a fact that Father would have at the minimum *tried* to contact us on the *Alexandria*, or even here in Simport, after the catastrophe at the palace. And if their whereabouts are so widely known that a bundle of Simport's courtiers know where they are, then what has actually befallen them?"

Jovin furrowed his forehead. "She has a point,"

"That she does." Conrad looked to his sister, "Your verdict?"

"This confirms that they were captured," Charlotte said breathlessly. "At the very least, they went underground. Either way, something is wrong in our government. There is a lie circulating in the babble circles, and here we have the heir and his sister at a party, socializing."

Saphir's eyes met Jovin's, "What are you thinking?" she asked.

"Simport was tipped off by Terrison that you were with us." Jovin analyzed his companions' faces. "I will try to talk to the King as soon as possible, we need to find somewhere else to sit through the winter before we can go back to Canston."

"I suggest we make it our business to seek out allies," Charlotte replied. "If we are to live securely after this passes, we should know whom we can trust."

Jovin looked past Merik. His nose twitched. "They are starting to dance. Conrad, we should be over there."

"Right," Conrad agreed.

Jovin exchanged a look with Saphir, "Be careful here," he whispered, low enough that Conrad and Charlotte did not hear.

"I'll be fine," louder, she said, "you both should go find allies."

Jovin raised an eyebrow and, with Conrad in tow, turned and smiled their way through the crowd.

Merik shifted uncomfortably as he watched his brother. "When I am old enough to ask a girl to dance, it won't be with the desperately flirtatious ones who bat their eyelashes and giggle every other breath."

"Why do you say that?" Charlotte inquired.

"Because then I'd be distracted and probably kick them in the knee." Merik made a face as though he had tasted something rancid. "And anyway," he went on, "there are always other girls who need the dance more."

Saphir watched Jovin invite a young lady in a pale green dress out to the dance floor. "You may have a point. But maybe the flirty girls need the dance as well."

Merik shrugged, "Maybe. I don't know yet… still too young to be taken seriously by anyone here."

Chapter 34

Static

Captain Donald had been in Simport Castle's dispatch room for nearly an hour. He was trying to send a message, but every time he tapped it out, the machine fuzzed with static and the connection failed. He had considered telephoning directly, but then there was the gamble of who may be listening.

It was near ten in the evening when there was a knock on the door and a communications worker entered. "Sir, have you finished?"

Donald gestured to the screen, "I seem to be running into a problem. Every time I send my message, the system glitches and shuts down."

The worker looked confused, "Where are you sending it?"

Donald considered not telling the worker, but there was no point in secrecy, it would be catalogued in the system regardless of whether he told the man or not. "To Canston,"

The worker nodded and punched a few buttons on the keyboard. "I don't see why it's not working…" he muttered, pulling up a chair. "Everything seems to be… Oh, you know, it's probably the weather. The system can't make the connection because the temperature dropped too quickly tonight. I thought they were changing out the receiver, but I guess not."

"How soon will I be able to send it?" Donald queried.

"It might have to wait until the receivers can be looked at—probably late morning tomorrow. I could request that they be changed first thing in the morning, but I can't guarantee a time."

"How is it that you communicate with your airships and neighbors in these cases?" Donald asked the worker.

"We have another tower for long-distance messages. We use our main tower locally because the static in the air is less than if we're trying to reach across the Channel," the worker explained. "Unless it's Canston's problem. It might be something on their end… a blizzard maybe?"

"You might be right."

"You could try telephoning."

"I am in no mood for lengthy discussions tonight." Donald gathered up his papers. "Thank you for your time. I will request again tomorrow," he rose, nodded to the worker, and left.

+++++

"Should we be worried, then?" Mister Carter asked.

"That is the dilemma." Captain Donald continued pacing his cabin. He had been hesitant to leave his wards in the castle by themselves, but felt that he needed to speak to Mister Carter and Baron Von Lorian without the possibility of being overheard. It was late in the evening, and the windows of the cabin were rimmed with condensation. The crew was below deck, as their captain had requested they stay on board and not take up lodging in the town.

"Should we move them from the castle?" Baron Von Lorian asked from the window, where Simport Castle was visible as a cataclove of lights above the subdued town.

"Sometimes the people with the most cheer are the people who are the most dangerous," Carter warned.

"Sheep can be wolves, and vice versa," he turned his attention back to Donald. "What do you think, Captain?"

Donald deliberated before answering. After releasing a long pent-up breath, he said, "I would like to think that the communication tower is really frozen and we are in no danger."

Baron Von Lorian moved away from the window, where the castle continued to reflect on the glass.

"Well, if anything suspicious comes up, we can leave," Carter advised.

"Not without proper protocol," the Baron reminded them.

"Yes, if we got up and left in the middle of dinner, that *would* put a slight damper on our camaraderie," Donald said.

"What then?" Carter looked to Donald. "You don't think this is just a problem with towers freezing and bad weather. It's not cold enough in Canston; it's not yet November. They will have had barely a dusting of snow there."

Baron Von Lorian reproached Carter, "You are accusing Simport of lying?"

Carter's face contorted in attempt to conceal frustration. "It's us or them. Canston is very particular about messages, and the King would be prone to keeping all connections available to us in case of further emergency," he said. "I have my doubts about Simport."

Baron Von Lorian looked repulsed. "Please do not jump to the worst conclusion before we have explored all possibilities."

Carter turned away from Baron Von Lorian so he would not notice the rolling of his eyes. "That's not the worst."

Donald ignored Carter's comment. "Let us wait out tonight. If something else arises, then we will tell the children."

"They're not children, Captain," Carter reminded him. "Jovin is hardly ten years younger than I am."

"Ten years is a long time when you are young," Baron Von Lorian said.

+++++

The festivities died down around a quarter to twelve, and everyone dispersed to their rooms or vacated the castle to their own homes. Conrad was able to slip through the milling crowd without much notice. He was grateful for the lull. He had danced with too many young ladies to count and had found it difficult to keep the ever-present smile from slipping from his face.

Conrad spotted Saphir in the entry hall near the double stairwells. She was talking to a tall, rather haughty-looking man a few years older than himself. Although Saphir was keeping a smile on her face as she spoke to the stranger, her eyes flitted over the crowd for a familiar face. Conrad altered course.

Saphir cut off the nobleman's lengthy monologue to welcome him. "Prince Conrad, hello."

Conrad took up her hand and found amusement in the way the nobleman's nose crinkled.

"I do not believe you have met Lord Avery, he is the sponsor of the ball day after next," Saphir said.

"Sponsor—what does that entail?" Conrad asked as they shook hands.

Lord Avery had the look of a man whose nose never dipped below eye level. Tidy hair, derisive smile, and a clean, pressed suit. The golden cufflinks he wore looked antique, and his shoes shone like the bald patch on a passing server's head. "None more than donating copious amounts of money to the state," Lord Avery said jovially. His attention landed on Saphir. "But it has its perks."

"I am sure it does," Conrad offered his arm to Saphir. "If you will excuse my rudeness, I think I will escort the princess away for the evening, we have a rather long day of politics tomorrow."

Lord Avery took up Saphir's other hand and kissed it for a few seconds longer than was necessary before turning his back on them and joining another conversation.

Conrad led Saphir up the staircase, purposely not glancing back. On the landing, he turned left.

"Well, he's a character," Conrad muttered, so as not to be overheard by the few people making their way through the hall.

Now that Saphir had stopped smiling, she looked exhausted. Her hair was coming undone from its elegant twist, and she held tightly onto Conrad's arm as they walked. "Thank you, that conversation was very uncomfortable. The nobility of Simport... well... I feel that they are a bit oppressive."

"Saphir, you are allowed to walk away."

Saphir huffed out a sigh. "I know, but then I have to worry about being rude. But if I smile, they take it as flirting." Saphir paused in front of the large window that occupied the wall. Conrad waited for her. "You can see the *Alexandria* from here," she said softly.

They walked in silence until they reached Saphir's door at the end of a corridor. "Thank you again, Conrad, I appreciate your timing."

"You're welcome," Conrad said.

"Good night," Saphir said with a smile, and slipped into her room.

Conrad knocked on Merik's door when he passed, and the young prince answered in a moment. He was glad Merik was in his room already, and from what the boy said, Charlotte was in her room as well. Merik disappeared mumbling "see you tomorrow," and "happy dreams," and his door closed again.

Conrad was on his way to his room when he doubled back and knocked on Jovin's door.

"Come in,"

Jovin was beside the window, his party jacket in his hands, his feet bare. His eyes were finally showing his sleep deprivation, and he was watching Conrad with a vacant sort of stare. "This is weird, Conrad, what are you doing here?"

Conrad ignored the judgment in Jovin's voice and closed the door behind him. "Jovin, are we getting along well enough to talk civilly?"

"We're doing fine," Jovin said, eyeing him suspiciously.

"Really?" Conrad said, "Because it is my impression that we ignore each other when not obligated to be amicable."

"Hey, I let you spar with the crew and I, that's pretty civil." Jovin retaliated.

"Look, I'm tired and I don't have the energy to counter sarcasm," Conrad rubbed his forehead. "I want to ask you about the girls here."

"They are girls, you approach, speak with, and win them over the same way you win over any other girl," Jovin sighed.

"Heavens no, not that," Conrad crossed his arms. "They're flighty and scared, and they don't talk about anything that's been going on, here, or in the rest of the world. Maybe it's the culture and social climate, maybe they're a bit more conservative, but we have two heartstrong young ladies with us..."

"We do," Jovin caught on.

"I think we need to watch out for them—especially your Saphir," Conrad said.

"She's not *my Saphir*," Jovin muttered, "she is her own person," he carelessly threw his ebony-and-gold embroidered party jacket over a chair.

Conrad raised his hands in surrender. "All I'm getting at, is that you made a point to claim her as your property. I'm just following the *stay away from her* guidelines you're striving for."

"I *did not* claim her," Jovin retorted.

Conrad ignored Jovin's outburst. "Regardless, we need to assure that she is being treated properly by everyone," he waited for Jovin to agree with him, or to interject that he was overreacting. But Jovin just stood there, expressionless, almost melancholy, and remained silent. "On a lighter note, the King should be speaking with you tomorrow."

"He should be," Jovin agreed. His mood shot back to something less gloomy. "Did you meet Lord...?" Jovin searched for a moment. "Uh, Lord Avery?"

"Briefly."

Jovin speculated Conrad's expression. "What did you think of him?"

Conrad snickered, "Why?"

"I find that he is degrading to everyone he comes in contact with. Our upbringing and social standings are different, but there is a level of politeness that should be shown to everyone," Jovin answered curtly. "It appears that he has misplaced his manners."

Conrad's eyebrows shot skyward, "Are you sure that you're not overreacting?"

"Not on this venture," was Jovin's reply. He picked up his jacket from where he had tossed it over a chair. "If that is all, I'm sure you can see yourself to the door."

Chapter 35

A Desperate and Reckless Action

The next day, Lord Avery cornered Jovin at breakfast, and before he had a moment to talk himself out of the situation, he found he was seated between a gnarled old aristocrat and the pompous Lord Avery. Jovin was searching for a suitable reason to extricate himself from the dulling conversation when he noticed Merik seated beside Conrad a few seats down. Conrad was in a deep conversation with Wendall Jackaby, but Merik's eyes were downcast as he picked at the quiche on his plate. Jovin found himself checking on Merik until the younger prince excused himself and walked, sullen, from the dining hall.

Lord Avery kept up a steady flow of remarks on his beloved country of Tavenly, making it difficult for Jovin to get a word in edgewise. "I, for one, am so thankful for the strong hand of our King. He has led our country from ruin and poverty to riches and tranquility."

Jovin nodded politely. "That is wonderful, would you excuse—"

"I cannot believe any ruler could have done such a fantastic job as our King," Lord Avery blabbered on. "Not even *Serinnia the Magnificent.*"

"Yes, I heard about—"

"History books are nothing to reality though, right now, in this time, we are making history."

"Yes, it is fantastic."

"Jovin, I have been meaning to ask you for some time. Of your princesses, which would you be willing to give up?"

Maybe it was the completely straight face with which he said it, or maybe it was the sheer nerve required to ask such a question, but Lord Avery's assumption was so unsettling that it took Jovin a moment to register his shock. "Excuse me?"

Lord Avery's face split into a sly grin. "Your traveling companions. Because I have a great desire to know them better," Lord Avery hinted.

Jovin involuntarily gagged. "Sorry, what?"

Thankfully for Jovin, Baron Von Lorian found him at this time. "Prince Jovin," he kept to protocol and bowed to the prince, then turned to Lord Avery and nodded in respect. "Captain Donald has requested to speak with you about this week's schedule."

"Would you excuse me?" Jovin did not wait for Lord Avery's reply before following the Baron up the stairs.

Baron Von Lorian looked slightly flustered. "King Phlurus has withdrawn from our negotiations," he told Jovin. "It seems that we must be content to wait until the King decides he wishes to speak with us."

"I see,"

"The Captain suggests we stay on neutral ground with Simport until we are successful in reaching Canston."

Jovin did not respond. His mind was spinning.

"Have you given any thought to Simport's court?" the Baron asked.

"There are some interesting people here," Jovin said after a moment. "I find the lack of authority upsetting."

"Authority to whom, pray tell?" Baron Von Lorian asked. When Jovin scowled, the Baron went on, "Could it be that the thought of answering to a younger man as an equal, or even as a greater power, is below their standards?"

Jovin wrinkled his nose at this comment.

Baron Von Lorian was hesitant to reinitiate conversation. Jovin picked up on this, but ignored it. They turned down the hallway to their wing of the castle.

Jovin strode up to Captain Donald's door and entered, "Captain?"

Donald was standing beside the window, his posture was ridged, and he seemed to be contemplating the airship yard at the end of the city, a letter held loosely in his hands.

Jovin moved farther into the room, followed by Baron Von Lorian, who closed the door behind them.

Donald held out the paper to Jovin. "We just received this from Terrison."

"I was able to contact a friend who was close to my King," the Baron said, "he thinks that it would be foolhardy to return now or in the near future."

Jovin stopped reading. "What about Terrison's current King and Queen?"

"The remaining royal family has not been seen recently. They vanished on the day of the attack," Donald explained. "Most of the court stayed behind to keep peace among the people, although a few have fled. The common people are confused and starting to panic. I will not be sending Charlotte and Conrad home. Which leads me into another matter."

"What *we* are going do," Jovin guessed.

"Yes," Donald said. "Do you find it safe here, Jovin?"

"I do not want to make this decision," Jovin said.

"You cannot pawn off responsibility. You will be a leader sooner than not. What does your intuition tell you?" Donald asked.

Jovin thought back to the atmosphere and mannerisms of the court the night prior. He was accustomed to chatter, and gossip was normal in partygoers, but there was an underlying uneasiness in the people of Tavenly. It sat like dread in the pit of his stomach.

"King Phlurus was not present at our welcoming gathering, and he has still not arranged to meet with us," Jovin deduced. "If Terrison is weak and without a leader, both Charlotte and Conrad are at risk. Saphir should be in hiding; it is reckless to allow her presence and whereabouts be known. Merik and I have shown where our allegiance lies by collecting the Terrison's, and as we are still denied a conference with the King of Tavenly, then we are no longer safe in Simport."

"Eloquently put," Donald approved. "As a leader, what would you have us do?"

Jovin took a breath, "We should leave."

"You would run again?" Donald raised his eyebrows.

"There is no one to fight," Jovin said. "We are not in immediate danger, but if we prolong our stay, we open ourselves to misfortune."

"When would you have us leave?" Donald asked.

"I don't know,"

The Baron cleared his throat. "If I may, we must remember that Princess Saphir has escaped death already, Prince Merik was kidnapped, and Simport already knew that they were with us."

Jovin straightened himself. "Then we must leave tonight."

"Then tonight it is," Donald agreed. He folded the note and placed it inside his jacket pocket. "We need to gather everyone together and meet here before the next hour."

Jovin was already moving to the door.

"Jovin," Donald said, calling him back. "You may be looked to for reassurance; especially from your brother."

Jovin paused. "I'll do the right thing," he said, and walked from the room and across the hall to Merik's. He did not knock but opened the door and slipped in without Merik's consent.

"What are you doing here?" Merik asked in curiosity. He was sitting on his bed, a sketch book open over his lap while the restored version of Sighter flitted about.

"He's pretty," Jovin commented.

"*What?*" Merik regarded Jovin with some hesitation.

Jovin sat down beside his brother and pulled Merik's head close to him. "We're leaving. Get ready. Be in Donald's room shortly," he whispered.

Merik flinched and sprang to his feet, he ran across the room to where Sighter had landed and was now nesting in his party clothes from the night before. Sighter launched into the air and began zipping back and forth between the brothers as though they were playing a game. Merik raced after his invention, "No Sighter, come back!" he jumped onto his bed to grab Sighter before he landed on the top of the bedframe post. "Come here!"

Jovin glanced back at his brother, who was still chasing Sighter about the room. With a wave that went unnoticed, Jovin stepped out of the room.

He ran into Conrad halfway down the corridor. "Conrad, you look cheerful today," he clasped Conrad on the back in greeting. Jovin whispered, "*We're leaving. Meet in Donald's room.*"

"As do you, Jovin." Conrad said, continuing their loud conversation. He gave the slightest nod, and the look in his eyes made it clear that he understood the message. "Where are you off to?"

"I'm off to look for our companions, I haven't seen them recently." Jovin said this in a manner light enough to make a passing server smile and hide her grin behind her hand. Jovin passed Conrad and started walking backward down the hall. "And if you see Captain Donald, would you tell him that Merik was looking for him—something about a new card game?" Jovin went on, ignoring the girl.

"Will do," Conrad said, playing along. "And as far as the princesses are concerned, I think they were on the veranda with Lord Avery."

Jovin's light expression drained from his face. "I see," he muttered. "Well, I'm off then."

The veranda was abuzz with the chatter of ladies and lords enjoying the sunlight. Many sported heavy overcoats and frill-covered scarves to protect them from the dusting of snow that had fallen the previous night. Gloved hands held steaming glasses. Earmuffs and high top hats adorned heads, but for the life of him, Jovin could not understand why such a large party of people would mingle in the bitter afternoon air when there was plenty of room indoors.

Jovin was about to go in search of Charlotte and Saphir when Wendall Jackaby caught his eye. Jovin redirected his path to intercept him before he entered the castle.

"Ah, Your Highness," Jackaby said in a flurry, seemingly caught off guard by Jovin's sudden appearance.

"Mister Jackaby, I was not certain who to ask," Jovin started. "Has your King given an answer as to when he will be available to speak with us? I do not believe he was present at his gathering last night, and your prime minister disappeared before we had a chance to meet. I had wished to speak with one of them on matters of strict importance. I apologize for my impertinence."

"Not at all, Your Highness, it is understandable." Jackaby's eyes swept the crowd. "Let me see, oh there is Mister Hucklosh; he is very pleasant, and there is a possibility that he might know the King's schedule, although he is a rambler. Have you met—"

Jovin caught his arm before the man moved past him. "Mister Jackaby, I appreciate your willingness, but I do not wish to be delayed in conversation. My request is to your King, not to another nobleman." Jovin released his arm. "Forgive my offense."

Jackaby's face whitened, he tried to recreate a supercilious manner. "I will send a request to the King to have a time devoted to you."

"Thank you. Please send word as soon as there is a schedule. I have been denied audience twice—last night and this morning. A third time would not be advised. Let your King know that I have a tendency to grow impatient when presented with disrespect."

Jackaby nodded once and disappeared into the castle without a word.

Jovin did not have trouble finding Charlotte and Saphir at the edge of the veranda. As Conrad had mentioned, they were accompanied by Lord Avery.

Saphir laughed animatedly, and Charlotte giggled, covering her mouth with her hand. Jovin got the impression that there was an unspoken nervousness between the princesses that Lord Avery was oblivious to.

Jovin stepped forward and was at their side in a moment, emulating civility in a matter of seconds. "Lord Avery, I thought I recognized you. I hate to be a bother, but please excuse me in borrowing the princesses for a moment; our captain has asked for their presence—something about wardrobe and formalities, all very confusing." Jovin smiled amiably.

"Oh, Jovin, how wonderful it is to see you," Saphir beamed, tucking her arms around his.

Under different circumstances, this gesture might have been sweet, but Jovin's understanding of Saphir was great enough to realize that she wanted out of this conversation. Her sidling up to him was a silent plea for escape.

Lord Avery looked Jovin over, noting Saphir on his arm and the fondness that followed her. A gleam of contempt for the young man was clearly written in Lord Avery's eyes. "And your captain sent you as messenger? I hope that has not injured your pride."

Jovin kept his face placid. "I volunteered, actually, something to do, and any time with my princesses is better than wondering which new stranger is attempting to win them over." The sarcastic edge disguised as charm made it clear that Lord Avery was no longer in control of the situation. "Shall we go then, ladies?" he offered Charlotte his other arm, and she took it without hesitation. Jovin refocused on Lord Avery. "Of course, I am sure you understand. Good day to you." Jovin did not give the nobleman time to reply before leading Charlotte and Saphir away. He could feel Lord Avery's eyes on him until they mixed into the crowd.

Jovin nodded at the doorman and waited for the heavy glass door to close behind them before quickening his stride. He turned a corner and stopped, Charlotte and Saphir clinging to each arm. Both were wide-eyed and white-faced.

"He is very strange, Jovin," Charlotte wrinkled her nose. "He has very little social etiquette and is *very* straightforward in his opinions and intentions. It feels invasive."

"I think he is the rudest and most disrespectful person I have ever met," Saphir added.

"We can discuss this later. The Captain wants to see us," Jovin said.

The girls nodded. Halfway up the staircase to their apartments, Saphir stopped, causing a minor pileup. "'*My princesses*'?" she stared at Jovin.

"I thought it was better than saying 'my ladies,' because I didn't want to make it sound like—"

"'*My princesses*' isn't any better!" Saphir interjected. She started climbing the stairs again, "*Honestly!* What were you thinking?"

"I was thinking that you both looked like you were about to have a minor panic attack, and I thought you needed to get out of there," Jovin told her.

Saphir stopped and glared intently at Jovin "Really, Jovin, thank you for our rescue, but the whole situation could have been handled differently—"

"What would you have had me do?" Jovin asked, cutting her off. They stood halfway up the staircase, glaring at each other with mild confusion and intense irritation.

"I don't know... *something else!*" Saphir said.

Jovin looked ready to retort when Charlotte cut across them. "I do believe that Captain Donald wishes to speak with us," she said quickly. She feigned being oblivious and made a show of investigating the ceiling's architecture. "Oh, that is pretty," she commented to herself. "Hurry it up, please," she called back over her shoulder.

The radio's music lolled through Captain Donald's apartments and bounced off the door, their thought being that if anyone was listening in the hall, they would be unable to hear the actual words of conversation over the music.

Jovin and Captain Donald explained their decision; Baron Von Lorian peered out the window and interjected once to remind everyone that Simport had been warned of their arrival. Jovin ended his explanation with: "We're leaving tonight, and that's that."

"Alright, I'm on board," Conrad agreed as he reclined in his chair.

"Quite literally," Saphir jested. "Get it, because *airship*... and..." she giggled, "because the *Alexandria* is an airship and you can be *on board*..." she looked around at the unamused faces. "Oh, come on, I'm just trying to lighten the atmosphere."

"Back on topic," Jovin said, breaking the tension. "We need to get out of here."

"What changed your mind on maintaining an alliance with Tavenly?" Charlotte said.

"At the moment, I would rather apologize for a misunderstanding and leave now, rather than fall into a trap set by our own ignorance," Jovin said.

"Shouldn't we at least *try* to talk to the King?" Conrad pointed out. "If he knew the backstory, he might be keen to listen."

"I think this is my fault... everything has gone to dust since you rescued me," Saphir said softly, "you should have sent me away."

"You would have been compromised anywhere else," Jovin said in defense. He turned his attention to the captain. "I think we are running out of time."

"If this is true, it won't be easy to slip out," Conrad observed. "They could be expecting an irrational form of escape."

Merik spazzed from where he had been slumped tinkering with Sighter. He suddenly straightened, his eyes alight with excitement, "Disguises?"

Jovin shot him down, "No, Merik."

"I propose that we leave tonight," Donald said, "they will realize it, but if we time it right, they may not catch on until after we have fled."

"Are you expecting them to follow us?" Saphir asked.

"I am uncertain," Donald said. "There is no logical reason to be onboard tonight, especially considering that we arrived merely yesterday. We will be searched for, and it will provoke suspicion if our entire party is seen on the airship docks."

"What argument is there against leaving while the castle is asleep?" Charlotte asked.

"It would be suspicious to be caught sneaking around at any hour of the night," Jovin mused.

"Would it be a bad idea to leave during dinner?" Conrad asked the room. "Everyone would be in the dining room, we could slip out before they are through the second course. Perhaps they would think we are running late."

"Running late *and* borrowing a motorcar for a quick escapade to the far side of town?" Jovin said.

Donald contemplated Conrad's proposal for a moment, tapping a finger on the desk. "It might be better than leaving in the early morning; there would be far less suspicion that way."

"*Or*"—Merik pipped up—"we could leave *right now*," he straightened up in his chair and looked around at his companions. "They wouldn't be expecting it. Why would we leave in the middle of the day? It seems absolutely idiotic while everyone is awake. But the guard is lazy in the afternoon, and we could walk right down to the *Alexandria*."

"If they plan to keep us here, the guard will be on alert and watching for us." Jovin stated. "It will be impossible to get to the *Alexandria* without rousing suspicion, even if we say we are resupplying. And do remember that this situation is not Terrison, we cannot walk to the *Alexandria* from the palace. They have to escort us through town."

"What if we showed the *Alexandria* off? We could make it seem like we're offering a tour this afternoon and use it as reason for our being on board," Saphir suggested.

"What would we do with the hostages once we lifted off?" Conrad asked. "Oh, come on, Saphir; you do realize they would turn into hostages once we left."

Jovin sighed, "Do we really want to engage other people in this?"

"If we go alone, it is too suspicious. We can leave them on shore, but there is no way to get down to the docks without being noticed," Saphir said.

A hesitant knock on the door silenced the room. Captain Donald held up a hand for their party to remain quiet. He walked the floor and opened the door.

"Excuse me, sir," a timid server girl's voice said, "I was requested to give this to Prince Jovin of Canston, but he did not answer the door. Would you know where I might find him?"

"I am on my way to meet him, would you like me to deliver it?" Donald replied.

"If you would like," the girl said. She handed over her parcel, and the door closed on her.

Donald walked back into the room, a fine stationary envelope in his hand.

"You can open it," Jovin said, "it is most likely my response from the King."

Donald read the letter and passed it to Jovin, "This king is losing my respect."

"Do you actually know this man?" Jovin asked Conrad.

Conrad shook his head. "I have never met him. Our father dealt with all of our settlements."

Jovin read the letter aloud, "'*Regret to inform you… Will not meet as of yet… Other matters to attend to.*' Oh, that makes everything better," he muttered sarcastically. "'*However, the Prime Minister has been made aware of your request and could be available to meet in a week.*' Oh really, this is ridiculous. And it's signed by... oh, why did I even ask him?"

Conrad muttered something about antiquated rudeness.

"This is too much… He knew we were coming, yet he has not shown himself. It is disrespectful and tasteless. Therefore, I am concerned for out safety." Jovin gave in. "Who do we trick into helping us get out of here?"

Charlotte and Saphir exchanged a sideways glance, "Saphir, might we be thinking similarly?"

"*Yes.*" Saphir grinned mischievously, "I think it would be very easy to request his company."

Charlotte flushed pink and hid behind her hand.

Merik was beside Jovin, and now whispered, "Remind me never to get on their bad side."

"I'm usually on their bad side; I don't think you should be asking me," Jovin replied in a whisper.

Merik gave Jovin an exasperated look and redirected to Conrad on his left. "Remind me never to get on their bad side," he repeated, hoping that Conrad would.

Conrad regarded the prince with a look that clearly stated his amusement. "I'll try," he said loosely.

Donald spoke, "I assume you are referring to Lord Avery."

"Yes," Saphir stated with confidence.

"I think Jovin and I can rally a few ladies. Any thoughts?" he inquired of Jovin.

Jovin nodded, "Actually, I have one in mind."

"Merik, you will accompany Baron Von Lorian and myself. Plan to arrive at the docks before people start to realize what we are up to," Donald said.

Merik peered up at the captain, "What, do you doubt my ability to charm women?"

"Merik, you're eleven," Jovin pointed out.

"Hey, I'm twelve in a month!" Merik retorted. "And you're only like twenty something!"

"There is a difference."

"I see no difference!" Merik exclaimed in defiance.

"There is most definitely a differ… Wait, do you not know how old I am?"

"Uhhhh… twenty… ish?" Merik guessed. He smiled cheerily in hopes that Jovin would forget about it.

"Merik, you will come with me; it will look less suspicious that way," Donald cut in.

"Everyone, dress warmly, but bring from here only what you *absolutely* need," Donald told the group at large.

"What about weapons?" Jovin asked. "I don't want the girls alone with Lord Avery without defense."

Chapter 36

Green Skies

"And here she is!" Saphir announced, "may I present to you, the beautiful, the spectacular, the awe inspiring, the airship *Alexandria*!" Saphir said, stretching out her arms in presentation.

"Fairly pretty," Lord Avery said, humoring Saphir.

Charlotte removed herself from the motorcar. Her eyes were drawn to the dock house at the far end of the square, and she wondered if they were being watched through the darkened windows. She scanned the dockyard in hopes of witnessing Conrad and Jovin's arrival, but there was no sign of them, only a few dock hands loading a pair of stately battle airships. Further on, a mechanic was yelling profanities at his punks as they worked on a smoking SkyRider.

"And how long have you been aboard?" Lord Avery asked lethargically.

The frigid afternoon was growing steadily colder, and although Saphir and Charlotte had opted for thick woolen overcoats along with gloves and high scarves, they were not without a chill as they began climbing the stairwell that connected to the gangplank. Saphir's eyes darted from the docking braces that securely held the hull of the airship, to the cliff below the dock, where they were mounted into the rock face.

"Probably a week," Charlotte answered, taking the hand Lord Avery offered her and stepping over the fifteen-inch gap between the stairwell and the gangplank.

"We boarded in Terrison and were aloft for a few days before we arrived—was it only yesterday?" Saphir glanced back to check the docks.

"Fascinating," Lord Avery replied sardonically. Following Saphir, they set foot onto the airship's top deck. "Do you find the accommodations comfortable? I have heard that the Canston airship designers have a tendency to under indulge where luxuries are concerned."

"It's lovely," Saphir replied. She glanced from the empty docks to Charlotte. "You know, I think we should start the tour."

"If you insist," Lord Avery said, sounding uninterested.

"Oh yes," Charlotte continued, walking in the direction of the middeck stairwell. "But let us warm up first. I am absolutely shivered." She held out her hand to Lord Avery, "Come. Tea first, then the tour."

+++++

From the landing outside of the wheelhouse, Mister Carter watched Lord Avery take Charlotte's hand. Then the three descended the middeck stairwell. Carter trotted inside and called to the kitchens over the intercom.

"*The kitchens. How can we be of assistance?*"

"Damn it, Goodwin, you sound like a bank teller," Carter chided the cook's assistant.

"*Sorry, sir,*" Ryan Goodwin replied.

"Anyway," Carter continued, "tell Chef Mason that our two princesses and a Simport nobleman are on their way down to have a cup of tea. Keep an eye on them. I don't like the look of this guy."

"*Yes sir,*" Goodwin said, "*any word from the Captain yet?*"

"He has just arrived with Merik and Baron Von Lorian," Carter said as the three figures walked across the gravel road from a motorcar parked at the gate. "I have seen nothing of Jovin or Conrad yet."

"*The princesses and the nobleman are here,*" Goodwin whispered. And with that, he hung up.

+++++

Lord Avery cast his lazy gaze around the greenhouse. The high glass stern windows bloomed light over the plants and gave an excellent view of the town. "I suppose this airship *is* rather charming... in a homely sort of way."

Charlotte's heeled boots clicked on the tiled floor as she approached the glass wall. Through a side window she observed a motorcar pull up to the gangway, and four familiar figures rambled out of it. She felt her anxiety lessen. "I like it," Charlotte said with a placid smile on her face. Her tolerance for this snotty man had expired long ago. "It makes me happy."

Lord Avery persisted in an uninterested manner, "Of course, you will be going back to Terrison shortly; and you, back to Ee'lin," he directed the last statement to Saphir, who was sitting on a cushioned bench along the starboard wall.

Saphir answered before Charlotte had a chance to, "Yes, I should say so."

Lord Avery took one sweeping glance around the room and made for the door. "I am done with the tour. Let us go back to the castle."

"Let's wait a moment," Saphir feared that he had heard the desperation in her tone, and backtracked. "I mean, you haven't yet seen the ballroom, it's rather pretty, and..."

From behind Lord Avery, Charlotte was staring in dread at Saphir. She mouthed: *"ballroom?"* with every emotion Saphir was currently feeling: panic, frustration, and the need to continue stalling until the rest of their company arrived. Charlotte mouthed something else: *"We do not have a ballroom!"* but Saphir decided staring at Charlotte in an attempt to decipher what she way saying came across as suspicious.

"Ballroom?" Lord Avery sounded skeptical, but he was paying attention to Saphir, which meant that he had currently given up on leaving.

"Oh yes," Saphir went on.

Charlotte gave in to Saphir's fib. "It is rather..."

"Grand," Saphir covered, "it's very grand. You should come see," she began walking to the starboard door, followed closely by Lord Avery and Charlotte. "It's on the sixth level," Saphir went on. "We're on level one right now, but I think you'll like it, it takes up an entire deck!" She kept up her lie, and soon they were descending the hidden staircase.

A few minutes later, they emerged into the sixth-level landing. The light that shone through the small, high-set windows was pale and made the entire level feel eerie and lonesome. The plasma cannons lining the walls, and the additional passenger cabins in the prow left most of the floor bare.

Saphir walked into the room, her footfalls sounded with a hollow echo. "Here we are," she announced. Her voice seemed altogether too loud for the abandoned deck.

Lord Avery laughed. The sound reverberated throughout the room. "And you actually use this place? It's complete rubbish."

Charlotte stepped up beside Lord Avery, her hands in her overcoat pockets, an innocent, wide-eyed expression on her face. "Oh, I like it, it reminds me of something," she said airily.

"And what's that, a graveyard?" Lord Avery asked dryly, taking a few steps away from her and out into the middle of the floor.

+++++

Miss Olivia Twill and Miss Meggan Rose gave simpering laughs as they stepped aboard the *Alexandria*.

"Oh, what a delight!" Miss Twill exclaimed. She took Jovin's outstretched hand, and Miss Rose took Conrad's.

As it turned out, asking the two girls to accompany them to the *Alexandria* was far easier than Jovin or Conrad had expected. Miss Olivia Twill was the daughter of the prime minister of Simport, and Miss Meggan Rose was a longtime family friend of the Twills, and they were delighted to be in the presence of the princes.

Captain Donald came to meet them, looking very dignified for a person who was using the two ladies to ensure the airship's freedom. "Welcome," he said, bowing to them and smiling amiably. "I am Captain Donald. Pleased to meet the pair of you."

The ladies curtsied in the Tavenly manner, with their heads to their right shoulders and their hands over their hearts.

"Olivia Twill,"

"Meggan Rose,"

Donald nodded to each. "Would you care for a cup of tea? Then we can show you around if you would like." He held out an arm to each of the ladies, who let go of their princes' arms to take the Captain's. Donald started up a conversation based on complimenting each lady in turn, and continued to lead them away while the two prattled and twittered.

Jovin and Conrad exchanged a look.

"I think we just got out-charmed," Conrad said.

Jovin raised his eyebrows, "Yeah..."

On the landing outside the doors, Conrad held Jovin back. "Do you think the girls are on board?"

"I don't know, but let's wait to be worried,"

+++++

Beep! Beep! Beep!

A high-pitched alarm sounded three times. There was a scuffle from above, and the muffled sound of the engines roared to life.

"I understand now," Lord Avery mused, walking to a small window and peering out. "Seems to me that everyone has arrived."

Charlotte and Saphir exchanged a petrified glance. Neither had planned this far.

"You thought I was clueless enough to let your feeble escape plan go over my head, didn't you?" Lord Avery said, turning on them.

Saphir tilted her head to one side, "I'm sorry?"

"Your chef and his assistant are both on board? So is the rest of your ragamuffin crew," Lord Avery said. "If *I* had been traveling for a while, *I* would want to get out, stretch my legs, go and see the town, not stay on board." His eyes darted between the two, searching for a fault, displaying both irritation and amusement simultaneously. "But *you* forget that other people observe things also; blindness is not an attribute I associate with. *You* have lured me down here, to the second-to-last level on your airship. You have also done this at a time when most servants have the afternoon off."

Charlotte folded her hands. "I do not understand where you are going with this."

Lord Avery began pacing the floor, his tone was slipping into frenzy. "It is a pretty airship, but still, why would the two of you bring me here in the late afternoon, when everyone in the palace has their guard down, just to show me your *pretty floating house?*"

Saphir flushed. "Because we like our *pretty floating house* and we wanted to show it off."

Lord Avery ignored her words. "If the pair of you cannot stand me, why, then, am I here?" he demanded.

Charlotte did not reply. She stared back at him and put her hands back into her pockets.

"You let too many things slip," Lord Avery went on. "Jovin made an obvious attempt to gather the two of you earlier, had he been more discrete, he would not have given you away."

Neither princess spoke. Saphir toyed with an alibi, and Charlotte kept her eyes fixed on Lord Avery.

"Ah, see? You are stalling," Lord Avery concluded. "But I doubt you would mind very much if I left? I don't have the patience to stay here while you try to kidnap me."

He made to walk back to the stairwell, but Saphir ran forward, placing a hand on his arm. She tried to keep an amused tone to her voice. "We're not trying to kidnap you; they only turned on the engines. They do that from time to time to keep—"

In a motion that caught Saphir off guard, Avery twisted her arm behind her back and clamped another over her mouth. "Princess, you should know better than to keep playing when you are found cheating at your own game." To Charlotte he said, "Would you walk ahead of us? I don't really want to give you a chance to club me over the head, and you would be so pretty leading our procession."

Charlotte stared him in the eye. "No, I would rather not," she spoke bravely.

"You think you're funny," Avery sneered. "No, but really, get a move on."

+++++

Merik burst into the captain's cabin. "We gotta go—*now!*" he shouted.

Miss Olivia Twill and Miss Meggan Rose gawked in confusion. Their nonsensical conversation with Jovin, Conrad, Captain Donald, and Baron Von Lorian fell with the lowering of their teacups.

Donald sprang to his feet, and without excusing himself, ran from the cabin up the stairs to the wheelhouse before anyone could react.

Jovin and Conrad followed suit and trotted after Donald.

"Merik, keep them company," Jovin called back over his shoulder.

"What? But—" Merik was cut off by the door slamming behind them.

"What is going on?" Miss Twill asked anxiously of Merik. She looked around at the Baron, who had paled and melted into his seat.

Merik blanched. "We're... uh... Just stay here and don't ask questions, because I don't like lying."

+++++

Avery's hand clamped over Saphir's mouth tasted of dust and sweat. She had deliberated fighting him off, but ultimately decided that it was wiser to wait for Charlotte's reaction before trying to force her way out of his grip.

Charlotte stared determinedly back at Avery, barely blinking while her hands remained thrust into her overcoat pockets. At length, she took a breath and spoke in an even tone, "Please let Saphir go."

Avery contemplated her. "Asking nicely. You would do that, wouldn't you, Charlotte?"

"Yes, of course, a lot can be gained by asking nicely. And now, I really would prefer you let her go." Charlotte's expression was not swayed. "Because the reality is, there is a whole deck of crewmen right above us, and *dragging* Saphir up six flights of stairs, *kicking and screaming*, will probably attract some attention."

"You're bluffing. Get moving." Avery commanded.

"*No.*" Charlotte said, standing her ground.

Confusion grew on Avery's face. "You're not supposed to do that. You're the docile one."

"Am I?" Charlotte kept her tone level so he would not target her for weakness. "And who told you that?"

Avery took a step back, dragging Saphir with him. He changed tactics: "No one will believe a high-minded princess. They will all think you're whining for attention, because you love drama, you *crave* it—well, here's the reality that you should get used to: no one will listen to you. My word will always win over yours."

Charlotte straightened. "What you are attempting to do is wrong. Regardless of who will believe me, we all know the truth of the situation. *I will not stand for it.* So, please, *let Saphir go.*" Charlotte spoke with confidence, and for Avery, who was not accustomed to any sort of backlash, it was terrifying.

Avery jerked Saphir back a step, keeping his focus on Charlotte. She could almost see the gears of his brain turning behind his wary expression.

Saphir took their standoff as an opportunity to elbow Avery in the ribs with her unrestrained arm. Taken by surprise, Avery was slow to react. Saphir pried his hand off her mouth, grabbed his wrist, and yanked down until his elbow locked; then she quickly tugged his locked arm forward, and he was sent staggering past them.

Avery regained his feet and rubbed his ribs where Saphir's elbow had hit him. He grimaced at her. "Oh yes, very princessy indeed. *You*——"

Avery darted after her. He took a firm grip on her wrist and forcibly pulled her to him, catching up a handful of her hair. "Who do you think you are? Hmm?" he yanked her head back. "You are nothing in the long run—a shadow."

Saphir yelped, thrashing against his grip, "Let go of me! *Let go!*"

"I have spent far too much time improving my status in the eyes of royalty. I have groveled and flattered my way to where I am now. Soon you won't matter, your ridiculous birthright will mean nothing." Avery began dragging her to the staircase. "I hope they let you live long enough to see the ruins of Ee'lin be consumed by the sea."

A sharp *click* made him stop dead in his tracks.

"*Let go of her.*"

Avery spun and came eye to eye with the end of a pistol. "What the hell are you doing, Charlotte?"

"*Let go of Saphir,*" Charlotte repeated.

Avery's face lit up with concern for his own life. He released Saphir, who staggered away to stand beside Charlotte, and took her own pistol from inside the pocket of her coat.

"I might sit if I were you," Charlotte suggested.

Avery moved to the floor and slowly put up his hands in mockery.

+++++

"They've tightened the braces, and we're latched in," Mister Carter relayed the moment Captain Donald entered the wheelhouse. "Unless we get the braces loosened, we're stuck."

Jovin and Conrad came stumbling into the wheelhouse after the captain.

"What's going on?" Jovin demanded.

"We are trapped in the docking braces," Mister Carter answered.

"Then unlock them!" Jovin exclaimed.

"We can't. They have to be unlocked from the shore," Carter replied shortly.

"Then how did you get out of Terrison?" Conrad asked.

"I released the braces manually in the docking house," Donald told him.

Jovin took in the concealed franticness of the men around him. "Was all this for nothing then?"

"The braces hold the hull together like a clamp, right?" Conrad said, thinking aloud. "Well, what about the hinges? What if we damage the hinges and the support that's attached to the cliffside? The braces might fall off once the hinges are loosened."

"That won't work," McCoy said frantically.

"It might," Carter countered. "The braces are attached under the dock."

"Fire into the cliffside. We condemn ourselves otherwise," Donald ordered. "Aim the cannons on the fifth and sixth levels into the cliff. If we do not hit the hinges, maybe we can dislodge enough earth to cause the automatic lock to malfunction. Prepare a volley of eight."

"On it!" Carter shouted.

Mister McCoy set to work preparing the cannons. "Ready, Captain!"

A magnified voice came from the port house. It was loud enough that the men in the wheelhouse could hear every word clearly. "*Occupants of the Canston airship* Alexandria, *we request complete surrender under orders of King Phlurus. Turn over the royalty, the captain, and the prisoners you have stolen. You will be guaranteed an audience with the King, who will determine your sentence. It is not an option to refuse.*"

"Captain," Conrad pointed to a large group of soldiers who were filing in from the dock house and gathering around their slip. Their guns were aimed at the airship, and a few were shouting as they prepared to climb the gangway. "They're either going to shoot or board us," Conrad announced.

"But they want us alive; they won't shoot," Jovin said.

"They look a little trigger happy to me," Conrad muttered under his breath.

"Hold fire," Donald commanded, moving to the starboard window.

Carter watched with apprehension. "Captain, orders?"

Donald turned back to his men. "On my command, fire. Then get us away as fast as you can. Jovin, Conrad, find Charlotte and Saphir, then get everyone into my cabin and stay there."

"Yes sir," Conrad said.

"What about Miss Rose and Twill?" Jovin asked.

"We will have to send them back another way. Right now they are not our focus," Donald held him back by the arm. "Jovin, there is more to this than what we see. Safeguard your company."

Jovin clasped the captain on the back, "I will." He and Conrad passed through the door and trotted down the stairs, aware that the Simport soldiers were watching them from the land.

"Where are Charlotte and Saphir?" Conrad asked Merik as they entered Donald's cabin and looked around at the petrified faces.

Merik was frantic, "I don't know, they're not here."

"Your Highnesses, you tricked us," Miss Twill stated in irritation. She and Miss Rose looked rather peeved.

"*Shh!*" Merik said with vigor. "We're not talking to you." He turned back to Jovin and Conrad, "I haven't seen either of them."

"Are they on board?" Jovin clarified.

Baron Von Lorian looked as though he was going to be sick. "Mister Carter said they came aboard with Lord Avery about half an hour ago,"

Jovin departed to the concealed staircase. "We need to find them," he motioned to Conrad to follow him but held up a hand to Merik. "Stay here and keep an eye on those two."

Merik exasperated, "But—"

"Stay here," Jovin ordered.

+++++

Avery had relaxed into a loll, leaning against his wrists and looking rather bored with the situation. "If you're not going to shoot me, at least make me feel like I've done something wrong. At the moment, the pair of you are anything but threatening."

For good measure, Saphir shot a spot three feet from his leg, leaving a plasma scorch in the polished wood flooring. "Shut up," she hissed.

"Not very princessy. You and Charlotte should start a club: *'The People Who've Been Brought Up Well and Become Turncoats'*. I think you might attract members rather quickly; just don't tell them you've got guns."

Saphir knit her eyebrows. "If anyone should start anything, it is you; you should start by dropping your false confidence and keeping your words to a minimum."

Avery's eyes refrained from meeting hers. "Fine, I'll just be quiet then."

Saphir moved closer to Charlotte, keeping her gun aimed at Avery. "What do you think is going on?" she whispered.

Charlotte cast a glace around the sixth level. The sun light coming in through the windows had faded considerably since their arrival, and a large portion of the floor was in the shadow of the cliff. Unless a light was switched on soon, it would be too dark to see clearly. Charlotte and Saphir were hesitant to move too far from each other for the fear that Avery might try something again.

"I think Captain Donald is a smart man and a good leader, and I trust him. I also trust that we will get out of this," Charlotte affirmed.

"I just wish we knew where everyone is." Saphir walked back to her earlier floor space.

Avery decided to press the boundaries. "They are probably all dead," he mused quietly.

"If you are going to speak, speak so you are heard," Saphir reprimanded.

"I *said* that your people are probably dead or dying because of your stupidity. What was there to be gained by setting your life into this folly of danger? You should have died along with your dearest mother and burned with the simpleton stretch of land you call a country."

"You are in no position to speak," Charlotte told Avery. She placed a hand on Saphir's arm to keep her from pouncing on the infuriating man. "Go back to your silence; it suits you better."

Avery shifted from leaning on his hands and made to get up. "Mind if I stand with you?"

"I would rather you stay seated," Charlotte replied.

He was up now, dusting off his coat. "Yes, but you see, I've been sitting for a while now, and I don't much care for—"

"*Sit,*" Saphir commanded.

"I don't really—"

Charlotte's gun was level with Avery's face. "I will shoot you, and I will not care what becomes of it."

Avery did not move. "You won't."

Charlotte's shot fell inches from Avery's foot, scorching the wood again.

He took a small step back. "That's the second time I've been shot at! What kind of—"

"*Sit down.*"

Avery sat.

+++++

"Hold," Captain Donald told Mister Carter, who was waiting to fire the starboard cannons into the side of the cliff face.

"How much longer can we wait?" Carter asked. His fingers were itching to press the cannon fire button. "We're going on ten minutes; they probably realize we're stalling."

"Hold for another moment," Donald told him. "I want them to think we are not moving."

"How much longer will that be?" McCoy asked as he looked out the window. "If we don't move soon, they're going to board us."

"You don't want that, do you, Captain?" Carter asked.

Donald was silent for a moment. "No,"

Mister Carter cleared his throat. "What are we waiting for, then? They are making to board, Captain,"

Donald watched the men on the landing dock, mentally marking their actions. The soldiers congregated at the gangplank as an officer moved forward to study the *Alexandria*.

"Hold," Donald held up his hand, "wait another moment."

The soldiers steadied the gangplank as the Simport officer set one foot on the stairwell.

"Carter, get ready." Donald silently counted to three. "And… *Now*," Donald commanded.

The starboard cannons fired, blasting beams of plasma into the cliff face. Chunks of rock flaked away, leaving the embedded braces exposed from their hiding place and vulnerable to the next volley.

The men on land shouted and retreated back to the safety of the port house as cascades of rock fell away from the cliff. The officer shouted to his men to stand their ground.

McCoy engaged the engines, steering the airship away from the cliff. The *Alexandria* jolted sideways as the force of the volley shot into the side of the cliff. Another cannon volley fired.

The *Alexandria*'s angle strained the beams and exhausted the hinges. Cannon fire blasted into the rock, causing an avalanche underneath the dock. The airship was still captive in the braces, slanting away from the cliff. Her passengers were knocked off balance; some fell and rolled across the floor to bump into furniture, while others were thrown into walls.

The three men in the wheelhouse were knocked sideways by the sudden angle of the deck. Mister Carter bashed his head against the edge of the control table. They desperately tried to regain their feet. The engines roared as the airship tried to right herself and cannons continued to fire.

"*Hold fire!*" Captain Donald shouted to Carter. Another cannon blast made contact with the dock, scattering the soldiers and leaving the dock in a shamble of rubble. The *Alexandria* slid again, and the cannon fire shot into the air above the airship yard.

"I said hold fire!"

"I'm trying! We'll rip the hull and disconnect from the balloon if we keep this up!" Carter shot back, wiping blood off his forehead.

McCoy stumbled over to Carter. "What's your mother's maiden name?"

"Uh, Jeannette."

"How many fingers am I holding up?" McCoy held up his hand.

"Two," Carter answered. "My head's fine— we're gonna fall out of the braces for crying out loud!"

McCoy ignored him. "If you had a choice between dying for a noble cause and living forever, which would you pick?"

"*What the hell is the point—*"

McCoy cut him off, shaking his shoulders. *"Answer the damn question, Lewis!"*

"Get off me!" Carter threatened. "I'll die when I'm good and ready, and not a moment before, but you're looking for a landing without a chute," he pulled himself back into his chair and furiously disengaged the cannons. "*Captain?*" he was scarcely heard as the stabilizers engaged and the engines exerted in a massive effort to right the slanting deck.

Captain Donald held on to the main console to keep balanced. "Hold fire. Release the next volley when we are level," he ordered.

"Holding." Carter was wiping at the gash in his head with his sleeve, the blue cloth was steadily becoming a bloody mess.

"McCoy, get us out as soon as the hinges giveway."

"Come on, come on, come on…" Carter muttered to himself while the slanting of the deck gradually righted. "We're stable!" Carter took a nod from the captain. "Three… two…"

The cannons fired.

The braces were weakening. The engines screamed, but the hinges held, and the roar of the engines reverberated throughout the airship.

"That can't be good," McCoy murmured to himself.

"Try to get us moving," Donald ordered. The soldiers on land were recovering from their initial shock and were beginning to regroup nearer to their slip. "They will engage as soon as they think—"

There was another jolt to the airship as the hinges snapped.

"We're out!" Carter whooped.

The *Alexandria* floated free for a moment, rocking under the balloon, then came back to collide abrasively against the cliff.

"McCoy, get us out of here!" Donald looked out the window, then pressed the intercom to the engine rooms. "Engines, this is your Captain. Status report?"

McCoy was turning cranks and pressing buttons, engaging the engines, and desperately trying to get them away from the cliff.

"*We're fine,*" an engineer's gruff voice answered. "*The engines are strained, but it looks like the parts from Tinseenwell are holding for the moment—still nowhere near full power though. And Captain, those soldiers shot through a window or two.*"

Mister Carter swore colorfully and pounded a fist on the control board.

"Go into lockdown," Donald said. He turned back to the room, "McCoy, get us moving."

McCoy tapped the controls. "I'm trying to. The braces are still attached to the hull and are weighing us down. I have to adjust the weight and the level—"

The amplified voice boomed out again. "*Occupants of the Canston airship* Alexandria, *you have broken our trust. If you try to flee, we have no choice but to attack. Stay where you are. You will be boarded and held in contempt. This is your final chance to surrender.*"

"*McCoy, get us out of here!*" Donald commanded.

"I'm trying!" McCoy shouted back. "The stabilizers aren't… wait…" McCoy started muttering to himself, calculating the weight of the braces with the buoyancy factor to configure forward propulsion. "Carter, put the stabilizers on manual."

"No! That's ridiculous!" Carter shouted as he switched the stabilizers to manual.

"Got it!" McCoy exclaimed.

The *Alexandria* lurched sideways.

+++++

Saphir wobbled as she regained her feet. In the confusion of the cannon fire, and being thrown sideways, she had lost hold of her gun and the heel of her boot was tangled in the skirt of her dress.

Avery was already on his feet. He spotted Saphir's gun where it had slid astern of the port wall and was running after it.

Saphir scrambled forward and grabbed Avery's ankle. He kicked out his leg, and his foot collided with the side of her head. She grunted, blinking in shock, and released his ankle. Avery ignored her and ran to reach the gun.

With a cry of pain, Avery lurched and fell, clutching his leg.

Charlotte huffed, picking herself up off the ground, *"I have had it with you."* She stumbled across the floor to where Avery was writhing. She leveled her gun to his chest. "If you so much as utter the slightest sound—"

"*You shot me!*" Avery screamed.

"Damn right she shot you," Saphir was up holding her head and struggling to stay balanced. She retrieved her lost gun. "And I think it's my turn to shoot you now,"

Avery let out a small whimper and clutched his leg.

"What the hell is going on down here?" Jovin came bounding down the stairs. He took three steps into the room, assessed the situation, and threw back his head in laughter. "What did you do, lure him down here then shoot him?" he asked, coming to meet them.

"*What?*" she demanded of him.

"Nothing," he said. Jovin's smile dropped from his face. "Are you all right?"

Saphir took a shaky breath. "I'm fine. I'll be fine."

Jovin trotted back to the stairwell. "Conrad, I found them!" he shouted to the upper level.

Conrad's stomping footsteps sounded from above as he came stumbling down the stairs. His eyes swept over the scene: Saphir clutching her head, Charlotte with a pointed pistol standing feet from the now cowering Avery, who had murder in his eyes.

Unlike Jovin, Conrad did not find the situation comical. Conrad walked to his sister and embraced her.

"We should get everyone upstairs," Jovin said, joining them.

Avery began scooting away, hoping to escape unnoticed. He let out another whimper of pain.

"Is there anything you would like to say?" Conrad inquired, stepping between his sister and Avery.

Avery strained to sit up as he held on to his injured leg, his face contorted as though he had tasted something extremely bitter. "No," he said through gritted teeth.

"Well then," Conrad scooped Avery up by the front of his shirt, making the man stand on his good leg. "How about an apology?"

Avery set his jaw and scowled at Conrad, then Jovin. "I will not apologize to them!" and he spat at the princesses.

Conrad dragged Avery forward, and the man grunted in pain.

"And why not?" Jovin asked, his temper rising.

"They are not worthy of apologies; they are nothing but deceiving creatures with petty lies and simple tricks," Avery jeered.

Saphir recoiled.

"You are in a bad situation right now, Lord Avery. I would advise you to stop talking," Charlotte said, bracing Saphir's shoulders to steady her.

Avery turned furious. He chided Charlotte, "You're nothing but worthless, lying, stupid, weak little—"

Charlotte pulled Saphir back just in time before Jovin's fist hit Avery across the jaw. He fell with a *thud* at their feet.

Saphir made a sound of disgust, and Charlotte gripped her hand.

Avery began sitting up, gawking and cursing in furry. His jaw was starting to turn red, but he stayed where he was, trying to stem the flow of blood coming from his leg.

"Let's go," Jovin said, herding his companions to the staircase.

"Do you think we're out of the—" the floor lurched from under them, cutting Conrad off. They went staggering again.

"Get up to Donald's cabin," Jovin instructed, "Conrad, give me your necktie." Jovin took off his tie and motioned to Conrad to do likewise. He trotted back to where Avery was watching them from the floor. "Stay down," Jovin tied Avery's hands behind his back, bound his ankles with the ties, and rolled him onto his stomach so he would have a harder time escaping. He ignored Avery's grunt of pain and the blood staining the floor. He rose and jogged to the stairwell in the stern, where Conrad was waiting for him, having made Charlotte and Saphir go first.

"Well, that's done," Conrad sounded relieved. He motioned to Avery's hogtied form, "At least he'll be down here for a while, but with that leg, I doubt he'll want to move anywhere."

"Maybe," Jovin started up the stairs, Conrad following. "How long were they down there? The girls looked rather uncomfortable when I found them."

"Charlotte had just shot a man and Saphir had to watch. Did you see the bruise on her head? I doubt they felt at home," Conrad said. "Charlotte usually doesn't shoot people."

Jovin ran up the stairs to the first level to where Charlotte and Saphir were waiting. The two of them had the same nervous, quiet energy about them. They huddled close together as though someone would try to snatch one of them away.

"What's been going on?" Saphir asked when Jovin and Conrad were before them.

"We're supposed to be escaping… Hopefully we are out by now," Conrad said, moving to peer out a side window. "Actually, um, we're still getting out."

The three joined him at the window.

On the port side of the *Alexandria*, another airship was poised, ready to give chase. They were close enough to see the airship's exposed rows of cannons, smoke rising slowly into the air. The crew was scurrying about on deck, passing weapons to each other and preparing to board the *Alexandria*.

"We're not even close to freedom," Saphir breathed.

"Alright, get upstairs," Jovin said, opening the door to the concealed staircase that led to Donald's cabin.

Saphir looked confused. "You are coming, right?" she asked him. Charlotte was already hurrying up the stairs.

"I'll be up shortly," Jovin told her.

Saphir hesitated for a moment, but followed after Charlotte.

Jovin held Conrad back, "We can't leave him down there,"

"Do we care?" Conrad asked.

"I have the feeling that if he's left alone too long, our trouble will increase," Jovin said.

Chapter 37

A New Ally

"We're going to crash…" Mister Carter whispered.

Two Simport airships, the *SunDance* and the *Veronica,* were blocking their flight path now; their sides were leveled to the *Alexandria*, their cannons exposed and aimed at the Canston airship, mocking, as they barred her from her freedom.

"They're going to fire on us," Mister Carter said to himself. "They're going to shoot us out of the sky…"

"*Captain!*" McCoy warned, "the engines are at half capacity!"

Donald looked between his two most trusted crewmen. "We may have to fight. If they attack, we will return their fire, but only if we must. We are worth too much to go down today."

His men nodded in solemn understanding. "We're with you, Captain," Carter said.

The *SunDance* and the *Veronica's* cannons blazed as they sent a warning volley at the *Alexandria*. McCoy turned in his seat to see the blasts hit the docked airship behind them. "They're reckless..."

Donald pressed the intercom button to the Captain's cabin, "Jovin, is everyone there? Jovin, answer."

"Shouldn't he have found them by now?" Carter asked.

"He should have," Donald said. He called through the intercom again, "Wallace, can you confirm that the princesses are safe?"

The airship lurched as McCoy manually fought to keep them level. The *SunDance* and the *Veronica* were angling to block the mouth of the port, and the only exit. The rest of the port was blocked off by the high walls that kept the outside winds at bay. The *Alexandria* was running out of airspace, and by the time they could come to a halt, they would have long since crashed into the opposing airships.

At his station, Mister Carter was swearing as though it would save him from the gates of hell.

"Hush, Carter," Donald said calmly as he took in the situation. "McCoy, angle us up."

"Sir," McCoy replied to his order.

"Captain, we won't make it, the braces are weighing us down and there's not enough space to clear them." Carter pointed out.

The intercom speaker came to life. "*Captain, the princesses are here, but Prince Conrad and Prince Jovin are not,*" Baron Von Lorian said, "*Merik is trying to keep the two ladies we brought aboard subdued, but they are nervous and becoming agitated.*"

"Where are Jovin and Conrad now?" Donald queried.

A scuffle was heard, and Saphir replaced the Baron over the intercom. "*They are on level six attending to Lord Avery.*"

"Thank you, Saphir. Stay where you are," Donald told her.

"They're brave little boys, but they don't think things through," Carter groused.

Donald ignored this remark and tried to reach Jovin and Conrad again, "Jovin, if you are going down to the lower levels, the intercom box is near the stern on the starboard wall. The oxygen masks are located in the bow, beside the washrooms. Respond."

"What about the air masks?" Carter questioned.

"Report from the engine rooms: we're at half capacity." McCoy relayed.

"When clear, go quickly. Head northwest. Mister Carter, when we are in the open sky, I give you permission to fire the cannons for defense," Donald said.

"Captain, we won't clear them unless the braces fall." Carter insisted.

The captain ignored this remark.

Jovin's hurried voice came over the intercom, *"Captain. Lord Avery is down on the sixth level with an injured leg and an injured ego, what do we do with him?"*

"Put an oxygen mask on him and leave him there. Then get back up to the others," Donald advised.

"*Will do,*" Jovin said. "*What's going on?*"

"We are still in a situation," Donald said.

"*Captain?*" Carter called.

Donald turned his attention from the intercom back to the two airships blocking their path. "McCoy?"

"The stabilizers are having a hard time readjusting when the braces move. They're just too bulky. We need them to fall soon, and preferably before we fly over any cities." McCoy said, scrambling over the control panel.

"What is beneath us now?"

"Rocks, maybe a few sheep," McCoy answered.

Donald weighed his options. "Engage High Elevation Protocol. Steer away from the city. Get us out of immediate danger."

Carter made to protest. "But Captain, the docking braces… The stabilizers won't—"

"As long as we are somewhat upright, we cannot care about the braces. Get us out of here."

McCoy nodded. "Yes sir," he engaged the engine.

The *Alexandria* lurched forward, still on a collision course with the two Simport airships. Donald detected McCoy's hesitation. "Start our ascent," Donald commanded, "Mister Carter, prepare the cannons for defense for when they follow us."

Carter began prepping the cannons. "I thought you weren't one to shoot people out of the sky?"

"Your backtalk has become irritating," Donald said. He switched his focus back to McCoy, "Can you get us out without colliding?"

McCoy let out a small squeak of panic. "Possibly… It will be close, but yes, I think so."

"Then make it close, just get us out."

The *Alexandria* rocked violently. Donald gripped the console to keep his balance. McCoy slipped sideways off his chair.

"*The braces are slipping!*" McCoy shouted.

"They'd better not be tearing up the windows," Carter said.

"Lock down on all doors and windows," Donald ordered. "Send out the alert for immediate ascent, announce it in the engine rooms. McCoy, status?"

They were gradually nearing the *SunDance* and the *Veronica*. "They're too close together. If we don't hit them, they'll hit each other," McCoy calculated. "It will be difficult for them to turn and chase us quickly. We'll have a lead of probably… five minutes."

"All levels are going into lockdown," Carter reported.

+++++

"What does the red light mean?" Charlotte clutched at Saphir's arm.

Saphir blanched. "Uh, Merik?"

A sheet of metal slunk soundlessly across the window wall and plunged the room into a lamp lit dimness. Merik paled. "It means we're preparing to fly into really high altitudes. They're locking down the windows in case any are broken."

Baron Von Lorian was trying to subdue the two hostages who were threatening to run out on deck and jump over the sides. "Now, please stay calm. We are going to return you as soon as we have a chance, please stay cal—"

Miss Olivia Twill slapped him across the face. "We have been taken hostage. We are all in very real danger because you weren't gutsy enough to hand yourself over!" she jabbed a finger at the Baron, "so don't you tell me what to do. I'll stay calm if I want to. Or maybe I'll just *scream*—and *keep screaming* until you release us!"

Charlotte gently patted the Baron's arm to get him out of the way. To Miss Twill and Rose, she spoke softly, "We plan to release you as soon as possible. It was not intended that you should be in any danger. We plan to see you to safety as soon as we are able."

Charlotte's words seemed to have a slight effect on Miss Twill. Her face remained sour, but she departed to perch on the sofa without another word.

Miss Rose stayed beside Charlotte. Her voice came out as a breathless declaration of her fear, "This is far more than we bargained for. I would prefer it if we contacted someone to see us safely aboard another airship."

"I would agree with you," Charlotte said, "if not for the airships that plan to shoot us out of the sky. There will be no negotiations if we are all dead." Charlotte said curtly. "If you have any influence to call off the attack, now is the best time to voice it."

Miss Twill rose abruptly from the sofa. "My father is the Prime Minister, I think I might have some influence."

"Then there may be a hope that everyone will come out of this unharmed," Charlotte said.

Merik called the wheelhouse from Donald's desk, "Captain?"

There was static, then Donald's voice, *"Merik?"*

"The ladies we took from Simport might be able to help us get out of here alive," Merik relayed.

Miss Twill walked over to the intercom. "My father is the Prime Minister; I will be able to call off the attack."

"If you would like to try, that would be ever so helpful," Donald replied. *"Merik, do you know how to contact the Simport castle from my desk?"*

"Uh, no."

"Bring her up to the wheelhouse," Donald said.

"Have we started rising yet?" Merik queried. His eyes flicked to the red light above the door.

"No, but we will any moment unless we are freed," Donald said.

"She'll be up shortly," Merik turned to Miss Twill. "Come on."

Miss Twill stalled in a brave attempt at defiance. She turned to Miss Rose, "Well, now I'm a traitor."

"Remember that we need you." Charlotte gently took up Miss Twill's arm as though they were longtime friends and led her to the hidden staircase at the front of the cabin. Charlotte glanced over her shoulder to Miss Rose, who was hesitating beside Merik. "Come along, you," she called to her. Miss Rose scampered up the stairs after them.

Chapter 38

An Impolite Face Card

Miss Twill wrung her hands as her attention flitted between Charlotte and Captain Donald. The wheelhouse was quiet enough that she could hear the frantic breathing of Miss Rose as she clung to her arm in quiet dejection.

"*Canston airship* Alexandria, *we have lost patience, surrender and relinquish our people.*"

Captain Donald gave her a slight nod.

Miss Twill took a breath and approached the microphone, "This is Olivia Twill, daughter of Prime Minister Belart Twill. I am aboard the Canston airship *Alexandria* with Meggan Rose. We voluntarily came aboard and are still aboard. Meggan and I have not been harmed, and I am in doubt that we will be by the occupants of the *Alexandria*; however, I do not have the same hope from my own people. I hope that the people of Simport have enough grace about them to release this airship without threatening murder."

"*You are unharmed?*" the voice on the other line asked.

"Yes, well, not yet anyway," Miss Twill confirmed.

"*And you say all this freely; they did not forced it on you?*"

"I volunteered to negotiate," Miss Twill said.

"*I see,*" the voice replied.

There was a pause.

"*Who else is there?"* the man on the line asked.

Donald exchanged a look with Charlotte: *They did not believe her.*

Charlotte pointed to herself and raised her eyebrows.

Donald nodded.

Charlotte stepped up to the microphone. "Excuse me. Thank you for trying," she said to Miss Twill. Charlotte took her place. "This is Princess Charlotte Luna Mimzy Goldwele of Terrison. My brother Prince Conrad and I, along with Prince Jovin and Prince Merik of Canston, and the fellow Princess Saphir of Ee'lin are aboard the *Alexandria*. Cease fire. You threaten the *Alexandria*, and we consider it a *very definite* threat on our lives. We have been ignored for two days by your king after multiple requests of an audience, fired upon, pursued, and made to be political prisoners during our stay in Simport. You are in a very bad position. As far as I am concerned, I will no longer be affiliated with Tavenly unless the attitude toward our party changes *immediately*. We have every right to leave, and your rejection of our free desire not only sullies the trust between Terrison and Tavenly, but also violates the contract we have held for over eighty years. In said contract it states that '*a diplomatic party has the right to abandon foreign ground if the receiving party is unwelcoming, or if the diplomatic party feels endangered.*' By our contract, we are free to leave, and as a sister country of Canston, you are under orders to protect the heirs to the Canston throne as well. Continuing to pursue us will not only make your country an enemy of Terrison *and* Canston but will also extinguish the possibility of trust and diplomacy in the future. I suggest you consider your options carefully."

The line was quiet.

Donald gave Charlotte a small approving nod.

The line came back to life, "*Princess Charlotte of Terrison*,"

"I am here,"

"*We understand your position, but I do not think you understand ours.*"

"Whatever it may be, you have no right to detain us," Charlotte told him.

The man on the other line sighed, "*I am sorry to inform you—*"

Charlotte cut him short, "To whom am I speaking?"

"*Maxwell Hafner, I am the head—*"

"Maxwell, I wish to speak to someone with negotiating power. If your king or prime minister is standing by, I will gladly speak to one of them, but until I am speaking to an authority, there is nothing left to say."

There was a pause on the line.

A new voice came onto the line, "*My apologies, Princess, but I was not—*"

"And who are you?" Charlotte asked.

"I understand that you are feeling mistreated."

"That is an understatement. I demand to know to whom I am speaking with," Charlotte insisted.

"Prime Minister Belart Twill," the man on the line told her.

"I take it you have been listening and you understand my position?" Charlotte asked.

"Yes," the Prime Minister replied.

"And you understand that your daughter is aboard? You did not respond to her."

"I was waiting to see what you would do," the Prime Minister said passively.

Charlotte looked to Donald for reassurance. "You will release us, and you will not peruse the *Alexandria*; do you understand?"

The line was quiet.

"Prime Minister Twill?" Charlotte said, "I am waiting for an answer."

"We understand," he replied at length.

"Good," Charlotte said, "We will send your daughter and Meggan Rose down shortly, along with one of your more irritating nobility. In the time it takes us to return them to you, please have your airships move aside so we may exit your harbor."

"How do I know I can trust what you say? You could easily keep our people," his tone was growing cold.

"On my honor, you may trust me."

The Prime Minister's reply reproached her, *"Princess, valuable though you may be where you hail from, your personal honor does not go far in these matters. I wish to speak to someone else."*

Charlotte stepped away from the console; her chest heaved as she tried to calm herself. Her throat felt dry. "This is ridiculous," she said softly.

Donald approached her gently. "Your Highness, allow me to take over?"

Charlotte shook her head to clear it. "No, I started this; I would be unhappy with myself if I did not finish it," she told him.

Charlotte reminded herself not to let her emotions cause a diplomatic landslide. She took a deep breath before returning to her opponent, "Prime Minister Twill," Charlotte was standing her ground for her brother, for her allies, and for herself. "I am not pleased with your last comment, and I am appalled you would say that in front of your daughter, as it discredits your own honor as a gentleman. But maybe this is the way in Tavenly. Lord Avery seemed to be of your same mind when we spoke earlier—"

"I want to speak to him, then," Twill said, cutting her off.

"He is not available," Charlotte insisted. She muted herself for a moment to speak to Donald, "Captain, how am I doing?"

"A little threatening, but I think you will produce the desired result," Donald replied.

"I should not care what anyone says about me. Today has tried my patience more than any other day," she confessed to him.

"You are doing well," Donald told her. He turned to Mister Carter at his station, "Prepare a launch, but keep the cannons ready."

Miss Twill said from beside Charlotte, "You do realize that they won't let you go even if you do send us back, right?"

"Yes," Charlotte responded. "I am hoping that we can buy enough time to get you to safety and possibly get a head start."

"Jovin is not answering," Donald muttered as he called the sixth level.

"Are they still down there?" Carter asked in apprehension.

"We have no way of knowing," Donald took a breath. "Carter, call Jovin and Conrad upstairs, tell them to leave Lord Avery."

"On it." Carter said, taking over the control table from Donald, and tapping a few buttons.

The line came back to life: *"Send us our people."*

Charlotte moved back to the console, "Have you decided to let us leave peacefully?"

"Send us our people," Minister Twill repeated, *"my daughter is scared for her life."*

Charlotte glanced over at Miss Twill, who was watching and listening quite calmly for a hostage. "I am sure she is," Charlotte lied defiantly.

When Minister Twill spoke again, it was with the concern of a father, *"Please let them go. We promise to let you go in peace. We will not follow you."*

Charlotte drew away from the microphone and exchanged a look with Donald.

"I think that until his daughter is safe, we are safe; but once they have her, we are in danger again," Donald said.

Charlotte weighed her options. "Should I agree, then?"

"Right now, I think you should," Donald replied.

Charlotte stepped back up to the microphone. "We will release your people on these conditions: you will allow us to pass, and you will not follow. We will send them over shortly. Have a party waiting on the docks to receive them. I am through speaking to you. Good evening, Prime Minister." Charlotte ended the transmission. She turned to Donald and began to speak, but her words got caught in her throat.

Chapter 39

Sunset

Miss Twill and Miss Rose stood uncomfortably by the stairs, gripping each other's hands so tightly their knuckles turned white. An emergency launch pod had been prepared, the engine was humming, and the glass roof was open, waiting for them to board. The craft itself resembled a small sea-fairing vessel, made of dark wood and sheets of polished brass. The engines and stabilizing wings were secured in the back, and the balloon was fixed over the pod, under which sat a disgruntled Lord Avery.

Avery had not yet spoken, and no one wanted him to. His locked-jaw gaze was fixed on Charlotte, who was purposely looking in his opposite direction.

Jovin arrived at the bottom of the stairs and almost bumped into Miss Twill and Miss Rose, who were blocking the walkway. "Excuse me, ladies," Jovin said. The ladies jumped about a foot in the air and continued huddling together.

"I apologize for dragging you into this chaos, I did not know this would happen," Jovin told them.

"I'm sure you had an idea," Miss Twill said briskly.

"At least this gives us something to gossip about at parties," Miss Rose said in a quivering attempt at humor.

"You won't be safe again until you are back in your country," Miss Twill said, ignoring her friend. "I don't know what's going on, or why Simport wanted so badly to keep you here, but I don't agree with how it has been handled. However, I do believe there is some integrity within you, since you are going through the steps to return us when you could have kept and ransomed us. So, if there comes a time when you need assistance, Meggan and I will answer your call."

"We did not discuss this," Miss Rose muttered. "But since we're here, I think we need a code,"

"We are not five-year-olds," Miss Twill rebuked.

"I bet the Landic Assassins use code words," Miss Rose responded in irritation.

"Yes, but they are trained killers," her friend said, taking a breath.

Charlotte came to join the three. "The launch is ready," she announced, then placed a hand on Jovin's arm. "I fear we are in more trouble than we realize."

"Really? Because I think we've realized that we're in a lot of trouble," Jovin countered.

Merik came scampering down the staircase. "Captain Donald wants everyone upstairs now!"

"What is a good code word for 'help'?" Miss Rose inquired of Merik.

"Agh, please stop asking me questions…" Merik scrunched his face. "'*Sunset'?* You could use it casually in a sentence: 'Did you see the *sunset* in, um… blankety-blank-blank,' or, um… 'I just went on holiday to… blank-blank location—*whereeveryouare*—and the *sunsets* were really great.'"

Saphir came down the stairs, panic stricken across her face. "We're not dilly-dallying, are we?"

"Oh, of course not," Charlotte said, breaking the tension. "Yes, well, when next we meet, I hope it is under better circumstances."

There was an awkward exchange of goodbyes while Charlotte took Saphir's arm and walked her away from the group. "Lord Avery has been staring," Charlotte whispered to her friend.

Saphir glanced over to where Avery was seated in the open launch. His leg had been tended to by Professor Hopkins, and his wound was now clean, wrapped, and braced with one of Hopkins' own patented splints from his days as a field doctor for the Canston Crown. His hands and feet were bound, and a blanket had been draped over his shoulders by a kindhearted crewmember.

Nevertheless, he was glaring menacingly at the two princesses through the pod's open doors.

"Oh," Saphir sighed. "Do you need to confront him?"

"I would rather forget about him," Charlotte said.

"You owe him nothing, Charlotte," Saphir assured her. "We are not weak, we are strong."

"I feel conflicted."

"It is not wrong to protect yourself, or your friends," Saphir said. "He will not apologize, but it is good to forgive him, not to clear his conscious, but for you."

Charlotte nodded somberly.

"My dear friend," Saphir said, taking her arm, "we are going to be alright."

Charlotte exhaled a strained breath, "I do not need the last word. I wish to move on now."

"I'm proud of you."

Charlotte gave Saphir a smile filled with exhaustion and confliction. "See you upstairs," and she left the seventh level.

Saphir turned back to Avery and gave him a look so saturated in distain and mockery, that the man had to avert his eyes away from her.

Merik was feeling uncomfortable and leaned his head against Saphir's shoulder.

The two ladies were instructed on how to fly the aircraft by a crewmember and were loaded into the launch. Then the bay doors in the stern were opened, the launch was released, and the noble ladies were gone, along with the insufferable Lord Avery.

Saphir watched as the launch slipped out of sight and wondered if they would make it ashore alive.

Merik let go of Saphir, yawning. "I'm hungry,"

"Why does that not surprise me?" Saphir smiled and followed Merik up the stairs.

Chapter 40

Leap of Faith

"They're letting us pass," Mister Carter informed Captain Donald.

"I did not think they would," Donald said, looking up from the control panel and surveying the scene. The two airships were flying white lights in the prows and sterns, signaling their neutrality; they were slowly crossing each other, altering their courses to be out of the *Alexandria*'s line of flight.

"Neither did I," Carter said, running a hand over his face. "For a second I thought we were gonna meet the sky spirits, like how they used to talk back in training…" he turned to Mister McCoy, "you know what I'm talking about, right? The older kids at the academy would say that if you messed up on a test you'd be left on a mountain and the sky spirits would take you?"

McCoy was starring slack-jawed at Carter. "I can honestly say, I have no idea what you are talking about."

"You know, the sky spirits!" Carter went on. "Captain, I know you've mentioned them. Didn't you say you had a run-in with one once?"

"Did I?" Donald replied as he checked the engine gauges.

"Yes, you said about ten years ago…" Carter trailed off, and became somber once again. "What are your orders, Captain?"

The intercom beeped, and Mister Carter answered it. "Wheelhouse,"

"*Everyone's here,*" Saphir announced. There was a scuffle from her end of the line as Merik tried to listen in. "*Captain, what's going on?*"

"They are letting us pass."

Merik's whooping was clearly audible through the intercom. "*Capt—*" Saphir tried to talk over the boy's joyous shouts.

"*We're alive! We're alive! We're alive!*" Merik cried.

"*Captain—*"

Merik cut off Saphir, "*Where are we going now?*" he asked frantically.

Donald did not answer Merik's question, for at that moment, a low *beep* sounded from the dashboard. McCoy and Carter exchanged a petrified glance and looked to their captain.

"Captain, they're turning," Carter said.

"Stay put, for now. Send Jovin up to the wheelhouse."

"*He's on his way,*" Merik said.

There was a sharp hiss of, "*Ow! That's my foot!*"

Merik then said, "*Sorry, Saphir.*"

"White lights are gone," Mister Carter verified. "They're not flying signal lights anymore."

Donald was desperately dialing Simport Castle again. "Castle of Simport, your airships, *SunDance* and *Veronica*, you are on a collision course with the *Alexandria*. Stand down."

The line beeped three times as Simport denied their message.

Donald dialed again, "Castle of Simport, call off your airships."

Simport did not reply.

"Captain, what are we going to do?" McCoy asked.

"Radio the entire harbor," Carter suggested, "we need to reach them before they sandwich us."

Donald changed the radio wave frequency on the control panel, "Simport airships *SunDance* and *Veronica*, stand down. You are on a collision course with the *Alexandria*. Stand down. I repeat, stand down."

The two airships were turning alright, now on a flight path that would force the *Alexandria* to pass between them. If they sailed forward, the *Alexandria* would be pinned between the *Sun Dance* and the *Veronica*, and at the mercy of their unpredictable wrath.

"Prepare the cannons again and alert the crew," Donald ordered, "double check and lock down the windows."

"Prepare the cannons? Captain, what are you planning to do?" Jovin asked as he stepped into the wheelhouse.

"*Airship* Alexandria," there came a reply at last, not from the opposing airships, but from the castle of Simport. It was Prime Minister Twill; and his voice was utterly broken, sorrowful, comparable to a man who has lost everything in the world. "*I send my apologies. I did not foresee this coming into play. I wish I could have honored my word to let you go free, but this was not my decision to make. May the sky spirits guide you on your journey to the next life, as we will not be seeing you again in this one. A blessing to you on your journey.*"

There was silence.

No one moved. No one dared breathe.

The weight of their impending finale was suffocating.

"We are strong and united. We, as leaders, will always do the right, and just, thing," King Raleigh had said before they left Canston. *"It is my responsibility to take care of our country and our people, and it is yours also."*

The Prime Minister leading Tavenly did not understand what it meant to be a leader. He did not understand the value of human life, and regardless of his apologies, there was no sincerity to his person. There was no reasoning with a man who lacks integrity.

Jovin took a breath, wishing he could speak with his father. His words at the beginning of their voyage meant something different now. It was his responsibility to take care of his people, of the *Alexandria* and her passengers, of his country, and of those who owed him nothing, but who needed someone to stand up for them.

Someone to make the right, and just, choice.

"Father, I hear you, my eyes are open. I am trying to understand."

"The time for running and waiting is over," Jovin said in the ringing silence. "While it might have saved us before, it will no longer. At this point, there *is only* forward. We will not cower away, spending our last moments in turmoil."

Donald placed a hand on Jovin's shoulder. "We have everything left to lose."

The prince clasped him on the back in return. "We must fight."

"I wholeheartedly agree, Your Highness," the captain affirmed. "I promised your father to keep you safe, and I have tried not to fail you."

"I wish Merik had stayed at the palace," Jovin confessed.

Donald cracked a smile, "Desperation makes fools of us all." He turned back to his crewmen, who were watching with baited breath. "You heard your Prince," he said with a nod to Jovin. "*We fight.*"

Mister Carter let out a whoop of triumph.

"McCoy," Donald barked, "Fly us between them on my mark. Carter, status on the cannons?"

"But the engines!" McCoy cried.

"We either weaken our engines or get shot out of the sky," Jovin said, catching on.

"Cannons are ready, Captain." Carter affirmed.

Jovin told himself not to second-guess. This action would be detrimental if it failed. If they stalled for even a moment, the *Alexandria* would be under attack, and everything they had gambled on over the last few months would have been for nothing. Rescuing and safeguarding Saphir, protecting Charlotte and Conrad; even sending Merik away from their homeland and on this mission would have all been for nothing.

What his father had told him months ago came back to him now: *"As a ruler, you must be prepared for everything, good and bad; as a father, I am making sure my children are safe."*

"We're sure this is the only exit?" Jovin asked.

"Yes. Harbors are designed with situations such as these in mind," the captain replied. He turned again to his crew, "When you are clear, reengage the High Elevation Protocol and get us into the open sky."

Jovin pressed the intercom button to the captain's cabin. "Stay away from the window wall, take cover."

Saphir began to reply in earnest, but Jovin muted the intercom before she had a chance to say anything beyond: "*Jovin? What's happening?*"

McCoy's hand was fidgeting on a leaver, waiting to accelerate the *Alexandria* into the path of potential peril.

"Steady," Jovin told the crew, his eyes remaining locked on the two Simport airships that were flying parallel towards them. "They're getting closer, wait until they're close enough to see the crew's faces. Then, give it everything you've got."

The *Alexandria* glided forward painstakingly slow. A knot was twisting in Jovin's stomach, his mind was made up, but every second he was doubting this decision.

"Steady," he repeated, and he was surprised at how steady his own voice sounded.

The prows of the two airships were nearing the *Alexandria*, Jovin was beginning to notice figures running about the decks of the two airships, moving long objects that could only be gangways. Jovin reminded himself to breathe as he realized that they could not risk being boarded.

"Steady," Jovin told the crew again, and the knot in his stomach loosened.

The prow of the *Alexandria* was two thousand feet away from being sandwiched between the *SunDance* and the *Veronica.*

"Here we go," Donald said to himself.

One thousand feet.

Their opponents were climbing the gangways, weapons in hand, shouting to each other over the wind as they prepared to board the *Alexandria.*

Seven hundred feet.

"As a father, I am making sure my children are safe," Jovin could hear his father's voice say.

Five hundred feet.

"We are not weak," he had told his father when they left Canston.

The three airships were almost upon each other. Jovin could see every cannon exposed and poised, ready to demolish and shoot them out of the sky.

"I need to be brave," a voice whispered in his mind.

Two hundred feet.

"I need to be brave," the voice whispered again.

"NOW!" Jovin commanded.

The *Alexandria* lurched forward as Mister McCoy punched the accelerator, flying her into the stretch of sky between the two airships, cannons blazing, engines screaming as they were pushed to their limit. Everyone in the wheelhouse was thrown off balance or knocked to the ground again. McCoy yelled in fright and scrambled back into his chair, desperate to keep them from colliding with the *SunDance* and *Veronica* on either side of them.

"Fire!" Donald shouted.

Mister Carter sent volley after volley of cannon fire into the *SunDance* and *Veronica*, pausing only for an instant to reload.

For a moment, their adversaries seemed stunned that they were being fired upon. A few of their gangways fell over the rails as the cannon fire hit their hulls. Jovin tried not to watch as some of their crew fell with them, tumbling through the sky and out of his view.

"It's our fault," Jovin murmured to himself, but no one could hear him.

Then, when the *Alexandria* was about a third of the way between the *SunDance* and *Veronica*, the two airships retaliated.

"Speed up! Damn it, McCoy!" Carter yelled over the cannons as they hit the *Alexandria's hull.*

Plasma blasts from the *SunDance* and *Veronica* shot across the deck, removing a chunk of the wooden railing in the prow and scorching the polished wood. McCoy fought to maintain their course as the airship was battered between the volleys like a couple of cats toying with a mouse. An alarm began blaring over the speakers and lights flashed as their airship recognized that it was being compromised.

"Captain we're on fire on level four!" a crewman shouted through the intercom. *"The engines are not going to last."*

"Captain, the hull is severely damaged in the prow. The multilevel windows aren't going to make it."

"Captain, we've lost two men already."

"Fire everything!" Donald barked.

"Captain!" Jovin shouted in the deafening roar. "Go up! Get us out of here!"

The *SunDance* on the port side was slowing their cannon fire, but to starboard, the crew of the *Veronica* was preparing their remaining three gangways to board them.

A sheet of metal slid across all but the front windows of the wheelhouse. The red light flashed over the door and the alarms were silenced.

"Give the engines everything you've got; just get us out of here!" Donald ordered.

The engines, who had hardly ever made a sound before today, screamed as they never had before. The men could feel the vibrations from where the cannons were hitting the stern sides of their airship. Jovin's mind raced to his companions, and it took everything in him to keep himself from running to make sure that they were alright.

Just as he was about to abandon the wheelhouse; the cannon fire stopped.

"We're gonna make it!" Carter whooped. "We're gonna make it! We're out!"

Jovin ran to the stern door and unfastened the airlock, yanking open the door and gazing out at the destruction they left in their wake.

The *Alexandria* had cleared the harbor walls and was ascending at a steady pace. The *SunDance* and *Veronica* would not be able to turn quickly enough to match speed and peruse her. With smoking hulls and cannon blasts through their sides, the two airships were hardly staying aloft. The *SunDance* was starting to descend slowly as a fire blazed its way through her stern. Bits of railing were now scattered wreckage across the decks, and flames burned in the gaping holes left by the plasma blasts.

Jovin felt the knot return to his stomach.

"We're free!" McCoy shouted in triumph behind him.

Carter was crying out profanities, thanking the universe for their getaway.

Jovin felt Captain Donald place a hand on his shoulder. "It is the price," he said, gazing out at the burning airships.

Jovin found he was unable to speak, so he only nodded, avoiding the captain's eyes. The setting sun was just kissing the horizon as they took one last look at the horror left in their wake.

"See to your companions." Donald advised.

"I can do that," Jovin said, finding his voice.

Carter and McCoy nodded in respect as he reentered the wheelhouse. "Your Highness," McCoy said, placing a hand to his heart and bowing his head, Mister Carter followed suit.

Jovin found a smile, and placed a hand to his own heart in response.

+++++

It felt all too familiar, Merik thought: the escape, the fear of pursuit, the tight oxygen mask strapped around his face. The window wall was covered in its thick wall of shining metal, the cabin door was on airlock, and the emergency lights glowed softly.

He glanced around at his friends, it was just the five of them now, as Captain Donald and Baron Von Lorian were in the wheelhouse. Conrad was sitting with his back to the wall with his eyes closed, and Charlotte was leaning against her brother. Saphir was acting as Merik's pillow, and Jovin was on Merik's other side, staring across the room.

It was after eleven in the evening when the green light above the door flashed, giving them clearance to remove their oxygen masks. Chef Mason brought up a plate of sandwiches a short while after. They ate sluggishly; all were far too exhausted for conversation, and too alert to sleep. Jovin disappeared after he had eaten and did not reappear again. Out of habit, Merik brought out a deck of cards and played on the rug with Conrad. Charlotte watched from a blanketed bundle on the sofa.

"Where are you going, Saphir?" Merik called across the room.

Saphir turned back to face him, her hand lingered on the stairway doorknob. "For a cup of tea," she told him. "I'm a little jumpy."

Merik contemplated her with a nod, and turned back to the card tower he had been building with Conrad.

Saphir's bare feet made little sound under the quavering hum of the engines. As she passed the crew's dining hall, she heard their chattering and a ruckus of singing. Saphir could not help but smile at their rambunctious celebrating.

She pushed open the kitchen door to find it deserted. She had expected to see Chef Mason or his assistant, now she wondered if she wanted to be alone after all.

Saphir looked to her left and was surprised to find Jovin seated on the countertop, watching her with speculation. "Hey there, Princess."

Saphir went about filling the kettle with water and did not answer him until she handed him a steaming cup of tea as he had slipped off the countertop.

Jovin cast his eyes around the room, but refocused on her after a moment. "How are you holding up?"

"As to be expected," she murmured.

"You've been rather alone lately, ever since you came aboard, and I haven't been helping," he said.

"I think I could have been a bit more decent to you, too."

"Saphir—"

"What's done is done. Let's move forward now."

Jovin nodded somberly.

Saphir's melancholic expression was replaced by something more pleasant. "Jovin, about Lord Avery…"

"Darling, you shouldn't be treated with such disrespect," he ran a hand through his hair. "I feel that the treatment you and Charlotte received in Simport was just that."

"And Merik?" she voiced finally. "He just wants to know his brother…"

Jovin was silent for a moment.

She found it difficult to look at him, opting instead on swirling the dregs of her teacup.

"Saphir?"

"Yes, Jovin?"

He deliberated saying more, but hesitated, and thought better of it. "Never mind... Well, I think I'll head upstairs. It was nice speaking to you without the immediate fear of dying or—"

"Oh, hush with the dramatics."

Chapter 41

Fear Will Make Them Act

"There is no sign of them; they were seen heading north, away from Simport, but after that, they lost them," Miss Shannon reported.

"Have Twill contact me in the next hour." Ganimead marked a spot in the southwest region of Tavenly on a map. "We do have the daughter, right?"

"Yes,"

"Are all three royal parties still together?" he asked his assistant.

Miss Shannon took a timid step forward to answer. "As far as we know."

"Ee'lin Princess?"

"There has been no evidence that she left their party. Likewise with the Terrison royalty," Miss Shannon said.

Ganimead contemplated the map spread out over his desk. "Where do they think they are going?" he muttered to himself.

"They are possibly searching for allies now that they are fugitives in Tavenly," Miss Shannon suggested.

Ganimead leaned against his desk, "I think they will try to find a way back to Canston before winter is through."

Miss Shannon blinked. "Once the temperature drops and winter sets in, they will not be able to get back across the Gemelle Channel safely, without their engine problem acting up."

"Which will make them easier to find." He moved back to his desk and scanned the list of Canston's known and suspected allies, deliberating which of the many places there would be left to run to; assuming they were intelligent enough not to dock out in the open. "We still have the tag in, right?"

"Yes," Shannon answered, "but it seems like they'll notice it at some point."

Ganimead did not immediately answer her. "Who thinks that?"

Miss Shannon shifted her weight. "Well, um, I do. I don't think they are as ignorant as we would like to believe."

Ganimead contemplated her for a long, uncomfortable moment. She lowered her gaze to her clipboard and waited for him to speak. "Iris, if you had your way, what would you do?"

"How do you mean, sir?"

Ganimead had grown tired of explaining himself. "How would you drive a royal heir out of hiding?"

Miss Shannon kept her eyes fixed on the evening report from the Landin Favar on her clipboard.

"Well?" Ganimead's expression sat on the bridge between anger and amusement.

Miss Shannon swallowed. Her voice was hardly above a whisper when she spoke, "Well, maybe I would find something they love and… threaten it…?"

"There you have it," Ganimead raised his hands in appreciation. "But we've already done that. It is difficult to burn a country twice."

"May I speak my mind?" Miss Shannon asked. When Ganimead nodded, she continued, "If the Ee'lin Princess hasn't done anything to reclaim her country by now, I doubt she will without further prompting. She must have heard the rumors and must know about Kellen by now."

"It's not been even two months yet, she hasn't had time to think about it, let alone to rally support." Ganimead said.

"But Canston will have had time. Have we considered that the King of Canston will find Ee'lin's new leadership disturbing?" Miss Shannon asked.

"Parents will only focus on finding their children," Ganimead looked her dead in the eye. "If we want to find the children, we must tempt them with what they desire. When they see it—or, in this case, when they hear rumors about their divided and dilapidated countries lacking proper leadership—they will try to act, and when they do, they will make themselves available to us."

Miss Shannon felt her throat close. She forced herself to keep her face pleasant.

Ganimead ignored her and wrote up a slip. "Here, send this out to Simport," he passed it to his assistant. "Iris, it is confidential."

"I understand. My allegiance is with you, sir." Miss Shannon placed it under the papers on her clipboard. "I do not have plans to do anything foolish," she said proudly.

Ganimead ignored her.

She passed him the Landin Favar report. "Have a pleasant night, sir."

Miss Shannon hastened from the office to the telegraph room. No one looked up as she entered. The light was low. The only sound was that of the tapping of codes and subdued coughs as the Graphers worked diligently over their stations. Miss Shannon had passed Ganimead's confidential information to each on multiple occasions and knew them all by name. But she was not allowed to be friendly with them. She was restricted from positioning herself as a friend.

She took a seat at a cubicle near the end of the line and carefully removed the slip from her clipboard. She put on the telegraph headset and scanned the paper's contents; then she set about coding the message to their contact in Tavenly.

Chapter 42

Bravery's Talk with Kindness

Charlotte's mind was a mess. After wandering about the airship all morning she found herself seated at the dining room table, staring absently out of the window, and clutching her tepid cup of tea in her hands. The door opened behind her, and she was surprised to receive Captain Donald as company.

"Hello, Captain,"

"Good morning, Charlotte."

"May I ask where we are now?"

"Three days from Ariden," Donald replied, taking the seat beside her. "You missed it at breakfast; Lady Eleanor's manor in Ariden has recently become free. She was unable to take us on earlier this week as a new mayor was being exceptionally nosy, and she feared for our safety. But now, she feels it is safe and we should be able to rest there for a while."

"Did you contact her from the wheelhouse?"

"There is a risk that it was intercepted, but there is no where we can dock to send a message." Donald said, folding his hands on the table and observing the patchwork clouds rolling past the window.

Charlotte fidgeted. "Captain, I want to apologize for yesterday. I was trying to do the right thing. I was thinking about how my parents would have handled the situation, but it resulted in danger."

"Your negotiations helped save everyone on board, Charlotte," Donald said. "If you had not held your ground, we might *be* on the ground."

Charlotte grinned at this feeble joke, but her smile quickly left her face. "It was frightening."

"But you were brave," Donald said, "you were strong, and I thank you for your strength."

Charlotte felt a small swoop of pride, which was slowly replaced by a nagging feeling in her stomach. "Yes, well, I still could have done better."

"You did very well. Considering what they were throwing at you, you handled yourself with grace. I am grateful for it."

Charlotte thought back to the anxiety she had felt while negotiating the *Alexandria*'s release, the fear of capture, the disrespect she experienced with the prime minister, and the numbness she felt while with Lord Avery. The image of him threatening Saphir haunted her mind even now. She could still hear his voice taunting her.

She thought Donald might have picked up on her train of thought because he said: "People believe that they must power over one another to gain power and respect, it is the way they are taught, and it is the only way they know. But my point is, Charlotte," Donald continued. "Your kindness is strength. You have a beautiful power, and your kindness should not be mistaken for weakness."

+++++

Everyone gathered in Donald's cabin after lunch. Charlotte and Saphir were cozied up in a quilt on the sofa while watching the gentlemen and Merik invent a card game on the rug before them.

"Righto," Merik finished sorting out hands. "Twos are wild, one-eyed jacks are instant death, and red threes mean you give up your three best cards and exchange them with the person on you right."

Baron Von Lorian looked over his hand, "What if you have a regular jack?"

"Nothing happens," Merik said.

Jovin leaned back on his hands. "You said something about fours earlier."

"Forget what I said about fours," Merik waved it off.

Captain Donald furrowed his eyebrows as he looked over his cards. "When are we allowed to fold?"

"What if your three best cards *include* a one-eyed jack?" Conrad asked. "When do you know if you die?"

Merik huffed, "On the second round, the dealer asks if there are any suicides. Then everyone with a one-eyed jack tosses in their cards and you can fold." Merik looked around at them expectantly. "Got it?"

Conrad ran a hand through his hair. "No, but let's start anyway."

Charlotte leaned close to Saphir, "What do you wager? Any bets?"

Her friend speculated their companions. "Merik is going to bluff everyone into folding, Captain Donald is going to go out on the second round, and Jovin is going to switch hands with the Baron."

Charlotte twittered a laugh. "Are you sure about that?"

"Just a guess," Saphir said, tucking her feet up closer to her. "I think your brother is going to win," she whispered to Charlotte.

Conrad overheard, "My eleven-time winning streak only lasted for the day; I've been beaten by Merik almost every hand since."

"I don't know why you're complaining, Conrad; isn't it better to win and win, and win, and win, and *win*, and win, *and* win, and win,"

"Are you done yet?" Conrad asked.

"Not yet," Merik replied. "*And win and win and win*, and lose to a child, than to have won *here and there* and still lose to a child?" Merik asked with a straight face.

Conrad chuckled.

"But Conrad, you've won since then," Saphir pointed out.

"Not as often," Merik commented. "Second round," he dealt everyone another three cards. "Any suicides jacks?"

Jovin tossed in his cards.

"Wait, I have a red three," Conrad changed his best cards with Donald.

Saphir raised her hands in surrender as Charlotte gave her an amused look. "Alright, so I was wrong this time. But on the next round, we should team up and beat them all."

Merik and Conrad exchanged a worried glance.

+++++

Jovin stood alone on the moonlit deck, now so different from when they had first set out on their voyage. Chunks of railing were missing from their run-in with the Simport airships, and there was still a gash in the deck from where Saphir's Windridge had crashed so many nights ago.

Far below him on the silent earth, lights popped in and out of existence. The lights reminded him of something long forgotten—a distant memory barely on the brink of imagination.

Jovin closed his eyes, letting the freezing air wash over him. All the confusion and fear he had felt during the last few weeks dissipated into the changing night, and in the space left in their wake, he found there was room for resilience and peace. He was reminded of a conversation he had with Captain Donald when they first began this voyage, back before the overwhelming confusion and fear had taken over, and there was still the prospect of maintaining peace.

As the *Alexandria* passed through the starry sky and the moon grew ever more distant, he kept his gaze straight ahead. Maybe it would turn out alright. Maybe there was still hope for them. Or maybe this was the start of something they could not control.

Jovin found himself whispering, almost unconsciously, "*What a way to begin an adventure.*"

Made in the USA
Columbia, SC
01 December 2020